THE DEVIL IN EDEN

Jeffrey Peter Clarke

THE DEVIL IN EDEN

FICTION4ALL

Fiction4All
www.fiction4all.com

This Edition
Published 2020

PROLOGUE
THE ONE WHO WOULD SEE

A new star appeared in the evening sky. The ground crew in their blue pressure suits watched it drift, watched it brighten until, reflected in their visors, the light of the shuttle's main engine speared down from the vault. Now they could make out her form; spider legs grasping from the silver shell as the blaze of her engines drove back the darkness. To a rolling drumbeat she steadied above the landing zone, raising curtains of dust that retreated in the tenuous air of a frozen twilight.

Then silence.

The vessel was down, a squatting mantis on the basalt platform beyond the far side of the runway. The door drew in then moved aside as three of the ground crew approached. The boarding ramp slid out and from the metal husk ten figures descended, anonymous in white pressure suits and tinted helmets, each to place a foot upon this new but very old world. They stood a while, not knowing true gravity since the day their journey had begun; a gravity one third that of Earth's but gravity, nonetheless. Ushered by the crewmen they crossed the landing strip, silhouettes against a burnished horizon where a violet glow hovered in spectral memory of the now vanished sun. In their approach to the main airlock they gazed in wonder at the great, domed complex rising from the red desert. For some this was the end of their journey, for others only a stepping-stone.

Amidst but not of them was one for whom this vision of human enterprise hardly mattered; one for whom there waited an assignment of which she as yet knew nothing, though the fate of all humanity on this arid world might hang upon it.

With the outer airlock doors sealed, they stamped their boots over the metal grill and awaited the rise to optimum atmospheric pressure whilst a muffled roar proclaimed the operation of dust extractors. Then a chime, followed by a call from one of the ground crew, 'All right everybody - we can take off our hats!'

Hands raised up to release airtight collars. Space helmets lifted clear of turning heads. One balanced his helmet on splayed fingers, raised and lowered it to test its weight in the new gravity. One, two, then a third jumped up and down, each laughing at the antics of the other. The inner airlock door was opening and with disarming normality a voice announced, 'Welcome to Mars, everyone! Welcome to Novamerica Five!'

'Oh, I smell grass!' smiled a young woman, shaking free her long hair.

'Hell, yes - and food!' exclaimed another, turning to one of the ground crew. 'That's real food I can smell. Tell me if it ain't!'

'Could be, sir,' replied the crewman. 'The biodome main restaurant is close by. It's open around the clock. And when you want to give your stomach a rest and walk around the gardens then the biodome is the place to go. It's almost like home. You'll think you never left Earth.'

They followed the crewmen, talking of the sights they had witnessed from the shuttle on their way down. Except for one. One who held back in the shadows as the rest moved away into the bright concourse. One who watched their faces glow in infra-red. Watched fumarole heat coil upward from the opened necks of their pressure suits. Processed and perverted their images to render them as grinning, chomping skulls in filtered light, lurid in shifting wavelengths. She captured, amplified their voices, heard the creak of their spacesuits, listened to the sound of their breathing, to the cacophony of beating hearts as they gathered to receive their welcome brief. But she would remain where she was until *he* sent for her.

One of the base crew re-entered the airlock, glancing about to ensure only the two of them remained there. He eyed the name badge on her suit. 'Officer Michaelis - welcome to our station - I'm to take you to your quarters. Chief Hammond is waiting to see you as soon as you have your gear stowed away.'

She had already scanned, already analysed his DNA, his micro-implants - those for gravity compensation, hormone and antibody levels, bone marrow, calcium stability. The man was as perfectly adapted as all the colonists had to be. 'I'll get out of this pressure suit and go directly to his office,' she responded. She needed to do that. Once having landed, then again when approaching the base, she had attempted direct contact but her mind had been unable to reach his.

Leaving the storage lockers she followed the orderly across the concourse. From his thoughts she resolved freeze-framed images of herself. He was appraising her slim figure, her attractively angular features, her dark, oddly expressionless eyes. Such banalities were of little importance but she wished he would move quicker in her desire to meet once more with Virgil Hammond. It was a year and a half, back on Earth, since they had spoken face to face yet there was his image as it had been when he stood before the silent faithful in that secret hall – the faithful whose message went unheeded on Earth. In her mind his words once more rang out. 'The wounds of Christ still bleed for the sins of mankind! On Mars those wounds will be healed. On Mars His word will be manifest. We have the means. We have the will to do what is demanded of us. Barriers will be raised in our path but they will be thrown down. We will prevail! On Mars His Kingdom will rise anew!'

For the message she cared nothing at all. It mattered only that the appointed time was close and that she would be there to serve and to obey. Trimensional pictures shifted before her eyes. The corridors and passages, every part of the complex had, since her arrival, become familiar through the minds of others. She knew exactly where to find Hammond. But she must be patient. The orderly must not become suspicious.

At the end of a plain, well-lit corridor stood the office of the man responsible for all facilities established by the United American States, a major power on Earth stretching from Alaska to Cape Horn, the man who was co-ordinator of the international mining consortium. Hovering against the door the words glowed. Virgil Hammond - Chief Executive. Frontier Mining.

The orderly touched the words.

The words reformed to read, 'You may enter.'

She found herself before a small township with stark white weatherboard church set amidst sunlit fields of golden corn. An idyllic scene basking beneath the blue skies of distant Earth, the whole accompanied by the retreating notes of a choir. The desk and figure behind it rotated to face them whilst the scene shivered, fragmented then altogether faded to reveal a sparsely appointed office interior. At the centre of the room a ring of lights glowed into life. The figure arose. 'Officer Michaelis - I did not expect you would come directly here from the concourse. You have caught me in a brief spell of self-indulgence. That was my hometown as a boy. Please - take a seat.'

She knew he was lying. She was certain he would have followed her every move as soon as she left the shuttle but she was unable to penetrate his mind as she could the minds of others. Intending to effect a formal introduction, the orderly had found himself pre-empted. His request for dismissal was also stillborn for his one-time charge moved away without a word whilst a brief glance from the Chief Executive told the man his presence was no longer required. The orderly shrugged then left the room.

She was, of course, familiar with the sturdy figure, with the big boned, heavy-jawed features. Familiar, too, with those steel-grey eyes, with the slightly twisted smile of the man who extended a hand to greet her. His was a smile quite as forthcoming as her own and quite as superficial. 'Welcome to our new world and to our humble outpost. I trust the journey out and the company on board were not too tiresome.'

'I experienced no problems, General,' she replied. 'Apart from a necessary minimum of dialogue I closed down for much of the time so the other passengers tended to leave me alone. As you appreciate, after a day or so in space, people usually switch between entertainment and hibernation. I sensed even their dreams were frozen. Two of them woke for a while then retreated from the emptiness beyond our vessel. They were afraid. They imagined that I also slept for most of the journey but of course I did not. Our transfer to the shuttle was without incident.'

'Well now you're here I'll arrange for refreshments then we can discuss the purpose of your journey. And we do not use the term "General" in the presence of others - with a small number of exceptions, of course. At least not yet. "Chief" will suffice because out here I as well as all of my staff are officially and strictly civilian. I believe I made that clear before you left Earth.'

'You did indeed, Chief,' she replied, 'but we are alone in this room and there are no active sensors other than those required for your personal security.'

'You are of course right, my dear Zena. 'I above all should never doubt your remarkable abilities.' He issued words to a small dome shimmering translucent green on the left side of the desk. A man's face appeared above it. To this Hammond addressed his order for food and drink then returned to his guest. 'As you are aware, the official reason for your visit is that you are to undertake environmental systems studies. That will be sufficient should anyone ask and it gives you ample reason to go when and wherever you wish. I expect you will see more of this world than most. More, perhaps, than any of them ever could.'

They made small talk. She appeared relaxed, but her expression belied the busy probing of her mind. She was aware of the real Hammond behind that benign and easy-going manner. Aware of the zealous, uncompromising mind of a man who would have nothing and no one stand in his way. That was no secret to others close to the General and yet - in spite of the screen that prevented her fully accessing his emotions, she perceived a dark shadow. Whatever cast that shadow, she realised, had brought her on the long voyage through space to serve him on this world as she had been programmed to serve on Earth. To search out, to reveal any who schemed to subvert. Any who thought to deceive. Following the near fatal accident on Earth, Frontier's biolab had restored her body, remodelled her mind, had made her what she now was. What she recalled from an earlier life was only what they had allowed her to remember. Much of what coloured her memories had never been.

With the arrival of refreshments she expected Hammond would remain at ease but he did not. When they were alone again he leaned toward her as if in fear of being overheard. 'You will understand,' he breathed, eyes hard upon hers, 'that what I am about to tell you is known to only a select few within this facility and to no one else on the entire planet. These are sensitive times. You will find speculation and rumour everywhere, my dear Zena. They seem to appear and disappear planet-wide like whirlwinds out there in the desert.'

'I sensed those rumours, Chief. I sensed them in the one who brought me here and in those who walked by. There are events, images they do not understand. There are things that have occurred recently. It fascinates them as rumour always fascinates.'

'Ah, yes,' he said, 'rumour is a black seed placed by the Devil and watered by the ignorance of the unwary. Opinion is its shoot waiting to blossom into dangerous conviction.' Hammond once more relaxed then continued, 'This office is, as you have gathered, electronically isolated and what I'm to tell you will be treated Class One confidential.'

'Information I am given in confidence will not be imparted to unauthorised persons, Chief. You know that better than anyone.'

'Oh, I know it very well, my dear Zena - I do indeed. But if we are to carry out His good work in this soulless place; if we are to unmask, if we are to crush the evil that has arisen to test our resolve then we must be on our guard at all times. At *all* times!'

***

The last personnel had entered the base. They had watched the outer airlock doors slide shut against the forbidding beauty of a starlit desert. Maintenance bots retreated to cluster inside their protective shells. A low mist advanced from the night to explore their domain. It drifted in spectral cortege, embraced parked vehicles, stole away their warmth and veiled them with carbon dioxide frost. Soon the mist would settle and thicken. Soon the complex would be obscured to leave the great biodome a pale bubble adrift in a phantom sea.

***

The General had finished speaking. His disclosure had been brief. Now she understood the nature of her mission as he leaned back in the chair, hands held prayer-like, fingertips touching his lips, eyes still fixed upon her. 'You don't appear surprised. Perhaps I should not have expected it.'

'Things are what they are, General, whether they surprise us or not. I will be vigilant and do nothing to arouse suspicion. I will report directly to you when the time comes.'

'That is what I expect, Zena, and I know I can depend upon you. Our resources on Mars are growing though as yet we have not been able to authorise suitable surveillance equipment. We have, however, the backing of others on Earth - some of considerable influence. We will accomplish His good work together and His hand will surely guide us.' Hammond's smile returned. 'But you have hardly set foot on the planet and here am I detaining you. You must go to your quarters then do a little exploring. Visit our biodome before your evening meal - the main pathways are lit throughout the night and I suspect it is the biodome where you should begin. We can discuss matters further before you retire. I'll recall the crewman to escort you.'

'Do you consider that necessary, General? Most people familiarise themselves with our complexes before they leave Earth.'

'We must play safe, my dear Zena. You must not appear over-familiar with finer details to those who know you are newly arrived. That could fuel more speculation. Let them continue with the rumours they already have for as long as it serves our purpose. After this evening you may go about as you please.'

The door slid aside to reveal the waiting orderly. Hammond remained motionless until the door had closed and sealed, then he raised fingers to the sides of his face and closed his eyes. Where had been the familiar surroundings of his office there now resolved corridor walls and overhead lights. The head and shoulders of the orderly swung in and out of the scene as he proceeded around a corner to approach the staircase. He appeared to look directly at Hammond whilst his lips moved in silence. He was, of course, speaking to Zena Michaelis. Hammond had no interest in hearing what was said, only in the picture that she unknowingly fed him through the secure link. Her eyes now were his eyes. Whatever evil moved amongst them would be revealed to him exactly as it appeared to her so that he would know at once. And once knowing, he would act.

He remained watching until they arrived at her quarters. A smile of satisfaction touched his lips. His gaze remained cold and unblinking.

She had become the eyes and the ears of a man whose motives she could never truly understand, in part because they involved emotions. And even though the senses conferred upon her ranged far beyond the keenest possessed by any human being, she was no more able to predict the future.

Nor could she foresee the coming of death and destruction.

CHAPTER 1
ENIGMA OF THE CRYSTALS

Most of that morning I'd spent working out in the gym with my old buddy, Leo - Leo McDowell, that is. He's a fellow pilot. Our ground leave had overlapped a few days this time around. As usual when the opportunity came up I'd done my best to outshine him but he always managed to haul more weight than me. I guess that's because he spent a deal longer working out than I did when he was down at base. Some people relax in the bar or the biodome, or get lost in programmed dreaming. Leo was no more interested in escaping from the real world than I was.

Stepping from the gymnasium, my thoughts had hovered over a session of further education rather than the bar room, where I knew Leo would be heading after our workout. Further education? Well, I was involved in an arts course though I was never too interested in the subject back on Earth. But after arriving on Mars, I'd come to realise the value of much that I'd left behind. Earlier that day I'd planned to have myself a tour around one of those virtual European art galleries, all trimensional images, all perfectly convincing, except that you had the illusion all to yourself – no crowds, no company at all, unless you wanted otherwise. By this time, however, my academic side was feeling less assertive. It backed down altogether when my left earlobe pinged. 'Hi, Brett - sorry to interrupt your free time but there's something I'd like to discuss right here in my office. How are you fixed?'

'Ten minutes Joe - okay?' I replied, wondering why I needed to go to his office in the flesh. He could in any case have joined me in the bar room as he occasionally did but the tone of his voice suggested this was something out of the ordinary. Something that maybe needed a private face-to-face.

'Sure, Brett,' he came back. 'See you in ten.'

Joe, our station commander, seldom interfered with people's leave schedules. It's no secret how jealous pilots get about their free time on the ground, though in my case it didn't matter so much. For me real freedom came when I was flying. On the other hand, it wasn't too often I could get together for a drink and a little reminiscing with Leo. Leo and I had been pals since we were kids. From the start we'd both dreamt about going into space, each of us telling the other that he himself would be the first to do it and maybe the other one would never get off the ground. But good old dependable Leo and I ended up in basic military training together. We graduated as pilots on wingships and shuttles and began flying at more or less the same time. We even fell out over the same girl. That could have terminated our friendship but when she threw us both out of her life that did it; Leo and I were pals again.

We made the journey out to Mars together, although our reasons for so doing were not the same. Leo wanted to fly wingships long enough to pile up the credits then return to Earth. He figured on having enough set aside to pursue his favourite sport, golf, in a big way. In the meantime, his ambition was to set up the first teams on Mars and eventually organise inter-base tournaments.

As for me, I wanted to fly wingships and go on flying wingships. I never thought there was enough peace and quiet to be had back on Earth. Never enough time to sit and think. I found life too complicated Earthside - over-regulated, overcrowded, with too many people retreating from a reality they figured was no longer worth having. It's very easy to interact with bionics, easy to be something you aren't in order to escape the pressures of life on the home planet. There's no sense of wonder for a lot of people. Maybe there never was. Plug yourself in and you can be and go and do almost anything you like as long as you don't shift your butt from the couch. It's what people were escaping to as much as from that bothered me.

I needed to find myself. I needed to live my own life and on Mars I could do that. I could think straight and metaphorically speaking I could breathe again, which is a pretty ironic thing to say about a planet where the outside air is unbreathable. And sure, there are people - there are forty or so bases and at least twice as many outstations. There were, when I arrived, the all-important uranium and rare metal mining operations as well as the automated factories, but the human population hadn't climbed much higher than a hundred thousand. A major percentage of them had been born on the planet, though, and never gotten closer to the real Earth than taking a stroll in the biodome or wandering through virtual Earthscapes.

With so few human beings on a land area roughly the same as Earth's, and almost all concentrated in the bases, you could say even then that the surface of Mars was practically devoid of humans. Most of the big ships plying the routes those days were just cargo platforms and most didn't carry people anymore, only manufactured goods and industrial equipment. But the big dream, the one that had initially lit the fuse, had proved too ambitious in the end. Mining the asteroid belt, siphoning up the organic atmosphere of Saturn's moon, Titan, then shipping the stuff back to Mars for processing - both had remained no more than that – stalled because of the war on Earth. And I for one hoped it would stay that way since I didn't care to live out my days on the factory planet some people had been intent on creating. Yes, I could wander over cratered deserts, around great volcanoes, through vast canyons, and the sky was mine. Above those ancient landscapes I imagined things a lot of people wouldn't understand. Some of it I didn't understand myself.

Then maybe I wasn't alone. Rumour had it that a few people, those who spent time at remote outstations, claimed they heard and saw things. Sounds. Images. No one ever used the word "haunted" but I knew what they meant. I'd felt it myself when I'd been grounded and asleep in my quarters. As if voices were calling from across some great divide, but it's not the kind of experience you advertise. Loneliness, remoteness, can have a strange effect on people. At least that's what I told myself.

Some might not consider the likes of Leo and me to have had particularly glamorous lives. We flew cargo containers and pallets to and from main distribution points as well as from base to base. On Earth that would be entirely automated and so would not require a pilot. Out here the powers that be still preferred a genuine human on board so whenever I carried passengers they would have someone to bitch at when life wasn't going their way. Apart from that, everyone on Mars had to be involved with something.

The cargo containers arrived after being released to aero-brake in the atmosphere and from those same main points, new ones were blasted up into space. They would rendezvous with the crewless freighters as they swung around our small world to begin the long return journey to Earth, oscillating back and forth across the solar system to the unheard beat of some celestial pendulum. When the big rockets did come in direct from the home planet, there were always people aboard. Sometimes they'd transfer passengers and equipment to the shuttles in orbit or onto the Isaac Newton space station; sometimes they'd come right down to the surface. When they did come down, when the sun was low and the sky clear - what a sight they were!

The passengers I mentioned might include technicians, engineers, scientists or administration staff. That's how I first met Karin - Karin Blomdahl, the first real complication in my life since I'd quit Earth. Karin worked for the Europeans but at that time she was using our base facilities for one of those co-operative ventures the powers-that-be got involved in. Sure, everyone joked about the male pilots and their women the way people used to about those old-time sailors on Earth. The innuendo some of us were subject to seldom matched reality, though I guess Leo and I didn't have much to complain about in that respect. But Karin was different - no, more than that as things turned out. Even so, it took a while for me to realise there could be more to life than sitting in the pilot's pod and musing over the scenery. Eventually, I found myself gazing at the mountains and the deserts but seeing her face, too. At first that worried me and I tried to convince myself it would soon pass. Karin didn't start out as a complication, however. I flew wingships whereas she was a geologist - a planetary scientist if you prefer - so the nature of her work kept her firmly on the ground most of the time. Anyhow, where there's a will - as they used to say. Except that in this case the will, initially, wasn't mine.

It might never have happened but for Joe – the very Joe I was now heading up to meet. Joe van Allen was not only my base commander - he was a good friend. He, too, belonged out here though he came initially on a five-year tour of duty. That's Earth years, by the way. We always reckon time out here in Earth years. The Martian year of six hundred and eighty-seven days gets too complicated, though it makes you sound a lot younger for a while. Anyhow, Joe came out to help further his career on the home planet. That was twenty-eight years ago. His partner hated Mars so much they split and she returned to Earth. Meantime, he'd been offered command of, and responsibility for, the expansion of what had been our first permanent base,

Novamerica One. It became his personal project and he saw it develop into what it is today. The place is ancient by colonial standards, getting on for a century old, though it's been modified so much over the decades the original structure got recycled somewhere in the process.

Karin made out that Joe was my father figure. I guess she was right. Joe always had a soft spot for me, maybe because he never had kids of his own. It was Joe's idea to have me show Karin around our station on her first visit. When I looked at those cool Nordic features, when I saw how they so easily dimpled into a smile when she spoke, he didn't need to hold a gun to my head. Well, it seemed innocent enough at the time, even when Joe arranged for the three of us to have dinner together in the biodome café away from the crowds then found, just before Karin and I arrived, that he had an unexpected inter-base meeting to deal with. Sure, I was slow off the mark but I figured out what he was up to when I found my rest and recreation periods falling as often as not at the same time as hers. Regardless of nationality and provided there was room on a wingship going in the right direction, personnel could spend their leave time in someone else's back yard. After a while we realised it was due to Joe and his counterpart at her patch, Europa Four, cooking our work schedules. Neither of us objected although the possibility did cross my mind. All right, only once, and it was totally without conviction. When I got around to broaching the subject with Joe, he swore it was nothing to do with him. In any case, as he was quick to point out, interfering with duty schedules without good reason was a breach of regulations. Regulations! Now that's not a word I ever associated with Joe and I don't recall he ever used it until that day.

I entered Joe's office to find him staring out over the runway. There were a couple of robots shifting sand from the external storage area, a never ending task if ever there was one, but nothing flying in or out. His office was the nearest thing to a suburban habitat back home I ever saw. How he got some of that stuff out here with space on the cargo ships at such a premium, I never discovered. And there was that nineteenth century mechanical clock of his - always ticking away. He never adjusted it to compensate for the slightly longer Martian day so it always measured the time at his hometown on Earth. Even more than the greenery of the biodomes, that office of his seemed so out of place on this planet that I felt at odds with reality whenever I went up there.

'Sit down, Brett,' he said, stepping over to the low table. Joe, a grey-haired, tall and slightly stooping man in his late-seventies, was usually pretty equable. Others might have chosen to retain a more youthful appearance but he didn't worry about that. Anyhow, when you know a guy as well as I knew Joe, a plain speaking, straightforward man, you can sense when something isn't right.

He pushed a cold beer my way then began, 'We've had an official decree from Chief Executive Hammond. I won't go into all the details and it isn't something that will affect everyone, at least not for a time. You, Brett, it will effect. Putting it simply, we're to put a hold on some joint scientific programs and *all* non-commercial operations with other nationalities plus we're to introduce security measures. I'm telling you first, and unofficially I might add, because – well, I'm telling you, that's all.'

'Security!' I responded. 'Who needs security out here? Security against what?'

'I wish I could answer that, son. Until now, earth left us to solve most of our problems as we saw fit, mainly because there were no realistic options. We had to help each other out regardless of nationality, regardless of political circumstances back home and no one bothered much over territorial boundaries.'

As Joe talked, I wondered about security. On Earth, almost everything anyone said or did was recorded and stored in case someone felt the need to refer to it later. That was the kind of over regulated insanity I was glad to shake off. That way of thinking hadn't taken a hold in the colonies because we had different priorities – the main one being to survive. Everyone had their responsibilities and if you got caught doing something you shouldn't be doing you couldn't exactly take to the hills! We were flexible about a lot of things that would have been tightly regulated on Earth. We needed to be to keep the show running.

'We have to accept the status quo is changing now,' continued Joe. 'With the asteroid and Titan projects stalled, the powers that be on Earth have been asking why the colonies don't produce more – why they don't pay their way. Mining operations are being intensified under the Consortium but outside that there's increasing pressure for people to stick to political boundaries – particularly the UAS, since through Frontier Mining they control by far the biggest slice of the Consortium. We're about to lose some of the freedoms we take for granted - freedoms we've known since the colonies were established. I guess our people committed the sin of settling down and multiplying instead of building everything up and seeing it out for a few years until it was time to head for home.'

As Joe and I knew, the biggest setback had raised its head years ago. Even before the war they'd realised back on Earth there was no way anyone was going to terraform this planet until long after the investment blew out. Generations they were saying when humans first arrived here. Generations became centuries until it landed on them like an avalanche: terraforming Mars was even less likely than those other big ideas flaunted by the academics. Theory is fine until you go and check out the show for yourself. The only major power on Earth that wasn't shedding quite as many tears was China. The Chinese had been so successful economically on the home planet they'd never considered it important enough to invest in as large a chunk of distant Mars as the other power blocks had.

'But what about the International Council,' I asked, 'don't they have anything to say about what Frontier is trying to push through?'

'Maybe they would but except for their representative on our space station the IC is still on Earth. We're a long way away and with that you have to add the influence of the industrial conglomerates with their financial clout. And I don't just mean their legitimate dealings, either.

Still, most of us are on the IC's side and they've always been on ours.'

Joe was right, of course. The International Council had looked after colonial interests ever since it had been established in the previous century, right after the war. Their space station was put into service to support the colonies. It operates as a docking facility for some interplanetary flights as well as for the shuttles and it holds supplies in case of emergency. Administrator for Colonial Affairs up there in orbit was Amalia Barbosa. Secretary Barbosa was respected by us all and worked for the interests of everyone on the planet. Like most of us, she had little time for the big business power jockeying and politics on Earth.

'The trouble now, Brett,' Joe continued, 'is that the colonists are becoming mutually suspicious. That's bad - real bad. There was never a hint of anything like that until recently. We've had no problems here at Number One but there's talk - undercurrents - things that don't make a lot of sense.'

'I've heard the occasional remark from my passengers, Joe, but nothing that sounded too serious.'

'No, son, you're way above it most of the time. You don't pick up some of the rumours that are filtering through from a number of the outstations in spite of Hammond trying to keep the lid on things. I've picked up tales of robot equipment going haywire, especially the new deep level stuff the Consortium recently sent out: crustal probes returning to the surface with nonsensical information or none at all. I also hear two or three probes have disappeared without trace but you know what happens when people speculate – hearsay becomes accepted fact. I have no idea what's going on though I guess someone could be trying to mess up schedules and operations – hence the security factor. That'd be real enough. Anyhow, some of the mining executives are levelling accusations. The Europeans, the Russians, the Chinese - our own people. They've all dusted off the word, "sabotage," without actually pointing a finger. Except for the Russians - they've accused just about everybody. At least their boss, Pazukhin, has.'

'From what I hear, that guy never won any prizes for diplomacy,' I put in.

'Sure, "Happy Pazukhin." After the shady deals he was involved in on Earth, his own government talked him into moving out here. They figured he'd do less harm to their image on a different planet. Earth's gain, our loss, you might say. Now Hammond's wearing the big hat and it's generally believed he holds a large personal stake in Frontier as well as having his fingers in other parts of the Consortium. From what I gather, he's moved around quite a bit since easing back from the military - getting involved with the senate then muscling in on colonial policies. Of late he's taken it on himself to issue directives without the courtesy of prior consultation. I've never had so much as a, "Good morning, Joe," out of him since he landed. He's never placed a foot outside of Number Five to my knowledge. If he's here to finger whoever or whatever might be causing the problems, he sure is keeping the lid on things. I could be wrong but my guess is that like the rest of us, he doesn't have a goddamned clue. Maybe there really isn't anything sinister – maybe we just had a few glitches. You know and I know, things *can* happen that way. Nevertheless, the feeling that there's something affecting operations isn't going to vanish overnight, I'm sure of that.'

Joe got up and strolled over to gaze out across the desert. 'I never met the General myself,' he said, 'but I understand you did.'

Joe was right about that. Leo and I had encountered Virgil Hammond before we graduated from the Academy. He once dropped by to lecture us on military affairs. He also talked at length about his grandfather, Saul Hammond, who was something of a hero during the last major conflict on Earth. The family had been high profile in the military for a century and a half so I reckon that's how little Virgil grew up to be a General, though I don't believe he ever saw any action. He described the last war as, "a crusade against the powers of darkness," and I guess that's the way a lot of people must have seen things in granddaddy Saul's time. Then there was the speech from our own president about the fortress of civilisation and democracy standing against a tide of medieval fundamentalism. I remember my father replaying that speech. He told me how his school lessons were cut on the network the day it was broadcast.'

'Sure,' I replied, after some thought, 'but a good few of us at the Academy regarded Hammond as a religious nut. Rumour was that he headed some hard-line underground sect that grew out of the war but none of us rookies ever got involved – leastways not as far as I know. That's the last thing we want out here when everyone should be working together. Virgil Hammond's no friend of the International Council either. He let us all know in his speeches at the Academy how hard granddaddy Saul campaigned against its establishment after the war ended. He was mighty proud of the fact.'

Joe turned away from the armaplast shell then said, 'Maybe that's why the UAS off-loaded him onto us. Maybe they figure he'll cause fewer problems on Mars. It worked with Pazukhin.'

'Could be, Joe,' I answered, 'but Pazukhin was never more than a small-time politician. Hammond's a much bigger fish as we're beginning to discover. But you said it was going to affect me sooner than other people. How so?'

'Brett, this should have been good news. I'd got something put by as a surprise for your next leave. We owe the Europeans a big favour and they're looking to call it in whilst they still can. For some time they've wanted to send a team over to the east side of Olympus, about two hundred and fifty kilometres due west of here. It's almost on our doorstep geographically speaking but we've never sent personnel, not even robots out there because aerial surveys never gave us reason to do that. You've flown around the volcano often enough - you know what that region is like.'

'Sure, it's a mixed desert terrain with broken plateaus, mesas and outcrops - not too good a place for even a shuttle landing I'd say.'

'Not only risky, Brett, but expensive, and it would require approval from the European General Administrator for them to send out a shuttle. It

28

would also mean the crew going a long way on foot because, as I understand it, what they want to look at is some distance from any practical landing site. They're pretty cagey about the mission but as the volcano area is undesignated territory we can't object. What they have admitted is that one of their pilots thinks there may be some kind of wreckage in one of those canyons, though they claim that's of secondary interest. Anyhow, I'm assured they won't tread on our feet because it's a scientific rather than a commercial survey. So, I felt obliged to help out with the proviso they keep us informed over whatever they turn up, whether it looks to be of commercial value or no. They agreed.'

'Okay,' I said, 'so how do I fit into the scheme?'

'Well, they've assigned the project to Karin. Planetary study is a major part of her work after all and in spite of her tender years she is senior science officer at Europa Four. I agreed to supply the ground vehicle as long as I also supplied the backup crew. They didn't like that one bit and I can see why. We know what can happen with new discoveries: you put in the initial effort to get the prestige, then there's a conflict of interests and someone else benefits. Anyhow, she talked them over.' Joe's face broke into a planet-sized smile as he continued. 'You volunteered your services as back-up, Brett - that's the surprise! Meanwhile, we're hoping to keep it from under Hammond's nose. I don't think the Chief Executive would approve. Oh, and Karin arrives here by wingship tomorrow.'

'Well, thanks, Joe, but I never went on an extended overland expedition before. Who else will be coming along?'

'Who else!' exclaimed Joe. 'What the hell makes you think there's anyone else?'

'Well - regulations. I understood that any trip over five kilometres -.'

'Sometimes you make me wonder, son.' he interrupted. 'Here am I breaking ten or more rules and doing my darnedest to -.'

'Okay - okay, three's a crowd,' I said, trying not to appear overly enthusiastic. 'You have my confirmation, Joe, whatever it is I'm letting myself in for.'

'I wouldn't authorise it if I didn't think it was safe, Brett, you know that - and the Europeans wouldn't take undue risks with Karin. The worst thing you have to contend with as far as I can see is around sixty kilometres of sand dunes inside some old crater they labelled Olympia two-eight-five. The ground vehicles are as safe and reliable as anything we've got and authorisation for their use never needed to go above base command level. You know, son, if it wasn't for the company you'll be keeping, your only problem might be downright boredom.' Joe fetched two more beers but continued talking. 'It looks like the last time we'll be able to act independently over anything like this. And I hate to say it after all the effort I now admit to having put in, but it may be difficult for you and Karin to get together again for a while - courtesy of Chief Executive goddamned Hammond!'

Were things going to turn out that difficult, I wondered? Nevertheless, the idea of the field trip was different and as Joe went on to explain, we'd just about make it inside a Martian day, which for the wilfully pedantic is a mite over twenty-four hours and thirty-seven minutes. I'd flown almost everywhere on the planet but unlike Karin, I'd travelled no great distance on the surface. There was nothing unusual about that since, with the exception of the outstation workers, not so many people had. Still, it would give the two of us a chance to reach some solid conclusions about our relationship. As much as I thought, or felt I ought to think about her, one side of me warned, 'Don't do it! Don't get hooked! You're a free spirit!' The other half said, 'Why worry, Brett? It's going to happen sooner or later unless you plan to spend your old age staring out of the biodome into a desert of memories. She was and is a genuine good-looker and unlike some she's actually as young as she appears.'

No one is supposed to have access to a person's real age unless they allow it but Mars didn't have Earth level security. She'd probably checked out my age, anyhow. And it's genuine if anyone asks.

As for the journey - in a world utterly hostile to human life, we would be totally alone.

***

I was used to getting in and out of bed at odd hours. That was the inevitable result of flying - of starting out in one time zone then ending up in another. Day, night - day, night - it ceased to matter after a while. You developed your own internal clock and lived mainly on that. I guess it was another form of isolation.

We were scheduled to be on board the ground vehicle and ready to leave at five-thirty, so with that in mind I took it for granted I'd be up and ready for breakfast whilst Karin was still in the land of dreams. Not so. I awoke to find an empty space at my side. Already taking her shower, she'd been too considerate to dig me in the ribs. I was perched on the edge of the bed, wondering if the dead-fish eyes that stared back reproachfully out of the mirror really belonged to me when her fresh, blue-eyed, flaxen haired smile zeroed in on me from around the doorway. I felt like a cornered animal.

'Ah - we're awake at last!' she said, fixing her red kimono. 'Who tried to convince me that pilots never really sleep? And as for snoring -!'

'Oh, Christ,' I groaned. It felt like my mouth needed a spell under the dust filters.

'You had too much to drink last night, my sweet,' she added, kissing me on the cheek. 'And as you never accepted a genetic catalyst you are not able to deal with it properly. Keep looking at yourself like that and you'll become depressed.'

'I'm depressed already,' I muttered, turning from my own stubbled image to watch her in the mirror as she moved about gathering her things. Slim and beautiful, she looked like she ought to be heading out somewhere classy for dinner, not into the freezing Martian desert at the crack of dawn. And whilst my enthusiasm was still cowering in bed, she was anxious to keep to a schedule we couldn't let slip. Once reinforced with a light breakfast, we were ready to go and, dressed in metallic blue service overalls, we headed out to the ground vehicle bay at just gone five o'clock. On the way she said to me, 'Brett, we'll have to wear these for our picnic today. Not very flattering, are they.'

'Oh, you're okay.' I answered. She could have wrapped herself in a tractor dustsheet and still turned people's heads. Particularly mine.

Everything we needed to take, in addition to standard equipment already on board, was contained in each of the two small cases carried by Karin and myself. I assumed both held her scientific equipment.

Unlike some larger service buildings, our ground vehicle facility was pressurised but, being an older station, you still had to pass through a standard airlock. We entered the bay to find the vehicle gleaming like a blue and white beetle with the base identification code in bright red on her sides. Her pair of claw-like manipulation arms were drawn back like she was about to groom herself for the journey. Two of the maintenance crew were standing by one of the shoulder-high tracks and a third, on the service platform, was still wiping over the transparent curves of the armaplast cabin where it protruded forward of the tracks.

We didn't expect a send-off committee but as we were stowing Karin's cases in the rear bay of the vehicle, next to rescue equipment and other paraphernalia, Joe's upper image materialised by the wall. 'Hi, you two. Have a good trip and take it easy out there. We'll keep an eye on your systems but report in before you leave the GV. And don't take any risks. I mean that, now - we have to keep this trip low profile. And take care of that old jalopy, especially if you steer her on manual. She's a third of our ground fleet. Any scratches or dents I make you pay for!'

'Don't worry, Joe,' grinned Karin, 'I'll keep an eye on him!'

'Who needs to drive this thing, anyhow,' I put in. 'And I'm on leave, Joe - remember!'

'I'll see you both for a late evening dinner,' smiled Joe, before fading out.

With co-ordinates in the vehicle's navigation system, she would take us as close as possible to the designated spot without my help. Still, I liked to take the controls when flying; I liked to take Delta Seven a little off course or down a bit lower to look at something interesting - against regulations, naturally. Secretly, I'd already adopted the same attitude toward the ground vehicle. It was when I closed the rear door I discovered someone with an anachronistic and shallow mentality had scrawled across it, 'Lovers' Express.' I pretended not to notice. Karin noticed me pretending not to notice and smiled to herself. I swore quietly I'd find the joker who did it and make them swallow the marker. Right then I was feeling a little sensitive but I saw the lighter side of it - eventually.

Once through the small airlock - it only squashed in four people at a time – or two with pressure suits and back-packs - we passed along the centre of the vehicle - between lockers, bunks, wash cabin and the small laboratory; each a triumph of ergonomics and engineering. It was designed to accommodate four people for a couple of weeks but the control cabin, reasonably spacious as it was, only seated two. I figured they didn't want to encourage sightseeing when there was work to be done on board. Karin, having guessed how much I wanted to play at being driver, said, 'You should take us out, Brett. I'm used to these things anyway. I'll sit here and watch the world go by and you can do the hard work.'

Our display showed the decrease in pressure inside the building. As it dipped below ten millibars, first the inner then the outer airlock door slid silently upward. The temperature reading for outside hovered around a bracing minus 85°C. 'Yeah,' I muttered, 'great day for a picnic.'

Fingers of red sand splayed over the floor then began running into the grid behind the open doors. The desert was coming in to meet us - beckoning with a frozen hand. The power plant whined at our rear, we shuddered a little then started forward. As we emerged, the horizon to our east smouldered a dim, lurid orange whilst our lights speared into a mist that hung in slowly shifting curtains. We turned to the west where, ahead as well as above, the sky was deep indigo, still ablaze with multi-coloured stars. There was no outside maintenance crew to wave goodbye as we moved off so we were straight away on our own. I felt fine and eager to go, whilst Karin sat back to gaze out at the sky. Our route from the base took us by the parking area on the opposite side of the runway where my wingship, Delta Seven, waited.

'Look at her standing all alone there,' I said. 'I hope she doesn't mind me going away for a while.'

Karin peered at the big aircraft, a ghost-like image in the glow of runway lights whilst her two big fins cut the horizon of a slowly brightening Martian dawn. To me that wingship proclaimed the triumph of humanity in a place that held precious little sympathy for any of us.

'Do you think she will miss you?' asked Karin

'Sure she will. I reckon she'll be jealous as hell.'

'Jealous?' smiled Karin, 'no, I don't think your big bird will be jealous of our big beetle.'

'No, I meant she'll be jealous of you - not the ground vehicle!'

'Jealous of me? I hope not. I wouldn't want to keep you both apart. I know you're truly happy when you're roaming the skies. Perhaps Leo will fly her whilst you are gone. I know you wouldn't want anyone else to do that.'

A bright spot was locked onto the route on the navigation screen. I could have released the steering and let the vehicle go automatic right then but I wanted to appear occupied as I thought about what Karin had said. Looking aside, I watched the last of our outbuildings pass by. To our rear, Delta Seven appeared abandoned to the shadows. I hoped that if Joe did need to send her out then it would be without a pilot.

Karin grabbed my attention when she pointed into the sky, saying, 'There, you must see it often when you're flying at night.' High up and slightly to our south drifted the spectral light of Phobos, larger and closer of the two small Martian moons. An enormous boulder, Phobos travels in its orbit much quicker than the planet rotates so those with nothing better to do can watch it cross from west to east three times through each Martian day. I must have seen it hundreds of times but it didn't look much different from ground level. If anyone had suggested one of those dead lumps of rock might soon play a critical part in human affairs, I'd have needed more than a little convincing.

During those minutes we spent discussing the Virgil Hammond phenomenon, Karin made it clear he was not on her list of favourites – after which she changed the subject by asking, 'Brett, how old is this vehicle? Joe called her an old - an old something - I didn't quite hear what.'

I felt she sensed my own misgivings about Hammond and wanted to get me into a more amiable frame of mind. 'An old jalopy,' I replied. 'That's a twentieth century term for a dilapidated automobile. As to how old - well that's not so easy to answer.'

'Not easy,' she smiled. 'Okay, I can tell you our ground vehicles are about fifteen years old. That wasn't too difficult.'

'Ah, there's a paradox,' I responded. 'Virtually everything in this buggy except the basic shell has been renewed over the years in our own plant. So you tell me - is she new or is she old? I don't know. I've heard some of them back there argue about it.'

'Like the Athenian state galley in ancient times,' she replied as our lights glared into an expanse of rock-strewn desert. 'The hull timbers, the sails and the rigging all had to be replaced over the years because they went rotten. So - one philosopher argued that it was a different boat because the materials were not original but another said it was really the same because the image remained unaltered.'

'Well then,' I answered, 'it sounds to me like those old guys had too much time on their hands. Anyhow, I checked under this old crate yesterday afternoon. The timbers are just fine and we had the sails patched up last week!'

We called up some music and before long the sky was brightening and the stars beginning to fade whilst ahead of us lay undulating emptiness. After a while, the strangeness, the vastness, began to press in on me. There can't have been much of this world I hadn't flown over at one time or another so I thought I knew it like the back of my hand. That went to prove how little I knew about the back of my hand. We were travelling along the ground, our movements governed by its every rise and fall. I couldn't lift off into the sky. I couldn't soar above it. I felt swallowed by an immensity I thought I had long ago come to terms with. The desert wasn't so off-putting to Karin because she knew why it was there, where it came from and where it would go. To her it was laid out in time as well as space - an exercise in geology, in silicates and iron oxides - the result of volcanism, wind erosion and mass wastage – an ongoing metamorphosis of the red planet's being and identity.

Now on more level ground, we were proceeding at a pretty respectable rate. Europa Four called in so Karin chatted to her people for a time. They commented on our being ahead of schedule, too. That was the result of my taking the ground vehicle along at a higher speed than I ought. Anyhow, that's what the control panel kept telling me. I hate machines that nag. Delta Seven seldom nagged - but that's because I'd found a way to cancel out some of her safety systems. Yeah, I know – it's against regulations.

By the time we were getting into full daylight I was more at ease. The steady whine of the power plant and the now almost imperceptible swaying of the vehicle, as well as Karin's self-assured good humour - I guess they all helped.

'You know,' I remarked, 'Delta Seven could have got us there in well under half an hour instead of over four.'

'Yes, dear, but as you wouldn't be able to land there, what would be the point?'

'Okay, so what's the point in what we're doing?' I asked. 'What Joe told me about the wreckage sounded pretty unlikely. He reckoned there was nothing in the area to take this much trouble over. I didn't want to push you too hard over that but since your people are being unduly secretive I figure there has to be enough to justify the time and trouble.'

'You're right, Brett - they need to be secretive and I haven't told you much, have I.' She brushed a wisp of hair from her cheek and looked at me with unaccustomed seriousness. 'And I have to tell you because we're sharing this journey together so you are going to find out anyway. Let's do a deal - right? Put her on autopilot, get us both some coffee and I promise to explain everything I know.'

'It's a deal,' I responded, swinging the seat around, quite certain I was about to learn a lot more than Joe had been told. I returned with the coffee and there was the part-risen sun already casting a shadow of the ground vehicle way ahead of us. We swivelled the seats to face each other though I couldn't help but keep a slice of my attention on the desert ahead.

'It's true, Brett,' she began, 'that the area around Olympus has always been of interest to the Europeans. In the past we've talked of exploring it on the ground. Survey robots or drones could be sent over to do that though drones don't work so well out here. But what is the point in people coming to this planet if we don't go and see things for ourselves?'

Now there was a sentiment with which I wholeheartedly agreed, even though my own observations tended to be from several kilometres up.

'Anyway,' she continued, 'a little over a year ago, one of our pilots reported something odd. A fluctuating glare of light was how she described it, and that was during the day. We had no reason to doubt her - she stored the co-ordinates so naturally we kept our eyes open. We really did think it might have been a piece of unrecorded wreckage catching the sun - maybe something from the early days – a failed probe that no one had wanted to admit was theirs but one that could be historically important. We studied close-up satellite images. They showed unusual landforms but there was no wreckage. It's not a region our own aircraft cross very often and though we kept a look out, none of our people reported anything like that again.

Now, Brett – please don't say anything about this, not even to Joe, but soon after that sighting we began to monitor the communications of other people's wingships passing over the area. Then three weeks ago we picked up a call from one of the Asian pilots. He reported seeing what he described as a bright glow. Both we and the Asians found excuses to divert pilots as well as satellites over the area to scan it in detail but there was still no sign of what caused the lights, though there are unusual rock formations. They knew nothing of our sighting and they didn't inform anyone else of theirs. But we know it cannot be wreckage and we know humans have never been there. Those lights we cannot explain.'

'I must have flown over that region a dozen times and more, day and night,' I said. 'I never noticed anything. Then I guess it would be unlikely unless I happened to be looking at exactly the right spot. On the other hand, maybe it's just coincidence.'

'Brett, it's no coincidence. Their pilot gave *exactly* the same co-ordinates as ours, and guess what - both observations occurred when the sun was at the same angle in the sky. Fascinating isn't it? Now you and I are going to find out what they both saw, so our scientific survey could end up being quite legitimate.'

***

By seven-fifteen we had negotiated a low ridge; the eroded wall of that ancient crater Joe had referred to as Olympia two-eight-five, and were entering the dune field. The temperature outside had risen to a balmy, minus 52°C - what we might have expected only twenty degrees north of the equator in early summer. Karin had taken over the controls to enjoy a spell of steering but once in the dunes we found it easier to let the ground vehicle take over and travel at her own pace. These dunes were quite modest compared with some since they averaged only around three metres from trough to peak. Our

41

vehicle rose and fell like a boat, cresting one rise then descending gently before climbing the next slope, the sound of her engines rising and falling with an easy, reassuring purr. That didn't stop me imagining conditions there during a sandstorm. You could be overwhelmed by the sand. If your location wasn't known you might well disappear without trace. Maybe they'd find you one day. Maybe they wouldn't. But for now, the sandscape was utterly still.

By eight forty-five we were clear of the dune field and trundling over the opposite side of the crater. Another kilometre saw the ground levelling off into a brick-dust plain with weird, wind-sculpted formations of pinkish-grey rock rising all about - some of them two, maybe three metres high. They made me think of unfinished stone animals, people even, trying to struggle up out of the sand from the grip of the bedrock. You'd never see them properly from the air so when Karin put a hand on my shoulder, when she breathed in my ear, 'Ooh, aren't they spooky?' it well summed up my own feelings. I tried to visualise what they must look like at night lit only by the stars and with a ground mist flowing close about. So striking were those bizarre forms that I was lost in my own weird imaginings when Karin exclaimed, 'Brett, look ahead!'

Gazing to the horizon I could make out an uneven, pinkish-mauve escarpment rising from the haze. After a while, what had appeared as a continuous line of cliffs resolved into a series of distinct mesas. Karin checked the display and said, 'Good, dead on target and we're still ahead of schedule.'

'Would anyone out there be upset if we were ten minutes late?' I asked.

She leaned over and kissed me. 'Now, now - pilots are supposed to set a good example. They are supposed to take schedules seriously.'

'I never get too up-tight about them,' I remarked, taking over the controls once more. 'I had enough of that Earthside.'

If I'd been less than enthusiastic over the scenery when we set out, by now I had changed my mind. At first, those mesas didn't appear too exciting but as we drew closer, they impressed me in a way they never had from above. The nearest looked awesome with dark basalt walls, tinged red with windblown sand rising sheer from the desert. Karin scanned the precipice closest to us, saying 'You wouldn't think it from here, Brett, but that cliff is over 200 metres high.'

It appeared close even though we were almost a kilometre away whilst others of its kind lay ahead and to each side. The mesas were not level but tilted this way and that like great, flat-topped bergs about to founder in a rolling sea of sand.

'How much d'you know about this area?' I asked.

'Oh, a little. What we see about us is the remains of an ancient lava plateau built up in layers as the Tharsis region and the volcano grew. It was stressed then began to fragment many millions of Earth years ago as the crust lifted and fell. You can't imagine the time that has passed since wind and frost began to erode the plateau away. The crust beneath the plateau was weak and that explains why the mesas have sunk in places after breaking apart.

43

It's mapped in detail from the air but there's always something new to find when you're here on the ground.'

It was her slight accent and the musical lilt of her voice as much her comments that kept my attention. But something else appeared further west to fuel our interest. Beyond the mesas, veiled by distance but running in a continuous line across the horizon, lay the Olympian Wall, an immense escarpment, roughly circular when seen from space. It defines much of the perimeter of Mount Olympus, greatest volcano in the Solar System. Soaring in places to a height of six kilometres the wall dwarfed that which now so dwarfed us. Flying close by it puts our greatest efforts on this planet into a very sobering perspective.

As for the volcano itself - well, that's something else. Spread across eighteen degrees of latitude, no one can see Olympus from the ground. Its immense bulk, rising gradually to a height of over twenty-two kilometres, lay beyond our field of view. The base diameter comes close to 600 kilometres and for those who like comparisons, that's big enough to blot out the state of Arizona! Only spacecraft fly over Olympus. Wingships skirt about her lower slopes, though most routes are planned to avoid this mother of all obstructions. Having passed by the first mesa, we were able to see the western side where the area falling within its shadow was streaked by carbon dioxide frost. Closer now loomed the other mesas - great tabular wrecks laying in disorder as far as the eye could see, with sunlight glowing on their weathered flanks. When the ground began to fall gently, levelling out into a broad natural trench, our navigator said we should be turning right by some sixty degrees to head north-west. I duly complied and as we climbed again we found ourselves approaching a tilted mesa that reared up directly across our path.

'That thing is broken in two,' I remarked. That much was obvious enough, one side being lower and out of alignment with the other.

'Ah - and look at the middle of it,' said Karin, pointing ahead.

Running diagonally down from the top was a black dislocation. It appeared as if the whole gigantic slab had been lifted by some monstrous hand then dropped back into the desert. The navigator told us we should head straight for the dislocation so we continued fifteen more minutes until it seemed we were almost under those towering walls. The ground, however - a mixture of sand and scree - was by then rising so steeply that I wondered how much further we could go before the vehicle started to lose traction. Our status display was telling us it would be pretty soon. As we continued to climb we passed by irregular fragments of basalt protruding through the sand. Nearer the cliff face, a few of these were considerably larger than the ground vehicle, becoming so numerous that I had to steer around them.

'I guess these have some time been detached from the walls of the mesa,' I remarked, not bothering to disguise my apprehension.

'Oh, more than likely,' answered Karin in her carefree manner. 'They will have been here for a long time though – millions of years most likely.'

'That's fine,' I remarked, 'but what d'you reckon are the chances of some more coming adrift over the next hour or so?'

Her face dimpled with amusement. 'I don't think so, Brett. Maybe in a hundred, maybe in another thousand years. I think you're a pessimist again because you're not flying.'

She was absolutely right. With that vast, dark wall rearing skyward to fill our vision, there was no denying I'd have been much happier had we been circling overhead. I visualised Delta Seven drifting in the sky high above like some great white manta. The navigator warned we were climbing too steeply to go on. If I ignored it we'd soon be churning grit and getting nowhere. It didn't seem like we could have gotten much further anyway because of those fallen chunks so I backed the GV off and put the controls in neutral. Directly before us lay the fracture, at its base an ominous twisted gap, blacker even than the black wall from which it opened.

'Doesn't feel too welcoming around here,' I remarked.

'No, not really,' she answered, peering through the armaplast shell. 'Makes me think of some great dark bat about to close its wings over us.'

'Gee, thanks,' I mumbled. I saw she was grinning.

According to our sensors, we were less than fifty metres away from the base of the precipice and that in turn was over a hundred and eighty metres to the top of the higher section. Then Karin noticed me staring at the navigation display and said, 'Do you see what it's telling us?'

'Yes but I -. Have *you* looked at what it's telling us?'

She peered by me for some moments. 'Of course I have, Brett, dear – long before we set out. It's quite interesting - don't you think?'

'Interesting? Yes, I guess you could say that. Er - very interesting.'

I followed her gaze as she turned her attention back to the basalt wall. Oblique sunlight was striking the fissure to pick out its jagged edges more clearly. The navigator displayed the co-ordinates for our intended destination. They placed it some distance inside the mesa.

'Well, Brett, it looks as if there's only one way we can go.'

'Are you serious?' I asked. 'We should send a spider in there to check things out first. There are three in the storage bay with nothing else to do.'

'If we do that we will have to wait until they return because they won't be able to transmit to us from inside the mesa. By then we may not have enough time left to go and see things for ourselves. I wouldn't want the spiders transmitting anyway. That might not be as secure as I hope our link to base is from your ground vehicle.'

'So we have to go inside the thing,' I mumbled. 'Sounds great.'

Before ten o'clock all the necessary checks were done, we were suited up and ready to squeeze into the airlock. Karin had called up her people to tell them we were going walkabout. I had informed Joe and he'd said, 'Okay, son, but don't you take any risks. Like I said, I want you both back here for dinner.'

In our white pressure suits we waited for the airlock to decompress. Karin climbed down the extended metal ladder. I followed, jumping most of the way, then we stood together just gazing about. Karin had enough enthusiasm for both of us, which was just as well since when I looked at the mesa, I didn't have any. The sand was a kind of orange-red, speckled with basalt grit. It felt soft underfoot as we trudged around to the stowage bay. She took out one of the small cases, grinned at me through her visor, moved around and clipped it under my backpack. 'There, now I have found a use for you.'

'There can't be much inside that,' I commented, sensing how light the case was.

'No, but I'll want to collect rock specimens so you had better be feeling fit.'

As we plodded up the rise, fine sand rose in flurries from our boots to swirl like vapour across the wide sunlit slope. 'There's quite a strong wind here,' I said, aware through my sensors of the thin air singing about my suit.

'It's because of the rock formations,' answered Karin. 'They channel the air like buildings in a city. Think what it must be like in a sandstorm.'

I didn't care to. I had something else on my mind and we were heading toward it.

Once you're away from anything built by humans, the scale of these landscapes and formations can be very deceptive. What had earlier appeared little more than a crack in the mesa had resolved itself as a fissure when we approached in the ground vehicle. Now we were only ten or so steps away, it had grown to a gallery around six metres across. A gap of six metres may not sound off-putting but standing at the foot of that cliff, I imagined us a pair of insects about to crawl beneath a barn door. When I glanced back down the slope at the ground vehicle, she was a bug lost in a vast ocean of sand. The sun was well up but once within the entrance to that passage, the way before us appeared totally black. Worse, the left hand wall of the gallery sloped upward quite noticeably to the left, which meant the dislocated but matching right hand wall was an overhang. As we moved inside, I felt we were entering a pair of black jaws that might at any moment close upon us. Karin switched on her suit lamps and grinned right at me. 'As we didn't send in the spider, you will have to do instead.' Her manner was disarmingly relaxed.

The perspective was so odd that I wasn't sure if I was standing upright or not so I needed to steady myself. I switched on my lamps and rangefinder, aiming them down the passage. 'I get a reading of less than eighteen metres,' I told her. 'It must be blocked or change direction. Have you any idea how far this goes?'

'I rechecked the satellite images whilst you were getting our suits ready,' she answered. 'It opens out into a valley at under one kilometre. There may have been a continuation of this passage on the other side but satellite images don't show it. Either it didn't open like this one or it's closed up since.'

Her last remark did nothing to bolster my confidence. Angling up my helmet lamp, I looked at the black wall curving over our heads. We'd be out of base contact all the time we were inside. I imagined our voices would echo like rolling thunder had this been on Earth.

As we reached the first bend she peered at me through her visor and said, 'I don't like this place either, Brett. If you were not with me I don't think I would care to go on.'

I was tempted to say, 'Fine by me - let's turn around right now,' but we'd travelled a long way so, what the hell, I wasn't going to quit and we both knew it. I took her hand in mine as we continued on. The walls reflected practically no light so that meant we relied on our beams picking out the paler floor of the chasm as it wound on into black nothingness. We started whistling, swinging arms to our tune in some kind of crazy defiance - two bright embers drifting in a fathomless vault. As we went in deeper, however, the gallery was beginning to narrow. Until then, we had walked on quite firm sand with, here and there, the odd chunk of basalt but as the gap narrowed further, something strange was happening. Instead of seeing solid ground we were wading through the shimmering ghost of a river. Because the space had become more constricted, the wind was flowing quicker, raising fine sand, carrying it out of the darkness to flood about our ankles like running water. We moved with greater caution, using our range finders in case the sand flow hid a dip in the ground - or worse.

A few metres further and we could no longer walk side by side. The thought crossed my mind that if it kept on narrowing we'd eventually have to stop. Pushing on in front I soon needed to walk at an angle whilst steadying myself against the wall at my left. The right hand side of the gallery sloped low over our heads like a caved-in ceiling. So close that our lamps picked out embedded crystals that glistened as tiny gems in the rough basalt. Claustrophobia? I was discovering it in full. I imagined the life support unit in my suit to have all departments on full alert right then and I was anxious neither of us should strike our helmets, tough as they were, against anything sharp. We had reckoned on thirty minutes at most to get through provided we didn't meet any obstructions but it seemed like we'd been in there much longer. I was beginning to think it would never end. I was wishing us both a light year away from there when two things happened. First, I noticed the gallery was opening out once more, then Karin's voice cut in, 'Brett, dear - did you remember to bring the food for our picnic - it may be in short supply at the other end!'

'What!' I exclaimed, stopping dead in my tracks, 'is your stomach all you can think of right now?'

She prodded my arm and laughed, 'At the moment, yes. Breakfast wasn't up to much at your place and the ground vehicle rations are pretty basic. So keep moving, lover boy - we haven't got all day!'

She had coped with the place far better than me but by now I was telling myself everything would be all right. I was greatly relieved when only a couple of minutes later we were seeing light. Vague and dim, but light! The gallery was rising gently, growing broader, and I knew at last we had made it to whatever lay beyond. Soon we were treading rubble - soon rounding what proved to be the last bend. Ahead of us appeared an irregular, tilted gash glowing pinkish apricot. The sky!

Emerging from the chasm, we found before us what at first struck me as the interior of an immense, open box - a roughly rectangular valley hemmed in by the high basalt walls of the mesa. The place was like some vast, empty theatre. I called out, 'Wow!' and Karin exclaimed, 'Oh, Brett, what a sight this is!'

With some features on the planet you lose your grip on perspective so that sheer size becomes meaningless. Here, it was not so and the grandeur of the place impressed itself upon us at once. For a while we stood in a kind of reverent silence, holding hands, gazing about - a couple of kids about to enter a magic kingdom. We were atop a moderate slope of black scree, no more than a couple of metres above a pavement of grey lava. This lava floor inclined downward from left to right across the canyon at an angle of around ten degrees. A fault line ran almost dead straight from below where we stood to the far end where it met the opposite wall. To the right of the fault, the ground dropped abruptly by over two metres. It then continued down into deeper shadow where it became buried under drifted, reddish-black sand that rose to form a smooth talus running all the way along the base of the cliff. In contrast, the walls further over to our left were bathed in sunlight some two-thirds the way down. A section of these cliffs were dislocated, tilted back as though some malignant giant had heaved parts of the mesa aside in a blind rage.

'Imagine standing here on the day that happened,' I breathed.

'I don't know, Brett. If it was sudden we might have been too busy trying to get away. On the other hand, it could have been gradual. More likely that.' Checking her rangefinder, Karin added, 'It's less than eight hundred metres to the far end and hardly more than seven hundred from side to side.' She produced a scanalyser, which she passed across the walls of the gallery from which we were about to emerge. 'The place is immensely old but we should have expected that. I register almost two billion Earth years. The plateau that once lay above us must go back to when Olympus was just a child.'

'What d'you think caused the mesa to break apart?' I asked.

'Something must have stressed it. The crust could have given way beneath or maybe it was blasted apart by the eruption that left the frozen lava floor we are going to cross.'

Both laughing, we half ran, half bounced down the slope whilst the scree of fine debris under our feet gave way no more than beach sand; then we landed on the lava pavement. Our boots on solid ground, we stepped a short distance from the cliff wall, away from the fault, then stopped. Karin raised a hand, saying, 'Brett - listen. Turn up your sound.'

I did so and waited. There was nothing - but I knew what she meant.

'This place is silent now we're in the open.' she added. 'Even the wind has gone.'

Yes, it was silent and utterly still. Not that you'd expect to hear or see anything move, apart from the occasional dust devil. But this silence was different - imposed by a solemn, monumental stage-set that made you want to lower your voice the way you might in some ancient, long deserted temple.

'Which direction d'you want to take?' I asked, gazing along the valley.

'I would prefer to head for the sunny side. We'd find the going difficult in the lower part with all that loose debris. In any case the light those pilots saw, and whatever caused it, was to the far left of the canyon and further toward the end.'

We tweaked our visor magnifications to see if we could make out anything significant. 'Look,' I said, pointing diagonally across to the base of the cliffs. 'What d'you make of that?'

'Oh, I see. Yes, it looks like -.'

'Like a group of columns?'

'Yes, that's definitely what it looks like. I think we should head straight over and check it out.'

'Okay,' I agreed, with renewed enthusiasm, 'let's go.'

It felt like we were crossing some great ceremonial plaza. And though the sun was only now making real inroads, diffused light from the sky had imparted the canyon walls with a subtle pink glow even at the lower side. The lava floor was free of sand, remarkably flat and laced with fine, polygonal cracks that promised to resolve into a regular hexagonal pattern but never actually did. Karin remarked how it had contracted upon cooling. As we walked on she busied herself recording what she felt was scientifically important. General views of the scenery, the tourist stuff, she left to me, so between us I hoped we'd capture enough of value to justify this part of the trip.

Three quarters the way across, what had attracted our attention stood out more clearly. We counted eleven columns, eight of which rose to a height of over two metres whilst the remaining three were broken or incomplete. They appeared no more than a half-metre thick and being perpendicular to the valley floor, were tilted slightly from the vertical.

'I've seen nothing like this on Mars,' said Karin. 'They must once have been a part of the mesa. They may first have been isolated by the forces that created the canyon then eroded over the passing years. And, Brett, look at the tops of those intact ones – that is *really* strange.'

Near the top of each column were clusters of a dark, crystalline material capped with basalt. Now only a few metres away she stopped to record these odd formations. Another minute and we were walking amongst the columns which, spaced well over a metre apart, reminded me of some ancient ruined temple. I could see that before long the sun would be full on them and I would have myself some great, 'how about these, folks,' sequences.

'We must take back samples,' came Karin's voice from behind as she unclipped the small case from my harness.

Lost in thought I gazed back across the valley then, walking around toward the cliff wall I found her kneeling by one of the shattered columns with the opened case at her side. The top half of the column lay by the rock wall and around it lay several crystals that must have broken loose when the thing hit the ground.

'Our ancestors were still picking nasty things out of each other's fur when this came down,' she remarked, placing five of the crystals into the case. For a time she was silent, clicking the scanalyser repeatedly, so I strolled a short way to where the basalt wall changed direction abruptly to the right. There, I discovered something else. I was about to call her over when -, 'Brett, this is most peculiar!'

I turned to see her walking toward me. 'What is?' I asked.

'Those crystals - the readings don't make sense. I've checked the scanalyser on other minerals and there's no problem. My readings from the crystals suggest that - no, that is stupid. I'll try again in the ground vehicle. What have you found?'

'It's a *very* deep hole.' I replied, because that's exactly what it appeared to be. What we had until then regarded as a solid lava floor had collapsed some three metres from the adjacent wall. A shaft, over a meter and a half across, sank into nameless black depths. Kneeling close to the edge, our suit lamps speared into darkness but revealed nothing. The words, 'Be careful!' were banging around inside my head.

'It must be an ancient lava conduit,' said Karin. 'Some areas of the planet are riddled with them. Record it, Brett, whilst I take out a sample.'

'You watch what you're doing!' I called, moving back to capture the scene as she crouched close to the edge. Too close, I thought. There was something wrong so I stepped back over.

'This will be older than -,' she started to say, but the ground was cracking where she knelt. She cried out and reached back her arm to hold on to something – anything, because the edge of the pit was giving way! I lurched forward to grab at the harness holding her life support pack but the thickness of my glove prevented me getting a hand underneath. She was going down! I was grasping at whatever I could, then her arm flew out again and I went for that, seizing it with both hands. She twisted about, kicking her legs over gaping blackness as her other hand clutched at the rock edge that itself crumbled in her grasp. I had to be quick. The pavement was giving under me as well! I hauled in desperation to drag her out. Hauled until her feet were scuffing hard against solid lava. The circulation pumps in my suit were humming like hornets but at last we were away from the pit. Even so, in spite of the lower gravity we'd almost fallen down there. Had we done so, no one would ever have known.

Karin rested on her knees, her breath coming in short gasps. She was badly shaken and so was I. Where the pavement had collapsed, the top of the shaft was no longer circular. It resembled a black mouth that grinned mockingly at us in our near misfortune. 'Next time! Next time!' it seemed to say.

My main concern was that her suit and life support pack had not suffered damage. We were three quarters of an hour away from the ground vehicle and even had I relayed a message for help via any satellite that might have passed overhead, I doubted anyone would risk getting a shuttle down onto that surface. Apart from some grazing, though, her suit and equipment were unharmed. I helped her to her feet but all she could say was, 'Oh, Brett, I'm so sorry. That was such a foolish thing to do.'

I held her tight, pressure suit or no. 'Don't you -,' I said, staring through her visor, 'don't you ever scare the shit out of me like that again! If you'd fallen, I don't know what I -! Well, I just don't!'

A tear glistened on her cheek so the two of us stood in silence until we felt calmer - until our heartbeats were closer to normal. When she smiled, when she pursed her lips at me, I knew everything was okay. I was about to ask what she next had in mind when her gaze shifted past me. Staring open-mouthed, she cried out, 'Brett - look! Look at them!'

One nasty incident had been enough but when I turned - when I saw what she was seeing, it wasn't like that. No - it wasn't like that at all.

During those traumatic minutes, the sun had risen higher above the cliffs on the opposite side of the valley. The light, creeping down the wall close by, had struck the tops of the columns nearest to it and was already falling upon the others. The crystals were aflame! They were radiating light! They were alive! They didn't shine as one but as many, stabbing out brilliant colours, each increasing in intensity, diminishing, brightening again to an uncoordinated, pulsing rhythm. Some flared bluish-white, others in vivid rainbow hues. Karin had the presence of mind to start recording the spectacle and I stepped back to capture the scene with her in it. Others began to glow as sunlight fell on them. We were witness to a dazzling, kaleidoscopic display, its glare tempered only by the safety filters in our visors.

'Brett, this is incredible!' Karin yelled. 'Really – it is too - too fantastic! This is what they saw from the air! How could anyone have guessed!'

She wasn't exaggerating. No, not a bit. The crystals blazed a symphony of light and colour intense enough to drown our thoughts. As I moved to her side she began to laugh. 'Oh, Brett, I've never seen anything so wonderful! Never!' We walked around the columns hand in hand, seeing the crystals shimmer radiance whilst colours shifted about the basalt wall behind them like some crazy light show. She grasped my arm and exclaimed, 'Brett, we're the first, the only people *ever* to witness this!'

I could think of nothing profound to say so all she got from me was, 'You bet! It's incredible!' Yet impressed as I was by the lights, a part of me was still thinking of what had happened only minutes before. I'd almost lost her - maybe both of us. And now this. What the hell was going on! As we stood in that nameless canyon bathed by the radiance of those crystals, I realised how precious Karin was to me.

'Brett!' Her words broke into my thoughts as though they'd been expressed in the lights. 'Brett, you're the only one I would want to share this with. The only one!'

Still hand in hand we backed away with no intention other than to stand in awe. Then came a sound - high-pitched like mosquitoes inside my helmet. 'Can you hear that?' I asked.

'Yes, I hear it. Is it our suit radios? Is that where it's coming from?'

The sound was increasing so I switched off my radio. It was still there so I switched my radio back on. 'It's travelling through the air. It must be the crystals.'

'Yes,' she laughed, 'that's what it is. They are singing! The crystals are singing!'

The sound grew no louder but soon began dropping in pitch. As it did we perceived the light of the crystals beginning to diminish. The ones near to the cliff wall darkened, then the others closer to us - fading in the order in which the sun had fallen on them.

'Oh, Brett,' cried Karin, 'the lights are dying!'

And that's what it seemed like - as though they had been alive - as though they had been speaking to just the two of us. The whole show had not lasted more than five minutes and before another minute had passed, the crystals were no more than fading embers with the sound entirely gone. However, when sunlight fell across those spilled upon the ground they, too, began to shimmer bright as flaming jewels against the lava. Walking over, I stooped to pick one up, taking care in case the thing was hot. Through the sensory pads of my glove it felt cold. Very cold. I was tempted to pick up some more crystals and add them to the few Karin had collected but I hesitated with my fingers stretched out above them. I felt like a thief about to grab gems from an opened casket. It didn't seem right to disturb them further so I figured just this one would be enough. Karin stood against the bright sun, watching as I rose to my feet. When the crystals on the ground had darkened we knew it was time to go. But in spite of that near disaster the place felt as if it belonged to the two of us. As if it could never belong to anyone else.

'Have you any idea how the crystals do that?' I asked as we set off, determined to stay in sunlight until reaching the chasm.

'No, but they must contain a lot of energy to release that much light. Perhaps all the sunlight they absorb by day is stored at night and alters them physically until they're triggered the following day. I hope we'll find out soon.' She hesitated, looked back then said, 'Brett, I'm beginning to think this is all a dream.'

Neither of us spoke again until we were over three quarters the way back across the canyon when I said, 'I'd like to show you more of this world from up there in the sky. Maybe sometimes you could fly with me. I'd like that a lot.'

'Yes, Brett, I'd like that, too. I'd love to go there often - to your world in the sky.'

We were discussing how that might be possible under the impending restrictions Joe had talked about when we arrived at the spot where we had entered the canyon. Needless to say, the prospect of our returning through the blackness of that chasm pushed other matters out of my mind for a while. I thought of it now as a passage joining one dimension to another.

***

She looked like she might have been abandoned to the desert but the ground vehicle was a welcoming sight as we half trudged, half ran down the slope in a cascade of sand. The sun was high overhead and searing bright when we knocked the sand off our boots prior to squeezing into the airlock. We couldn't hurry that part; residual dust, some of it fine as smoke, had to be de-ionised then sucked out.

With our pressure suits stowed on recharge Karin called her people and, full of enthusiasm, gave them an outline briefing on what we had discovered in the canyon. All the while, though, something told me she ought not to be doing that. One thing we had agreed upon, however; we wouldn't mention her near fatal mishap until we got back in case someone above base command level found out and decided to give all concerned a hard time.

Our survey route around some of the mesas would account for the best part of three hours plus any time we stopped to go grubbing around outside. Once the ground vehicle was away from those fallen rocks, we set her on autopilot because it would give us time to talk over what had happened in the canyon. It also gave me chance to chat with Joe van Allen at Number One, after which I heated up a couple of food packs. During that time Karin had occupied herself with the crystals in the mini-lab. When I poked my face inside I found her holding one of the crystals on the palm of her hand. She was simply staring at it. Next to her glowed trimensional, shifting molecular structures that reminded me of my college chemistry course.

'Have you figured those things out, yet?' I asked.

She seemed at first not to hear me then she placed the crystal down by the side of the image. 'Brett, I -. These things are unlike anything I ever heard of. They show structured domains of incredible complexity. Yet beyond these, at molecular level, they are comprised of relatively simple repeating units. They resemble genetic structures but some of the chains seem incomplete as if they – as if they continue on somewhere we can't see. Somewhere into some other universe.'

'Genetic structures? Are you saying they contain some sort of life code?'

'Perhaps they do but they defy all attempts at analysis right now. But what I am saying, Brett, is that - well, if we'd not found them where we did, I would have no doubt, none at all, that these crystals are synthetic.' She thought for a moment then added, 'No – nature could produce nothing like this. They *are* synthetic!'

'You mean they're a product of intelligent life?' If she was right, the implications were staggering.

'Brett, there was life on this planet early in its evolution when the climate was warmer, when the atmosphere was thicker and open water existed on the surface. But no one ever found traces of anything advanced. And what evidence we do have is so old and degraded it has never told us much.'

'Maybe the crystals didn't originate here,' I offered. 'Maybe they arrived from outside our system.'

'A fascinating possibility either way,' she said, placing the crystals into a vacuum container. 'Let's hope our laboratory is able to solve the mystery. I'd rather not transmit more data from here.'

I readily agreed with her over that.

Until then, I'd been oblivious to the sound of our engine but when the tone began to lower and the ground vehicle swayed slightly I said, 'We've come to a standstill. I guess it's our next call.'

From the cabin we were confronted by another mesa; this one tilted so much it looked about to take a final plunge beneath the desert sand. I took the controls and drove around it whilst Karin recorded whatever information she felt might be of use. Since the events of that morning neither of us were able to stoke up further enthusiasm in spite of the sights all around. As Karin put it, 'We have to go through the motions, Brett. We have to make the whole thing appear the way we intended. I think now I should have said nothing about the crystals until we got back.'

'Oh, why?' I asked, wishing more than ever I'd spoken up at the time and persuaded her not to do it.

'It's a feeling I have,' she sighed.

***

It was seventeen-forty hours by the time her work was logged and the ground vehicle instructed to take us home. As we were now going east, the westerly sun was behind us and we were heading in the direction of those weird red rock formations on the way back to the dune field. Karin wasn't going back to Europa Four for a couple of days because there were no flights. Maybe because of that her base commander came on and ordered her to transmit *all* of her recorded data to Europa Four. That had to include the results of her attempted crystal analysis. She tried to talk her way out of doing it but she was firmly overruled.

We were passing through the formations and I was gazing out with strange notions drifting through my head when she called, 'Brett, I transmitted the data to Europa Four but there's been no response. And – and I can no longer pick up transmissions from them. We have no communications!'

Now that was guaranteed to nail my attention so I got our equipment to self-check. The result was not what it ought to have been. 'Hell - our communications are being blocked!'

'Blocked! But that's impossible. Who could do that? Who would want to do it?'

Communication problems were all but unheard of except in cases of severe solar flare activity and there had been no warnings of that. 'Don't ask me,' I said, running the check again. 'Ah, we do have a channel open.'

'Who is it, Brett?'

'It's my own base. It's Novamerica One.'

I made a priority call to Joe van Allen. His face appeared like he'd just been handed a long-term posting to the south polar cap. 'Joe, what's going on?' I asked. 'Our communications with everyone except you are completely out.'

'You're not going to like this, Brett,' he answered. 'Neither of you are.' I'd not heard Joe sound that serious for a long time. 'I've only just been informed of it myself and I was about to call you. Our Chief Executive found out about the trip whilst you were still at the mesas. Looks like he's had you monitored from the time you were back on the road. I've had plenty of explaining to do and it wasn't easy. Hammond claims all rights to your data and the samples you collected. He demands those crystals go to his lab at Novamerica Five. He reckons as there was no official agreement at higher executive level, it's a UAS show, using our transport and our crew - you, that is. I'm sorry, son, I can't debate with him over the legalities.'

'Come on Joe - this expedition was on the books before Hammond set foot on Mars even if it was only finalised a short while back. You said yourself we owed the Europeans a favour. And what the hell right does anyone have to interfere with our communications? It isn't done, Joe. And if I'm not mistaken it's a breach of the law here on Mars same as it would be on Earth!'

'Brett, there's no need to tell me but last thing we need right now is a major incident over this. I have to play it cool for the time being. We all do. I'll see you both in a few hours then we can talk it over.'

'You bet we will, Joe.'

Karin stared at me as Joe's image faded. She put into words what I was thinking. 'From what Joe said they might still be listening to us. What d'you think is behind this, Brett? What is that man Hammond trying to do?'

'That guy has got it into his head to reorganise everyone's lives the way he sees fit. He wants the consortium to start paying big dividends back on Earth no matter what the cost to everyone out here.'

The truth, as we had yet to learn, went far beyond that.

There was nothing we could do about it - leastways not for the time being, and we didn't feel like sitting around to watch a backwards replay of the desert scenery for the next three and a half hours. Through much of the following day, Karin would be in discussion with her fellow scientists via satellite and the morning after that, she would be gone. This could be our last chance to be alone together for a while so we figured on making the best of it. The ground vehicle could earn its keep for the remainder of our journey and make its own way home.

CHAPTER 2
VISITATION

Our return that evening should have made for a minor celebration. Instead, Karin was formally requested by Joe to hand over the vacuum container with the crystals it contained. She shrugged the situation off but I knew how angry and upset she was. 'This is going to make things difficult, Joe,' she said. 'My people will not like it. We had an agreement.'

Joe, too, was far from happy and did his best to be sympathetic. 'I'm trying to iron this out with Europa Four, Karin, believe me, but it's Hammond's responsibility to talk to the European General Administrator. I assure you I do not go along with what has happened and that will be on the record. I've already briefed Amelia up there on the space station and the whole damned episode will be in my next transmission to the International Council back on Earth. I have no idea what difference, if any, it will make.'

'Hammond may not take too kindly to that,' I said.

'Maybe he won't but it's going through anyway.'

***

We had dinner together as planned, but not in private, where we would have discussed the expedition. Instead, we met up in the crowded main restaurant where a new show from Earth was downloading via Marsnet. That was usually a special occasion particularly if, like me, you were away from base much of the time. It occupied us for a while but Karin remained subdued. Back in my quarters that evening, we were careful not to bring up the subject of the crystals or Virgil Hammond. We didn't want that guy spoiling any more of our time altogether.

Next morning, Karin was out of circulation as I had expected - involved in one of those specialist planet-wide conferences. She still had to earn her keep but as for me, well, Leo was no longer at home base though I did spend a while in the gymnasium. I thought of doing some study work, then a spell of jogging around the biodome perimeter. I did neither. I just hung around the bar in idle conversation with whoever happened to be there. For someone who got on mighty well with his own company, it took a while for me to admit that I was feeling lonely. I thought most of the time about Karin, about our journey to the valley of the crystals, about how difficult it might be to meet up again once she had gone back to Europa Four.

She appeared just after lunch - earlier than I had expected and without first having contacted me. A few jaws dropped when she walked into the bar with her hair let down, wearing a big smile and a cute little metallic silver dress. All at once the sun was shining. When I said, 'Hi, how did you know I'd be here?' she answered, 'Brett, dear, there are some things I can take for granted.'

'Feel like something to eat?' I asked.

'No, I had lunch during the conference. What I need is a walk.'

'The biodome?' I suggested. It was an easy choice since there were no real alternatives, unless we suited up and went outside.

'Yes, Brett, you can show me around the gardens. I never spent much time in your biodome.'

Our biodome, like all biodomes, had a main and subsidiary airlocks. It wasn't a precaution to keep the wildlife from getting out since everything living in there was programmed never to try, but a safety measure in case of major emergency. Most people at this base - at any base - took the biodomes for granted. I suppose that was natural enough but perceptions changed completely after what happened at -. Well, I'll get around to that in due course.

Much as I loved the mountains, the deserts and the open skies of Mars I never took the biodomes for granted. Maybe because of that. To me our own biodome was a place of wonder - an island full of life and colour surrounded by the merciless aridity of the world outside. Beneath the great, bioplast bubble you'd find yourself in wooded parkland, complete with insects, birds and small animals; all of them designed to play their part in a closed ecosystem. Even the sky looked Earth-like through much of the day because the bioplast shell made Martian daylight appear that way.

As we strolled hand in hand along the main concourse Karin said, 'Brett, I'm sorry I was so put out over the crystals yesterday. I appreciate the position I have placed Joe in and maybe you as well.'

'Forget it,' I smiled. 'Things might not be that bad.'

'Oh, and why is that?'

There were a few people close by, mainly kids chasing each other about. We had only walked in a short distance but before I could answer, a couple of small, brown, rodent-like creatures with large eyes and ears scurried out of the bushes close by, screeching their heads off. They were part of our biodome maintenance system - scavenging for expired insects, clearing dead vegetation and generally keeping the place tidy. Karin grinned as they scampered about us. She laughed aloud when, whiskers twitching, they squawked my name and jumped up like they were trying to climb my trouser leg.

'Brett, don't tell me you've adopted them as pets! You of all people!

Hugely amused, she watched me self-consciously stroke each before shooing them away.

'I thought you didn't have time for that kind of thing - big, independent man flying around the sky.'

'They just - you know - they just latch onto people now and then.'

'Oh, do they, now! Why don't you confess, Brett? They seem to know you very well. Sometimes I think you're so old fashioned – really, you can be so funny.'

'Yeah, maybe. If it's old fashioned to want to belong in the real world, then I'm Neanderthal Man.'

'But this isn't the real world - not here on Mars. And none of these artificial creatures could survive naturally on Earth.'

'Well it's as real as it's ever going to be as far as I'm concerned.' I responded. 'You know what

I'm saying - it doesn't jump out of a box of electronics to take over your brain. Anyhow, whilst we're out of earshot, there's something I have to talk to you about.'

'You mean the other crystal, Brett, the one *you* picked up - is that it? I hadn't forgotten.'

'That's exactly what I mean.'

'You didn't tell Joe about it did you? At least you didn't when I was there.'

'No, I've said nothing to anyone. Joe doesn't know it exists, though I feel he ought to.'

'So, what are you planning to do with it?'

'I'm giving it to you, Karin. You're going to take it back to Europa Four and have it checked out by your own laboratories. That way there's less chance of Hammond finding out.'

'Oh, Brett, that *is* taking a chance. If it proves to be alien origin after all then we will have to declare the fact sooner or later. Then what will Virgil Hammond have to say? And what about you? You will have disobeyed his orders.'

'No Karin, I haven't disobeyed anything. I didn't tell anyone I had it and no one ever asked me. They assumed you brought back the only ones. Why should I disillusion anyone – especially Hammond?'

'But he'll be mad all the same. He won't let you get away with that. And what about Joe?'

'He can't blame Joe because Joe's entirely innocent. And as far as I'm concerned, Virgil Hammond can go poke a drum of rocket fuel up his ass and blast himself back to Earth where he belongs.'

'That sounds a little drastic,' she smiled, 'but I don't suppose he needs to know you gave it to me. I'm not sure what he could do if I said I had kept it back for my own people.'

'Well, I don't want you getting into trouble, either. As for me - I guess they'll always need pilots out here. Then there'd be the publicity. No, it wouldn't do Hammond any good sending me back to Earth.'

'And I wouldn't want that to happen, Brett,' she said, squeezing my hand.

We had reached the first of a group of ornamental fountains when a chime swooped through the air like a bird song. Karin must have noticed it but she said nothing until it sounded out again two minutes later – less tuneful, more abrupt. 'Brett, what was that last signal? It sounded like a warning.'

'It means they're going to switch on the rain. There'll be another signal in a couple more minutes then, five minutes after that, we'll have to be out of the biodome or find shelter by the perimeter. I doubt the trees around here will offer enough protection though there's shelter around the far side.'

'Rain!' she exclaimed. 'Oh yes, I've heard about that but I've never been around to see it happen.'

By now the only people still in sight were headed for the main exit.

'Yes,' I said, 'two or three of our biodomes have the real thing. The rest will be converted whenever or if ever we can allocate resources to do it.'

'I wish ours had rain. Most of them still use boring old irrigation feeds. You know, on a warm summer day I used to enjoy the rain. There's a park in Stockholm where I played as a little girl. Our winters were so long and cold that when spring came and the days grew longer, they couldn't keep me away from that park. I loved it so much, I didn't mind getting wet from time to time. It's one of the things I really miss since I left Earth.'

'Then I promise our rain won't disappoint you. If we're not out of here or find shelter pretty soon, we'll get soaked!'

'Well, I don't care,' she answered. 'I'm going to stick around. I'm going to enjoy it!'

'What! You mean you -?'

'Yes,' she laughed, 'I want to get soaked! Brett, you must stay with me. Just let yourself go - forget we're on Mars. Let's have a little Earthly fun. It won't hurt!'

'Get soaked - have fun,' I groaned as she hurried off toward the central fountain. By the time I'd caught up with her the first spots were splashing here and there as a prelude to what I knew was going to be a heavy, if short-lived, downpour. But I have to admit the air smelled wonderful and I no longer cared about getting wet. The rain came on full, drumming loudly on the pathway whilst we chased like a pair of kids around the fountain. Pretty soon we were both drenched, our hair and clothes plastered to our bodies. As I held her, she looked up. 'Oh, Brett, see how slowly the rain falls.'

I hadn't thought about it until then but my mind was on something else altogether as we headed toward the nearest grove of trees. I'd heard on Earth of people making love in wet grass but to tell the truth, I'd never gotten around to doing so myself. Trust me to experience it for the first time on a planet that hadn't seen natural rain in billions of years! Needless to say, as we walked back to my quarters trailing water through the corridors, dogged by a frantic trio of maintenance bots busily cleaning up, we got some mighty peculiar looks.

* * *

Next morning the aircraft was due in and Karin had to be on it for her return to Europa Four. After breakfast, I took her to the main airlock where I helped her on with her pressure suit. The wingship was down and being rotated for take-off. Her incoming passengers were heading from the strip toward the airlock when we arrived before the inner doors. We stood and kissed for a while - not an unusual sight at any base when people are leaving, so those hanging around the concourse took no more than passing notice. As the inner doors opened I picked up Karin's helmet from where it rested next to her holdall. 'Brett,' she whispered, 'the crystal – do you have it?'

'No, you do' I smiled, kissing her for the last time, 'It's in your vanity box. I dropped in there before breakfast.' As I helped fix her helmet, the new arrivals were stepping from the airlock. There were six including a couple of technicians from our own base returning from duties elsewhere. With Karin about to leave I took little notice of the rest. I tapped on her helmet and wiggled my fingers. She smiled, said goodbye through her suit microphone then stepped into the airlock with the holdall that contained her small vanity box. The doors slid shut to blot out her image and I stood for a while staring at the blank space in front of me, seeing the valley of the crystals and wishing we were back there together in that place of wonder that had for a time been ours.

When I turned to go, all but one of the new arrivals had left the concourse.

***

Zena Michaelis was aware of the two as soon as she stepped from the airlock into the concourse, cradling her space helmet. She had given them no more than a cursory glance but even without that, she would have sensed their guilt. She hesitated to express superficial niceties with the orderly who met her so as to remain in the concourse until the man and the girl had parted. Yes, there was guilt, a guilt she suspected was born of deception, but their other emotions and the distraction of the attentive orderly prevented her delving deeper into their minds. Theirs were the emotions of two people who did not wish to be parted from each other. Emotions that to her had once mattered but now no longer could, though memories sometimes haunted her dreams; dreams like footprints that said once, long ago, someone unknown had passed that way. Could their guilt be of any importance? She could think of no connection the pair might have with her mission. Yet there *was* something. Something elusive.

No, she could not allow herself to be distracted by the trivialities of people's affairs. Only with the crystals and with her mission must she concern herself. The crystals and what secrets might be revealed by them. She would later go to the station commander, the one who she considered ought to have been there in person to meet her but was not, and formally request their handing over. Once she had emerged from the pressure suit store, the orderly led the way to the main corridor then on to her quarters. It was her first visit to Novamerica One but, of course, she knew exactly which way they would go.

***

Now I really was at a loose end and I had, so I thought, another two days hanging around the base with little more than routine studies to occupy myself. And though Leo was due in next day, it wasn't for a break but a scheduled cargo drop, so he wouldn't be hanging around any longer than necessary. I was in my quarters later that afternoon and had, through a supreme act of willpower resumed my course work, when Joe van Allen's image materialised.

'Brett - sorry to interrupt you but am I right in thinking you want out of here now Karin is gone?'

'If you need to cut short my ground leave, Joe, I wouldn't object - nothing personal.'

'I'm sure it isn't, Brett. You know how I felt about making her hand those things over - mean as hell! Especially as you and she are - well, you know what I'm saying.'

'If you're going to feel guilty about anything, Joe, it should be over that.'

'Well I don't, son, she's what you needed and I reckon you're what she needed. Anyhow, I've had to organise an unscheduled flight at the request of our Chief goddamned Executive. I don't expect you're going to like it but you and Leo are the only two pilots I have around at present. Leo's back here tomorrow but only for a couple of hours.' He eyed me straight so I knew this was serious. 'You have a special passenger, Brett. She came in this morning from Novamerica Five on the same wingship Karin took out.'

'Direct from Hammond, you mean?'

'That's right, direct from Hammond - she's his personal representative and is to be afforded priority status. She arrived on Mars a few days ago. He told me that back on Earth she was also a security officer.'

'A security officer! Has this got to do with the sabotage allegations we were discussing a while back?'

'You may well ask, Brett, but your guess is as good as mine. Now listen - I'm not supposed to discuss this with anyone but she's going to be your passenger so you have to know. Just keep the details to yourself - okay?'

'Sure I will, Joe. I suppose it has to do with those crystals – am I right?'

'That's it, son. She's already found her way up here and taken possession of them. Acts like she owns the place in her own quiet way. She expected me to be there when she arrived, which is exactly why I didn't bother. Anyhow you'll be responsible for getting her back home because Hammond doesn't want her hanging around here for a scheduled flight. She is to leave early tomorrow morning. Look, if you're not happy about this I'll arrange to swap your schedules.'

'No fuss, Joe, I'll do it, but don't tell me we're running a flight just for one person - and without a cargo? That isn't the kind of luxury they can afford on Earth, let alone out here.'

'Not exactly,' he replied, 'It will appear more or less a normal flight. I've had a cargo made up for Europa Six – we had some processed metals and other stuff due for them anyway. You'll drop down there and collect another cargo straight away. We can justify the trip quite easily as it happens. There's a ship due in direct from Earth with a cargo to be distributed, so Hammond prioritised his flight with that in mind.'

'Yeah, *Cassiopeia*. She's bringing over more people, so I hear.'

'That's right but you won't be taking any of them aboard - just the cargo. After that, it's due east to Huygens crater and Novamerica Five. As soon as you've dropped her and the pallet on Hammond's doorstep, there'll be another cargo and with that you kind of slot back into a normal schedule. You can grab your spare time back later on or pick up extra credits against it. I'll make sure you don't lose out.'

'Okay, Joe, I'll think about that. Maybe after flying halfway around the planet with her and those crystals I'll need another break. I don't expect I'll be top of her popularity list at the end of it, either. Where is she right now? Am I to have the pleasure of an introduction?'

'I doubt it, son - she's given instructions she isn't to be disturbed so you'll have to curb your enthusiasm until the morning. I get the impression she doesn't care to mix with any of us. Too goddamned important.' Joe leaned back, hands clasped behind his head. 'Now maybe she's not my idea of good company – hardly a laugh a minute -

but she is a VIP. I don't want the Chief Executive to have any further reason to gripe at us so try to be pleasant. Do whatever she asks - even if she wants you to loop the loop. Hammond insists on radio silence, too, so I've ordered our people not to call you on any account. I don't know what the hell he's up to but that's the way things are. Maybe we'll tread carefully for the time being.'

Joe knew I wasn't overly impressed with the situation so before we closed I offered a reassuring, 'Depend on me, Joe. I won't let our side down.'

***

It was late evening when Zena Michaelis entered the biodome. Passing through the inner airlock doors she stepped onto the wide path where the lights were bright to find there were still a number of people strolling about and the restaurant busy. She had not expected to see any children at that time but there were three of them, shouting, playing tag around the bushes. Two of them broke off and hurried by, chasing a small maintenance bot that scampered just far enough ahead not to be caught.

She saw them as she had seen the people in the concourse on her arrival. Watched their heat stream out behind, listened to hearts beating rapidly above the sound of their laughter. Walking on, she sensed hidden movement all about - heard chattering, clicking, scurrying. A flutter of wings. Her eyes beheld the dancing lights of living things, all devised, all attuned to an ecosystem that mimicked that of a distant, more hospitable world. Turning aside, she reached out a foot to disturb one of the small rodent-like creatures that, crouching beneath a bush, thought itself hidden from prying eyes. It sensed the touch of her mind. Its nose quivered. Its eyelids flickered. Other minds it was familiar with. Some, it knew well, like the man who travelled the skies, the one who sometimes came into its domain and had become a friend. But this mind! No - there was something wrong. Then the creature was gone - fleeing into the deeper obscurity of the undergrowth.

Further along the path a woman called, 'Come along you kids - it's way past your bedtime!' The three children were ushered by, finally racing along to see who would be first into the airlock.

Zena Michaelis walked on until reaching the central fountain then, sensing there were no humans close by she took an unlit side path that meandered through the trees. Above the gardens and the trees, beyond the protecting shell, the stars shone brighter than ever they did on Earth. Peering up, she hesitated to analyse the spectra of the more prominent suns - to her a simple exercise, yet mildly satisfying for one who regarded the glory of the Martian skies with little more than academic interest. She continued on until reaching the edge of the biodome shell and its low, supporting wall. There she stood a while, gazing out into an intensely frigid stillness, the starlit stage-set of a desert night.

There was a presence.

She turned to peer along the curve of the perimeter path. Whatever it was had not been there until that moment. It was something she did not understand. Something she had never before encountered. It hovered tantalisingly close yet was

81

diffused as a misted image. As her mind reached out, the presence retreated as though wishing to elude her amidst the shadows.

Now it was gone.

With her extraordinary senses fully alert, she set off slowly along the path where it curved inward to skirt a small service airlock. For a short way the path led among the trees but she could see and hear no one, see and hear nothing to explain what she had sensed only minutes earlier. The path returned to the perimeter and by the light of the stars she continued on a short way beyond the airlock.

Again the presence. This time closer.

It knew her. It understood who - understood what she was. It excited her curiosity as never before. Gripped it irresistibly. Stepping from the path, she pushed through dense bushes and beneath spreading branches, the words, 'Who are you?' forming on her lips. In the darkness she halted.

She sensed it move closer though all about her was still.

The presence whispered her name. It entered her mind.

***

The flat expanse of Sinai plateau, and Europa Six where I was scheduled to go, lay due south-east in the southern hemisphere. The base itself, around fifteen degrees below the equator, stood at a distance of little under three thousand kilometres. In between lay the spectacular Tharsis mountains - three giant volcanoes, Ascraeus, Pavonis and Arsia, each bigger by far than anything on Earth. Amongst the most spectacular features on Mars, these march south-westwards from the northern into the southern hemisphere with the middle one, Pavonis, sitting astride the equator. They rise as much as eight kilometres high on the so-called Tharsis bulge, itself some ten kilometres elevation above the surrounding plains. There's no way a wingship could fly over those mountains, not even on rocket power because the air is too thin. No more than with the daddy of them all, Olympus, which lay over to the northwest of them. Well topography or no, people still have to get to wherever they need. As it happened, my route was a conveniently straight line, passing between Ascraeus and Pavonis, then over the western extension of another great feature on the red planet, the Mariner Valley. This vast canyon system stretches some four thousand kilometres eastwards in a gentle dip below the equator. From space it looks like some angry cosmic beast clawed a long gash in the planet's surface then had a couple or so more attempts at it before giving up to move on somewhere else.

But I didn't have the scenery on my mind when I suited up that morning. I'd expected to meet up with my passenger when I arrived at the concourse because that's where Joe had said she would be waiting. When I asked the duty officer where she was, he told me she had already gone out to the ship. That struck me as out of order, not to say downright impolite, but then I thought of what Joe had told me and decided maybe she was impatient and played on her authority.

Travel case in hand, I left the airlock and stepped into early morning light. The sun was just above the eastern horizon with a deep red haze reaching out either side to grade upwards into pale apricot. The clean, white form of Delta Seven sat on the turntable, rotated to face along the runway with her cargo pallet clamped in position under the broad body of the ship. Three of our maintenance personnel in blue pressure suits stood by the low-loader waiting to see me lift off. As I reached the ventral access ramp, I got grinned at by a couple of guys who had been doing a routine check on the landing gear. One of them described a female figure in the air with his hands whilst his voice came over my radio. 'You're doin' okay this time around, Captain!'

Doing okay? They must have seen her before she suited up and that intrigued me. After the way Joe had spoken of Zena Michaelis I had naturally reached the conclusion she'd be anything but glamorous. I'd pictured in my mind a hard-bitten old stick of a woman though I'd never inquired about her age. If those maintenance guys were having me on it wouldn't be the first time.

Once inside Delta Seven's airlock, I waited until the ramp was up and sealed. With the air pressure optimised I eased out of my suit then went to stow it and my case in the storage compartment. The compartment will hold up to ten suits but there were only three inside, apart from mine. I checked that they were all correctly stowed, all connected up for life support recharge, but I couldn't have said which was hers since only mine carried an ID strip. Checking them was important, you understand; you have to care for your pressure suit like you care of yourself, only more so. The fact that she hadn't left her ID or her travel bag in there skipped through my mind but didn't seem too important right then.

Stepping into the pod, I couldn't make her out at first because, even with the filters, the sky was bright outside the windows and I'd become accustomed to dimmer light at the rear. She was perched before the console so little more than the top of her head was visible resting against the back of the seat.

As I approached she swung around to face me. 'Good morning, Captain Anderson - I am Zena Michaelis.'

I don't recall if my mouth fell open but I do know I stared hard before summoning up my first words. 'Oh - er, welcome aboard, Officer Michaelis, even if you did manage to get up here ahead of me.'

I had determined some time back that, whilst I was going to be polite, I would also be coldly correct so that by the time she quit Delta Seven she would be in no doubt as to my feelings. Now, it was too late. I'd smiled - maybe too hard. And why? Well, she was quite beautiful. Black hair cascaded like obsidian glass over the shoulders of her blue crew suit. Her eyes were lynx eyes and jade green, her high cheekbones suggested a Slavic or maybe eastern origin. As I took my place close by in the captain's seat her appearance blew away any thoughts I'd harboured over being offhanded.

I smiled again. A little reservedly this time - but I still smiled.

'How long before we leave?' she asked as I checked our destination in the ship's navigation system.

'Any minute now,' I told her. 'I don't hang around.'

As if on cue, the ground controller cut in. 'If you're all tucked up cosy, Brett, you're fine for take-off. The air is clear and calm all the way to Sinai so enjoy the sight of those little old hills on the way - if you can find time to look out the window, that is!'

'Okay,' I replied, switching the controls over to automatic. 'We're ready.'

From what Joe had said, this would be the last communication with my own base for some time.

A slight jolt ran through ship as the booster vehicle coupled to our rear. The big turbines were singing and as they wound up to a high-pitched howl, Delta Seven began to roll. Feeling the power of the engines as the ship gathered speed I was in my element. I was going airborne again. The big fans were on full take-off power - sweet music to my ears - and I was pushed gently back into the seat as, aglow in morning light, the desert sped by. For the first time, my trip out with Karin in the ground vehicle slipped from my mind.

'Feel her lifting?' I enthused as the ground fell away under us. 'It's not like on Earth where the big jets go up steep. The air is too thin out here - we have to take it nice and easy.'

I figured she knew all about wingships, of course, just as she must have known about conditions on the planet long before she arrived. Still, being told about something then actually finding yourself there are two different things, and there was my own enthusiasm to contend with. The horizon tilted lazily across our vision, shafts of sunlight speared around the pod as we banked to swing in a wide circle toward the south. Again I thought of Joe's comments. Maybe he was missing something. Or maybe he'd been so put out over the crystals he'd decided what Zena Michaelis *ought* to be like. At least I wouldn't need to hold back on conversation and maybe I'd uncover more about what was going on. That was the excuse I allowed myself in advance to justify being sociable when I ought to have been otherwise.

At an optimum height of around two thousand metres we levelled off, the turbines quietened down to cruise mode and we were on our way.

***

Two maintenance men in white pressure suits stood by their tractor to watch Delta Seven rise clear of the runway with a small posse of dust devils scurrying in her wake. They continued to watch as she swept into the sky to catch the morning sun. The blast from her engines had washed away loose sand banked at the edges of the strip and, as their gaze followed the booster vehicle returning along its metal track, one of the men spotted something at the far side of the runway. 'What d'you figure that is?'

'Dunno,' replied his companion. 'A piece of scrap, maybe. Probably nothing.'

'Can't be nothing. Maybe something fell off the ship. If something fell off the ship, that could be serious.'

'Nothing fell off the ship. We'd have seen it happen. His systems or ours would have alerted him. Bit it ain't nothing. You'll see when we finish on this side and get around there.'

***

From the sand protruded an arm. The frozen hand reached out with bird-claw fingers spread wide. Beneath the arm, as the sand shifted, a human face emerged. Deep-chilled flesh glistened like fine-glazed china in the harsh sun. Sand poured from a rust-stained mouth that gaped as a grotesque theatre mask. Blood-streaked eyes stared into an empty sky.

***

Over an hour had passed since Joe van Allen watched Delta Seven head south-east and diminish to a vague, distant speck vanishing into morning haze. Sitting before his desk to review flight schedules, Joe had called up another coffee when moments later the communicator pulsed with unaccustomed urgency. A space helmet materialised before him. An agitated voice issued from within it. The eyes behind the visor stared out in alarm. Joe backed away with hands raised. 'Okay - okay! You have an emergency – now slow down and tell me what is going on!'

'Commander, there's someone lying dead out here!'

'What! Who the hell is it?' Joe glanced out along the runway where the tractor and two men could be seen.

'Who? Commander, I – you want the name?'

'Yes, fella, the name - that's what I want to know!'

'But commander I can't find no -.'

'Check the pressure suit ID, goddammit! Do I have to -?'

'Pressure suit? No, sir – this one ain't wearing no pressure suit! Really she ain't!'

'What – it's a she! Now don't you guys fool around with me - no one can go outside without a goddamned pressure suit and no one's been signalled as compromised or missing!'

'Commander, it's exactly like we say - there's no pressure suit. I mean it - none!'

'Okay – okay! Get the body into the tractor and head straight into medical. I'll warn Petra Giordano and I'll be down there as soon as it's arrived. And if you guys are having me on I promise you *will* be sorry!'

Frowning, Joe stepped over peer out across the runway. By the tractor the two men lifted an object from the sand then placed it into the storage bay of their vehicle. Joe watched the tractor swing about to begin its journey back toward the complex. 'No pressure suit,' he muttered. 'If this is someone's idea of a joke, I'll have them transferred for duty down at the goddamned south pole on the next flight and that's for sure!'

Joe van Allen entered the medilab, heading past test and diagnostic equipment toward the group of four people standing over a narrow, transparent shell-enclosed table that protruded out from one wall. One of them turned. 'Commander, we have the body here. We're trying to keep it frozen but – but the head and spinal cord seem to be warming up by themselves since it was brought in here.'

'Have you any idea who this is, Commander?' asked chief medical officer, Petra Giordano. 'We can find no record of this person and all personnel presently assigned to this base are accounted for.'

'Have I any idea -.' breathed Joe, his eyes fixed upon the grimly contorted face. 'It's Zena Michaelis. She's on the staff of our Chief Executive and is – was, here on a special mission. D'you people have any idea how she died - or better still, how she managed to get herself through our safety systems then outside the base without a pressure suit?'

'No, sir,' answered his medical officer. 'There are no marks except where body fluids escaped. She appears to have died as a result of decompression some time before midnight.'

'Oh, did she now - died from decompression! Died then had herself an evening stroll over halfway down the goddamned landing strip. That must have taken some doing. Examine her and tell me just how she managed to do that - and tell me quickly!'

'Commander,' declared Petra Giordano, 'I must point out that we, any of us, yourself included, are not authorised to undertake autopsies without permission of an officer from another base, especially when -'

'Thank you for your advice on protocol, Doctor Giordano. I admire your concern for the rules and you must put everything in your records. Now she's in that fancy contraption of yours I order you to scan every molecule in her body if you have to! I intend to find out what's been happening around my goddamned patch - rules or no rules! And after you've done that you can inform Novamerica Five we've had ourselves an incident. I now have something equally important to deal with!'

Hurrying from the medilab, Joe reached the top of the stairs leading up to the administration area. There he hesitated to consider the question that had occupied him since seeing the body. 'If that's Zena Michaelis down there then who the hell does Brett have on board Delta Seven!'

***

They slid the body into the diagnostic scanner. The shell closed and displays pulsed colour. Seated before them, Petra Giordano's assistant began running her tests. She hesitated for some moments, staring in silence, then - 'Petra! I don't understand these readings. Please – take a look!'

Petra Giordano moved to peer at the display.

'Petra,' said her assistant, 'there's electrical activity in her brain as though she - as though she's kind of – alive!'

Tense moments passed then the girl added, 'See what the scanner's telling us. She's – she's trying to self-repair. Doesn't that make her some kind of – of enhanced android? Aren't they illegal at this level?'

'Android – really!' responded a puzzled Petra Giordano, peering closer. 'Well whatever is happening, most of her vital organs are way beyond repair. Her body's basically had it and even with our facilities it's going to stay that way. Wait! What was that spike? Play the event back - slow it down.'

'I've never seen anything like it,' responded the girl as both intently watched the display.

'Play it through again and slow it even more,' ordered Petra Giordano. 'Slow it down a thousand times.'

The spike, no longer a spike, resolved into a series of complex waves and pulses.

'Interesting,' breathed another assistant who stood peering over the operator's shoulder. 'What are we to make of it?'

'That,' declared Petra Giordano, 'is some kind of transmission sequence. Dead or no, part of her is communicating with someone. But not here - not in this base. It must be a satellite. Concentrate on her brain and try to maintain activity. This is something we need to figure out and quickly!'

She had moved away to consult with two of her team when a cry cut through the room. She spun about to see the girl leap from the chair which she heaved aside before stumbling back. Turning wide-eyed to face Giordano she pointed to the shell. 'Petra, her eyes moved! She - she was staring at me!'

CHAPTER 3
VALLEY OF THE SHADOW

Over the great plains of the Tharsis Rise we made small talk, or at least, I did. I asked if I could get her a drink but she said she didn't want anything. She didn't strike me as officious or offhanded, which is what I had expected, but detached as though her thoughts were elsewhere. Oddly, and very much so when I considered her looks, I had no desire to have her any closer to me than she already was - no desire at all to touch her even had the opportunity presented itself.

'Is this your first time on our glorified rust ball?' I queried.

'It is my first time,' she breathed.

'What d'you think of our scenery?' I asked, waving my hand at the panorama drifting toward us. 'Isn't it something? Empty and still unspoiled by human beings - at least most of it is.' I planned to angle the conversation so as to pull in a few comments from her about the mining operations.

'Yes,' she answered, 'empty and unspoiled.'

'Some people say we should leave it all alone - just let it be. To others it's real estate, resources, something to exploit, maybe another place to send all of those people who cause so many problems back on Earth. How do you feel about that?'

For a while she stared ahead whilst the desert and an occasional crater passed beneath us. Then she said, 'It would be wrong if this was spoiled, even as we see it now.'

'How d'you mean, as we see it now?'

'You travel much about this world, Brett. You know it was not always as it is.'

'Oh, sure, it's long been accepted there was once life here - life, seas and oceans. We've had people over the years who maintain there's still some form of life on the planet apart from us and our machines. They describe odd experiences when they're alone but no one's ever provided anything to back it up. Nothing has ever been recorded.'

'And what do you think, Brett?'

'People dream. I dream a lot. It's what you make of it. Me - I'm a born sceptic. I think there are people who want to believe in mysteries for their own sake – like there's always something hidden in a box somewhere. They still go on believing after the box is opened and they find there's nothing inside. Some of them say there is something in the box but the rest of us don't see it. Others say your box isn't the real box because only they have the genuine article. Maybe you people have found something. Is that it? Something that isn't a product of nature or hasn't been left lying around by human beings? Maybe those crystals Hammond's had you collect?'

I hadn't thought about the crystals again until that moment. Strange, because now it was as if their image had been inside my head all the time, glowing bright, bouncing up and down for attention. And her voice – I had the oddest feeling I'd heard it before, so familiar did it sound

'We have to find out,' she answered. 'We have to understand.'

'Yes, I suppose a lot of people have that priority, for whatever reason.'

She turned to look at me, unblinking. 'And what are your priorities, Brett?'

It wasn't the kind of question I got asked every day so I needed to think it over. I wanted to be honest because I felt the question was important. Honest with myself as much as with her. 'I guess that - well, when I'm flying I just want to be where I am because it gives me time to think - to watch and wait.'

'To watch and wait? For what?'

'That's a simple enough question but I can't say for sure. Maybe I'm not waiting for anything. Maybe I enjoy the journey because the destination isn't worth getting heated up about.'

'There must be something at the end for you, Brett.'

'Could be there is of late,' I answered, thoughts of Karin springing into my mind as suddenly as had my image of the crystals, 'but when I'm flying, I feel I have something special - something personal.'

'What is so special for you?'

Her voice, now a whisper, was as much in my head as in my ears but it seemed perfectly natural. What wasn't natural, at least for me, was the way she had me moving into verbal excess – something I was seldom inclined to do. 'Well, how can I put it,' I went on, 'I find this world - I find it a place you can fill with images all your own. The deserts, the mountains, the valleys - they're so cold, so empty. But for me Mars is haunted by ancient memories. It's an empty stage with the players about to come on. You can fill it with people and adventures all of your own making. You can have dreams and no one can say they aren't real. Do you understand that?'

'I understand it well,' she replied.

'Okay - the landscapes change throughout the day. Often, around sunrise, there's a heavy mist. You can look down and see the hills rise up out of it like islands. There are bays, shorelines, promontories, great bastions of crater walls enclosing dream cities. And when the mist ripples in the wind, you can imagine this world as it once was - with a great ocean of water.'

She was watching me with eyes like the eyes of a big cat. She seemed to dwell upon my every word. Then she said, 'The landscapes, the dreams are yours, Brett, and to you they are of great value.'

'Sure they are. The planet might be empty and devoid of life now, but when I see them digging the heart out of it I think that's wrong. People like Hammond don't give a damn about what they destroy and you should know that even if you don't want to hear it.'

'I understand, Brett. You are at one with this world.'

I'd only ever expressed my feelings that way to Karin, who chided me for being an old romantic, and maybe in shorter measure to Leo who was too much of a good pal to deal out the ridicule even though he never quite regarded Mars that way. Why I was expressing my thoughts so readily to someone I shouldn't have placed an atom of trust in, I didn't know, and at the time, I didn't care.

'But not everyone thinks as you, Brett,' she continued. 'That is not why most of them come here.'

'I can't speak for other people,' I answered. 'They all have their reasons. I reckon for a good many it's the high pay more than anything else. A few years on Mars and you can retire comfortably back on Earth. Or at least you could. Things have changed over the years. Mars is costing too much. I guess that's why Virgil Hammond is here.'

We were an hour out of base when what appeared at first like a shallow hill, appeared hazily on the horizon a degree or so to the right of our flight path. It was the first feature of real significance since we'd passed close to the great escarpment of Olympus. We were approaching the second of the three great volcanoes that straddled the equator to the south-east of Olympus. 'See that,' I said. 'That's Pavonis sitting dead on zero latitude. Doesn't look all that impressive right now, does it? Out of sight to our left is Ascraeus. Arsia, is way over the horizon beyond Pavonis. They're over seven hundred kilometres from crater to crater.'

She continued to gaze ahead in silence as I added, 'Our flight path takes us close by the volcano, then it'll sure look impressive. Before reaching orbit, that's a good time to see all three as well as Olympus. Did you get to see them from space?'

'No,' she answered quietly.

As we flew on, as the volcano grew against the horizon, my passenger seemed absorbed by its presence. I wondered briefly why she had not observed it and its companions on approach, or from Mars orbit when the Tharsis region and the Mariner Valley are 'must see' features. The ship buffeted a little because of the airflow being disturbed by the great mass ahead of us but that wasn't unusual.

Pavonis had earlier appeared a muted grey, shading up to rose tints at the crater summit. Now its eastern flank glowed in the morning sun. When we skirted the volcano it was at an altitude well below the summit. Soaring upward to our right, her awesome bulk belying our real distance, the lower slopes of Pavonis and the mountain proper were draped with a fabric of golden sunlight. Whenever I flew over the Tharsis region I imagined there was some kind of inexplicable, brooding presence around those immense volcanoes. That same feeling had taken me over right then so I was lost in thought when she next spoke.

'Brett - we are to make an unscheduled landing.'

'A what?' I responded, wondering if I'd heard her right.

'We must land before we reach Sinai. I will show you where.'

Her expression was cool, I'll say that. I guess mine was less so. When I asked her what it was about and if it had been authorised by Joe van Allen, she answered, 'Commander Van Allen was not informed. It is classified.'

'Classified or no,' I said. 'We're due to enter Europa Six navigational space in an hour and a half. How do I explain things when we show up late?'

'That has been taken care of, Brett. The schedule was revised earlier.'

'Oh, was it, now. But I guess you won't mind if I call up Novamerica One and check this out. I fly for Joe van Allen - not Virgil Hammond.'

She stared hard at me. 'No, Brett, you cannot do that. Your broadcast will not be secure. You must accept what I say. There is much at risk.'

Hell - I believed her. I concluded this must be some venture connected to her work as a security officer. And there were of course the orders from Joe himself to do anything she asked as well as keeping radio silence. 'All right, where's this big operation to take place? I suppose you do have exact co-ordinates?'

'It is a small diversion from our flight path,' she answered. 'We land within the Labyrinth. Show the central region on your display and I will indicate the place.'

'The Labyrinth!' I exclaimed. 'You have to be kidding!'

'It is the Labyrinth,' she responded. She wasn't kidding.

'But the co-ordinates - surely you -.'

'I will indicate on the display,' she cut in. She already knew the question.

I'd accepted it to that point because I had no idea what she intended - but the Labyrinth! We all know a labyrinth is a maze, and a maze isn't the kind of place where you expect to put down an aircraft. As for this particular labyrinth - in the early days it was known as *Noctis Labyrinthus* - Labyrinth of the Night. It extends westwards of the great Mariner Valley and covers an area of over a hundred thousand square kilometres. It's an expanse of chaotic terrain riddled with canyons, gullies and ravines and it spread right across our route. Nobody had ever been down there, not even by shuttle, so with that in mind I wavered on outright refusal.

She gazed up at the display and said, 'Move your cursor to the right.'

I moved it the way she asked.

'Down a short way.'

I did that, too.

'Now, enlarge the area around it.'

'Exactly what am I looking for?' I asked.

'It is there,' she answered, 'just below the cursor. Enlarge it further.'

The image before us showed a gash in the landscape aligned north-east to south-west and looking pretty well like all others in that part of the world. By that I mean, inaccessible.

'The canyon is deep,' she said, 'but it is broad and long enough for you to land safely. At the southern end, it widens out further. There you can turn Delta Seven around.'

'You have to be kidding,' I said again. 'Has anyone done a ground scan?'

'The ground there is firm and smooth,' she assured me.

'And when - if, we get down there in one piece - what then?'

'Brett, there is much you cannot yet know. Soon you will understand.'

The choice was mine. She might have been a VIP but this was *my* ship - more to the point it was my life and to that I'd grown kind of attached. With the precise co-ordinates in my navigation system I checked the situation out in some detail. There was little comfort to be had from the data. It showed the canyon almost two kilometres deep. This was the last place anyone would expect to take a wingship or anything else and you'd have to be out of your skull to consider doing it. Maybe at the time I was.

As for total secrecy - if others found out where we were headed they would certainly have satellites diverted over the area to see what we were up to. Everyone wanted to know what everyone else was doing even before the colonists started getting wound up with suspicions over sabotage. Anyhow, whilst I figured this had to be something way out important, it still looked suicidal. But she was taking the same risk and she appeared not in the least concerned over it. So - I decided I wouldn't back out unless otherwise faced with probable death. I watched the navigation display as, with Pavonis at our rear, we made a slight course change toward the south. If nothing else, life was becoming more of a challenge.

With the steady hum of our turbines, with the desert flowing by, I was pondering over this new development when something caught my attention. Something high up and ahead of us far to the southeast. It hung as a brilliant sapphire – living, moving against a velvet pink sky.

'Hey!' I exclaimed. 'Take a look there! That's *Cassiopeia*, heading in direct from Earth - she's dropping down to Europa Six. She'll be waiting when we arrive.'

Seeing rockets come in like that is really something. I couldn't help but feel proud even though they might be shipping over a little more of the home planet I came out here to avoid. But they were less frequent than they once were and it was highly unusual to have another arrive so soon after the one that had delivered my passenger.

'How many people are on that ship?' she asked as I watched the descending glow.

'Ten as far as I know, but mainly she'll have priority cargo – stuff that needs to get here quicker than the freighters could do it. Some of it we'll be picking up.' I turned to ask her, 'Only ships with priority cargoes come right in. Didn't they tell you all about this back home?'

She did not reply.

Most of the freighters pass by and offload cargo pods close to Mars where they go into braking orbit. They collect those that are boosted out to catch them up then head out into space again on some crazy orbit that can take a year or more to complete. I continued to watch the rocket, which by now was much lower in the sky. Another minute would have her out of sight below the horizon.

Beneath us, meanwhile, the landscape was transforming from a relatively flat plain to a series of great linear ridges fingering toward us from the south. We were passing over the northern reaches of the Labyrinth. After a while, these features became less directional, breaking up into hills and meandering ravines, all the time getting larger; all the time becoming more chaotic. The ships sensors told me we were beginning to lose height. Over non-designated terrain her safety systems would not allow her to descend below a certain altitude so that meant I would soon have to take control.

Something odd happened. From the corner of my eye, I thought I saw the communications panel flash, though I didn't hear any sound from it. When I looked directly at the panel it was dead. Of course it was dead. It had to be. I was supposed to be strictly incommunicado. All the same I glanced at it a couple more times whilst thinking that a few minutes would have us within visual distance of the canyon.

That small incident with the panel was like one of those dreams where someone has been talking. When you wake up, you still hear the voices in your mind like echoes from an unreal world that once seemed real. Could be some of those imaginary scenarios, those make-believe conversations I got involved in whilst up there alone had carved out a piece of territory in the back of my head and declared their independence. Talking to her at this point helped me relax - something I needed to do. When the readouts told me we were close enough, I decoupled all but my peripheral safety systems – against regulations, naturally - and took the controls.

It happened again. I could have sworn the communications panel blinked. She was staring directly at me so I asked, 'Did you see that? Did you see the panel flash?'

'No,' she replied, 'there was nothing.'

Even so, I stared hard at the panel. And still there were those echoes.

Below us raced pinnacles, gullies and escarpments, twisting crazily, careering off in all directions. The prospect of attempting to land in there struck me with a kind of dark resignation. I could hardly believe I was doing it, especially when warning lights began to flash inside the control pod. The sound of our turbines intermittently rose and fell as the wings began to reconfigure for landing.

This was it. We were slowing for our final approach.

***

'To hell with radio silence! To hell with the so-called mission!' exclaimed Joe van Allen to the startled communications officer. 'If that's Zena Michaelis downstairs he has no mission. Get him on air - now!'

'Delta Seven, do you hear me?' called the girl.

Silence.

'Sir, Delta Seven herself acknowledges the signal but I have no response from Captain Anderson. Shall I check his onboard systems?'

'Do that,' responded Joe.

'All systems are functioning normally,' she confirmed. 'Captain Anderson must know we're trying to contact him even with his communications panel switched off – even if he's left his controls.'

Joe van Allen took a deep breath. 'All right, try again.'

From the other side of the control room, a woman called, 'Sir, Chief Hammond is on our priority-one channel demanding to speak with you. He's also calling your office and your personal communicator.'

'Tell him I'll call back!'

'Sir, he insists it *is* urgent!'

'Tell him I'm out walking the dog! My priority right now is we contact our pilot!'

'Captain Anderson is still not responding,' replied the operator. 'I don't understand why – and he seems to be going off course. Oh – his primary safety systems just closed down!'

'Okay, lock into the control pod directly. Let's hear what is happening.'

In the background arose the irate, insistent voice of Virgil Hammond. But it was to another, calmer voice they listened. The voice of Delta Seven's captain.

'He's talking to someone, sir,' said the communications officer. 'He sounds perfectly -.'

'Wait!' interrupted Joe. 'Can we hear who is with him?'

'Sounds like the captain's talking to himself,' another remarked.

'All right, forget the goddamned privacy rules,' snapped Joe. 'Get him on vision!'

'Sir!' called the woman in almost tearful desperation 'The Chief Executive is *very* angry! Please!'

Joe van Allen ignored her as the image sprang to life. He and the four operatives stared at it in puzzled silence whilst the crescendo voice of Virgil Hammond rolled by as a furious tide. In those seconds, the image before them shimmered like a rising spectre until it burst the shell of disbelief.

'Oh - oh, God! What's that next to him?' wailed the girl.

One of the men called out, 'Hey - this is some kind of fuckin' joke!'

Then another male; 'What the hell are we looking at here? Just what *is* that!'

'Captain Anderson is - he's just sitting there as though -,' exclaimed the other woman.

'Switch it off!' ordered Joe van Allen. 'Switch it off now!' The image dissolved. 'Right, let's get our act together! Run a complete systems check! If someone's fooling around, I'll -.'

'Commander Van Allen!' raged the voice from the steel-eyed image hovering above a desk nearby.

Joe turned at last to address a grim-faced Virgil Hammond. 'Sorry, Chief - we kinda have a problem on our hands at the moment. You will understand if -.'

'A problem, commander!' barked the Chief Executive, eyes smouldering. 'You have a problem all right! I have received a communication from your medical officer regarding the death of Zena Michaelis. From your medical officer! That report should have come from you personally, Commander Van Allen - not from a damned subordinate! And you have my officer in *your* diagnostic! This is a serious – no – it is a major breach of rules!'

'Well, I'm sorry about that, Chief, but right now *we* have a major incident that demands my full attention. We may be about to lose one of our pilots and that damned subordinate as you called her is one of the finest medical officers on the planet!'

Joe swung around to the girl at the main console. 'How are our systems looking?'

'There are no problems with the systems, sir.'

'Okay, get Delta Seven back on vision!'

The image shivered into life but gone was the spectacle that had so confounded them. The image was disintegrating into chaotic fragments, the sound had become an electronic babble. Above the disorder arose the girl's voice. 'Delta Seven is over the Labyrinth! Sir, she's going down!'

The tumult of sound and light vanished, the image darkened then proclaimed in flashing red - 'CONTACT TERMINATED.'

The image of Virgil Hammond, too, had gone and there was now only silence. For some moments Joe van Allen gazed out at the empty skies and the red desert, then turned back to the communications officer. 'Give me a position for Delta Four!'

'Delta Four, sir – yes. Delta Four is two hours away and due west of Ascraeus.'

'Then get Captain McDowell on vision.'

A neatly bearded face and keen blue eyes materialised above the group.

'Hi everyone,' smiled Leo. 'How are we all keeping?'

'Leo,' said Joe, 'this is no social call. We have an emergency. You need to divert southward over the Labyrinth. We'll send you co-ordinates then I'll explain ...'

***

We were close to the northern end of the canyon and losing height. Fearsome looking crags sped close beneath - then the edges of the canyon rim, fluctuating at the left and right of us some two hundred metres each side. I held my breath as Delta Seven flared out, and we slowed further, dropping now below the canyon walls. Peering forward and down did nothing to bolster my self-confidence. Iron-rust cliffs fell into a chasm of oblivion then I was greeted by an alarming sight. From the obscurity below arose spires of rock, eroded from the canyon walls by the winds, arrayed like the teeth of some impossible jaw-gaping beast. A slip too far either way would have us strike one of those things,

107

then we'd have continued down gracefully in a cloud of metal and plastic. The sound of my own voice startled me. 'Hell - I must be insane!'

The ship's sensors were reaching out ahead and either side, probing, testing, feeling our way into the chasm with invisible fingers. Delta Seven shivered, constantly adjusting her attitude, the sound of her turbines shifting up and down as we left behind the realm of sunlight and open skies. I cancelled the warning lights that had become more a pyrotechnics show, and wavered on the point of taking the ship right out of there. My passenger appeared quite relaxed, just staring straight ahead, so I began to talk again. 'It isn't the best time of the year for this kind of thing - you know that? It's winter down south so right now more of our atmosphere is frozen into the south polar cap. How about we try this later in the season?'

All I got out of her was, 'The canyon widens further along, Brett. You will see.'

Fine, I thought - but it's in the nature of canyons to get narrower as they get deeper. With the walls towering high above, with the sky flowing overhead like a river, Delta Seven seemed to breathe. She flexed herself as a living thing, extending every control surface, every segment of wing to maintain precious lift as we descended further. When Delta ships flare out over a runway it looks like they're coming apart at the seams. If some alien gopher had stuck its head out of a hole in the canyon wall, that's what he would have thought. And that was how I felt!

We were close on halfway down when the canyon suddenly lightened. Ahead, to our left, the sky opened out where a huge section of the wall had slid away into the depths leaving a semi-circular scallop over a kilometre long and reaching almost down to our level. Evidence of landslips is common in the canyon regions though I don't recall anybody ever witnessed one happening. As the gloom closed in again, I imagined Delta Seven a white moth drifting into an open grave. There was modest consolation in the fact that the pinnacles had fallen behind to leave the walls appearing less of a threat.

Though the sun wouldn't be overhead for some time, I could by now make out the canyon bottom - meandering a little but reassuringly flat and solid according to my sensors. In a gesture of renewed confidence, or was it surrender to what seemed inevitable, I deployed the landing gear, lifted the ship's nose a little then slowed to touchdown speed. With the ground rising quickly, I was distracted for a moment by something dead ahead of us. A splash of colour that soon became a blaze of vivid red. I had no time to analyse it for with the walls rushing by only a few metres beyond my wingtips we were almost at the bottom and I needed full concentration. If any kind of obstacle lay in our path now, we were past the point where I could manage normal lift-off. Mightily reassuring was the fact that our sensors indicated no such problems whilst the way ahead still appeared flat.

There was a slight jolt as our wheels touched solid ground. We bounced a couple of times as the turbines went into reverse with what sounded like a howl of despair. It might have complimented my own feelings had I not been so preoccupied with the ship's status. That seemed okay as we rolled along the canyon floor with the sky a ribbon of bright pink way above. The ship swayed a little on a less than perfectly level surface but at least we were still in one piece.

'How about that?' I smiled, wiping sweat from my forehead. 'So eeeasy when you know how!'

Who was I fooling? I'd just taken us into the abyss of a bad dream. Delta Seven, the 'big bird,' as Karin had called her, was now a cumbersome truck rumbling along the weirdest ever highway. But at last I could make out what lay further ahead of us. The glow defined a line of cliffs directly in our path, though still nearly three kilometres away. As we continued on, the canyon began to broaden as my passenger had said it would, opening further until the precipice ahead resolved itself as a vast curtain of stone, ablaze with sunlight over two thirds the way down to its base. At the end of the canyon, over to our right, I noted a tumble of shattered rock slabs, some as big as our ground vehicle. They must have plummeted from the heights above but at the time they were still in deep shadow.

Another minute saw us rolling out from those grim confines into a vast natural amphitheatre with ribbed walls towering all about in total disdain for anything on a mere human scale but I did feel some relief at being out in a more open space. The eastern walls to our left were out of the sun but the whole place glowed with reflected light. Unfortunately, even had there not been several oversized rocks to get in the way, I realised I could never effect a take-off from within the amphitheatre because of the distance across it and the height of those cliffs. As with the valley of the crystals, there was only one way out and that was the way we had come in.

'We should stop now, Brett,' said my passenger as if she was running some kind of conducted tour.

'Sorry, lady,' I answered, 'but we don't stop until this ship is positioned for take-off.'

Even as I spoke, even as I took Delta Seven around in a wide circle to face the way we had entered, the thought of piling on speed along that canyon floor and attempting to lift back out under normal turbine power with the cargo pallet made me groan inwardly. It was one hell of a way up and it looked like you wouldn't squeeze a goose through there let alone a wingship. I was going to keep the turbines running. The ship was going to stay alive and ready to fly us out as soon as my VIP had done whatever it was she needed to do and that was that. We came to a standstill and as the sound of our turbines dropped to a low moan I asked, 'Are you ready to suit up?'

'Yes, Brett. Please go first and I will follow you.'

'Follow me?' I said. 'I'm sorry but you can't do that - you're my responsibility. I have to help you with your suit and check everything out before we leave the ship. It's one of the few regulations I stick to.'

Her eyes fixed on mine. Her expression confirmed this was not an option as she said, 'You must go first, Brett. You need not concern yourself about regulations. The responsibility will be mine alone.'

Something nagged inside my head telling me I shouldn't argue so I muttered, 'Okay, your funeral.'

111

I let down the boarding ramp and left my seat wondering why I should be concerned at all over someone so pig-headed. Then I thought maybe she had some piece of equipment to sort out that I was not meant to see. Where she might have stowed it I had no idea unless it was tucked inside her crew suit. I wanted to get this over with as quickly as possible then have us both out of there. At the inner airlock door I called back. 'See you outside. I'll be the first human being down there if that's what you want.'

'I will follow you shortly, Brett,' came the reply and I took her word for it.

Once suited up I passed through the airlock and down the ramp, stopping at the bottom to savour the moment. As I moved from under the ship, the scale of that great encirclement struck me as ever more daunting but didn't impart the same child-like wonder as when Karin and I explored the valley of crystals. Around me soared an illuminated stage set that might have been built by the hands of giants long since passed from this world. I hurriedly recorded the view and wished Karin could be with me to share the experience. What she would have made of my passenger I could only guess. Not far from the ship I located a basalt slab of suitable height on which to park myself. There I could take in the scenery until my passenger appeared. My attention returned to the ship where her two big turbines spun slowly in their cowls with the white fins rising above. Dwarfed by those immense walls she might have been but Delta Seven stood proud and defiant as a testament to the human spirit and I was mightily reassured by that. When at last I observed a figure in white pressure suit descend the boarding ramp I raised up and called over the radio, 'So you made it. Now maybe we'll see what this is all about.'

I expected her to respond but no, she turned in the opposite direction to the one I had taken, setting off toward the mouth of the canyon like she knew exactly where she was going. 'Oh, well,' I groused, 'working for the likes of Virgil Hammond I guess you don't need good manners.'

By the time I had covered the distance to the other side of the ship, my passenger was already close to the rock fall, now part illuminated because the sun had shifted higher above the canyon.

'Care to tell me where you're heading?' I called and I noted at that point she was not carrying any piece of equipment. There was no reply so I called again and began to hurry. 'Hey, Officer Michaelis! Answer me! Check out your radio!'

Silence was all I got for my efforts and by now, still some fifteen metres in front, she was heading around that heaped mass of slabs. I called repeatedly, bounding along through the sand, wondering what the hell she was up to. By the time I reached the rock fall she had disappeared around it. Glancing into the canyon I observed the sun beginning to peer over the edge, spilling down to lighten the depths. What a sight that was if only I'd had time to spend in recording it properly. By now I was pretty angry over her tramping off the way she had and I was determined to let her know it, VIP or no, but when I arrived around the other side of the rocks she had altogether vanished.

Right in front of me was something quite unexpected. Partly hidden by the boulders there arose a narrow opening some four metres high, topped by an irregular natural arch. Further within was total blackness. It was obvious she had gone inside since she could have gone nowhere else. Again I tried to contact her over the radio - again with the same result. Nothing. 'All right,' I called as I approached the entrance, 'this is pushing things too far. Come on out - now!'

Maybe she knew what was inside there, maybe not. Either way, she really was my responsibility in this situation even if she outranked me ten times over. Stepping forward I switched on my suit lamps then peered inside. There was a gallery, sloping gradually down before twisting out of sight, its walls of fused volcanic glass suggesting the gut of some gigantic organism shining with digestive juices. Reaching out, I felt the side through the sensor pads of my glove. It was cold and smooth as polished steel. This wasn't quite *déjà vu,* but here I was once more in the middle of nowhere, staring into some place I'd rather stay out of but this time with no clue as to where I might end up. I was reflecting on this when her voice cut in. 'Brett, you must follow me. It is quite safe.'

'No thanks!' I responded. 'You come out of there right now and tell me just what this is about!'

With my suit microphones on, I heard my voice echo from within. I imagined her getting stuck, or worse still, falling down some nameless pit the way Karin almost had. She didn't answer so I stepped a little way inside and called, 'Stop fooling around and come right out!'

'Brett,' came the reply, 'we must speak with you. There are things you must know.'

Why the hell couldn't I see her suit light? How was she communicating? It didn't sound like it came over the radio. Why was she behaving this way in so hostile an environment and what did she mean by "we"? Fine, I could wait it out, I could kick sand around in the hope she wouldn't be too long or I could go inside and see what she was playing at. I decided I would go and haul her out of there, yelling and kicking if that's what it took.

Now sometimes a guy gets a lucky break and that's how it seemed at the time. I hesitated, backed out and looked behind me to find my ship was out of sight, hidden by those fallen slabs. I was about to move back inside when from the corner of my eye I saw something oh, so briefly dart from right to left. A shadow that fell across the rock fall and was gone in the blink of an eye. I stepped away from the entrance. I moved into sunlight thinking what the hell could have caused a shadow. On Earth you would have taken it as a passing bird or an aircraft, but not out here. There were no birds on Mars outside the biodomes. As for an aircraft, my whereabouts were supposed to be secret. Peering up, I saw a shape in the sky, a shape I knew very well but was the last thing I expected to see. She swooped gracefully in a wide arc over the amphitheatre. As she was about to disappear from sight over the rim, I used my helmet magnification and made out the number emblazoned on her wing. It was Delta Four – Leo's ship! What was Leo doing here unless Joe had sent him? I moved out further and waited, once more in sight of my own ship. My suit radio crackled to life before I spotted him again. 'Brett - do you hear me?' came Leo's voice with undisguised urgency. There he was, way up there, following the line of the canyon, flared out at low speed to keep in line of contact with me for as long as possible. 'Leo!' I called. 'What the hell is going on?'

'Brett, are you okay? Can you get out of there?'

'Sure I'm okay! Why shouldn't I be okay?'

'Brett - can you get back to your ship? Can you lift off? If you can then do it right now!'

'Leo, my passenger's gone walkabout. What the hell is -?'

He was over the amphitheatre again and in a tight turn. Too tight from the looks of it for he was beginning to spiral down. He'd got himself into a dangerous situation on manual control and it was obvious something was very wrong as he called, 'Brett - get back on the fuckin' ship! Get the ramp up. Get on vision! Please, old buddy do it for me right now!'

He couldn't hold the circle any longer and putting on full power to gain lift, he disappeared once more over the rim. I started back toward the ship, hesitating twice to see if my passenger had reappeared. With the situation pressing urgent, I only vaguely registered the fact that there should have been two sets of footprints leading to that rock fall when there was only one. Mine. There was still no sign of her when I kicked sand off my boots before ascending the ramp. Once through the inner airlock door, I uncoupled my helmet, hesitated until the dust extractors shut down then headed on past the open door of the suit locker, giving it no more than a casual glance. Normally, I would have stowed the helmet inside but, as I expected soon to have to put it back on, I hooked it over the passenger's seat before switching on my communications. Delta Four was back above me when Leo's face appeared. 'Brett, are you alone?'

'She hasn't shown up yet, Leo. What's this all about? What happened to my secret mission?' I watched him sweep by in an arc above the amphitheatre.

'Brett - what you've got ain't Zena Michaelis because she's dead! Brett - it ain't fuckin' human! Believe me - I've seen the playback! Get yourself out of there! Just go – go - go!'

No point pretending I wasn't confused - especially when I looked over toward the rock fall to see the white pressure suit reappear from behind then start out into sunlight.

'She's coming back!' I called to Leo. 'Can't you see?'

Leo closed his eyes and groaned, 'Oh, shit - why won't you listen?'

Then it hit me like a whacked gong. The pressure suit! There should have been only two in the storage locker but I swear I had seen three! No! I *knew* I had seen three! With Delta Four moving out of sight again, Leo's image vanished. The figure was quite close when I activated the boarding ramp and moments later was out of sight, having moved under the ship as the ramp sealed. I waited, expecting any moment to hear the voice of Zena Michaelis demanding to know why I had locked her out. Then Leo was back. 'Brett - What's happening?'

'Nothing, Leo. The ship is sealed but -.'

'Then why are you hanging around? Get yourself out of there!'

'Leo, I can't just -!'

Then another voice, 'Brett, you must lower the ramp.'

Leo was still talking when I answered her. 'Officer Michaelis, walk in front of the ship! Let me see you!'

'Brett, do not leave. Return with me.'

It was the voice I knew but I couldn't tell from where it came. Not my radio, that's for sure because the voice seemed closer than Leo's. I was getting scared as though something crawled over my flesh. Something cold and evil! I put the ship into take-off mode. The turbines were whining up high but there were voices all around me, fluttering like bats in every corner of the pod. Leo was calling but I couldn't make out what he said so I swiped at the panel to shut him off. I needed to get a hold on myself.

She appeared in front of the pod but – but now it was Karin. Karin without a pressure suit! And it was her voice! 'Brett, don't leave me! Please!'

'No!' I yelled. 'No - you're not real! You can't exist out there!'

She moved closer, arms raised - hands reaching up toward me. 'Brett you must not go! Not now!'

The voice was inside my head, echoing all about, rising above the howl of the turbines, drowning my thoughts. 'No!' I shouted. 'I won't listen!' But I couldn't stop her. The image was getting closer, growing larger, the voice louder, now joined by others - pleading, clawing at my brain, filling my head until I thought any moment she, or it, would rise up, pass through the armaplast then into the pod where it would reach out to touch me! The turbines were screaming. I felt my world was coming apart. There's a code word you call and a control you hit for emergency lift-off. I did both right then!

Thunder bellowed about me as the auxiliary rockets started up, then a jolt as the cargo container dropped clear. The ship lurched forward, seized by forces now beyond my control. The blast must have been terrific for we were enveloped by a surge of incandescent gases as Delta Seven, rocking, pitching on her suspension, accelerated at a truly alarming rate. Exactly when the voice stopped I couldn't say but as we drove clear of that inferno, bouncing along the canyon floor at high speed, it was gone. The turbines howled like banshees over the roar of the rockets and the canyon walls were just a blur.

'Come on sweetheart! Come on!' I yelled as her nose lifted. Then we were airborne. Not in the normal way a wingship is airborne but reconfigured for high speed, blasting up at a crazy angle on a spear of flame. What a sight she must have been, rising between those grim walls, soaring sunward like a great white bird until at last we were out of there beneath an open sky. As soon as we levelled off, the ship reconfigured for normal flight and her rockets cut with what sounded like a sigh of relief. It was nothing compared with the sigh of relief that escaped from me as I regained full control.

I swung around in a broad arc, cutting my altitude, following the canyon, at the same time calling up a view of the area I'd just left. All I could make out down there was a long pall of smoke and dust that obscured anything that might have remained, including the abandoned cargo pod. The cargo pod was, however, transmitting its own location and my sensors showed it laying where it had dropped.

A wingship appeared in the sky to my right and as I came around my communications panel signalled for attention. A face appeared and I called, 'Leo, I'm just fine!'

'Glad you made it out of there, buddy,' he smiled. 'I do hope you're on your own this time.'

'I no longer have a passenger,' I replied, setting course for Novamerica One.

Moments later Joe's image appeared so I relayed my experiences to him as well as anyone else out there who happened to be listening. It was well and truly out of the bag, planet-wide and most likely on its way to Earth because neither of us had thought to secure our transmissions. As we drifted over the deserts, as we passed like two white motes between the great Tharsis volcanoes, everyone was trying to get through to us. We locked our transmissions into Novamerica One so communications had to go via there. It also gave priority to Joe, although I expected our Chief Executive to muscle in at any time. I guess Leo and others were thinking very much the same as I was during our flight home.

In the arid remoteness, in the hidden depths of this world, there was life - intelligent life that must have been moving amongst us unrecognised. The experience had shaken me but now I had time to think about it I asked myself a few questions - the most important of them being, 'What would have happened to me had Leo not shown up in time? And why - why had it happened at all?

***

It was well into the afternoon when Leo and I entered our own navigational space only to find ourselves locked into a holding pattern some ten kilometres out. We asked each other what was going on but before we could contact Joe the answer appeared literally before our eyes. Lifting clear of our base on a jet of flame was a shuttle. I judged from her angle of ascent she must be going sub-orbital. I didn't need any clues as to her destination since the identification on her side read, NA-05. She had come from Virgil Hammond's station so I had no doubt it was to there she would return.

After the shuttle had cleared I went in, followed by Leo. I knew he wasn't going to be hanging about since he'd lost several hours and still had an important cargo to deliver. My priority was different. Joe ordered me to speak to no one but to enter the complex via one of the service building airlocks, stash away my pressure suit there then head straight for his office.

***

That Joe had been much concerned over my safety was obvious as soon as he spoke.

'I tell you, son, when Leo radioed you were out of there, I started to breathe again. What a turn-up, Brett - what a hell of a turn-up! This whole planet is buzzing and on top of that I have every goddamned government on Earth as well as the space station howling for information. The European General

Administrator wants to interview me on a secure link and our people on Earth are intent on setting up a conference to include ourselves and the International Council. The only one who isn't bugging me is our Chief Executive and that's a real surprise though I guess he's got enough to think about with Zena Michaelis. Soon, Brett, I'm gonna wake up and find all this never happened!'

'Oh, it happened, Joe. It's still sinking in but it happened all right. Now we really are awake.'

'And the turmoil is only just beginning. This next half hour is the only chance we'll have to go over things because that's about as long as I can hold some of those people off.'

'What about the shuttle? Don't tell me Hammond's been over here.'

'No, he sent a couple of guys to collect Zena Michaelis and the crystals. And, Brett, we still don't know what happened - we don't know why she ended up out there without a pressure suit. There were no signs of violence - no signs of a struggle. It's as though she somehow overrode the airlock controls and - and just walked out. The safety systems wouldn't allow a person to do that without a suit unless they were reprogrammed but then I would have been informed before that could happen. And we thought she was dead! Well, to all intents and purposes she was - about as dead as any human being could be and frozen solid when they found her.

Human being did I say? I had Petra Giordano scan her - I guess we weren't supposed to do that. She was more a product of the laboratory than anyone I ever heard about – blood, heart, pituitary and thyroid glands – you name it. Inside her brain, too: Giordano says she had a mass of synthetics in her sensory cortex plus more things I don't pretend to understand. Even her goddamned eyes and ears came out of someone's biolab back on Earth, able, she assured me, to see and hear way beyond those of even an enhanced human. She was a syntho but not off-the-shelf androids like the military once used on Earth that are now illegal. If only we'd had her down there a while longer.'

Joe relaxed for the first time since I had entered his office then went on, 'Call me old-fashioned, Brett, but you're either basically a human being or a syntho, and I don't reckon she'd fit either description since she still had enough left of her original brain. That'd still make her illegal on Earth as well as out here. Giordano confirms she could have survived long enough to get that far down the runway before seizing up through cold and lack of oxygen. Part of her was still operational and started transmitting when she warmed up - and it could only have been to Virgil Hammond. It's a pity we didn't have enough time to download the contents of her skull.'

'Mm, I wonder who she was before they got their hands on her - but it means Hammond knew what had happened before anyone else here - except for whoever -.'

'Except for whoever or whatever killed her! Too right he did, but he wasn't admitting anything - no sir! Even so, he had that shuttle on its way the minute news was out. It must have been standing by ready - and unless I'm mistaken, he'll know we scanned the body and he'll know what we found out.'

'There has to be a connection, Joe. Maybe she was killed to stop her going with me so I ended up with - with some kind of illusion. I'll say this - I still find it difficult to believe that woman wasn't real. My eyes and ears said the image was real, even in that canyon when it was Karin standing there without a suit. It almost took me in, Joe, whatever it was.'

'You didn't see it, son, did you - you didn't see what the thing really looked like.'

'No,' I answered, 'I have no idea apart from what Leo told me.'

'Well, we saw it - or we thought we did, on screen. It was none too clear because it was changing shape all the time like some goddamned amoeba. I had Giordano try to analyse the images from the recording but I reckon it frightened her and her staff more than it frightened you. All he or any of us can be certain about is that it was well and truly alive.'

'There's no arguing over that, Joe.'

'Brett after what you've been through - you must be phased out. You can stay on leave for as long as you need, naturally. Karin's been on to me so she knows you're still in one piece. I guess you'd better call her as soon as you can. After that, son, you may feel inclined to lie low for a time, especially since Roy Kendrick is aiming to drop in on us. You won't want to -.'

'Roy Kendrick!' I cut in. 'What's he doing back on Mars?'

'SolaNews sent him over on *Cassiopeia* when word got to Earth of possible sabotage. He'll sniff out a story at a hundred light years even if there isn't one.'

'Especially if there isn't one,' I put in, recalling Roy's antics in the past.

'Well, Brett, he'll be flying here from Europa Six, so we have few hours left before he shows up.'

Roy Kendrick – a name I hoped never to hear again. Fact is I never did care for newsmen but in my personal register of undesirables, Roy Kendrick occupied place of dishonour at the top of the list. I didn't hate the guy - he was only doing his job, if that's what people want to call it. I didn't hate anybody in particular at that time, but until Virgil Hammond arrived on the scene, Roy would have been the most promising candidate with Konstantin Pazukhin trailing a poor second.

'Now, Joe,' I said, 'I don't want to be laying low in my own back yard to avoid the likes of Kendrick. I was due to resume my schedule again, anyway - so how about it?'

'If that's what you want, son, then you have it. Nobody keeps a pilot on the ground for the fun of it. We'll have to route all communications through here, mind, otherwise they'll be hounding you every minute of the day and night. Now, you and I have a lot of talking to do before then, and I do mean a lot! I know you want to speak to Karin and I have to report to the Chief Executive. Meantime there's something you may want to see before you do anything else.'

I had to see the recording before I contacted Karin because Joe had already shown it to her. I watched myself in the pilot's seat, my mouth moving, then sitting quiet as I listened to - to no other speech at all. To nothing. Whatever hovered near me was as Joe had described it; ill defined, shifting, expanding and contracting - changing all the time. Some kind of ectoplasm moving about like it was trying to examine me from every angle without actually touching. I could hardly believe it was me sitting there with that thing.

With that visual treat ended I called Karin. When her image appeared she looked exactly like the illusion in the canyon. So much so that I wanted to reach out and touch her hair to know this really was her.

'Brett, I've been worried sick. The stories - they're so confusing. Joe told me as much as he could whilst you were on your way back so I won't ask you to go through it all again. Is our conversation secure?'

'I guess it's as secure as anything can be with the likes of Hammond around.'

'My side too - I hope, but if that man is listening then let him; he has no jurisdiction over me. Brett, I want to talk to you as long as I can - as long as you want. The five crystals I handed over to Joe - have you heard anything?'

'Joe told me they were found in Zena Michaelis' quarters and put on the shuttle back to Novamerica Five with her body.'

She hesitated over her next words. 'I should not risk talking to anyone about this, Brett, but I'm going to tell you. The crystal I brought back went straight into our laboratory for analysis. Our people are certain they were laid down in the remote past and later buried by natural processes. There is no doubt whatsoever that they are a product of intelligent life. The crystal lattices contain a complex molecular code that is activated by ultra-violet light. We think fluctuations and colours in the light they give out may express the kind of information each one holds but that is hardly more than guesswork.'

I hung onto her words then said, 'Finding these and what's happened as a result of it has to be the most important event since human beings set foot on Mars.'

'Yes, it has to be. But even though we're unable to break the code within the crystals we are sure that just a few of them, perhaps each one, must contain truly staggering amounts of information at a quantum level – perhaps equal to the sum of all recorded human knowledge. There are several domains within the crystal we hold, each exhibiting subtle differences in its subatomic structure. We believe each domain could be interface to a parallel universe - to an alternative space-time. Brett, it's as if those crystals will speak to whoever is able to understand their message but it is not a message intended for us. I believe what you and I discovered out there is an ancient repository - stored information on – on we don't know what. We're certain they must have been left on Mars by a life form that existed here many millions of years ago and that whoever or whatever created them must have been utterly different and very much ahead scientifically of ourselves. We've examined our crystal as far we are able without risking damage to it. Nothing more will be done with it for the time being.'

'Karin, I don't think the owners ever left. I think we've been walking by them every day in the recreation area and the biodome. It looks like I carried one of them down into the canyon inside my ship!'

'Brett, don't say that - you frighten me. How can such life forms have existed for so long? The sooner we have security measures in place, the better. You must have been so close to –.'

'To being snuffed out - yes. I've been thinking hard about that, Karin - especially since speaking to Joe. Why the hell did they have me fly into the Labyrinth? What I'm saying is - why didn't it, or they, do for me like I'm beginning to suspect they did for Zena Michaelis? Why? That's the question I'm asking myself and I have no answer. It would have been so easy to haul me into that cave. I was half inside before Leo showed up. I'm beginning to wonder if, just maybe, they were trying to communicate.'

'Communicate? But why do it like that? Why not make themselves known on the way out instead of having you risk going into that awful place?'

'I don't have an answer right now, Karin, but there has to be one, I'm sure of it.'

'Brett, be careful. Don't take any more chances. Please don't!'

'It'll be okay. I'm flying out tomorrow before Roy Kendrick gets on my back. Joe has a cargo standing by for the Russian prime base.'

'Will we be able to keep in touch?'

'Of course we will. I'll talk to Joe about it before I leave. As soon as I'm airborne, I'll call you up from the wide pink yonder via our base. That's a promise!'

**

'I'm sorry I didn't contact you earlier, sir,' said the technician, 'but I had nothing of significance to report on the crystals during our tests late this afternoon. Not, er - not until now, that is.'

The laboratory was almost dark, illuminated by little more than the light shining upon the crystal where it sat within a transparent enclosure in front of him. The man was nervous even though the image of Virgil Hammond regarded him with an expression of disarming amiability. 'Then kindly update me on what you have discovered since we last spoke.'

'Well, sir, they - the crystals, oscillate and re-radiate fluctuating colours after a wavelength stimulus of ten to the fifteenth Hertz and up – that is in the ultra-violet band. Our work until nineteen hundred hours involved attempting to analyse their behaviour during that phase - but -.'

Hammond's expression did not change though a hint of impatience was evident in his voice. 'But by now you must have had the opportunity to pursue your analysis somewhat further.'

'That is so - yes. When I applied stimulus at higher frequencies to this specimen, something very odd happened.'

There was a brief silence then Hammond said, 'I take it you *are* alone in there, Friedland.'

'Alone? Oh, yes, quite alone, I assure you. None of the others saw me return.' His assurances

did not prevent him glancing nervously aside into the obscurity of the room before continuing. 'An hour ago I began to probe one of the crystals in the lower X-ray band. It absorbed energy at ten to the eighteenth Hertz but without re-emission at any wavelength. That was very odd indeed – yes, very odd. The lattice, however, appeared to undergo molecular reorganisation then the crystal became totally opaque. After that I was unable to observe anything at all. It may have been expressing energy through that reorganisation. Five minutes ago it became clear again.'

There was no mistaking the irritation in Hammond's response. 'Apart from enumerating frequencies that are of little interest to me, are you saying there is more that can be done or are you not?'

'Well, I – I have to say Doctor Robertson considers that if we apply too much energy to the specimen, it may be damaged or destroyed. Because the crystals are the product of an advanced technology she is reluctant to do this. It will be in her report to you.'

'Doctor Robertson is over-cautious in my estimation. If we can shake these things hard enough they might give us a clue as to their contents. What is your opinion, Friedland? I take it you have an opinion?'

'An opinion? Oh, yes, I do indeed. I think it's worth going on. Even if one of the crystals is destroyed, there will be four remaining.'

'Quite so,' agreed Hammond, his image moving closer, 'and we know where there are plenty more of them to be had if the worst comes to the

worst. The information locked inside those crystals could be of the highest importance to our interests. They may well be a gift of providence – yes, a revelation. But I need results quickly, Friedland. Results! As you say, you have enough of the things to play around with so test one of them to destruction if necessary. You have my direct authorisation to carry on as you see fit. If you achieve anything positive, I will ensure the credit goes in full to you. You have my word on that.'

'I understand, sir. Thank you.'

Hammond stared hard at him then his image vanished.

Friedland ran through the details of his previous tests and those obtained during their journey by the earlier expedition that had been passed on to him. Here was an opportunity to discover that which others might only dream of and to make his name known. Perhaps more than that. He watched closely as the energy levels increased. Watched the read-out as the frequency input soared to a point well beyond that authorised by his superior earlier that day. Then higher still.

'Ten to the nineteenth Hertz and still nothing,' he breathed. The crystal had turned black some minutes earlier. 'Now then, let's see how you respond to Gamma frequencies.'

His instruments indicated no output to compensate for the energy pouring into the crystal. Moving closer, Friedland peered hard through the protective wall of the analyser then at his readout. It told him the specimen was increasing rapidly in mass – a totally inexplicable phenomenon. He regarded the crystal as he might a large spider of dubious origin. 'Ah! What's this! It's rotating! The thing is spinning!'

The crystal spun on its pedestal, humming like an insect, reflecting multicoloured light as would the polished facets of a dark jewel - fascinating, mesmerising, compelling him simply to sit and stare. The sound increased in frequency to touch Friedland as a tuning fork. More rapidly it spun until it became a blur reflected in the eyes of the technician. The sound grew louder, increased yet further in pitch until it began to hurt his ears. The reflected glare was becoming unbearable. Friedland lifted hands to the sides of his face, squeezed shut his eyes then groped with splayed, quivering fingers to shut off the power.

**

The emergency light was still flashing above the door when they entered the darkened laboratory. A burning odour hung in the air, sweet, cloying, not at first unpleasant. With the lights switched on the room appeared normal except about the bench where Friedland had been working. Here was charred chaos. The analyser and the equipment close about it appeared to have melted. The crystal, seemingly quite intact, lay in a far corner where it had come to rest after rolling across the floor. Friedland lay face down, part covered by the bench. When they turned him over, they saw that his face and his hands were altogether burned away.

CHAPTER 4
ANGEL OF DEATH

Kurt Hoffman, a pilot flying for the Europeans, looked forward to the break as his wingship began its descent over the desert. He would soon be meeting an old friend, would soon be taking things easy over a welcome meal and a few drinks. On the horizon appeared the new complex of Europa Six - still under construction but already one of the largest, most impressive bases on the planet. Destined to become the first true town on Mars, it lay close to the ramparts of the hundred kilometre wide Nicholson crater, itself some three thousand kilometres to the west of the Tharsis volcanoes and, like Pavonis, sitting astride the equator.

The day had advanced beyond mid-morning yet the sun appeared as a disk of smoke-veiled bronze, the sky a shimmering orange haze, the runway indistinct against an encroaching tide of sand. The wingship flared out to circle above the complex, skirting wide to avoid the big cranes as wraiths of ingested sand spiralled from her turbines. The sandstorm was developing quickly.

'Paolo, the strip is almost obscured - I'm seeing sand ripples from up here but my sensors tell me it's still safe to land.'

'Sure it is, Kurt,' came the reply, 'we're talking only centimetres so far. It'll get worse before long then there's no way anyone will be flying out of here for the rest of today.'

'Flying out!' responded Kurt. 'Don't talk to me about flying out! Didn't you check out my schedule? I'm down with you for two days.'

'Sure I did - that's great! I'm over at one of our construction sites right now but by the time you're down I'll be there for real to meet you.'

On final approach Kurt observed the bright blue tractor standing like a child's toy at the far end of the runway, waiting to turn his ship around. The big turntable was temporarily out of use because of building work. Beyond the cluster of domes and blocks towered the yellow cranes - two sentinels casting long shadows across the growing complex with, scattered between them, a mayhem of steel pipe-work. Streamers of sand spun across Kurt's vision, the desert flashed beneath then his sensors told him he was over the runway. The wheels touched once, twice, hurling up fountains of sand - then Early Bird was down.

'Not a bad landing for a novice!' grinned the image of round-faced, dark eyed Paolo Romano.

'Careful, big mouth. You got me hanging about for some time – remember.'

The wingship rolled to a halt but Kurt waited until Early Bird was tractored around into take-off position. Watching dust shrouds writhe across the strip, he was well aware how sand would cover the runway faster than maintenance bots or humans could clear it.

'Captain Hoffman, good to see you again,' came the voice from one of the blue pressure-suited crew as the bulky figure of Kurt descended the ship's ramp.

'Hi there,' he answered. 'I hear nobody predicted the sandstorm.'

'No, Captain, not until it got started further west. The place is closing down now so we'll be the last crew out here until it clears. It's local but pretty extensive so there's nothing to be done once it gets a hold.'

The low-loader loomed from an encroaching haze, circled Early Bird then manoeuvred under the cargo pallet. As they walked across the strip toward the main airlock, the footprints of Kurt and the crewmen were quickly obliterated. Five people stood in the airlock awaiting recompression whilst the dust filters ran on full power. As they removed their helmets, the tractor man gestured up at newly installed detectors and smiled at Kurt. 'Glad to see you're a genuine human, Captain. Whatever lives here might have fooled the Americans but they won't get by our electronics.'

'Nice to know I qualify,' muttered Kurt as the inner doors slid open.

Framed against the bright lights and vibrant colours of the concourse a figure stepped forward, arms outstretched. 'Hoffman, you overstuffed Kraut - won't anyone else take you in for ground leave?'

'Romano, you Dago bastard,' grinned the bigger man as they hugged, 'show me the menu so I can check out the crap you're serving up. And what's with the crazy walls? I don't remember any of that from last time.'

'Ah, our active mural,' replied Paolo, gesturing toward abstract forms that flowed in liquid iridescence over the concourse walls, forming then reforming in trimensional polychrome complexity.

We're moving away from mundane functionalism into a world of self-indulgence - it is home to most of us after all. You like our mural - yes?'

'Fucking decadent,' muttered Kurt, attempting with difficulty to focus on the nearest of the patterns. 'And they tell me the colonies are costing too much.'

'That mural didn't cost Earth a bean,' responded Paolo, 'It's home grown. Yes - designed by our own artist. She's the best on Mars I tell you.' As they walked toward the pressure suit storage area Paolo added, 'Hey, seriously Kurt, you'll appreciate it here even more now. Since you were last in, our food synthesisers are fully operational and the main restaurant section is opened – *and* we got the best menu on the planet. If those lousy Martians everyone's going on about are real, they'll want to move in here just for the food. We have five kinds of fish as well as all the -.'

'You mean *real* fish, Paolo – fish meat that doesn't taste like wood shavings?'

'I mean *real* fish – well, as real as it gets most of the time including back on Earth. Any organic complex we can match. Yes, with the right texture and perfect flavour - not like the shit they feed you at Number Three. And we're running out some decent wines to go with anything you like - so how about that. Next time you're down, the northern section should be pressurised and -.'

'Hey – you mentioned booze!' Kurt stopped abruptly. 'Good job you reminded me before I got my suit off. You won't guess what I left aboard Early Bird.'

'You left something behind? Does it matter right now?'

'I'll say it matters! I did the Russkies a favour and I got myself two good size flasks of vodka in return.'

'Vodka!' responded Paolo. 'I didn't think Earth would allow that. When did it come over?'

'It didn't come over - they've been synthesising the stuff at some of their bases from who-knows-what but I can tell you, my friend, it tastes pretty damn good.'

'Christ - what if Pazukhin finds out?'

'Pazukhin!' exclaimed Kurt. 'It's only feeding him a regular supply of the stuff that keeps the miserable bastard off their backs!'

'Okay, Kurt, I'll do a deal. You go and get it before conditions are too bad out there and maybe we'll feed you top class chow this evening. Then our lab can analyse a sample of your booze for the future.'

'You got a deal, Paolo. Better have a decent lunch ready or you don't get a fucking sniff.'

It took little time for Kurt to return to Early Bird where he collected a case containing the flasks. Once again he found himself trudging toward the complex but now the sun was a vague pink smear, the horizon obliterated by curtains of sand that had turned once bright day into a smothering twilight with rapidly falling temperature. Soon, the modest distance between the base and his wingship would be totally obscured. The world was closing in.

Not ten minutes had elapsed since he last stood waiting in the airlock for the inner door to slide open. Not wishing to place his case down until he had passed through, Kurt had kept his helmet on so had failed to notice the flashing readout on the air pressure level indicators. When the inner door opened, things were not as he expected. Across the once busy concourse hurried two small groups of men and women, some with loudly wailing children clutched in their arms. Alarms sounded whilst at the centre of the area, above the corridor exits, blue lights pulsed. When two men rushed by, Kurt removed his helmet and called, 'Hey - what's going on?' In their haste they ignored him. Like others, they were heading in the direction of the biodome. Kurt looked up as a voice echoed across the now deserted space. 'Repeat! All personnel to the main biodome! This is a Class One emergency! All personnel to the main biodome!'

There was an odour of burning, then a dull rumble like a detonation echoed by. Kurt was aware of something else - breathing was not as easy as it should be. Only now did he check the environment status read-out by the airlock. It told him what no one would want to see. The air pressure was falling steadily. In a few minutes time it would drop below six hundred millibars and reach danger level. Hurrying to the main corridor, which lay off-axis to the centre of the concourse, he perceived a tide of brown dust billowing toward him - as if the sandstorm in full spate outside had gained access to the complex. He stared hard into it, muttering, 'What the hell,' then called over his suit radio, 'Does anyone hear me?'

There was no reply. Changing to the emergency band he was assailed by a babble of voices all intent on delivering the same message over their personal phones. 'Everyone get to the main biodome! Get to the biodome!'

Pain assailed his ears. Kurt fitted back his helmet.

He moved on to find the next corridor brightly lit but also hazed with drifting dust. Another, much louder echo and he stepped back to the first corridor. The dust there had thickened but having advanced no further, was instead receding, swirling, pulsating like some bizarre living organism. Peering into the haze he concluded a strong flow of air must be passing away from the concourse and down the passage. Confounded by this vision of horror Kurt strode quickly across, snatched up his case then stabbed at the airlock controls. The inner door was only part opened when he squeezed through and within seconds he had it closed. The indicator confirmed pressure within the airlock was already below three hundred millibars and falling. It reached two hundred - one hundred then lower still. As soon as the outer doors opened he would go outside, he would radio for help even though alarm signals must have been triggered planet-wide.

The lights went out. The air pumps ceased. The emergency lights were on and Kurt peered about to find the status and communication indicators blank. There was provision to release the outer doors for anyone trapped inside the airlock and suited up, as long as pressure was low enough. This panel still glowed but though he stabbed at it repeatedly the outer doors would not open. He stepped back to the inner doors to press his visor against the window. The emergency lights about the concourse shone pallid but the wall mural no longer shimmered colour. Because of the sandstorm, only the faintest daylight entered via windows higher up in the walls.

'This cannot be real,' he breathed, splaying fingers against the door. 'No, it cannot be.'

There was no response to his radio calls. No more babble – only silence. He remained some minutes staring into eerie emptiness, numbed by what he had witnessed and thinking soon that the nightmare must end. Again he tried the outer door. Again no response. After a while he carried out what he knew he had to do; he opened the small panel on the right arm of his pressure suit, turned his life support system to minimum, slid down against the wall and closed his eyes.

***

When the news broke I was taking on cargo at Novaya Granitsa, largest of the Russian bases and centre of their administration. That was far enough to the south-west of Nicholson to have avoided the sandstorm and we had ourselves a fine, clear morning. But as we were closer than anyone else to Europa Six the European General Administrator, Adelle Saint-Leger, had put out a request for assistance to the Russians. Everyone's satellites would meanwhile be trying to get a look-in and I imagined them bouncing off each other up there like old-style pool balls. Joe had contacted me directly from our home base and requested I attend a conference with himself, Adelle Saint-Leger and Russian Chief Executive, Konstantin Pazukhin. Yeah, that's the one, Happy Pazukhin – and he'd be there in the flesh. Involved also would be Amalia Barbosa. You'll doubtless recall that, based on the International Space Station, she was Secretary for

140

Colonial Affairs on behalf of the International Council.

I was in Pazukhin's office with images of the others appearing before us. It wasn't the first time I had seen the Russian supremo close up but I'd had little to do with him directly until now. He was a grumbling bear of a man - dour and humourless as his reputation implied. It was an aspect he appeared keen to perpetuate though I could never figure out why. I think if he'd tried to smile, that tombstone face of his would have cracked open. He informed me our conversations were to be encrypted for transmission by light pulse over Marsnet. Being highly directional, light-pulse is difficult to intercept. It was obvious they had security in mind though what it would achieve at that point wasn't clear to me nor, I think, to any of them.

The one party we expected would preside, head of the mining consortium, Virgil Hammond, wasn't in evidence at all. It turned out he had nominated Joe to stand in for our side and I saw that as a ploy to avoid anyone asking awkward questions. I figured, though, he would be monitoring us via relay from my base the way he'd been snooping on Karin and myself on the way back from our field trip. He may or may not have had a right to do that but just then there were more urgent matters to consider.

The image of perennially attractive though solemn-faced Adelle Saint-Leger was last to appear. Adelle's true age was subject of frequent speculation but everybody agreed she could not possibly have remained so young for the many Earth years she had resided on Mars, though on the home planet such cosmetic time-freezes are common enough. I well remember her face on that day; her eyes were bright, her mouth set firm as she looked at each of us in turn.

'You will understand if I waive the usual formalities,' she began. 'Circumstances of a most pressing nature have fallen upon us. Shortly after ten thirty-five hours local time, our station at Nicholson ceased communication. There were automated alarm signals from various sections of the complex but no human call for assistance and, due to work being carried out on her communications systems, Europa Six was temporarily offline to our central monitoring facility.

We at first considered the possibility of a meteor strike but any object large enough to pose a threat would have been detected out in space and measures taken to destroy it. Numerous satellites have been passed low over the area in the last hour and a half since the emergency. Visible light observation will not be possible until the sandstorm has cleared but scanning at microwave frequencies has revealed no sign of damage to the structure - impact or otherwise – and the biodome appears to be intact. We should, however, have been able to detect an infra-red signature. There was a weak signature from the base and from an aircraft that had arrived there a short time before but both were residual.'

Adelle took a deep breath then continued. 'Europa Six has for some time been too cold to support human life. The only activity we have detected is from emergency lighting systems and alert calls from those maintenance bots designed to operate under hostile conditions.' She hesitated, looking once more at each of us in turn. 'Even a massive power failure could not have caused this to happen. Auxiliary back-ups outside the complex would have cut in to provide full power for at least a week. Our base had all the normal self-repair as well as more advanced maintenance facilities. Whatever happened must have been sudden and catastrophic.'

There was utter silence then Pazukhin leaned forward to speak in that growling voice of his. 'You have requested our assistance but as our wingships are a long way from here, Commander Van Allen has agreed his pilot should remain with us to assist. I will supply a crew should a reconnaissance or a landing be considered when the sandstorm is over. We have also one of your people from Europa Five. He is an engineer and is familiar with Europa Six. He should go too.'

'I agree,' replied Adelle. 'Who is it you have there?'

'His name is Gary Holloway.'

It would be natural to think old granite-face was doing his duty by offering to help out. To be fair, perhaps that was his main reason but I suspected high on his list also was the chance to have his crew take a close-up look at the latest, most advanced project of another party.

'What's your assessment of the situation, Brett?' asked Joe.

'We're all agreed conditions are no-go at present but I'll be ready to fly out as soon as the sandstorm begins to clear.'

143

'We passed over the area a few minutes ago,' said Amalia Barbosa. 'We predict the storm will soon begin to decay. We predict conditions will be clear enough at Europa Six before mid-afternoon.'

'In that case,' I answered, 'we'll give it a shot as soon as we can.'

'I doubt you'll be able to set down with the strip under so much sand,' said Joe, 'but maybe you'll get close enough to figure out just what has happened before a shuttle gets there.'

'We'll see, Joe,' I replied. 'Sometimes there are ways and means.'

'Brett,' snapped Joe, his gaze hard on me, 'I don't want to hear about that. Take no chances, understand? I mean *no* chances!'

***

There were six on board including Gary Holloway and myself. We didn't figure we needed as many as four Russians but Pazukhin had insisted on it. The fact that each of them had some kind of fancy recording device clipped to his suit didn't surprise me. We lifted off without the aid of their booster vehicle since it was out of order, same as last time I was in there, so I was glad to have left the cargo pallet behind. Gazing from the control pod as we circled about it struck me, as it usually did, how untidy these people were. Disused containers, cables and pipe sections lay everywhere around the complex even though this was an area replete with craters – any of them ideal for storing what you didn't need until it could be recycled.

Gaining height, we all relaxed and got better introduced to one another. Away from the dour gaze of Pazukhin, the Russians talked freely as we

144

headed almost due east in the direction of Nicholson. With a flight of almost fifteen hundred kilometres before reaching Europa Six, we could only speculate for the next two hours over what we might find there. One thing we all agreed on; it was unlikely to have been a natural disaster.

'That creature you encountered,' said Alexei, one of the Russian team, 'I hear it looked like a human being. Was that so?'

'It sure was,' I answered. 'Exactly like a human being - and a damn good looking one.'

'It was so real then, 'he continued, 'so real that without electronic screening, any of us could be fooled by them?'

'Yeah,' put in Gary, 'makes you wonder who the hell is who, doesn't it?'

'I've thought about that a lot,' I responded, 'and I don't think they could get away with it again so easily.'

'You mean you could tell them apart from us?' asked one of the other Russians.

'Maybe next time I might. There was no warmth, no sensuality about her like you'd get with a real woman. And the way she - it talked - simple, direct phrasing - no elaboration, no real dialogue. Of course, not knowing what we do now, I had no reason to suspect anything. It must be difficult for them. They surely can't laugh or joke, or even indulge in the kind of rhetoric we do. At least I hope they can't.'

I and others had assumed from the very beginning there must be many of these beings and I'd heard several stations had already installed detectors of one kind or another. Now I wondered if any measures we took would be of much use. My thoughts were broken when Gary cut in with. 'We'll need to defend ourselves against them, don't you think?'

'Oh, and how d'you propose we do that?' I asked as the landscape drifted by.

'We bring over guns from Earth and we shoot them, yes?' said Alexei, pointing his finger into the air and cocking back his thumb in the manner of someone using an old fashioned pistol.

'I think what Brett is saying,' put in Gary, 'is that you can only do anything about it if you know they're there.'

'Quite so,' I agreed, 'only if you can recognise them. The way they appear, the way they sound must be based on what they take from our own minds. They reflect our behaviour as best they can.'

'Our own bots can do better than that,' remarked Alexei. 'If these things are intelligent, why don't they not do it as well?'

'He's got a point,' said Gary. 'Or maybe they're just getting in a little practice.'

'Well, they've had quite a long time to do that,' I replied, 'but our bots speak our own language, they employ in part our own biochemistry and neural networks and they mimic our own life processes. Whatever we've come upon here could be utterly different at every level.'

'Ah, maybe so,' countered Alexei, 'but you said they had a long time to get used to us and I think so, too. They could have been moving amongst us since the first humans arrived. They could have watched the very first landing party set up their flag. They could have watched them set up their scientific instruments and walk about this planet believing they were the first to take possession of it.'

'That's right,' Gary agreed, 'they could have been infiltrating the colonies since the earliest times.' 'It gives me the creeps just to think about it. And I'm wondering if these things have anything to do with what's happened at our base.'

'Well, there's no law against people speculating,' I said, 'and there seems to have been plenty of that around lately. I wouldn't be so sure about any of it.'

There was no law against drinking plenty of coffee, either. We did that, too. We also spent a while familiarising ourselves with the layout of Europa Six.

***

We were entering Europa Six navigational space but there was no contact - no communication with myself or Delta Seven. At last the complex appeared, bathed in afternoon sun, set out in the desert haze less than a half-kilometre to the south of Nicholson crater, which was as good a landmark as anyone could wish for. As we expected, the sandstorm was on its way out, though thin sheets of the stuff still drifted through the air and the sun hung like a disk of brightly polished copper. I took over the controls to begin our descent. It was during our first banking pass over the base that Gary called out, 'Hey - there's Kurt Hoffman's ship!'

I also spotted her, though with sand spread over her horizontal surfaces, she was not immediately obvious. The runway was impossible to make out visually but the ship's sensors displayed it perfectly well before me. We were lower now, circling not much higher than the big cranes when Gary said, 'I can't see anything - no sign of damage - but the biodome; Oh Christ, look at it!'

It was obvious to all of us. The whole structure appeared pallid, like a great translucent pearl rather than a transparent bubble. No one could doubt the terrible significance of that but just then none of us cared to say it. At that point my communications flashed on and a familiar face appeared. 'Brett, we have complications. Don't take her down any further.'

'What's the problem, Joe?'

'The Euros have a shuttle ready and are asking our Chief Executive and Pazukhin to call your mission off. Hammond is leaving matters to me. Pazukhin says it's no concern of his since it isn't one of his wingships. Amalia has a shuttle standing by at the space station, too, but Adelle Saint-Leger has refused further help including theirs. I understand the General Administrator has been in touch with Earth and the Europeans have made it clear who they want and who they don't want snooping about their site.'

'That's out of order!' I responded. 'Earth is back there and we're out here. Whoever first gets to the scene of an emergency here on Mars is obliged by international agreement to offer whatever assistance they can. There are *no* exclusions so they can squawk all they like!'

'That's absolutely right, son, and the final decision has to be made by the individual on the spot - you. But I have to advise you of their request and I have to point out that a shuttle landing would be safer and easier by far under present conditions. That's my advice, Brett - no more.'

I thought about it - but not for long. 'I didn't fly these guys all the way over just to turn around and head back. You can see I'm circling the base right now so we are definitely going in!'

Joe gazed at me in a way that said he approved but with considerable reservation. 'Very well, Brett, we're keeping an eye on you and I'll be standing by. But definitely *no* risk-taking.'

'Wouldn't dream of it, Joe.'

With the desert rising up to meet us Gary Holloway asked, 'What are you planning to do? Surely you can't go straight down onto that runway without taking a closer look.'

'Time we fastened our seat belts,' I answered casually, letting down the landing gear whilst flaring the ship out. Our safety systems I had already shut down. Against regulations or no.

As we dropped low, as we approached the obscured runway, I raised the nose of the ship. None of the guys behind me spoke but I sensed they were eyeing me and each other uneasily. They may have guessed what I was about to attempt and experienced a sudden lapse of enthusiasm. Slowing further with the hidden runway's position locked in, we were speeding along only twenty metres above the ground when one of the Russians called out, 'You should not do this!'

'This is none-standard procedure!' exclaimed another. 'It is not allowed!'

There was no denying he sounded nervous. I couldn't blame him.

We were lined up directly on Kurt's ship with our nose still lifting. So many warnings flashed about the control panel the whole thing looked about to explode. I didn't want the distraction of additional displays but the Delta ships had good forward vision otherwise I wouldn't have been able to see ahead so well. When we were only four metres from the ground the ship began to buffet and I could hear animated chatter behind me. There was no time to sweet-talk anyone for we were getting real close to the strip. Lower still we settled, almost touching the sand, then I powered up the big turbines and we began to accelerate. I raised the ship's nose even more to shed lift so we stayed close to the ground.

The turbines howled, Delta Seven steadied then we really began to put on speed with Early Bird lying dead in my sights. I figured the guys in the back must be sweating some but I didn't let that worry me any and I didn't have time to sweat! Leaving things as late as I dared, I pushed the engines up to emergency take-off power, gave the rockets a three-second burst whilst lowering our nose so Delta Seven would generate more lift. We passed right over the parked wingship with the complex rushing at us and I froze as, engines howling, we gained height. Had those guys behind been able to see the expression on my face it would have done nothing whatsoever to improve their day.

We were almost on the main buildings, too near for me to use the rocket boosters again and as we swooped upward an unfinished section passed so close beneath that I half expected to lose our landing gear. Some kind of oath drifted by from one

150

of the Russians and I imagined them all squashing their eyes with whitened knuckles and saying goodbye to their dear ones. Those still intent on looking would by then have realised there was no chance of our gaining sufficient altitude to clear the two cranes even with the rockets. Worse - in the thin Martian air you cannot do fancy turns like on Earth without risking a fatal sideslip. I guess we had all quit breathing by then and the cranes came at us so quickly there was no time for anyone to wonder if there was enough room to get through. Our Delta ships had a wingspan of fifty metres, their sensors were pretty damned accurate and when I switched them back in I must have been on good terms with the ship's control and safety systems despite the fact we'd not been eye to eye earlier. Even so, I'll swear the distance between those two cranes was little more than fifty-one!

I thought of Joe and was all but tempted to call him up just to see the expression on his face. Most importantly, however, the manoeuvre had worked. At a more respectable altitude I brought the ship around again so we could see how enough sand had been dispersed by the blast of my engines to make the runway usable. Glancing over my shoulder, I saw the Russians slumped back with their eyes half closed. They were just starting to breathe again. Gary, still clutching the arm rests, stared straight ahead but, like the rest, appeared somewhat relieved at having survived my unorthodox sand clearing technique.

The sun was well past its zenith when we rolled up to Kurt Hoffman's ship. As was my habit when no turntable was on hand, I manoeuvred Delta

Seven around into take-off position before powering down.

'Kurt's ship has no cargo pallet,' observed Gary, his voice dry, his expression still strained. 'They had time to unload her before it happened so it must have been sudden. Really, very sudden.'

I cut in our sensors and we had a close-up look at everything in sight. There was no human activity. Nothing moved except for the occasional dust devil that scampered aimlessly, detached from the coat-tails of the retreating sandstorm.

'We should go out there now,' said one of the Russians. 'We may need much time.'

He was right, of course. We had no idea how long this might take and being at the equator, darkness would be on us quickly. The ship's sensors showed the outside temperature to be a deal lower than it ought to have been. Despite our location, despite the time of day, it was down past -50C because the sandstorm had blotted out the sun's heat.

All six of us suited up and left the ship. I saw no point in anyone staying on board unless it was myself and I had no intention of doing that. We gathered at the bottom of the ramp to look about but could see nothing we hadn't already observed from the air. Nearest to us stood the admin building with factory and accommodation facilities behind that. To the left lay the cargo storage building with close by the vehicle and aircraft maintenance units, whilst to the right, set back some way, a section of the huge biodome was visible. Something else struck me as peculiar whilst we stood there. In a pressure suit you hear things - the faint hum of your life support system, the sounds you make and the sounds of others when your radio and microphones are active. In spite of that, I was aware of the silence, of an utter stillness about the complex. Even the wind had died to leave the sand no longer shifting around. Like the valley of the crystals, the place seemed surreal – a projected image on some vast stage.

'We should get moving,' prompted Alexei. 'The sun will go down in less than four hours.'

So lost in thought was I, his voice startled me.

We set off across the sand with nobody speaking until we reached the main airlock of the reception and administration building. There, we stopped before the blank face of the outer doors, half expecting, maybe just hoping, to see something meaningful.

'They're fully sealed,' announced Gary, having stepped over to place fingers against the smooth, white surface.

'How many people were inside this base?' I asked him.

'Getting on for three hundred. And they were due for a big intake of people from other bases in twelve days' time.'

'What next?' asked one of the Russians.'

'I reckon we keep walking around the base,' I said. 'The worse we can do is end up back where we started.'

There were no objections but we agreed to stay together rather than splitting up. I suppose it gave us a false sense of security, which was better than no sense of security at all.

'How far is it to walk around this place?' asked one of the Russians.

'The completed section is roughly six kilometres,' answered Gary.

'A long walk,' said Alexei.

'We should head for the biodome first,' I said. 'We ought to take a look through the bioplast shell if that's possible.'

The biodome was, of course, transparent to visible light except for the circular stone base upon which these structures usually rested and from which they were organically grown, becoming larger, more ambitious as the years went by. So we trudged on through loose sand until we'd passed around the admin block. Soon we stood before the biodome, which rose up to curve away against a mauve tinted, ochre sky. We couldn't see inside to begin with because we were below the top of the basalt supporting wall. At that point the ground formed a natural depression and did not rise up to level out again until further around, at which point we reached the first auxiliary airlock. It came as no surprise to find that shut tight as well. Stepping to the side of the airlock housing where was fixed a service ladder, Gary announced, 'I'll get up onto the wall and take a look inside. The lower part appears to be clear of frost.'

'I'll be right behind you,' I said, giving him a helping push as he started up the ladder.

Pressure suit or no, he was up there pretty quick, scuffing sand from the ledge then pressing his helmet against the bioplast. As I hauled myself up his voice cut in, 'I can see in there. Oh, this - this is terrible!'

I reached the ledge with one of the Russians clambering up behind as Joe came over on my radio. 'Brett, we'll keep with you and let the others do their thing.'

Seconds later I was peering into the biodome myself, knowing that Joe and the others would be seeing pretty much the same picture as I talked them through. 'Everything is white in there. Everything frozen!' With one hand resting against the shell, I tripped in my helmet magnification. 'There are bodies further back! There are dozens - no, wait – lots more - all frozen! I can't see very far but -.' My voice trailed off. I was beginning to appreciate the full horror of what had happened to these people.

'Yes, everyone is dead,' added the Russian, sending back his own images. 'Birds, animals, plants - all dead. The biodome has lost its atmosphere.'

'We can't see beyond the trees,' I said. 'There must be more bodies over the other side.'

'Brett,' cut in Gary, 'we ought to go on. There's nothing anyone can do here.'

'Maybe not,' I answered, 'but we still have to find a way inside - you know that.'

Gary was outwardly calm but I could feel how the situation was gnawing away at him.

Continuing along the wall, we reached a point where the perimeter path within the dome curved out then widened to join one of the radials. Here were more bodies, some of them part hidden by frosted undergrowth. They lay where they had fallen - men, women and children, their flesh pallid, their mouths agape, rusted with blood where life had convulsed from them.

'They must have been in here when it happened,' said Gary. 'Out for a picnic or a stroll.'

'I do not think death was instantaneous,' said the Russian. 'I think it must have taken minutes.'

'You mean the air escaped gradually,' said Gary.

'Yes, that is what happened, I am sure. The air could not have escaped suddenly unless there was great damage to the dome, yet we saw none.'

I was inclined to agree. Rapid decompression would also have caused more damage to the human body than we were seeing. Jumping down from the wall, we caught up with the three Russians who had gone to take a look further along then all of us continued around the broad curve of the biodome.

Having skirted almost a half of the biodome perimeter, a distance of nearly two kilometres, we reached other intersecting domes and structures. Some we could see into, others not, though for a while we observed no more corpses. Two of the structures joined to a main group, the housing for Europa Six's power core and the back-up unit that should have continued to supply energy in the event of its failure. They would have been of prime interest but, being enclosed by blank walls and sealed doors that showed no sign of damage, they would only be accessible from within the complex.

We were passing between the shadows of the two big cranes, stark and motionless over to our right where they framed the afternoon sun against the empty sky, when we found ourselves entering a building site. Metal, concrete and plastic sections, stone blocks, pipes and containers lay about in a kind of loose order; most of them topped by a layer of sand. The ribs of unfinished buildings and part-grown bioplast shells to the south and west of the complex stood in silent counterpoint to the cranes.

Witnessing all of this brought home to me the great feats of engineering these projects represented. Use was made of local materials where possible, mainly volcanic rock. Equipment to generate the vast domes, the internal organs of cables and pipes - the nerves and blood vessels of the complexes - all once came across the great void from Earth. Getting people and materials over to construct the fabric of the colonies had been the greatest feat in human history. Now, they were manufactured on Mars by the colonies themselves and had been for almost thirty Earth years. Yet in spite of our confidence, in spite of our achievements on this planet since the previous century, something quite unknown had occurred to destroy this oasis of human life. And apparently with great ease.

Passing through this starkly surreal-looking assemblage, we eventually reached the metals processing facility that spread out behind the administration building. Still we could find no evidence of damage or any airlock that was not sealed against the outside. We looked into the complex wherever we were able but saw only a few more bodies.

'Nearly everyone must have headed for the biodome,' remarked Gary. 'Whatever happened, it seems as if they had time to do that.'

I estimated we were halfway around the site when, turning a next corner, we came upon the rail track. From the main storage building it passed across in front of us and continued on to a small crater that I checked as being a kilometre and a half distant. The track passed through the crater wall then into the basin that had been adapted for shuttles as well as for the much less frequent big rockets.

'I think that's the only way we can go,' said Gary, pointing to where the basalt-paved sections of a road lay part exposed beneath drifted sand. The road led along the ravine and under a low bridge that carried the track. Having passed beneath to emerge on the other side we scrambled back up and I peered along the rail track to where it joined the cargo building. 'Gary!' I called as he went ahead. 'We could climb up onto the track and follow it into there. Maybe we'll find access to the complex from inside.'

'It's worth a try,' he agreed, as did the others. Apart from anything else, the sun was getting lower and the shadows longer. Time was not on our side.

Clambering up the embankment we reached the metal walkway by the side of the rails. Moving toward the cargo building, we saw that a section of the track had been drawn inside and the door above it lowered to keep out the sand when the storm blew up.

'Look,' I said, not wanting to give up this avenue of approach, 'there's a small door by the side of the main one. They wouldn't seal that, would they - not in an unpressurised area?'

'Can't think of any reason why they should,' replied Gary.

'Then that could be our way in,' enthused Alexei in a manner not entirely appropriate to the circumstances. It served to remind me that the

Russians' purpose here might not be wholly humanitarian.

We'd traversed half the walkway when something caught my attention and caught it for one simple reason - it appeared part concealed, but not by the sand. It was a solid looking basalt structure, built into the side of the ravine further along, surrounded by broken blocks and topped with desert rubble. Beyond, screening it from the runway, lay the newly completed ore smelting plant. I suspected concealment of the structure to have been deliberate. Certainly, it would not have been visible from the air other than as a heap of rubble and it seemed at odds with the general arrangement of buildings at other bases.

'What's that, Gary?' I asked, pointing to the structure whilst switching in my helmet magnification. Though it was in deep shadow, I could make out what appeared to be a sealed entrance. It also proved of interest to the Russians, with one of them quick to record it.

'I really don't know,' answered Gary, 'I've not been around this part of the complex before.'

'Could it be a store for explosives or chemicals,' asked one of the Russians.

'You don't need to put up a special building for that,' I responded. 'Not on this planet.'

'Well,' said Gary, 'your guess is as good as mine but it looks to me no more than a site for discarded building materials. Does it matter right now?'

I let the subject go but I didn't believe that and I wasn't convinced he did either. You don't abandon building materials on Mars - you reuse as much as you can. You reuse almost everything for something, then you use it again for something else.

We found upon reaching the small service entrance that it opened easily. As the door swung inward, I peered through but could see nothing for the whole of the vast interior was in darkness. Normally, it would have been lit around the clock. 'We're going to need our suit lights,' I said.

'There could be damage or an open airlock inside here,' said Alexei. 'That would explain why we saw no sign of anything from outside.'

'And if there isn't,' added Gary, 'then we may as well take a short cut through it and save ourselves a bit of time. We should be able to access the service building then get out to the front again.'

'What about emergency access through mechanically operated doors?' asked Alexei.

'Not in our bases anymore,' replied Gary. 'They're only electrically operated.'

'And in ours too,' I added. 'We did away with the older type years ago.'

In fact I was wrong - we hadn't, but that would be of no significance until sometime later. But a damaged service airlock would not allow the atmosphere to escape before the people at Europa Six were able to do anything about it, never mind the built-in safety systems. Once inside, our suit lamps illuminated the end of the rail track plus sections of two of the big elevator platforms then several metres of the metal catwalk that continued into blackness beyond. To the eerie, clanging of our own footsteps we walked on, the beams of our lamps stabbing darkness to pick out the occasional airlock on this as well as the lower level. At the first

160

intersection, we could have gone directly to any of the airlocks but decided a visual inspection from the catwalk would be enough. They were all closed and appeared intact.

We were aware of how quickly time was passing. We were aware, too, that if we couldn't get out the other end we would have to come all the way back again then still trudge the remainder of the distance around the complex. After several more minutes in that grimly unwelcoming place, we reached the end of the catwalk. There was no door to be seen, at least not on that level. Only when we made our way down the ramp to the lower floor did we find a way through to the aircraft service building that was lit by natural daylight. It took little time to discover we were not going to access the sealed part of the base through there, either. Apart from test and maintenance equipment, the only other thing of significance in there was one of Europa Six's new ground vehicles.

We emerged from the service building to find the sun further down toward the horizon, the landscape picked out in a vivid light that made the deep shadows even deeper. Beyond the strip where Delta Seven and Early Bird stood waiting the ramparts of Nicholson crater arose sun-flamed against the sky. We started back in the direction of the aircraft then as one we stopped to gaze back at the complex.

'Dammit! There must be a way inside!' declared Gary. 'There's no visible damage - there's no sign of entry! What the hell are we supposed to do?'

'If it was one of our bases,' I offered, 'I know what I'd do.'

'Okay, tell me! What d'you have in mind?'

'Your answer lies over there,' I said, pointing at the blue tractor I'd noticed when we first arrived. It was parked a short way beyond Kurt Hoffman's ship but I hadn't given it any thought until then.

'What the hell are you saying?' asked Gary.

'I'm saying we break in through the main airlock. The place is dead - what more harm can it do?'

Gary switched off his communications with us then stepped away to hold conversation with his own people. Returning, he announced that, much to his surprise as well as to ours, the General Administrator had agreed. He was more than a little irritated to see Alexei already raising sand as he hurried off toward the tractor. Gary must have assumed, as did I, that the Russians had tapped into his conversation from their station then relayed it straight back to at least one of the four with us. Unethical as it doubtless was, we had no time to stand around arguing.

The whine of tractor engine drifted by. She was heading our way as we walked back to the main airlock. Alexei called, 'I will turn the tractor around so I can use the coupling bar as a battering ram!'

A few metres from the big doors a cloud of sand arose as Alexei swung the vehicle about on its tracks. It looked as if he'd been driving one of the things all his life. Once it stood poised with the coupling bar lined up on the airlock, Gary raised an arm then called, 'If you're going to do it, let's go!'

I had no doubt this was a decision Gary Holloway hated to make. No one in their right mind would try to damage, let alone smash airlock doors. I don't recall anyone on the planet ever had. The tractor lurched backward, spewing rubble, with Alexei peering out the side. I for one held my breath as the coupling bar struck the left hand door with a dull clang. Alexei was almost thrown out of his seat but quickly brought the tractor forward again. The door had buckled under the impact so when the dust settled, a gap of some thirty centimetres was visible close to the bottom. Gary raised an arm once more, ready to order the next move when a voice cut in on our short-range personal frequencies, 'Hey! What the fuck!'

We stood staring at each other, trying to figure who had called out, then at Alexei since it seemed it could only have been him. Alexei's helmet protruded from the cab. He was puzzled as the rest of us.

'Who is this and where are you?' I radioed.

'It's me, Kurt!' came the reply. 'Kurt Hoffman! I'm trapped inside the airlock!'

'There's someone alive in there!' exclaimed Gary.

'Kurt, this is Brett Anderson. Are you all right? We have to break in.'

'Yes I'm all right but there's no power. How long will it take?'

'Not long,' I answered, glancing up at the tractor. 'Alexei, back up real careful so you can push the coupling bar through the gap.'

Alexei reversed cautiously until the bar ground against the edges.

'That's fine!' I called. 'Now rotate the bar a quarter turn to your left.' I saw that by doing this, the coupling bar would form a hook behind the right hand door. 'Okay, Kurt, we're ready! Better you keep clear of the door!'

'Go ahead!' came the answer so I waved Alexei forward.

We backed off as the tractor engine whined. At first, nothing happened then the door gave. A crack, a screech of tortured metal and the tractor lurched forward in a hail of grit. The door tore from its mountings then fell forward with a thud we felt through our boots, blasting out clouds of dust to obscure just about everything, including the tractor. As the dust drifted away, there stood Kurt Hoffmann framed in the airlock where the right hand door had been, a small case clutched in his left hand. I had the impression, the way he stood peering at us through his visor, that he was trying to convince himself we were real.

'Kurt, what happened?' asked Gary, trudging forward. 'Is anyone else alive?'

'I don't know what happened!' responded Kurt, stepping out to meet him. 'They were all running for safety because the pressure was going down – some of them panicking. There was an explosion, maybe - I don't know. As soon as I got into the airlock, everything shut off. I couldn't get out so I turned down my life support and fell asleep.'

'Kurt - what else did you see?' I asked.

'I can't say for sure, no I can't. There was smoke heading toward me, twisting and turning - not like anything I ever saw before, then there was a hell of a bang and it was rushing back down the corridor. I guess that's one direction the air was escaping.'

'Alexei,' I called, 'let's get that other door off then back her inside to break through the inside doors. We go in there now or not at all!'

Kurt tried to explain in more detail what he'd experienced but left off as Alexei went about a repeat performance on the left hand inner door. I'd all but forgotten I was being monitored by my own people then, as the second door crashed down, Joe's voice cut in. 'Brett, if you go inside there, you could be taking one hell of a risk. You ought to hold back until more people come over. Send a couple of spiders in first. See if they can ascertain what happened.'

'It's all right, Joe - I don't think we'll be in any danger.'

'You can't be sure of that, son.'

'Joe, we'll be okay, believe me.' I was quite convinced of that without really knowing why. But I *was* convinced. Then another voice - a voice I hardly expected just then but one I was mighty glad to hear. 'Brett, don't take any chances – please. Wait until help arrives.'

'Karin, don't worry – we don't have time to wait for anyone else - it's going to be dark here soon.'

It was the turn of the inner doors now. Using the fallen outer doors as a kind of shallow ramp, Alexei backed the tractor right into the airlock then slammed it straight into the doors. The resulting crash told us he had succeeded. As the tractor emerged we could see the inner doors, not as robust as the outer, were demolished. The fact that there was no rush of air from the opening served to confirm what we already knew. When we entered the concourse, there was no need for our suit lamps because as well as the still glowing emergency lights there was adequate daylight. The corridors running off it, however, passed under the upper floors so would have no natural illumination at all.

'D'you want to come with us, Kurt?' I asked, thinking maybe he'd had enough and might prefer to get back to his ship.

'Sure I'm coming with you,' he answered. 'I must try to find Paolo - he was my good friend. Maybe he's still alive somewhere.' He gestured towards the main corridor. 'Look, over there - that is where I saw most of that the smoke and – and heard whatever sounds I heard.'

We started over to that first corridor with our suit lamps on full, our footsteps echoing about the deserted concourse like we were in some kind of natural cavern. We would record sound and images from within the base then relay everything back as soon as we were out of there. At the mouth of the passage we stopped to angle our lights down its length because the emergency lighting had gone. Although the corridor was fairly long, our lamps should have been able to illuminate the far end on narrow beam – but they didn't. We could see no detail whatsoever so we set off walking. Well before reaching the halfway point we discovered why our lights had picked nothing out. The walls and ceiling were streaked with soot that became heavier as we went on.

'There must have been one hell of a fire,' said Gary. 'Seems as if it came from the recreation area right at the end.'

Two-thirds the way down, the walls and ceiling were entirely black. We spoke in whispers, our lights stabbing fitfully about like we were a bunch of scouts lost within the dark lair of some malignant beast. I kept telling myself there was nothing here that could harm us but we were all pretty jumpy.

'The fire can't have lasted long.' I remarked. 'There wouldn't have been enough air to support it.'

What happened next did nothing to help the situation. From behind came a thud like someone had landed on their feet from a height. We spun about to see black dust billowing straight at us. We all stopped breathing as our lamps probed into it. As it drifted by, Gary, who was then behind the rest of us called out, 'A ceiling panel just came down! A fucking panel! Must have been loosened by the heat.'

Ahead, in what Gary informed us was the recreation centre, where there had been warmth, light and life, the answer to what we sought was to confront us in the most graphic and shocking way. There was light at the far side - a ghastly light that showed how the whole place had been reduced to a blackened shambles. But as we stood there it was more than the wreckage that appalled us, more even than the twisted, soot-covered bodies lying frozen and part exposed amidst it, something that in those initial moments we found difficult to comprehend. 'The wall!' gasped Alexei. 'What has happened to the wall?'

167

Most of the wall that formed the far end of the recreation area and much of the floor above it, had gone. It seemed, looking at the amount of rubble, that the upper floor section must have come down with it to lay the entire building open.

'This whole section is hidden by the power core enclosure,' said Gary, 'that's why we couldn't see any damage from outside. This part wasn't finished, either. It shouldn't have been in use yet but they were under a lot of pressure from the Consortium.'

'Well now we know how the atmosphere escaped so quickly,' I said. 'It must have blasted out of here before anyone knew what was happening. Their self-repair systems could never cope with this.'

But there was something else. Close to where the wall had been was an irregularly shaped hole some three to four metres across into which a part of the floor had vanished. Making my way through wreckage and fallen panels, I peered down into it. 'There's a shaft here,' I called, pointing my light into the depths. It appeared as if the wall had collapsed where the pit had weakened its foundations. There was no point in asking Gary or anyone else what the pit was doing there. I knew just as the rest of them must have known, it couldn't have been there before the collapse. People in the recreation area and close by would have had no chance of escape even if others managed to survive elsewhere.

'Only part of the complex was pressurised,' said Gary. 'That would have made the loss of atmosphere all the more rapid.'

The Russians also joined us around the shaft to shine their beams into it. Despite the rubble we could see that it narrowed down somewhat, grading from coarse reddish-brown to smoother, black rock. My rangefinder said the depth where it curved out of sight was under twelve metres.

'It is a tunnel down to hell,' muttered one of the Russians.

Gary moved off, skirting the edge of the shaft. We followed, avoiding furniture and bodies - in particular the bodies, which in some cases were not immediately obvious. 'That's what cut the power!' he exclaimed, indicating the far corner. 'See - that column gave way and smashed right through the main inlet from the power core. It must have caused a fire that burned until the air ran out.'

'That will be the smoke I saw,' put in Kurt.

'What about the back-up generators?' I asked.

'They feed through the same distribution system,' he answered. 'There was never any reason why they shouldn't. In most of our bases they do.'

'Whatever caused this,' I said, gesturing to the pit, 'must have been evident before the structure collapsed. People in here must have seen the floor give way and never understood what was going on.'

'That must be so,' agreed Kurt. 'Then after that happened the alarms went off and everyone who could rushed for the biodome.'

'They should have been safe in there until help arrived,' said Gary 'even if the rest of the complex died. We have to discover what went wrong.'

We groped our way back through the wreckage, back into darkness, our boots raising black dust as the beams of our lamps darted here and there. One of the Russians, spotting something close to the exit, called, 'Hey - what is that?' then stepped over for a closer look.

At first, I could make out only a fallen panel - but it wasn't the panel that had caught his attention; it was that which lay part hidden beneath. Then we all saw it. Something glittered, reflecting our light as a patch of wetness in a place where there should be no wetness. I stepped over, took one end of the two-metre panel and with the help of the Russian, heaved it up, spilling off a layer of rubble that raised swirls of dust.

Like pressure-suited mannequins, we stood in that beleaguered oasis of light, staring in grim fascination at what we had discovered. The thing - the body, I can only describe as looking like some disgusting great polyp marooned on a desolate black beach. I recalled a large jellyfish I once saw washed up by the sea when I was a kid at school and I can't say the sight of it aroused too much enthusiasm in me even then. The creature appeared to be ruptured because a viscous fluid of some kind was oozing from it into the dirt. What the stuff might consist of we had no idea and none of us thought it appropriate right then to start messing with a scanalyser. It couldn't be water or those remains would have ended up a slab of ice.

As the dust settled, as we peered closer I knew what lay in front of us even before Gary exclaimed, 'Holy shit! It's one of them isn't it?'

'You mean it's a fucking Martian?' came Kurt's voice. 'So it could be those bastards were responsible for this! Maybe they came out of that pit!'

'There are things inside it!' exclaimed Gary, stepping abruptly back. 'Christ, see that! Some of them are moving!'

One of the Russians darted away then returned with a twisted metal bar raised in one hand. 'Alive!' he exclaimed. 'If it's alive I'll beat its damned brains out!'

'You'll have to find them first,' I countered, staying his hand. 'Wait! Don't touch it!'

Within the form, vague shapes stirred, some of them translucent, expanding, contracting like smaller hydroids; others like pale, coiled worms turning slowly in oil, sometimes visible, glowing a dull iridescent blue, sometimes not.

'I reckon they're internal organs,' I said. 'They're shifting because we've disturbed it.'

'Bastard must have got killed when the ceiling fell in,' muttered Kurt.

'We can't be sure it's dead,' put in Gary. 'What if it isn't dead? What if it's still alive?'

'It's got to be dead,' I answered. 'If it wasn't it wouldn't still be laying around. Let's find something to put it in and get it out of here.'

'You want to take it back?' exclaimed Gary. 'It might be carrying some kind of bug! I don't want to end up in quarantine. We should wait until we can contact our people. We need advice on this before we do anything else. This is European property so the thing has to remain under our jurisdiction.'

'That's stupid,' insisted one of the Russians. 'It is in all our interests to take it away for examination whoever -.'

'Look,' I cut in, 'we don't have time to argue! We take what's left of this thing now or not at all. If

171

it worries anyone, it can go in my ship. We'll let those in charge debate its future once we're out of here.'

'I'll go along with that,' said Kurt. 'We should do it quickly in case its pals come back to collect it. As for who's ship it goes in – I don't give a damn.'

'Then whatever happens is your responsibility,' responded Gary. His eyes glared with anger behind his visor.

We needed something to put the body in since neither I nor any of the others felt inclined to lay a hand directly on it. Fortunately, if that's the way you want to look at it, the kitchens were nearby so we got ourselves one of those long, white food storage containers everyone uses. Getting the thing inside threatened to use up more precious time but in the end, Alexei and I manoeuvred the ceiling panel underneath and eased it into the box like so much garbage together with some of the rubble. Two of us carried it back along the blackened corridor. No one spoke.

When we arrived back at the concourse, late afternoon sun smeared patterns of garish orange across walls that once flowed with mobile art. The food container we left on the floor close to the wrecked airlock.

There was one place we now had to visit. The biodome.

As we trudged on in silence I asked myself why the biodome had failed to do what it had been designed to do - serve as a safe haven of retreat for all those people? Everyone knew that in the event of a serious loss of pressure, the biodome airlocks would close automatically as part of a fail-safe

172

system. Unlike most other airlocks, however, they could still be opened manually to let people through, but only the inner or the outer doors at any one time – for obvious reasons.

Before we reached our destination we came upon more bodies. Six adults and two children lay sprawled about in semi- darkness, pallid and frozen, their open mouths seeming to gasp in death as they had during those final, agonised seconds of life.

'These people never even made the biodome,' I said as we hesitated. 'The power failure must have slowed them right down.'

'Or maybe they were asleep in their quarters,' said Gary. 'There could be a lot more of them down there. There should have been more safeguards whilst work was going on. There were too many people here. Too many too soon. Everything was push, push, push.'

'Paolo,' I heard Kurt mutter, 'where are you my friend?'

In all the newer bases there were few internal airtight doors and in public areas no more than screens, in part because it helped the free circulation of air throughout the complexes. I reflected on the fact that had such features been retained at key points, they might have closed off the damaged area and given more people time to find refuge. So assured were we folk from Earth, such was our confidence in ourselves and so good was the safety record throughout the colonies, the possibility of such a disaster had never been seriously considered. Or if they had, it would have been apparent how much extra safety measures might have added to construction costs.

When we reached the concourse before the biodome main and subsidiary airlocks there was enough natural light to see what had taken place. Here lay upwards of twenty dead, scaled in frost, as were the walls and ceiling from the warm, humid air that had rushed from the biodome.

'Look at the main airlock!' cried Gary.

I figured fifty or more people had been struggling to get through when death seized them. Some had been crushed, others almost dismembered as the big doors tried unsuccessfully to seal off the biodome. Most were squeezed inside the space between the inner and outer doors, frozen in grotesque attitudes like broken and cast-off dolls. Beneath them, the floor was caked with frozen blood. The situation at the smaller airlocks was much the same.

Most of us have an episode in our lives we'd afterwards rather wipe from our minds. In my case, and I guess for the others, it was when we pushed between the doors, when we had to clamber over those heaped corpses in order to get inside the biodome. Things cracked under my boots but I had no desire to look down and see exactly what I'd trodden on. We need not have gone in there once we'd discovered what had happened. We could have sent in spiders and waited somewhere else to watch the images. At the time, though, we felt we had to do it. We felt we needed to gather as full a picture as possible. Some people choose to remove such memories altogether but I don't go along with that. Good or bad it's a part of your life whether you want it or not and I'll always remember the sight as we gathered inside. Always. Only hours before, the biodome had basked in warmth and light. The air had been alive with sound, with colour, with greenery and perfumed flowers. People had rested, talked, listened to the birds, laughed at the antics of those small animals programmed to keep the place neat and tidy. Kids had chased each other about the fountains as I'd so often seen them do at my home base. The flame of humanity had burned bright. Within Europa Six now, the dream of Mars had been subverted by a nightmare.

The words, "frozen wonderland," passed through my mind. I don't know why when I was standing before a frozen hell. Beneath the great bioplast shell lay a monochrome stillness grading from white to shadow. A stillness all the more profound because it never should have been. A stillness so overwhelming that for a time none of us spoke or moved.

Beyond stark coral-like formations that had been living trees, the far side of the dome was blemished by a diffused, pallid sun low down enough in a sky grading from apricot to mauve to be part hidden by iced foliage. Above me hung the ice-sugared blossoms of a once green tree. I reached up to touch one of them. It snapped, falling slowly to the path at my feet where it shattered like eggshell porcelain.

Frost encrusted bodies lay all about, fingers clutching the memory of agony in their grasp, jaws wide in soundless protest. Close by lay the corpse of a woman, knees drawn up, hands frozen over her face as though wishing to hide the scene from sightless eyes. Further away was a child preserved as though asleep in a fine wrap of crystalline gossamer, and huddled beyond, two who may have been the parents, clutching one another as they had in those final moments. On pathways, amongst skeletal bushes they lay - writhing forms – carved alabaster figures of a medieval frieze conceived to illustrate the plight of the damned. The biodome had become a sepulchre. And just as, centuries ago on Earth, they might have embellished a tomb with ornate artistry, here the hand of nature had created a scene of macabre beauty.

We talked quietly about whether or not we should try to count the dead or at least carry out some kind of reconnaissance. Kurt had wanted to locate Paolo Romano but realised the difficulty we would have in identifying anyone even if we'd had enough time. In the end, we agreed there was no point in attempting anything of the kind because our small number and the lateness of the day.

'The Europeans,' said Alexei, 'they will have to organise teams of people to -.'

He didn't finish because what happened next almost scared us out of our wits. A shower of ice crystals burst from the bushes to our right and something headed straight at us. No one had time to move as it stopped right in front of us, forelegs waving in the air, antennae twitching inquisitively.

'Oh, shit!' gasped Gary. 'It's one of the maintenance bots. It's asking for instructions.'

'Then you'd better tell it to take things easy for a while,' I responded. 'Let's get moving.'

Minutes later we were out of the biodome, passing through the wrecked airlock with myself and one of the Russians carrying the storage box between us. The half-disk of the sun glared from the western horizon like a reptile eye to cast a spectral glow over everything. By the time the container was stowed, the sky was grading into purple, with a speckle of stars already showing to the east. Between the big crater and Europa Six hung a thin white mist that descended shroud-like over the desert landscape. I wondered what else might lie in wait beyond this fragile world of ours.

***

The Russians had boarded Early Bird to return with Kurt Hoffman - their station was closer to his than mine. I had my passenger tucked away in Delta Seven's deep-freeze bay as our prize, as a gleam of optimism amid growing turmoil. It would be analysed in the hope that we'd have some idea of what we were up against. At least that's the way I saw things as I watched Early Bird lift off into the night. Prior to boarding Delta Seven I transmitted back to base everything I had recorded then, once in the control pod I spent some minutes in conversation with Joe via our secure link. He informed me the Europeans were on his back demanding I fly the thing to them as Kurt had already relayed the essentials. I could see their point all right and I imagined they would be giving Kurt and Gary a hard time for not hanging onto it. 'Maybe it would be better,' said Joe, 'if we get it up to the space station where its pals can't drop by to grab it back.'

As I lifted off to head back home I expected our planet would soon be bombarded with transmissions from Earth demanding to know what Joe and the rest of us couldn't tell them. Next would come flooding in all the advice we didn't need from those on the home planet who had never been into space, let alone out to Mars. I was discussing with Joe how we might deal with people here on our own planet who were already clamouring when our conversation was interrupted. As Joe's image faded, a voice from the message panel declared, 'Captain Anderson, you have a Class One priority transmission from Novamerica Five.'

I guessed what was coming next but that didn't help any when Virgil Hammond's face appeared. Nail-head eyes stared at me. Maybe he remembered me from Earth – maybe he didn't, but this was the first time we had spoken since his arrival on Mars.

'Captain Anderson,' he announced in a manner of over-contrived calm,' I have naturally been party to exchanges between you and Commander Van Allen regarding this disaster.'

'I bet you have,' I remarked. He'd once again muscled in on our supposedly secure link and we both knew such actions were illegal.

'We must do our utmost to get to the bottom of this dreadful event,' he went on. 'You will fly the corpse straight here for preliminary examination. We have all the facilities at our disposal.'

I hesitated before replying, though it was obvious he expected my instant acquiescence. 'I will require confirmation from Commander Van Allen and I'll comply with whatever instructions he -.'

'I am not concerned with your requirements, Captain Anderson. Whatever has brought about this appalling event is a threat to all operations on this planet - not just to that of the Europeans. Matters affecting UAS security and interests of the entire

Consortium are *my* responsibility as your base commander is well aware and I should not be obliged to remind you of that. You will alter course immediately then proceed westward. You will maintain radio silence until your arrival at Novamerica Five. After that, Captain, I am sure you will wish to resume your schedule. The Europeans may do as they see fit.'

Hammond glanced down for a moment then stared at me even harder. 'You seem prone to involvement in matters outside your duties, Captain Anderson. It is a pity you and certain others choose to neglect the gift of prudence that is handed down to us all. Let us hope you are not precipitated into any more controversial situations. Take my advice and be wary, Captain Anderson. Very wary indeed.'

'Yes, General, I hear what you say.'

I assumed by "certain others," that he was referring to Joe Van Allen. Only after Hammond's image faded did I realise I had used his military title. Could be he hadn't noticed or perhaps he just chose to ignore it. Orders from him or no, I tried to raise Joe again but found I couldn't get through. It didn't take much guesswork to figure out why. Had the disaster occurred at a UAS base, Hammond would doubtless have sent one of our own shuttles over to avoid delay. But now, one of his wingships, mine, had violated European air space at a time when, because of the affair of the crystals, relations were for the first time ever openly tense. My taking the corpse back to Hammond without the Europeans being consulted wasn't about to improve matters and I expected the governments on Earth would take all of this just as seriously once they had the facts.

The fathomless desert drifted below in near blackness whilst the stars, though in the familiar patterns you see from Earth, shone here like coloured jewels. They, together with the steady sound of my engines, offered a degree of consolation as I thought hard over what I and others had witnessed: the frozen horror of Europa Six, my descent into the labyrinth, the crystals, the bizarre death of Zena Michaelis and the unwelcome presence of Virgil Hammond. I thought about the strange life forms that, having remained hidden for so long, had at last revealed themselves with such disastrous results. But why had they killed all those people and not me? All of these events must be connected - of that I was certain. I thought, too, about Karin, about those eyes that sparkled so brightly when she laughed. She travelled about the planet as part of her work. She could well have been at Europa Six when it happened. I thought hard upon what I had witnessed there. I gazed again at the stars. I gazed for a long time and I began to ask myself what the hell are we? What is this all about - we, the colonies, the damned consortium, Earth, Mars, any of it? We were an insignificant blip in a timeless infinity that cared nothing for any of us; not for our dreams, not for our living nightmares, not for anything. Time, yes, given enough time we wouldn't even be a memory because there would be no one around to remember. Then I got to thinking, fine, but this is here and now. Here and now - and I'm a part of it so, maybe it mattered a lot.

You may recall that Novamerica Five was close to the big Huygens crater. Huygens covers an area from ten to eighteen degrees south of the equator and is roughly eight thousand, four hundred kilometres west of Nicholson. That meant I had a journey lasting through some twelve hours of darkness before reaching Hammond's base. Okay, he'd blocked my communications with Novamerica One but I saw no reason why he should object to my holding conversation with Karin. I tried to get through to Europa Four on several of the bands allocated to personal usage but these were blocked also. Nor was I able to contact Leo. Hammond's interference with communications to that extent was a blatant breach of international law. I had a feeling it would be a none too happy occasion for one of us when mine and Virgil Hammond's paths finally crossed – as one day they surely would.

With the ship flying herself I lapsed briefly into sleep. I was seldom enthusiastic about programmed dreams and usually got on quite well with my own though not for the first time of late I had woken up imagining someone had called my name. Odd – an echo of the voice still lingered as I peered ahead into darkness. It was as though something out there, something in that frigid, desolate night was trying to speak to me – if only I would, or could listen.

***

Night still ruled when a wingship landed at Europa Six, though the mist had fragmented and was drifting as an army of spectres across a deserted plain of battle. To the whine of his engines the pilot taxied along the strip with the ramparts of Nicholson crater looming darkly at his right. To his

181

left the twin cranes arose vague against the stars and closer, the ghostly buildings of the complex. The aircraft turned about to face along the runway and powered down. From it emerged it a small arachnoid that glinted starlight. It hesitated. It tasted the night air with quivering antennae. It flexed spider-legs then scurried across the sand to halt before the shattered airlock, switching crystal eyes about with chameleon oddity. The pilot, as well as others much further away, saw what it saw, heard what it heard and knew what it knew. Images shifted before the pilot. From the console emerged its voice. 'Nothing to get excited about so far, Wernher. Shall I go on?'

'Yes, Smoochy, proceed inside as far as the entrance to the canteen area.'

A uniformed woman's image materialised by the pilot's controls. 'The picture we have is fine Wernher. Let her go in as far as you think.'

'Okay, Smoochy - you heard that. Go straight along to the pit so we can take a good look.'

'Yes, Wernher, dear, I heard. I'm heading there right now. All the other bots like me are asleep – are we going to wake them up?'

'No, Smoochy, not in the cold, not until they have their full energy input like you.'

The image shifted, there was the deserted main concourse illuminated by the spider, stabilised, synthesised to appear in bright detail. They saw next the corridor with blackened walls and ceiling. The fallen panel. Now the grim chaos of the blackened recreation area.

'You have the images, Wernher? Good Images, yes?'

'Good images from you Smoochy but not a good sight for us. You'd better go around the edge then take a look down that shaft. Be careful.'

'I'll be careful, Wernher - I know how much you treasure little Smoochy.'

Fallen rubble shivered across the screen. The part-charred, pop-eyed death mask of a face. The gaping mouth of the pit with sand spilling through the void left by the missing wall.

'Okay, Wernher, I'm spinning my thread. I'm going down. It's steep and rough near the top but you can see it gets smoother then starts to level out once I'm over the rubble. Yes, it levels out and goes a long way. I hope you know what you're about, Wernher, dear, you mustn't risk Smoochy just for the sake of it.'

An endoscope that probed living intestines is what Wernher compared the passage with as he stared at the screen. The passage stopped at a crevasse. Crystal eyes peered over. 'Can you see the galleries down there, Wernher? There are three. Do you want me to risk my little neck and go inside one of them?'

'You don't have a neck to risk, Smoochy, but better stop right there so we can decide which way we ought to go.'

Light reflected from fused glass walls that shone as blood-laced ice. 'Smoochy doesn't like it down here, Wernher - nothing to get hold of. Like being in a bubble under the water. You'd better think about who gets the bill if something falls in on me. I don't come cheap like those standard models.'

'Please don't exaggerate, Smoochy, there are thousands of you. Take a look inside those galleries - the nearest one first.'

'Yes, Wernher, I'm swinging myself across right now so you can -. Oh, I say!'

'Smoochy, what is it?'

'For a moment I sensed... It's nothing. Nothing at all. I'll carry on as soon as you're ready.'

'All right, go on slowly and - Smoochy, what's that clicking?'

'Clicking, Wernher, dear? Oh, no - there's no clicking. No clicking at all down here.'

'You're transmitting it back, Smoochy. Better stop!'

'Anything you like, Wernher, though I like it down here now I have company.'

'Company? Smoochy, what the hell are you talking about?'

'Friends, Wernher, dear. You never said I'd meet friends did you? Was it to be a surprise?'

'Smoochy switch your vision around. Show me!'

'I can't see them yet. They're waiting further along the gallery and, oh, I have a new set of parameters. That is nice. I have to pull in the thread now, Wernher. It might get in the way.'

'Smoochy - come out of there now! That's an order!'

'Orders, orders and more orders. Orders from you, orders from them. You'll overload my little mind if it doesn't stop. I need a break from orders. Need a break - need a break - need a break!'

The image from the spider dissolved into a disordered kaleidoscope of lights.

'Wernher!' The woman's image reappeared. 'Wernher, forget that spider. Drop three more to keep an eye around the biodome exterior then lift off out of there now!'

***

Once down at our prime base, Hammond got his dead creature and I managed something to eat as well as a few hours break. I didn't get to see the great man face-to-face or otherwise but maybe that was just as well since I was of a mind to let him know how I felt over his cutting my communications, Chief Executive or no. His staff were not particularly welcoming and I had the impression that the sooner I was out of there the better they'd like it. As if to prove the point I was woken up sooner than expected to be informed by the image of some guy I never saw before that a cargo was loading and I should be ready to lift off in one hour.

It would be another long flight - longer by over four hours than the last one; right around the opposite side of the planet. I'd carry on westward, staying this time in daylight as I headed home to Novamerica One.

Airborne in the morning sun and gaining altitude over the southern ramparts of Huygens, I checked out my communications and found everything back to normal. People had been clamouring to get through to me but Joe van Allen had kept them at bay and came on first. It turned out Hammond had told him virtually nothing and had persuaded Konstantin Pazukhin and Adelle Saint-Leger to keep the lid on things as well until he saw fit. His attitude was also rattling other parties on the planet since beyond the disaster at Europa Six they were told nothing.

It would be an understatement to say that Joe was unhappy about the situation. Even so, he suggested I call Europa Four and speak to Karin before continuing dialogue with him as she also had been trying to contact me. Naturally, she wanted to hear what had happened and wanted to know why the silence. All I could do was assure her I was all right, that I would be back to her as soon as I'd sorted things out with Joe. Minutes later, I was conversing with Joe again, filling him in on those details and impressions the images from Europa Six didn't show. He had no desire for me to spend too long over it, however.

'Brett, I'd rather we were sitting together in private before we discuss this further. The whole thing is terrible – just terrible. I half expected there would be widespread panic but so far there's been little sign of it. The big boys and girls are planning something and all base commanders, including yours truly, have been told by the Chief Executive Almighty to keep themselves available for communication around the clock.'

'Any idea what he's up to?' I asked.

'Not yet, son, but I'm sure we'll find out sooner or later. If I were you, meanwhile, I'd accept calls only via this base or you won't get a moment's peace.'

'I'll go with that, Joe.'

'You-know-who is waiting to pounce as soon as you land, if he hasn't blown a goddamned blood vessel in the meantime.'

'You mean Roy Kendrick is still down there? I thought SolaNews would have found some way of getting him over to Europa Six by now.'

'No they haven't but it isn't for lack of trying. The European General Administrator won't let Roy or anyone else near the place until they've investigated it for themselves even though a vital part of the evidence is now with Virgil Hammond. You're the big star on Roy's horizon now, Brett, but to be fair, we ought to give him something even if he has to hang around here until you come in.'

'Like a kick up the ass?' I offered. They could have used an investigative bot instead of Roy Kendrick, like they usually do on Earth. I'd rather talk to a machine than being pestered by him. Maybe I'd let Roy into my life later. Maybe I wouldn't. For now, as I drifted over the cratered wastes of the southern uplands, I was going to talk to Karin. A while later I'd check if Leo was awake and somewhere out there. If he wasn't flying or sleeping the chances are he'd be practising his golf. After that, I'd get myself some coffee and relax to a little music.

CHAPTER 5
COUNCIL OF DECEPTION

On my return I entered the base by a service airlock to avoid Roy, having already blocked him and most everyone else from accessing my earlobe communicator. Joe had forewarned me he was hovering about the main concourse. Roy was difficult to avoid and pretty agile. I guess he had to be in order to creep around corners unnoticed and snoop on others without being set upon and beaten to the ground by people like me who didn't want to be assailed with questions as soon as they walked in the front door. Roy wasn't above underhand methods, either, including some of dubious legality. Maybe that's why they kept him on board rather than using a bot in spite of the fact he took up more space and they had to feed him.

Meantime, Joe had been in constant dialogue with other bases planet-wide as well as the space station. When I reached his office I found things were not going too well for him in a number of ways.

'Security, security, security!' he said, turning from his view of the runway beyond the bioplast shell. 'That's all they're talking about! Everyone is asking everyone else what they're doing but nobody seems to have any ideas other than to put up surveillance equipment in the goddamned airlocks – equipment turned out by our workshops when they ought to be doing other things!' He made straight for the coffee dispenser. 'I don't know, son, how can you fight life forms you can't see unless you have more detectors around the place than there are people. And what can anyone do about something that comes up out of the blasted ground - I ask you?'

'Joe, whatever we're dealing with is intelligent – highly intelligent in my opinion. The death of Zena Michaelis, the attack on Europa Six and what happened to me - there has to be a reason.'

He drew out two coffees then we sat facing one another. 'A reason you say? Interesting, but I don't think that's going to help the three hundred folk who're lying dead in that base. If Europa Six had been completed the death toll could have been several times higher though I guess by then they'd have had all their safety systems in place and would have avoided the worst. You saw what had happened up close, Brett. What reason can there be for all those deaths?'

'Beats me, Joe, except I'm sure of one thing; if whatever did it wanted to wipe the rest of us out, they could have done so long before now – and I mean the entire human population on Mars.'

Joe stared down at his drink. 'Goddamned real coffee. It's the one thing I miss from Earth.'

'I think what comes out of our labs is pretty good,' I said.

'Yes, I guess you're right. Maybe I just feel like bitching a little.' He shrugged and pushed the coffee away. 'You know what some damned-fool people on Earth are saying? They're saying Mars has become too dangerous for human habitation. They're saying all spending should be cut and everyone evacuated back to Earth. Now that's what

189

I call a knee-jerk reaction from people who know nothing!'

'It's ridiculous, Joe. No way could it be done.'

'No, son, not in ten Earth years it couldn't! Earth doesn't have the resources. Anyhow, now we're all but self-sufficient I reckon most people would prefer to stay as long as they felt safe enough.'

'Joe, you mentioned earlier something was happening at executive level. Any news on that?'

'Sure there is,' he answered, leaning back in his chair, 'and that's the next thing I was going to discuss with you. Hammond, Pazukhin and a few others have arranged a conference on the space station to include senior base commanders and a number of experts who they think might have something to add.'

'Why have these people in one place when there's no need for it?' I asked.

'Maybe they figure getting everyone together up there is a lot safer than staying down here. I thought at first they were planning a council of war but I don't see the good in that since we don't have anything to make war with. I gather now the idea is to hold dialogue with Earth and form some kind of strategy without risk of interference.'

'I take it you'll be heading up there?'

A smile touched Joe's gaunt features. 'That was the idea, Brett, but no, I'm not. I haven't been in space for years and I do not have the slightest desire to go back now. I've nominated you as my representative, son, even though it will mean some of our cargos go flying in Delta Seven without a pilot. I hope you'll accept but - well - I'll understand if you don't. Our Chief Executive didn't take kindly to the idea but I won't be losing any sleep over that.'

'Well thanks a million, Joe, but how do I fit in? I don't have executive status. I'm no expert in anything except what I see when I'm flying.'

'I'm no expert in anything either, Brett, at least nothing that could be of any use to them. On the other hand, people like you and Leo know the layout of this world better than most. Apart from that, you are the only person as far as we're aware to have had direct experience of these – whatever they are, and lived to tell the tale. That surely makes your input worthwhile. As far as status is concerned, son, I'll appoint you as my official representative but if you want to speak your own mind that'll be fine by me. Anyhow, you should know that Karin will be up there as well in her scientific capacity. One thing I can't tell you yet is when she'll be going. Hammond is keeping a tight lid on all the flight schedules.'

'All right, Joe, I'll do it but there are questions I wouldn't mind asking right now.'

'Fine - ask me whatever you like.'

'Mining operations,' I said, recalling that odd structure I'd spotted in the ravine when we were trying to find a way into the European base. 'D'you know what they were doing at Europa Six, apart from the manufacturing and metals processing most people know about?'

Joe looked puzzled. 'No, not in any detail I don't, though it's common knowledge they intended to start major mining operations in the area. The Europeans are inclined to keep their pet projects under wraps same as everyone else. Paolo Romano and I chatted occasionally but he never gave much away.'

'Okay, then what about our own people in the mining sector? Are they doing anything unusual or anything they weren't doing before?'

'Not that I'm aware of, Brett, but as you know we never undertook large scale mining at this base since we're on the wrong part of the planet. All we've undertaken here for years is scientific research and specialised manufacturing. Why are you so interested?'

'It's just a hunch I have, Joe, but since Frontier's operations are being intensified planet wide I wonder if that hasn't triggered off some kind of response from whatever lives here. As you said yourself, Hammond is upping secrecy and winding down some areas of co-operation. Frontier Mining and the top dogs of the Consortium might be up to something they don't want us mere mortals to know about.'

'Well, son, if they are, they're not informing the likes of me. They were never too liberal with information and since Hammond arrived on Mars they're becoming a law unto themselves. I doubt we'll get to know much about anything unless they decide there's good enough reason to tell us. Maybe you'll find out more from Virgil Hammond direct - he's nominated himself head of the committee, naturally.'

'What makes you think he or any of them will be more forthcoming in orbit than they are down here?' I asked. 'And what about those accusations over robot equipment sabotage that were flying about until recently? If they blame that on our native life forms they may be right. It could have been a warning.'

'In the case of Europa Six, Brett, they *are* right. If these things can destroy an entire base I don't see how robot probes or a few pieces of mining equipment would present much of a challenge. Anyhow, the general will have to be forthcoming about something because the discussions are going to be broadcast planet-wide as well as being relayed to Earth. Frankly, son, the whole thing smells like a publicity stunt.'

'A publicity stunt!' I responded. 'Knowing what I do about Hammond, I wouldn't be surprised if it turns out more a front for something else – and I don't mean one of his prayer meetings.'

***

After my discussion with Joe, I contacted Karin. She had her suspicions about Hammond as well but they weren't quite so deep-seated as mine. Still, if there were any benefits to be had from going up to the station it was in our meeting up with each other. It occurred to me again just how quickly this relationship of ours had developed so you'll have gathered how it still surprised me - yes, me, something of a self-confessed one-time loner. Anyhow, it turned out Karin's flight was scheduled for late that night and mine not until early the following day even though we were in close time zones. That meant I was stuck on the same part of the planet as Roy Kendrick. I couldn't take refuge with Joe because he was too busy with other things. There was the biodome, of course, but knowing Roy, he'd call it up section by section and locate me there unless I had myself screened out. As soon as he figured that one he'd resort to bribing the kids who play around in there to track me down.

On the positive side, Leo was due in that evening and although he had a prior engagement we would enjoy a spell in the gymnasium and some gossip the following day. Roy wouldn't dare hang about the gymnasium in case he suffered a nasty accident. Such a thing had never happened - but you never could tell.

Not long after Leo had arrived I was unexpectedly invited to join him in the biodome café with Helen Verhaeren, his latest female partner. He and Helen had been in touch with each other frequently over the last few weeks though without Karin to take along I didn't want to be the third party that made a crowd. Leo persuaded me, however, and Helen, having less opportunity to travel than she would have wished, was also eager to hear first-hand about everything I had witnessed.

Helen was slim and attractive with long auburn hair and feline green eyes. Leo was ready on occasion to boast of her as a genuine twenty-five rather than a cosmetic refurb, convincing though the latter could be; none more so than Adelle Saint-Leger who might have fooled either of us. Helen had two jobs; one was to monitor the general ambience and quality of life within the complex and our outstations, the other to council those who needed to discuss their problems with a genuine, yes, *genuine* human. Some people considered her a luxury but Joe always insisted her role was important and could not be left to synthetic entities no matter how sophisticated. Maybe she'd been doing a counselling job on me without my knowing for I did feel more relaxed after getting things off my chest.

After a modest intake of biodome wine, Leo brought up the subject of golf as he usually did sooner or later though I couldn't say for sure if Helen shared that particular interest.

'I've at least one high-up in each of our stations hooked on the idea, old buddy.' he announced. 'As soon as this present mess is sorted out, I'm planning to go for it big time. You see, once we have our first team, it'll catch on with the rest – even with the Chinese and the Russians.'

'Well you can count me in,' I offered, 'if you don't mind having a complete rookie on the team.'

'That won't matter,' smiled Leo. 'We'll all be rookies until we adjust to the conditions out here.'

'Golf?' queried Helen. 'How can anyone play golf on Mars? Not in the biodome, surely? Whacking golf balls around wouldn't be a good idea.'

'Of course not,' answered Leo. 'We play outside.'

'Outside!' she responded, staring at us with a mixture of amazement and pity. 'You're mad, both of you. Quite mad.'

She was probably right. Well, to a point.

'Playing off whilst wearing a pressure suit, in lower gravity,' insisted Leo, as Helen pretended to soothe his brow, 'will present new and interesting problems. I know – I've been practising. Of course we'll have intelligent golf balls able to dig themselves out of the sand. The rules will have to be revised for conditions out here but we'll be the ones to work it all out, see. We'll establish the new rules. We'll have a monopoly on the game planet-wide!'

Conditions on Mars were not going to deter Leo. As he'd pointed out on several occasions, it was way back in the days of the Apollo moon landings that one of those early astronauts started the idea with the first extra-terrestrial tee-off. Should the colonies be threatened with extinction, I guess Leo would have to fit in a last round of golf. I stayed with them longer than I ought to have that evening. Their company seemed more special than on previous occasions.

***

The shuttles, each looking like some kind of big silver insect, were our link to the space station and a great way to see the planet, even sub-orbital. Trouble is they were fuel-hungry and fuel was even more precious on Mars than on Earth. Our shuttles couldn't carry as much cargo as the wingships but they were more agile and, of course, a hell of a lot better if you needed to get around the surface of the planet in a hurry.

We blasted off at seven-thirty local time. It was with some misgiving I watched my home base, our biodome and the two wingships drop away below. Aboard the shuttle were three of Hammond's people from our Number Five as well as four who had been picked up earlier from elsewhere. Optimum use was made of shuttle capacity whenever possible but on this occasion there were four empty seats. I'd half expected to see our Chief Executive but it turned out he was already up at the station with most of his pals. The other passengers, and one in particular, I declined even to look at in the hope of avoiding those ever-pressing questions.

Seated on the inside curve of our trajectory, I had a good view of the scenery below from the virtual window as we ascended. Seeing the sprawling bulk of Olympus like a ruptured abscess on the horizon, then the chaotic terrain where lay the valley of crystals, I wondered what other secrets the planet held. So preoccupied was I that I remained unaware of someone easing down in the seat next to mine. I'd had a few unpleasant encounters over the last week or so. If I had thought the trip upstairs was going to spare me from any more, I was about to be disappointed when I turned to find myself face to face with Roy Kendrick.

Roy's features were known, or should I say notorious, throughout the colonies. He was a wiry little guy with a big pointed nose. Those sharp, pale blue eyes, slightly too close together and set in a hatchet face under wisps of thin, brown hair, had startled many unsuspecting people. I guess it worked for him, which is why he never chose to alter his appearance. It must have cost SolaNews a fortune to run him around Mars but they evidently considered it worthwhile. He was nothing if not persistent and unlike a normal investigative bot he didn't respect any barriers, physical or emotional. His ploy was to ease his victim into conversation without asking too many direct questions, but ratcheting down all the time until they were cornered and felt there was no way out but to tell him what he wanted to know. Joe had kept him off my back at home base. Now he was sitting next to me on the shuttle and there was nowhere to hide.

'Good day to you, Captain Anderson,' he smiled as the rockets eased back. 'I take it you're glad to be getting clear of the troubles down there for a while.'

Still rising, though now at a shallow angle, we were passing south of Ascraeus, drifting toward the equator at an altitude of fifteen hundred kilometres.

'Shouldn't you be in your seat and wearing your safety belt, Roy?' I asked.

Roy ignored my question.

'I studied the records of what you and the others saw at Europa Six,' he went on. 'That must have been a terrible experience, Captain, and the ordeal you went through down in the Labyrinth. D'you think your own people are in any danger?'

'Who can say, Roy. If I knew that, I might not have bothered coming up here.'

'I've heard people talk of evacuating the planet. That must make you feel very insecure.'

'Oh, really? Well, when we're through on the space station, I for one am going straight back down to carry on with my job.'

'So you consider your base as well as Science Officer Blomdahl's any safer than Europa Six? Does that mean people there are less concerned over the situation?'

'I didn't say anyone was less concerned, Roy.'

'But what about Officer Blomdahl?' he asked. 'You must feel concern about her safety now you have formed a partnership?'

I peered out again. The vessel was manoeuvring, levelling off at under a thousand kilometres in readiness for our rendezvous with the space station. From my side of the ship the view was mainly desert with the isolated volcanic peak of Tharsis Tholus visible way to the north. That particular feature, lying due east of Ascraeus, is about the size of Mount Everest on Earth but from our height appeared little more than a speck. Roy was still waiting for my answer but why, I thought, should I make his life easy when he'd been snooping into my personal life? Any opinion I expressed was bound to be misconstrued by SolaNews if not by Roy - dressed up with lurid speculation and presented on Earth as a fact with my name engraved on it.

'If you want to find everything out,' I said, turning to him, 'get in on the conference.'

'Come on Captain – give me a break. We both know that's going out to everyone on both planets. I'm looking for the personal angle, not the official one. What you have to say will interest people back on Earth a lot more. I could make it worth your while discussing things with me once we're aboard the station.'

'Oh? Worth my while?'

'Sure, you experienced things no one else ever did. SolaNews can be generous when it comes to a good story straight from source. You and Kurt Hoffman could have a fine time on Earth with the credits you'd get from it.'

'Roy,' I said, 'firstly, I have no desire to return to Earth. Secondly, I won't be emptying my heart out to you or to anyone else until all this is over - and I have a feeling it may be far from that. Thirdly, I really would prefer to be left alone right now '

'Ah, so you're saying what's happened is only the beginning. Then what is your opinion about -.'

'Roy,' I cut in, half rising from the seat, 'don't make me angry!'

Maybe I sounded more aggressive than I actually felt because he got up quickly and before returning to his seat, said, 'You'll want time to think about my offer, Captain Anderson, but please do consider it.'

I left my place and moved to a spare seat on the opposite side of the shuttle to get a different view. Far below to the south, now drifting slowly behind, lay the vast Mariner Valley, or at least a part of it. Closer, running parallel with the main canyon were the lesser valleys of Candor and Ophir, the former around eight hundred kilometres in length and over four kilometres deep in places. Both were picked out beautifully by the low angle of the sun and each was part-filled with a milk of white mist - a relic of the departed night.

I recalled it was in Candor, during the earliest phase of human exploration, that a three man Russian crew disappeared without trace. Few people have been to that spectacular place since and no one ever found out what happened to the Russians. I wondered about their fate each time I passed over Candor on my travels. I was still wondering when a chime sounded, abstract images pulsed for attention and a voice announced, 'We will commence docking at the Isaac Newton space station in eight minutes. Please ensure all personal belongings are removed from the shuttle when you leave.'

The images dissolved then in front of us materialised an image of the space station a few kilometres ahead and turning against the stars. Anyone seeing it for the first time would get the impression of a squat silver cylinder consisting of huge joined-up ring segments floating above the brightly rusted, scarred and cratered ball of Mars. The station spun on its axis to simulate gravity, except for the cluster of interlocked, modular hexagonal structures close by that contained the observatory and various laboratories as well as a docking facility used by the big rockets from earth.

Suspended within the cylinder at one end was the service hub containing the power core together with various other utilities. The service hub and first ring segment had been sent out from Earth for assembly during the earlier part of the last century and would then have appeared as a giant rotating wheel. More ring sections with laboratories and living accommodation had been added over the decades by the participating nations as and when resources permitted. Those assigned to the station lived and worked between the pressurised inner and outer walls of the cylinder so the inner wall was their ceiling and the outer wall their floor. Ironically, many of the operations once undertaken there had been transferred to the surface as the colonists became more self-sufficient. That left a very expensive piece of orbiting real estate partly unoccupied much of the time.

The station could accept up to five shuttles at any one time – that is one to each segment except for the original wheel where the hub was located. Docking was a weird, disorientating sensation. I looked out as we passed by the rim to enter the illuminated interior of the cylinder. The station's control systems had meshed with ours, causing us to match our speed to that of the rotating body whilst turning the shuttle about until we were perpendicular to the cylinder's axis of rotation with our stern facing the inner wall. We began drifting toward the wall, which had now become our downward direction with station's centrifugal motion giving us our new source of gravity. After that fancy piece of co-ordination and at last docked, things began to feel normal again. Well, as normal as anything could be out here.

The access elevator housing telescoped upward from the inner wall of the station then clamped onto the shuttle. The elevator being pressurised meant we had no need to fix on our helmets though they advised everyone to do so as a precaution. We descended in one group to find ourselves inside the departure area and pressure suit storage room. I wasted no time in stowing away my suit on the life-support recharge unit as I didn't want another confrontation with Roy Kendrick. Bypassing the two female officers who waited to greet those unfamiliar with the station, I headed along to the recreation area where most of the passengers would end up anyway.

I never envied people living on the space station. Some of them, like the International Council Administrator and her staff, spent years there, albeit with periodic leave down on the planet. The station reminded me in one respect of Earth; you couldn't get far enough away from anybody unless you escaped into fantasyland or headed into one of the unused areas. Station gravity didn't bother people from Mars as it wasn't much lower than they were already adjusted to. There is, however, a problem associated with centrifugal gravity. It's the difference between that and the real thing, and I was reminded of it right then. When you hurry off at an angle away from the direction of rotation, you find yourself veering aside from the route you wanted to go. Believe me, after a few drinks at the bar that can be somewhat disconcerting!

The recreation area was awash with sound and light. One wall appeared completely dissolved away so that you imagined you were looking straight through the side of the space station at a stabilised image of Mars. You could shift from claustrophobia to agoraphobia in an instant if you didn't have too keen a trust in technology. People were sitting or standing around tables in the centre of the room. If you moved too far away, the gentle curve of floor and ceiling, to which you were generally perpendicular, created disarmingly odd perspectives for the unwary. There was much animated conversation and it soon became clear what the subject was. I was looking for Karin or anyone else I knew, when a hand touched my elbow.

'Brett, dear, I wondered when you'd drop by.'

'Hi, Karin,' I smiled as she planted a kiss on my cheek. 'Have you been here long?'

'Oh, only an hour. We went via three different bases. Adelle Saint-Leger came up on the same shuttle as me. I've been listening to some of the people here - they have all the answers, you know, but I'm not sure they understand the problem.'

She was right about that. As we moved closer and found a place to sit, various ideas were being aired on how the Martians, by now agreed upon as being our number one enemy, ought to be dealt with. It was an informal debate but not, I concluded, altogether unrehearsed. As food and drink were handed out by station staff people were glancing at me. That was inevitable since my face had of late been paraded in front of everybody, but the main focus of attention at that point was a big guy standing ten or so metres away - a rough character, the sort you imagine could be a serious rabble-rouser given half the chance. Leaning against a table by him stood a shorter, greasy looking individual with peak cap tilted above heavy, black eyebrows. Their crew suits identified both as Frontier Mining personnel. With one hand on his hip and the other gesturing up in the air, the big guy figured he'd solved the problem all right.

'I say we pump rocket fuel and oxidiser down there and burn those bastards out like they used to do with termites. New life form or no, that's all they are ain't it – murderin' termites!'

'Right on!' agreed his companion, knocking back something from a small flask that I imagined was not for the good of his complexion. More than likely it originated from one of Pazukhin's boys.

A number of others found themselves in sympathy with the sentiment as one called, 'Damned right - look how many of our people have been killed. It's either them or us!'

'Them or us!' agreed a few more, including the sidekick.

By now, I'd been spotted by the big man, who wagged a finger straight at me. 'Hey, now here's the guy who met up with those things! You, mister - you know how dangerous they are. What d'you reckon on frying the whole lot of 'em before anyone else gets hurt?'

'Yeah, how's about that?' added the sidekick, waving the flask from side to side.

Everyone quietened. I'd already decided those two would not be getting an invite to my next dinner party. Faces turned toward me. 'Well,' I answered, 'since you ask, I don't see how we can do that. It would take trillions of tonnes of fuel that Earth, let alone the colonies, cannot spare and years to get enough of it out here even if they could. In that time anything could happen.'

The big man's frown said he didn't like my answer.

'Biological agents!' someone declared. 'That's got to be the most effective way! Those things won't have resistance to our bugs!'

'Maybe we'll have to pull the colonists out,' suggested another, glancing my way.'

'No deal,' I said, recalling Joe van Allen's words. 'That would take even longer than getting the fuel over. We have to find another answer.'

'I must agree,' came a voice from the far side of the area. Our attention turned to a slim, casually dressed man with grey hair that looked like a failed exercise in topiary. His voice, though, was one of calm authority. 'We cannot simply wipe out another life form,' he continued, taking a step forward. 'It is the first intelligent alien life discovered by man. Other means must be found to prevent further deaths.'

'Intelligent!' exclaimed someone from a couple of tables away. 'Then *you* go down there and tell 'em to behave themselves!'

That triggered laughter and the big man said, 'Sure, Ingvar, why don't you get your ass down there? Ask them if they'd be good boys and not mind killing too many of our people for a while. How about that? You ain't been near the surface since all this started so what the hell do you know?'

I turned to Karin and asked, 'Who's he?'

'Ingvar Svendsen,' she answered. 'He is environmental consultant to the International Council. He finishes here then goes back to Earth in a month's time.'

The name I'd heard somewhere but of the man himself I knew little. At least the debate was keeping Roy Kendrick away from me. I noticed him over the other side of the crowd, no doubt recording the whole thing for his reports.

'We should try to communicate with these beings,' maintained Svendsen, in spite of the contempt shown by the big man's expression, not to mention the one-fingered gesture blatantly offered by his leering companion. 'They must,' Svendsen continued, 'have existed on Mars very much longer than ourselves.'

'How can you say that?' asked someone. 'We mapped every square centimetre from space before and after getting established here. In all that time we never saw a thing. They could be from somewhere else - somewhere outside our system.'

'I doubt that,' replied Svendsen. 'They are indigenous to the planet and -.'

'But they've proved they're hostile to us!' cut in a woman nearby. 'They waited until our colonies were established before making themselves known and now all they've done is killed people.'

'Yes, but they have left us alone until now,' insisted Svendsen. 'We must consider the

206

possibility that we have in some way provoked them. We should consider what we are doing. We should try to find out if that is not the cause.'

There was a rumble of disagreement. The big man and his pal appeared vexed and impatient. The latter, taking another swig from his flask, looked ready to call out something abusive when a woman officer challenged, 'Excuse me, Ingvar, but if they'd taken the trouble to make themselves known to us in the first place, the disaster might have been avoided?'

'That's right,' someone added. 'Murdering our people is no way to go about it,'

'We cannot answer that until we have established some kind of communication,' replied Svendsen. 'What would we do if they came to Earth, began constructing bases and -.'

'Don't give us that crap, Ingvar!' shouted the big man.

'Yeah, go get your fuckin' brains sorted out!' snorted his companion.

I'd already asked myself what a couple of jerks like these were doing here. The big man grinned across his audience then turned back to Svendsen. 'If they did that, Ingvar, somebody would at least walk over to them and say, "Good morning, sir. Welcome to our planet, sir. And what fuckin' parts would you like to take over first, sir?"'

'Then we'd go shoot the bastards!' sniggered his sidekick.

The big man returned his attention to me. 'Well, fella, they almost had your neck down in the Labyrinth. You must have *some* idea on how we get to kick their butts!'

'In all the time I've been flying,' I answered, 'I never saw anything to indicate there was organised life of any kind other than ourselves on this planet. Maybe they wanted to keep themselves to themselves. Maybe Ingvar Svendsen is right. Maybe we are doing something of late that's started to affect them.'

More murmuring and the big guy looked about to mouth off at me when Karin spoke out. 'Much of this world is still a mystery to us. We've been too intent upon exploiting it to find out many of the things we originally intended.' She next touched on that which I'd already raised with Joe. 'We should look at the mining operations to see if that is not the cause of their aggression toward us.'

'Jesus Christ, lady!' responded the big man, waving dismissively towards Svendsen, 'You're as mixed up as he is!'

'Maybe she ain't gettin' enough of what she needs,' sneered the sidekick with an unambiguous gesture of his arm and fist. His eyes were rolling as he spoke. The drink had taken over. On Earth he'd have been evicted and charged but some people still regarded Mars as a frontier town and behaved accordingly. There followed an awkward silence punctuated by some throat clearing.

'You can take that back and apologise, buddy,' I said, rising from my seat.

'What?' he asked, screwing those heavy-browed eyes at me with an expression of incredulity.

'Brett, it doesn't matter,' said Karin in a whisper that seemed to pass around the room.

I held his gaze and repeated. 'I said, you can take that back and apologise. Are you hard of hearing?'

'Go screw yourself, fella!' he grinned.

The big man winked at him. 'You've upset the captain, Mister Rigby - how about that.'

I was pushing toward them when Rigby, banging down the flask, narrow-eyed me, his head jerking, his lips pursed in defiance. Others close to them started backing off. You could have heard a sand grain hit the floor as I stopped three metres away from where Rigby stood posturing and stated as calmly as I could, 'I'm asking you one more time and it's going to be the last. Take back what you said and apologise!'

Fist raised, he started forward with a twisted snarl. 'Man, I'll fuckin' take *you* back if you don't get your ass outa here!'

I slugged Rigby hard on the side of his face. He reeled back then fell to the floor close to the big guy who remained watching but did nothing. Rigby, blood smeared across his mouth, was soon up and coming at me with both fists raised. I felt the wind on my cheek as he lashed out but I dodged that one. Then I was on him, slamming hard under his ribs and into his jaw. Mouth agape, he staggered back before crashing against a table then hitting the deck once more. I stood ready to hand out another dose if that was what he wanted. 'Okay,' I put it to him as politely as I still felt able, '*now* are you going to apologise?'

Grasping the table, he attempted to get up but stepping over, the big guy held him by the arm then raised an opened hand at me. 'Okay, fella, let it rest! He didn't mean no offence.'

'Then let me hear it from him!' I insisted, moving closer. I was in no mood to let this one go.

'He takes it back, don't you Mister Rigby,' said the big man, pulling the other to his feet by the collar of his jacket. 'And he's mighty sorry. It was just a mistake.'

'Yeah, anything you say, Milligan,' coughed Rigby, wiping his mouth, resting against the table and looking like he wanted to rip me apart. I don't think it suited the big man to let him have another try though it would have suited me just fine.

A hand touched my shoulder. 'Leave it, Brett, that's enough.'

Common sense stepped in alongside Karin and I let her usher me toward the exit. People were murmuring again and as we left I glanced about to see them sitting back down. Roy Kendrick had doubtless recorded what happened and was now busy cornering some other poor sucker. Ingvar Svendsen stood watching us intently from the other side of the room. As we passed along the corridor, Karin said, 'Brett, you should not have become involved. Those two men are just ignorant fools - anyone can see that. They should never have been allowed to come out here.' She landed a sudden kiss on the side of my mouth. 'But thank you anyway.'

'What you mentioned about the mining operations,' I said, 'it's been on my mind for a while. Hammond's covering something up - I'm damned sure of it.'

'There's nothing we can prove though, is there, Brett. You don't know anything. I don't know anything. All the same I think you're right.'

'I'd bet a year's credits on it. Where are we heading now?'

'I didn't get chance to tell you. We're to have a meeting with Amalia Barbosa. I spoke to her before we left base and she agreed to see us when you arrived.'

'Fine by me. But what's behind it?'

'Well apart from the fact that Amalia is an old friend, she is worried for the same reason you, me and Joe are worried. She wants to talk to us where it's more secure but she doesn't have much time. She is supposed to be meeting other people, then after the last shuttle arrives she is to open the formal discussion.'

We made our way through the complex of passages and soon reached the door of the Administrator for Colonial Affairs. As Karin reached out to touch, it glowed the words, 'SECRETARY BARBOSA WELCOMES YOU TO ENTER.'

Hers was a comfortable, softly lit office. As we approached the desk at the far side, a smiling Amalia arose with hand stretched out to greet us. This was my first visit to her headquarters, though we'd met on the planet a couple of times and I'd spoken to her occasionally by link. With those warm brown eyes and big smile she had a way of making everyone feel important. 'Please sit down. Would you like coffee?'

Over coffee we discussed the situation in general, the disaster at Europa Six in particular. I didn't know Secretary Barbosa as well as Karin did but as we talked I sensed within her a deep unease.

'Amalia,' I said. 'I realise we don't have much time to discuss this but I - both of us - feel things are other than they seem with Frontier Mining – this gathering of theirs in particular. You appreciate, however, that whilst I am here in place of Commander Van Allen, I'm expressing my views and not necessarily his.'

'But they are the views of others as well,' added Karin as we expressed our concerns further.

Amalia listened patiently and when we felt we'd talked enough she said, 'Brett, Karin, please take my advice - do not express those opinions at the meeting, especially not in front of Virgil Hammond or Konstantin Pazukhin. And there is something else I must tell you, for I do not believe anyone else will.' She stared at us for a second or so. There was no smile now. 'They have planned two meetings. The first you know about. It will be as public as everyone has been led to expect. The second you do not know of because it will be strictly private. I am not supposed to know about it either but I was warned earlier. I cannot say by whom. If either or both of you are invited to remain for this second meeting you should not accept.

'But why,' I asked. 'Everyone has a right to know what these people are planning - we're all supposed to be in this together.'

'Because - and this is strictly between ourselves - Virgil Hammond intends to disclose information that must not be imparted to the colonists or to the Martian life forms themselves. It means those who are a party to it will not be allowed to return to the surface. That he will enforce. He has men up here to do it.'

'I take it,' said Karin, 'it is because he – they, believe our bases have been infiltrated.'

'So it is generally accepted, yes – though I do not believe that is his real reason.'

'And afterwards?' I asked, realising now what Hammond's pair of goons were doing back there.

Secretary Barbosa frowned at us in turn. 'I cannot tell you any more - believe me. I cannot because I do not know. But I beg of you both - be careful.'

***

'She is very worried,' said Karin as we headed away from the office. 'I really don't think she knows much more than we do - maybe not even as much.'

Karin was more familiar than I with the space station so, during the delay caused by arrivals from other time zones on the planet, she located a disused office. It was useful to stay away from the rest – and not just to avoid Roy Kendrick. The memory of what happened in the recreation area was sufficiently fresh in my mind that, had Roy appeared just then and started pestering, I might have let him have the remainder of what I meted out to the other guy.

The office was not large but had what we needed - somewhere comfortable to sit, hot coffee plus the facility to screen ourselves from second and third level detection. Through the virtual window we had a fine view of Mars turning slowly beneath. The space station was approaching the planet's evening terminator, after which night-time ruled.

You could forget the station was rotating for, like the image in the recreation area, this gave the illusion of being viewed from a static platform.

'Karin,' I said, 'I don't want you to go back down there. Not for the time being. Not until things are sorted out.'

'Oh dear, Brett - I don't want you to go back either but I know you will. And if you are going back then so am I. Apart from anything else, I still have my job to do and it may be more important than ever.'

Watching the planet and the stars ought to have inspired a little romance but there was too much else on our minds. Whilst we talked, the night side of the planet spread across until the western limb became a vivid red crescent. Within the arc nothing was visible - not a light, not the faintest glimmer showed to indicate the existence of human life.

'You know,' I said, gazing into the blackness, 'people used to think there was something out there; something that controlled all our lives. I guess conquering space, colonising Mars and constructing all those bases made us the big shots. Now look what's happened - the whole show is in danger of being run off the road by something that hasn't even left one stone on top of another.'

'Apart from the crystals, Brett.' Karin took my arm. 'There is so much we don't understand. Perhaps we never will. We are on a journey with no destination. It goes on forever.'

As the western limb of the planet faded to dull redness, the eastern side was brightening to a thin crescent of flame-orange. I'd downed the last of my coffee when Karin exclaimed, 'Oh, Brett, look at that!'

A tiny glow was moving against the darkness, crossing the black disk - slowly at first but getting brighter as it speeded up toward the eastern limb. In moments it was a blazing arrow intersecting the crescent as though propelled outwards by some great celestial bow. The moving glare cut as we watched then became short bursts of light as the shuttle, still rising, manoeuvred to match our orbit.

'They will be the last to arrive,' said Karin as the vessel drifted from our view. 'I wonder which bases they are from.'

The arc was much brighter now and we were transfixed by the sight of it. At its centre edge flared a blazing light - a diamond set upon a golden tiara. The sun was rising again.

***

We entered the circular conference suite, a relaxing space of subtle greens and blues, to be greeted from the far side by Amalia. We were amongst the last to show up of the roughly forty people in there and as I squeezed along to one of the few vacant seats, Karin was ushered over to join the other specialists on call, clustered together near the committee of V.I.P.s.

Perched in their midst like some old-style priest ready to pronounce judgement, was Virgil Hammond. He glanced my way as I sat down but offered no acknowledgement even though I was there to represent his senior base commander. Not a bad start, I thought, looking at the rest of them. A dour-faced Konstantin Pazukhin sat on Hammond's right and at his left, Chief Executive of the Asian

Block, Liang Donghan, the only one of that merry trio I had never met first-hand. Few outsiders had, since he was perpetually involved in committee meetings. By contrast to the Russian, Liang wore a fixed smile that people said had been there since birth and wouldn't go away. Being in the company of the other two I guess it didn't have anywhere to go.

A little aside from them was seated the eternally young Adelle Saint-Leger, strikingly attractive and dressed as if she was going out on a date. All credit to the European General Administrator - her smile, though brief, was at least genuine. Why, when sitting with those three jokers, I couldn't imagine. It was no secret she'd never hit it off with Pazukhin but no one could blame her for that. Karin had told me there was no love lost between her and Virgil Hammond, either, and the recent events in which I had been involved had done nothing to help.

There were others whose faces I recognised, including a number of senior base commanders, plus a few more people I wasn't sure about. Behind the committee, with Amalia Barbosa, sat Ingvar Svendsen. What surprised me was the one notable absentee - Roy Kendrick. Anyhow, we didn't have long to wait before Amalia handed the show over to the guy who was really pressing the buttons.

Hammond arose without a nod of thanks to Amalia then looked about, arms folded, before beginning. 'I am going to be brief. I see no reason to reiterate at length the events that have obliged us to leave our duties in order to attend this meeting. It is my intention that we sum up what we know of the situation in a secure environment then impart this to the authorities on Earth with a view to initiating a plan of action. Earth is presently at a distance from us of some two hundred million kilometres, which means we have a communication delay of around eleven minutes. We cannot, of course, engage in live dialogue but will broadcast everything we have to say here so that they may later respond.

Now the creatures that have visited affliction on our people appear to have emerged out from beneath the surface of the planet. For that reason I suggest Officer Blomdahl of Europa Four gives an outline of Martian geology for the benefit of those on Earth who may be less familiar with the subject.'

Karin zapped her program up for everyone to view. The diagrams started to appear as she stood up to speak. Maybe it was an oversight, maybe not, but she did not offer Hammond customary thanks for the invitation before starting. 'Most of what we know, or thought we knew about the interior of the planet was gained in the early days of exploration. Since the establishment of the colonies, exploratory work has been carried out mainly for commercial programmes.'

She glanced about and pushed the hair back from her cheek. I could tell she was not happy about addressing this audience. 'Mars,' she continued, 'does not have the active plate movements that have modified the surface of Earth over many hundreds of millions of years. This little world lost most of the primordial heat from its upper regions long ago. In the lower gravity and with no tectonic processes, great volcanoes have risen above a thickened lithosphere. Enormous stresses have developed. In

217

part because of these stresses and subsequent fracturing, much of the upper as well as parts of the lower crust contain extensive regions of chaotic voids at a far deeper level than the higher gravity of Earth would permit. This is fortunate for us because many contain liquid water that would not exist for long on the surface, circulated by residual heat from the planet's core. Robot probes have gone down there many times but have revealed little we did not expect. Perhaps that in itself should have surprised us but it did not. Why should it until now? We believe these regions extend in places to areas of considerably higher temperature and pressure. In view of what has happened, we must consider the possibility that there may be, deep beneath the surface, a vast and complex ecosystem whose existence has remained hidden since humans set foot on the planet.'

I'd been watching the so-called committee. I could see the expression on Hammond's face as she went on to discuss the implications of finding life down there. He was not happy and pulled her up on several points before suggesting it was time to move on to the next speaker. That proved to be one of Pazukhin's men - a sharp-eyed, pallid looking character who Hammond introduced as Leonid Temirkanov.

'Doctor Temirkanov,' he went on, 'flew over from Novaya Granitsa as soon as the body of the alien found at Europa Six had been placed in one of our wingships. He has worked closely with my own team to undertake a thorough examination of those remains.'

The expression on Hammond's face changed to one of benign satisfaction as Temirkanov cleared his throat. 'Our studies of the creature,' he began in the condescending manner one might use in lecturing a crowd of first year students, 'have led us to conclude that it represented a form of life bearing little resemblance to anything on our home planet except, perhaps, certain organisms found at microscopic level. Even so, the biochemistry was quite different. True proteins or anything akin to blood were not present. Instead, we found a viscous organo-crystalline fluid with high hydrocarbon content that acted as a kind of endoplasm. No doubt this served to transport nutrients. Also, we believe it would have been able to generate a strong electrical field. The specimen we examined was not a multicellular structure but exhibited a polynucleate system without true cell walls. The nuclei themselves contained organo-metallic complexes that may have served the purpose of primitive genetic material.'

Even to me his remarks seemed a pretty crude assessment of something they'd had plenty of time to study. I had seen an expression of surprise on Karin's face that I hoped had not registered with Hammond as well. With the remark about organo-metallic complexes, Temirkanov might have been describing the crystals Karin and I had discovered. He'd used the word, 'primitive,' yet her people had already confirmed the crystals were anything but, so I regarded his speech was a well-rehearsed lie. I was convinced Hammond knew it, too – and Pazukhin, though maybe not the other V.I.P.s.

'Some of you may be aware,' Temirkanov continued, 'that the way I described the creature made it sound amoeboid. Indeed, its internal organs consisted of numerous entities in intimate association with each other, rather like the organelles we typically observe in such free-living creatures. This might be thought of as a multiple symbiosis - an association of previously independent species that have degenerated, that have come together in a kind of reverse evolution. I suspect this to be a result of increasingly adverse conditions on the planet in ancient times - surface cooling accompanied by loss of atmosphere.'

He then came out with something that explained, to me at least, the vagueness of what had gone before.

'You may have noticed my references to our findings were expressed largely in the past tense. When the creature arrived at the laboratory, we realised it had undergone some chemical decomposition in spite of the short time since death and the low temperature at which they had been stored. Its nuclei were already breaking down to diffuse through the endoplasm. Decomposition continued until we were left with a kind of semi-organic soup. It would appear our specimen carried the seeds of its own dissolution but in case anyone is concerned let me assure you this example did not harbour any microbial or viral entities.'

Karin glanced across at me then someone asked, 'Can you tell us anything about their brains or their mental abilities?'

'What degree of consciousness they possess,' replied Temirkanov, 'we might best consider in the light of some of our own machines from early in the last century. They evidently possess the facility of limited interaction with humans but we were unable to locate any evidence of higher cognitive faculties before the thing broke down altogether.'

'Are you saying the creature had no brain?' put in Liang.

'I assure you,' replied Temirkanov, 'we found no trace of such an organ. We consider the specimen to represent a degenerate life form whose presence may act upon the human mind rather in the manner of a hallucinogenic drug. The attack upon Europa Six was probably not a response to anything human beings have done, rather the blind, unthinking act of an insect in stinging someone who passes too close to its nest. It is also possible that a metabolic by-product of these creatures acts to alter the state of our own minds, creating illusions such as the one experienced by Commander Van Allen's pilot. In other words, they seem able to feed upon and recycle our own thoughts and fears.'

That was too much. I should have kept my mouth shut - but I didn't.

'Now wait a minute!' I said, raising up to side-track their star performer. 'Whatever killed Zena Michaelis knew about airlocks and was smart enough to get her outside. And whatever travelled on board Delta Seven with me managed to hold a perfectly rational conversation by any -.'

'Except, of course,' interrupted Hammond, straightening up in his chair, 'that only your voice was on the recording, Captain Anderson. Is that not so?'

His expression made me think of some guy who just invited you down a pleasant path beneath which was concealed a pit of sharpened stakes. I think he wanted me to see those stakes, wanted me to hold back, but I continued all the same. 'Sure, that was the case but I heard it and it persuaded me to go down into the canyon. That I did not invent!'

Temirkanov scrutinised me like some kind of laboratory specimen before saying, 'The death of Officer Michaelis is not a matter we consider relevant to this discussion. We believe that to have been the result of human involvement.'

'Exactly so,' agreed Hammond, 'and that makes it a problem for Commander Van Allen to investigate on his home ground!'

'As for your own account, Captain Anderson,' continued Temirkanov, 'you have not, I understand, been subject to an official medical examination since your encounter. We do not know to what extent the electrochemistry of the creature may have affected your own mind. We might have found an alternative reason for your behaviour had that been the case.'

'What the hell!' I began. 'Are you trying to suggest I -.'

'We are not here to argue with you, Captain Anderson!' interrupted Hammond, rising abruptly. 'Our purpose is to analyse the threat to our colonies and to put an end to it! Please continue, Doctor Temirkanov.'

Okay, I was smouldering. Okay, I wouldn't have minded getting my hands around that smug bastard Temirkanov's throat. He'd just made out one of our own people was a murderer and that I needed my head examining. I guess that wouldn't have gone down well with anybody. Then there was the shaft beneath Europa Six – that wasn't made by an illusion. He was talking again when I turned to find Karin at my side.

'Brett, I think we should leave,' she whispered.

'This whole thing is a damned charade.' I muttered, aware of Hammond glancing our way.

Someone else was looking at us, too, and looking hard. Someone Hammond couldn't see from where he was sitting. Ingvar Svendsen. We didn't move out right then because I wanted to know what else was going on. Temirkanov finished what he had to say and it turned out the remainder of the group were to answer, or try to answer, questions on short-term security matters. The committee, with the exception of Adelle Saint-Leger, seemed less interested in what was being said now and busied themselves in passing whispered remarks to one another.

Eventually, Virgil Hammond stood up to announce, 'We are all agreed the safety of the colonies must at present be our sole consideration.' He looked about as they all concurred that it had to be so then went on to reveal the next stage in his plans. 'Interim measures have been put in hand to counter the threat we face. The nature of these will be discussed in due course. Some of you will be returning to the surface but executive staff are to remain, except for those few who have already registered urgent business below.'

Karin and I were heading for the exit when his voice pinged into my earlobe communicator.

'Captain Anderson - you of all people should welcome the opportunity to stay with us at this point - together with Officer Blomdahl, of course.'

'No, Chief,' I answered, turning to meet his gaze, 'we don't welcome the opportunity - so if you will excuse us.'

'As you please, Captain Anderson, but you should at least give some thought to your safety and that of Officer Blomdahl. I assure you, remaining with us will most certainly be in your best interests. Perhaps before long you may reconsider.'

He was smiling like a contented Buddha as he spoke. I took that as a bad sign.

Once returned to the spare office I tried to persuade Karin to remain in orbit for her own safety as well as my piece of mind but she wasn't having it. Accordingly, I confirmed our places for departure by shuttle together with others who were going back down. Because of scheduling, or so I thought at the time, we had been allocated seats on the last departure. There had been a shuttle in each of the docking bays but an announcement informed us one was about to leave. With the wall vision on, we watched it stabbing light as it dropped away against the then night side disk of the planet. Our shuttle would not be leaving for over an hour and no more would be coming up until Hammond sanctioned it. It was obvious he had assumed authority over everyone, including Amalia Barbosa. I imagined he could only do that with at least the acquiescence if not the full backing of the other executives.

Karin drew coffee from the dispenser and we settled down, having assumed all along that our presence in that isolated room was not known to anybody but ourselves. It caused us no little surprise when, after thirty minutes of privacy, the door chimed.

'Who the hell -?' I muttered but neither of us moved. I had already conjured up the unwelcome prospect of Roy Kendrick hovering out there.

'Please,' came a voice. 'Please, I must talk to you face to face.'

It was a voice Karin recognised. We let open the door to be confronted by the troubled features of Ingvar Svendsen.

'It is important that you hear me right now,' he said, pushing into the room.

'How the hell did you find us?' I asked, glancing outside before I closed the door.

'I - look, never mind - I don't think anyone else knows.'

Karin pulled out another coffee and handed it to him as we sat down. He seemed like he needed something stronger.

'I must tell you what I know,' he began, grasping the cup. 'Hammond's men have taken charge of our communication centre. They have guns. They will allow nothing other than authorised broadcasts to Earth or to the colonies. Private transmissions are also blocked.'

'Taken over!' gasped Karin. 'He cannot do that!'

'Well I am telling you he has,' Svendsen responded. 'It was done during the meeting and no one is in any position to argue with him. And this you should know if you don't already - Hammond himself is executive director of Frontier Mining. Through his dealings he has financial control over the entire consortium. Konstantin Pazukhin and Liang Donghan hold interests in the operation as well, as did Paolo Romano of Europa Six. I believe Hammond had a hold over him as I'm sure he has over Pazukhin. The only one of the top people here who is not directly involved is Adelle Saint-Leger. Many of those base commanders who came up here have been persuaded to remain including all directly under Hammond. There are powerful interests on Earth backing Hammond and demanding more of the Consortium. Much has been kept secret from his own government and the International Council. You must -.'

'Hold on,' I interrupted, 'that isn't what they were supposed to be discussing back there.'

'No, of course not – they wouldn't. What they also have kept quiet about is that some time ago Frontier began using deep level plasma drills at several sites as have other members directly involved within the Consortium. I believe they have penetrated the Martian habitat far below the surface and it has caused them to react to this. Hammond suspects this also.'

'Deep level plasma drills,' I said. 'Yes, it makes sense. Those things need their own fusion cores as well and that would have to be concealed. I saw a building of some sort at Europa Six that could have contained a separate power source.'

'You are right, Captain Anderson,' he continued, 'such installations had recently begun operation at Europa Six and elsewhere. Only those with direct involvement have any idea how far this has gone because the automated mining systems employ few people.'

226

'How did you get to know all this?' Karin asked.

'Oh, I trained in military electronics before I took on my present work. Hammond may not be aware of this since he and I have had nothing to do with each other until very recently. I know the station research facilities very well - I have worked here on and off for almost two years. That's how I located you even though you are screened. When Hammond arrived on the space station, I tapped into his personal communications. This station has no military level security systems so Hammond uses his own and thinks himself secure. It was difficult. I felt like a criminal. I was afraid of being found out but knowing the kind of man he is - knowing what has happened on the surface, I considered it my duty. His conversations with Novamerica Five and others I have recorded but have not been able to transmit to Earth.'

He produced what appeared an ordinary pen, saying, 'Take this. It contains all the proof you will need but let it also record what I am about to tell you then transfer everything into your personal data before you leave here.'

'D'you know what they decided on back there?' I asked, taking the pen.

'Yes. Saint-Leger, Liang, Pazukhin and some of the others talked about bringing over troops and weapons. Hammond informed them that he had already called for military assistance from Earth and -.'

'Military!' I exclaimed. 'But even with Earth and Mars in their present positions that will take weeks. There could be thousands dead by then and

227

anyway, what the hell can the military hope to achieve?'

'No, Captain Anderson, it will not take weeks. They will be here in five days. Hammond persuaded the UAS senate to send out *Aurora*!'

'*Aurora*, Brett?' asked Karin. 'What is that?'

'She is - or was, a test vehicle for the so-called universal field drive. I thought they were still playing around with that.'

'So did most people,' continued Svendsen. 'It was their intention to have them think so. *Aurora* started out as a research project to harness dark energy, the very fabric of space-time itself, but was given priority status by the military some years ago. They used an earlier experimental model to have people think there were still problems and that little progress was being made. The real *Aurora* is operational with other powers working on similar projects. I tell you now - *Aurora* and her like will do to rocket power what steam did to the age of sail, but very much quicker. Her technology may one day take us to the stars – but now she is to be used against us. She will carry troops and Hammond has nominated the crew through his military connections so it will consist entirely of his own men. Some of these will be modified humans with greatly enhanced senses like Zena Michaelis. Entirely illegal - and I wonder about Virgil Hammond himself. He will establish a council to operate from here as well as controlling base facilities on the surface. All flights - shuttles and wingships will be under his control. There can be no opposition because his men will possess the only weapons on Mars.'

228

'Hold on there!' I interrupted. 'Armed or no, how can a few dozen, even a hundred or so men possibly hope to control all our bases?'

'They will have no need to do that. *Aurora* carries a cargo of military robots; surveillance micros, thousands of the things - enough to infest every base, and spiders armed for anti-personnel work. These he will activate as soon as he can integrate them into your own control systems. Fortunately *Aurora* is not equipped to handle them because they did not have enough time to adapt her equipment. To Hammond this is not just about Frontier and the Consortium, not just about boosting the Martian economy. He plans to establish a new order on Mars and to manufacture weapons here. He will use the increased resources of the Consortium and the zeal of his followers to do it. This was planned long before we knew there was life on the planet. Now he intends to exterminate the Martians before anyone on Earth realises what is happening. Creatures of the Devil is what he calls them. Hammond believes some greater power is guiding his hand. He believes his task is pre-ordained. He claims to hear the voice of God!'

'The man is insane!' responded Karin. 'There could be millions of these life forms beneath our feet. The human population on Mars could be wiped out in a matter of hours!'

'Europa Six died in minutes,' I added. 'But surely the rest of the big noises aren't caught up in this crazy agenda. How could they be? It would surely have leaked out back on Earth.'

'No, they are not – they know nothing of it except maybe Pazukhin. But in a few days that will not matter. They will have no choice other than to comply with his demands. Once he is established it will be impossible for anyone to do anything about it so the truth may never be known. Records will be altered to suit the account he has already given to Earth. We are a distant colony; it is not so convenient for others to come and see for themselves until the likes of *Aurora* are brought into service years from now. By then it will be too late.'

Svendsen lifted his hands in despair. 'I fear also what could happen on Earth if he succeeds? Others will see the UAS as taking control of Mars for its own ends. There has been no major conflict on Earth since early in the previous century but other powers will not tolerate what they see as American domination of Martian resources and colonists for whatever reason. It could lead to a difficult situation back home - perhaps war. Such a disaster would place Hammond in an even stronger position on Mars. He would claim it justified his actions. He would be unassailable!'

'This gets worse by the minute,' I said.

'If an account of what is really happening here reaches the International Council in time,' Svendsen continued, 'the UAS and major powers on Earth will have to respond. They will put a stop to this madness before it's too late. You are both due to leave on the last shuttle - I checked that before I came to speak with you. You must have Commander Van Allen contact the International Council with the information I have given you. Everything will depend on it. The colonists must be informed so they can prepare to resist. Hammond must not be allowed to establish military forces on Mars.'

'Let's hope he doesn't know you're in here telling us about it.' I said.

'I fear that if he does, none of us will be saying anything to anybody, and that includes Amalia Barbosa. I imagine we all will burn up in the Martian atmosphere like meteorites.'

Svendsen jerked back the chair, leaving his coffee untouched. 'I dare not stay longer. I feel he is becoming suspicious of me. He may be wondering where I am and trying to locate me. I will send further information to your base by light-pulse when I'm able but it will not be possible for you to reply.'

Svendsen was across the room and opening the door. Glancing from side to side, he turned back to us briefly. 'I wish you luck.'

As the door closed, Karin said, 'Brett, we have a missile defence system to deal with incoming bodies from space; could this not be used against *Aurora*?'

'If only,' I replied, 'but there's a difference between a lump of rock whose set course you know about weeks or even months in advance and a military space vehicle with *Aurora*'s capability. She'll be anything but a passive target and won't hang about to be shot at even if we picked her up on the way in.'

We had little choice but to stay where we were for the time being in the hope that no one else would locate us. Screened or no for most purposes, anyone in charge of the station control centre might track us through our ear-lobe communicators. The fact that this procedure is never followed unless absolutely necessary would not concern the likes of Hammond.

'You see what he's done,' I said. 'He's got most of the colony's decision makers up here unable to communicate even with their own people. They may not have realised it yet but they're his prisoners.'

'Svendsen is right, Brett. Hammond will attempt to destroy the native life forms and take us over at whatever cost. But he has to move quickly. He knows that if Earth discovers the truth in time, Frontier Mining, perhaps the entire consortium, will be placed under International Council control and he will be condemned as a criminal.'

The planet passed below whilst we talked - day to night - night to day, as though human affairs were of no consequence. I was checking the time when the public address announced, 'BAY FIVE SHUTTLE DEPARTURE IN TWENTY MINUTES.'

We shut off the view then made our way across the room. There was no hurry so we planned on taking a route through the unoccupied sections to avoid being noticed. Karin was right behind me as I opened the door. Standing square in front of us were Milligan and Rigby, the two undesirables I'd brushed with in the recreation area. Milligan, the big guy, moved forward with that same leer-daubed expression I'd noted earlier.

'The General told us how much he values these people's company,' announced Milligan. 'Isn't that right, Mister Rigby?'

His face-twitching sidekick snarled, 'Yeah, that's right, Mister Milligan. He'd be real fuckin' disappointed if they pulled out now!'

'Disappointed, Mister Rigby,' grinned the big man. 'That's exactly right.'

'I bet he would!' I responded, whacking Milligan on the jaw hard as I could in the confined space of the doorway. Not hard enough as it happened, though he staggered back a short way. Karin cried out as both of them lunged forward, pushing inside to fall on me with fists swinging. I managed to avoid the worst of it, landing a couple of blows myself whilst yelling, 'Karin - get out now!'

She scrambled by as Rigby made a furious grab at her, bawling, 'Come back you fuckin' bitch!' but she was already at the door and in the distraction I landed another good punch on Milligan's jaw, only too aware it would need more than that to bring down a man of his size. Seeing Karin disappear Rigby cursed aloud then the two of them fell on me like wild animals, hoping to finish me off quickly so they could chase after her. That wasn't what I had in mind and in a mêlée of swinging fists I was desperate to keep them occupied no matter what. Struggling free, I managed to grab a chair and swing it at them. It kept the pair at bay for precious moments then the furniture started to get badly disorganised as they closed in. Milligan tried to wrestle me down whilst his greasy pal, an arm locked about my neck, yelled in my ear, 'Your fuckin' number's up, shithead! '

Ignoring the verbal delicacies, I used Rigby as a prop, jerked a knee hard into Milligan's groin, causing him to gasp, then levered a foot against his stomach to heave him back. An overturned chair was on my side at that point when he staggered against it and fell sprawling. In Earth gravity he might have stunned himself but unfortunately didn't do so now. But the low gravity worked for me as well. I grasped Rigby's arm, heaving him up and over, intending to land him on top of Milligan. Nice thought but it didn't work. The big guy was already clambering to his feet so Rigby slid along the floor to slam up against the wall. The tussle with Rigby had thrown me off balance as well when Milligan came at me again. He struck me on the side of the face. I went down dazed and before I could struggle to my feet, both of them were leaping on top to pin me against the deck. Gravity or no, they had me. I couldn't get up. Then Rigby landed a chest punch that took my breath away. I remember seeing the big guy silhouetted against the illuminated ceiling, one arm lifted high with a fist the size of a plucked turkey about to descend on full power. I closed my eyes, aware of a mocking voice that seemed meant only for me as it announced shuttle departure in fifteen minutes. A gong sounded close by. He must have hit me real hard, I thought, because I was too numb to feel anything. Then my eyes were open and I knew he hadn't hit me at all because he was falling aside with blood streaming past his ear. Behind him stood Karin, oxygen cylinder raised to deliver another blow. Rigby gaped in disbelief. Lower gravity might have made that cylinder feel light but it sure hadn't affected its mass when it touched base with Milligan's skull. That's a brief lesson in physics for you.

Rigby cursed, struggled to his feet, at the same time reaching inside his jacket but I leapt up, kicked away his leg then threw him down against the overturned table. The small pistol he was attempting to grab fell out to skitter across the floor where Karin kicked it aside. Scrambling to his feet again, he fought back, swearing, lashing out with fists and boots but I went in to punch him in the guts then slam him back hard against the bulkhead. That stunned him. It gave me the chance I needed. I landed a blow to his jaw that felt like it ought to recalibrate his teeth and that was enough. He slumped to the floor in a heap, coughed, let out a groan and stayed there.

Brett, you're hurt!' said Karin, clutching my arm.

'Not as bad as those two monkeys,' I mumbled.

Milligan lay face down in a spreading pool of blood. He wasn't moving. Karin stared horrified and I needed to get my breath back. She slipped an arm around me but I couldn't say much right then. It was the next announcement from the public address that brought me fully to my senses. 'BAY FIVE SHUTTLE DEPARTURE IN TEN MINUTES. THIS IS A FINAL CALL!'

We glanced at each other then made for the door. With precious seconds scattering in the winds of urgency we headed along the corridors as quickly as we could, finding that our feet didn't quite want to go in the direction our brains intended. You already know why. We realised just how little time we had - if any at all - and we couldn't call up the control room to request a few minutes delay.

235

There were times when we didn't know if we were jogging along the floor or the walls but we dared not slow down. In what seemed a hell of a long time we got to the departure area unchallenged but there was further delay at the lockers. We had to suit up double quick though fortunately there was no need for us to pressurise at this end of the journey. The elevator doors were open but the readout close by already showed final countdown with only ten seconds to go. Karin dashed inside the elevator, clutching her helmet. I made three stabs at the numeric panel above the readout.

It now flashed, 'BAY FIVE DEPARTURE INTERRUPT – STAND BY.'

She stared at me in dismay. 'Brett, what are you doing?'

'It's the emergency override,' I informed her. 'The shuttle can't undock until it's cleared.'

'But that means we can't leave!'

'No problem!' I responded as she operated the elevator controls.

Footsteps rang from the passage as the doors began to slide across. Rigby appeared, gun in hand. There was a flash. His bullet smacked against one of the doors - then we were rising.

On the short journey up, Karin asked, 'Brett, how are we going to get away from here?'

Moments before the doors to the docking passage opened, I kissed her. 'Trust me, it's okay.'

Slipping the gun into his jacket, Rigby stood back to watch the flashing message, a grin of satisfaction spreading across his swollen, pain-pulsing mouth. Automatic departure sequence had been broken. Only those in charge of central communications, Hammond's own men, could cancel it. All he had to do was inform Hammond then wait until the elevator returned.

The grin was replaced by a rabid scowl when the panel ceased flashing to display a new message: 'BAY FIVE SHUTTLE DEPARTURE RESUMED AND IN PROGRESS.'

***

Virgil Hammond relaxed, swilling a straight bourbon about his cup then downing it with satisfaction as the image materialised across his office wall. Within the hollow interior of the space station the shuttle appeared ready for departure. He watched it detach from the inner wall and begin to rotate with short spurts of light from the manoeuvring jets. He was pouring himself a second measure when the desk communicator pulsed urgently. He regarded the intrusion with annoyance, ignoring it for a moment to take another gulp before demanding, 'What is it?'

Before him arose a bruised and bloodied face. Hammond stared hard as the voice croaked, 'General, sir - they made it to the shuttle, Milligan is dead.'

Rising from the chair, Hammond hissed, 'You mean you let them -!' His cup rapped against the table, part of its contents spattering across the surface. 'You stupid bastard!'

Swiping out Rigby's image, he barked a short code. Another face appeared. 'Control room, sir.'

'Taylor - stop that shuttle! Get it back into bay five! Stop it!'

The controller turned aside before announcing, 'No can do, General. Someone on board blocked the

237

override and reset her programme. She's already locked into descent sequence.'

Hammond stared at the big image as the shuttle distanced itself from the space station to drift bright in the sun. He watched retro-jets flare, watched the shuttle drop away, watched it pass westward, diminishing inexorably against the planet's half-lit disk.

'Cross me will you - you ass-hole,' he breathed harshly. 'Well make the most of it. The Lord's hand is with me. Yes - in the end I will prevail.' A sharp command caused the scene to vanish. Turning again to the desk, he ordered, 'Get me *Aurora* - code, "Trinity Alpha!"'

CHAPTER 6
THE BLACK MOUNTAIN

A violet glow on the horizon announced the approach of morning when we hovered for final descent above Novamerica One. Naturally there had been some confusion on board the shuttle - people shouting, demanding to know what the hell I was up to in taking over the controls when the vessel was already programmed. Someone did try to stop me. I don't know who the guy was but I whacked him hard with my helmet and that was enough. I had no time to explain though Karin did her best to convince the passengers that everything would be just fine.

My one regret was finding Roy Kendrick on board though under the circumstances he'd not been too eager to get near me. I wondered why they hadn't kept him of all people locked up in orbit but as I learned later, Hammond had banned him from the so-called public meeting. Roy might well have found some means of monitoring that but even so he would have come away with no more than was imparted to the people on the ground and to the authorities on Earth.

Once landed I reinstated the original programme, waved goodbye to those on board then had the shuttle continue on its way without a pilot as originally intended. I had expected Roy would home in on me soon afterwards but to my surprise he'd remained on the shuttle in order, as I later discovered, to pick up a connection down south at Karin's base, Europa Four. Karin had opted to remain with me rather than return home on the shuttle.

Joe walked over from the drinks dispenser with three coffees. 'Well, Brett, I have to say it isn't every morning someone hi-jacks a shuttle then strolls into the place with news like yours. I've already had Liang Donghan's second in command on at me as it was their shuttle - but without him in direct charge she couldn't fire off an official complaint. Even if she had, it wouldn't have gone any further than Virgil Hammond.'

Naturally, Joe was taken aback by what we had to report, particularly over *Aurora*, but that didn't prevent him handing us something of a shock in return.

'Brett, Karin - what I have to tell you puts an even more difficult complexion on things. During your descent from the space station we - the entire planet, lost contact with Earth. It isn't a signal blackout like you get with a solar flair. There's something blocking this as well as other bases on all frequencies. It's a situation we never encountered before though our own satellites are still functioning normally. The fact that it hasn't affected Marsnet or signals coming in from other directions in space would indicate the source of the problem as being located between here and Earth.'

It was becoming as obvious to Joe as it was to us what had caused the situation but before Karin or I had chance to add further comment his communications panel demanded attention. The face of the guy who appeared was not one any of us recognised, if he existed at all. He announced in a matter-of-fact way, 'This message is for the attention of personnel planet-wide. In view of the threat to the colonies on Mars, the authorities on Earth have sanctioned the despatch of a team equipped to render specialist assistance. This left the home planet some time ago on the high-speed research vehicle, *Aurora*. Problems with her engines when employed at full power have caused temporary disruption to communications with Earth. All personnel should remain vigilant. Please stand by for further transmissions.'

'Well, I guess they had to give something away to keep the folks at home happy,' remarked Joe as the image dissolved. 'I don't know much about *Aurora*, except that she's highly classified - the big secret of the century, so I heard, but I'm damned sure they would have figured out well in advance some way to stop her fouling up communications with Earth.'

'Well, deliberate or not, Joe,' I said, 'and it surely is deliberate, we have to do something. Hammond cannot be aware of what Svendsen told us, otherwise Karin and I would have had more than a couple of his gorillas to contend with - and I doubt we'd be here talking to you now.'

'But those men,' put in Karin. 'One of them was badly hurt, perhaps worse. Hammond may have guessed why we were so desperate to leave.'

'No,' I said. 'He can't know the full story - not unless -.'

'Unless he's got a tag on Ingvar Svendsen,' put in Joe.

'We should know soon,' said Karin. 'Svendsen promised to contact us by light pulse as soon as he finds out more.'

'I think you're right,' said Joe, 'Hammond might not know what Svendsen told you but he isn't taking any chances. Could be the communications blackout is as much a precaution against one of Amalia Barbosa's people yelling for help. The space station is big and Hammond can't have many of his cronies up there. If one of her staff got to a transmitter -.'

'He'd blow it,' I put in. 'Once they realised what he was up to our government would have to drop him, like it or not, and his name would stink from here to Neptune!'

'Frankly,' said Joe, after some moments of deliberation, 'I don't see what can be done for the time being. As soon as any of us opens our mouths, Hammond will realise we're on to him. And then what? We still can't call on Earth for help.'

'But, Joe,' Karin insisted, 'we must open our mouths - and loud.'

'Karin's right, Joe. Talk to whoever is in charge at the other bases on our secure link. Tell them everything - plasma drills, the attempt to stop us getting off the space station and the fact that *Aurora* is carrying military - Hammond's military, and enough armed bots to do his dirty work. The Russians and Asians won't like that one bit – especially as their own governments can't get military out here in anything like enough time. The Europeans will have still greater reason to object - even without Adelle Saint-Leger.'

'Persuade them to seal off their bases, Joe,' urged Karin. 'They must Deny *Aurora*'s men facilities for landing. They must deny them access to provisions and -.'

'Do it Joe!' I cut in. 'They couldn't hold out for too long up there. Unlike the early days - the space station depends largely on the colonies for provisions - not the other way around.'

'Now hold on you two! I have little enough sympathy for the goddamned General but it is one of our own ships on the way from Earth and what you're suggesting is some kind of insurrection. Even if most people agreed, it would only take one to back down and the rest of us would be in it up to our necks. It has to be everyone or no one. I'll sound people out as diplomatically as I can but don't expect anything dramatic. This guy Svendsen just might have a grudge we don't know about. Have you considered that?'

'Joe, please - Brett and I know Svendsen was telling the truth. We saw what was happening - and those two men of Hammond's were not playing games! If you doubt it, try talking to Amalia Barbosa and see what happens. There may still be a channel open to her. Try it Joe! When I return to Europa Four I'm willing to contact all our people in the absence of Adelle if you will do the same with the others.'

'Joe,' I added, 'you're the one person left down here who most people will take seriously. If Hammond, Pazukhin and whoever else is involved carry on the way they are, we'll all be sacrificed and the real victims will get the blame.'

'Now, wait on!' exclaimed Joe. 'No way do I see those – those whatever they are as victims. Certainly not after Europa Six! And after what happened to you, Brett, not to mention Zena Michaelis, none of us can be certain who we're standing next to anymore. I've got people staring at me and I'm staring at them. Why, I can't walk into the bar for a drink or a mouthful of food without someone wondering if I'm who I'm supposed to be. Now I'm doing it, too!'

'Perhaps touching is the answer,' offered Karin. 'The illusions may not extend to our sense of touch. Brett, did - I mean, did you -?'

'Touch her? No, I didn't -, okay, Joe, there's no need to stare at me like that!'

'Sorry, son, I don't suppose if you were something other than yourself you'd be looking beat up, talking the way you are or walking around with that grease mark on the sleeve of your crew suit.'

'Joe, I - look, you pointed out a while back how I'd lived to tell the tale after being so close to one of those things. I've thought about that a lot. I've thought about what Ingvar Svendsen said and I had a hunch on the way down from the space station. I can't explain Europa Six. I can't explain all those people we saw lying dead in the biodome but I'm convinced the life forms were trying to communicate with me out there in the canyon. Nothing else makes sense. Nothing at all!'

Joe stared hard. 'Fine, Brett, but why you when you're up there flying much of the time? Why not Karin or me - or anybody down here on the ground? And why take the trouble to go all the way to the Labyrinth? Why stage the illusion of that girl you saw and then another looking like Karin?'

'That was my reaction when Brett first suggested it,' said Karin, 'but now I'm sure he is right.'

244

'There are more questions than answers,' I went on, 'but I'll hang everything on these - whatever they are - being highly intelligent. Maybe not the kind of intelligence we understand. But they surely must possess the will to survive and if we're a threat, as Svendsen believes, as we now believe, it might be that -.' I hesitated. 'Joe are you sure neither of our out-stations have started using plasma drills?'

I asked the question because out-stations, ours as well as other people's, were something I never got close to because most of them didn't have a landing strip.

'Our outstations are not involved in deep-level drilling operations,' Joe assured me. 'Apart from pumping up subsurface water they are purely research facilities.'

'And your people Karin,' I said. 'What about Europa Four?'

'I very much doubt it though our industrial facility is automated like everyone else's and out of bounds to all except a few technicians. I will have to find out more won't I? The same as Joe is going to have to find things out, otherwise -.'

***

A spire soared darkly from the desert to pierce a glowing sky. Here was once a furnace that bellowed elemental fire. Long ago the beast had faltered, long ago it had died. Flickering centuries, rolling ages had stolen away its mantle of ash, spreading it over a waiting desert to expose the blackened needle-heart.

Humans were now its companions, descending from the sky to break eternal silence, to pry into its secrets, to chisel out its core. Close by they had built their landing strip, their complex and their biodome. They scurried about as sand grains in the wind, always busy, their machines probing ever deeper into realms they ought never to have entered.

Commander Andrei Nikolayev, recently appointed head of Chornaya Gora, gazed from his office whilst running fingers over a short, neatly trimmed beard. Beyond the biodome towered that which gave the base its name - an eroded volcanic core - a shaft of weirdly sculpted basalt rising over a kilometre high.

The bright-eyed, smartly dressed Nikolayev had members of the Consortium to thank for this placement. He was their prime nominee and with good reason. He had overseen the installation of robot drilling equipment within the newly excavated base of the black mountain - equipment his team had designed and helped to develop whilst on Earth. Equipment that would penetrate to great depths even more efficiently and in less time than anything the other powers possessed. Pazukhin had not wanted him up at the space station - not whilst operations required his personal attention. If everything performed as planned, Nikolayev might be offered a place on the board of Frontier Mining; a situation he would not wish to have jeopardised.

Turning to his deputy, Nikolayev said, 'I understand your misgivings, Alexei, but I see no reason to halt operations until Frontier and other members of the Consortium agree to it. I do not think Pazukhin would take it upon himself to go that far.'

Alexei shuffled uneasily. 'But commander, some of our people are wondering about Europa Six. There are rumours -.'

This was Nikolayev's first command. He did not intend to acquire a reputation for reticence or indecision. 'Yes, Alexei, I have heard the rumours. I have been hearing rumours ever since I set foot on Mars but we are not where those unfortunate Europeans were. Beneath this complex is a volcanic sill, a solid raft of basalt over three kilometres thick. There are no underground channels. There are no passages for little Martian moles to crawl out of. Our pilot drill has gone through it like butter and soon we will harvest the minerals trapped deep within the lithosphere including, Alexei, more diamonds than we will know what to do with - if our crustal probes and our geologists are right. Even so, I have had sensors placed around the complex as other bases have done. Remember, we do not know what they were doing at Europa Six and I'm quite certain others cannot know what we are doing within the black mountain. No part of our operations can be observed from ground level nor can they be detected from above.'

His deputy stared out across the complex to the basalt spine. 'That thing is like a rotten tooth, commander. One day it will loosen. One day it will fall out.'

'One day, perhaps, but it will not be today or tomorrow. It will not come loose for a very long time. Meanwhile, Alexei, I have been contacted by Van Allen at Novamerica One. He tells me the Americans are sending help from Earth. If he is to be believed, their vessel will be full of armed soldiers as well as military equipment even though Hammond himself has not admitted as much. I have no doubt our own people and others will do the same once they learn the truth, if truth it is, even if they are several weeks behind. Our government will not tolerate an American take-over any more than will the Asians or the Europeans - of that I am certain. They maintain Frontier Mining already has too much power within the Consortium.'

'I have heard about *Aurora*,' said Alexei. 'We should remember the first shots fired in our own country by another *Aurora* early in the twentieth century. You may recall what that led to.'

'Alexei,' responded Nikolayev with a condescending smile, 'we should never allow ourselves to be influenced by analogies from the past - they seldom withstand close examination. Take my advice - have more confidence in the present and the future. Affairs on Mars may have become a little complicated but I hardly think we are on the verge of a revolution.'

***

Two days had passed when late in the afternoon a European wingship came in and Karin went on board. From it emerged Roy Kendrick after a news gathering exercise at Europa Six. I heard a while later that recovery teams had flown over to bring out the bodies for mass disposal. It seemed Roy had got his tip-off from one of the shuttle passengers on our way down from the space station then managed to wangle his way in via Europa Four. He then figured there could be some advantage in hanging around my back yard for the time being. He approached me in the bar a couple of times without being too pushy. I guess he'd digested the fact that I wasn't going to be pressured though in spite of my animosity I couldn't blame him for trying.

Barely a morsel of food and not a single drink went on my account when Roy was close by. Had we been back on Earth I might quickly have developed a liking for vintage champagne but here on Mars no one had gotten around to producing it. Meanwhile I was convinced, as was Joe, that the next move had to come from Hammond. On that account we were to be proved wrong in a manner we could never have imagined.

Joe informed me early next morning that contact with Earth remained blocked and there had as yet been no meaningful exchange with the space station. 'I guess they're waiting it out,' he said, 'so they don't feel any need to hold dialogue with us at present. I've tried several times to contact Amalia since you landed but each time they make out she's engaged in consultation with Hammond and co. and can't be interrupted.'

'She can't be in consultation for ever, Joe,' I responded.

It felt as if we were in the eye of a storm. There was a mood of expectancy as people went about their business - which they had to do of course, as sooner or later so would I. There were still consignments of equipment and goods as well as personnel to be shifted around the planet no matter what else was going on. Meanwhile, I had little inclination to play cat and mouse with Roy Kendrick, free lunches or no. Leo was down for a break at our number six base so I spoke to him briefly a couple of times but did not refer to what had happened in orbit.

I saw nothing of Joe until nineteen hundred hours when he asked me to join him for dinner in the biodome main restaurant. The illusion of sitting outside on a warm evening back on Earth was agreeable enough even with the possibility of Roy spotting us, as if by chance.

'I've been in conference with people around the planet a good part of yesterday, the day before and much of last night as well as through most of today,' Joe began. 'Everyone is apprehensive - some of them downright jumpy. They all want to see things resolved. On the other hand, a good number won't commit themselves to anything as yet. All our own people will back me up if it comes to it and I think Karin will do a pretty good job with her side. But if Hammond's men landed right now, I don't imagine they'd have much problem in finding a home base even if it wasn't one of ours or the Europeans. I tell you, son, the goddamned Russians are the ones I have real doubts about because of Pazukhin's tie-up with Frontier. The Asians don't trust Hammond but aren't willing to come down on one side or the other for the time being. One thing I'm glad of – our planet-wide communications have remained secure. Nobody has blown the whistle on my conversations - otherwise I expect we'd have had a reaction from upstairs.'

'Aren't the Russians concerned about our military?' I asked.

'Yes, most of them are but they're waiting for a word from Pazukhin. Then again, a few feel it's not so much a problem for them as it is for the authorities on Earth or the International Council.'

'That I find difficult to believe,' I said. 'Let's hope it doesn't take another disaster to bring them to their senses.' Those were words I would soon have cause to remember.

There was one situation in our favour at the time however and Joe had seen it from the beginning. As Virgil Hammond had shuttled his cronies up into orbit together with the armed men he needed to take control of the space station, it meant there could be very few if any of them left on the ground. His plan would have been rolling along just fine if Karin and I hadn't wriggled out of his clutches.

At daybreak I was lifting off with a cargo destined for Europa Six. You may recall that was the base at Sinai plateau where I'd been headed that day when I ended up, or should I say down, in the Labyrinth. *Cassiopeia*, the big rocket from Earth, had departed late afternoon on the following day and there were no more scheduled to arrive for ninety or so days. I had company for the first stage of my journey as three of our own people were taking their leave at the European base. Inevitably, there were questions for which I had few answers - but I couldn't blame them for asking.

After Europa Six, I was to have continued due east but because of a last minute alteration to my flight plan, result of a reassigned cargo, I would instead continue south-east for another two thousand, two hundred odd kilometres, way south of the Mariner valley. Including a half-hour turn-around time at Europa Six that would give me a journey of about eight hours. It would be well through the afternoon by the time I showed up at my second destination. When the sun was lower in the sky you got to see the main feature of the place at its spectacular best - a great basalt spire rising out of the desert. The Russians had named their station after it - Chornaya Gora - the Black Mountain.

*****

Joe van Allen was again in conference when the call came on his priority channel. The features of his chief technician materialised. 'Commander, I'm sorry for the interruption but this is important.'

'Fine - what's the problem?'

'We ran an in-depth check on our communication systems as you requested. As a result we located an unauthorised device.'

'You located a what?'

'It's a relay device - a microbot probe attached to the main optical input. Someone's been monitoring our light-pulse transmissions.'

'Jesus Christ! Are you sure about that?'

'Absolutely, commander. Do you want to see it before it's removed?'

'Too damned right I do! I'll be up there in a couple of minutes!'

Joe closed his other conversations then hurried from the office. Ascending the stairs to the area above the main administration block, he emerged under the small dome where was housed the satellite communications equipment.

'That's it, commander,' said the technician, pointing to a diminutive, grey bug-shaped object flattened against but part hidden behind an optical cable that had itself been concealed by panelling.

'We think it flew in here at night, squeezed through a gap in the conduit then crawled up the cable. As we don't have a security field no one would have known about the thing until our check-up. One of our own bugs located it and flashed back a warning.'

Joe van Allen scrutinised the object as the technician continued. 'It punctured the cable then inserted a probe, somewhat like an aphid on the stem of a plant. The probe extends in far enough to intercept light-pulses but doesn't interfere with the signal. The bug processes the information then emits the message as a highly compressed, short-range radio pulse. We've logged its transmission frequencies.'

'I take it the transmitted signal was encrypted,' said Joe.

'Yes, commander, highly encrypted. Whoever was picking that signal up must have very sophisticated equipment in order to read it. This creature - device, or whatever we care to call it, is unlike anything we have on Mars as far as I'm aware, except for specialised bugs in the biodomes and the one that found this. We were concerned it might self-destruct. That could have damaged the cable but it doesn't seem programmed to do that. Back on Earth these things were used for sabotage as well as espionage.'

'Oh, were they, now,' breathed Joe, his gaze fixed upon the offending object. 'And it transmits only limited range, you say – possibly no further than this base?'

'Hardly further than the main complex, commander. It deactivated itself as soon as it sensed it was detected then attempted to hide behind the pipe work.'

'Yeah,' breathed Joe, 'I'll bet it did.'

'D'you have any idea where it might have originated, commander? We can find no means of identification. We can't say how long it's been here so it could be hours, days, even weeks. We're continuing further checks in case there are more of them.'

'Oh, I doubt you'll find any more - and I don't think it's been here very long, fortunately. And, yes, I have a pretty good idea who the owner is.'

'Really - who?' asked the technician, reaching out a gloved hand in which was poised a pair of plastic tweezers.

'I'll let you know in due course,' answered Joe, watching intently as the technician extracted the now wriggling object from the cable to place it inside a small transparent capsule. 'But just for now, let me say it belongs to the lowest form of life that ever crawled on this or any other planet.' Turning to leave, he added, 'And when I get hold of him I'm going to flog his lousy hide around the station before I have him shipped down to the goddamned south polar cap for the next ten years! And I mean Martian years!'

***

'So you think you can walk into my base and hijack my communications do you, Roy? That is highly illegal - you do know that, don't you? You're damned lucky I came off the boil before you were rounded up. Why, I'd be quite within my rights in having you strip-searched, body-scanned then locked away so you see no one and go nowhere

254

until this – until this whole goddamned mess blows over!'

'Commander Van Allen - I'm on your side. I have to do my job as best I can but I *am* on your side in all this - believe me!'

Joe faced him as Roy perched rigidly upright in the chair, eyes shifting about, nervous hands thrust out of sight beneath the edge of the desk.

'Roy, whoever's side you're on - and no way can I be sure about that - you do not under *any* circumstances tap into base communications. Certainly not on my territory you don't! The situation is not good right now and it may get a lot worse. The last thing I will tolerate, Roy, is having our security compromised and I don't intend to let you out of here to carry on doing it somewhere else.'

'Maybe I can help to -.' began Roy.

'Maybe nothing!' cut in Joe. 'For all I know, you could be in the pay of Frontier Mining as well as SolaNews. You seem to get yourself flown about this planet far easier than almost anyone else and I can't help asking myself how and why. Until this is over, your goddamned equipment stays locked away and you, Roy - you stay confined to this base.'

'But, SolaNews -,' began Roy, 'I still have to do my job. It's what they -.'

'I don't give a damn about SolaNews,' cut in Joe, leaning closer to narrow-eye Roy, 'just as I don't give a damn about Frontier Mining, the Consortium or Virgil blasted Hammond! Now I am not a vindictive man by nature, Roy, so you still have freedom of the ground floor recreation areas as well as the biodome. But on *no* account will you go

255

near the upper levels, nor will you pester *any* of my staff.' Joe rose from his chair to add with uncharacteristic gravity, 'If I find you've done either, Roy, I promise you'll be thrown into an auxiliary airlock and kept on a diet of bread and water just the way they did with old time criminals. Now get your lousy ass out of my office before I find something creative to do with my boots!'

***

Because my flight path south had taken us over the Labyrinth, it needed but a small detour to pass over the canyon where I had earlier experienced that bizarre encounter. I felt compelled to take another look whilst understandably, my curiosity was shared by my three passengers. Magnifying the image, however, showed no evidence of anyone having been down there. I wondered if the cargo container or whatever was left of it might be lost in shadow, but I didn't really believe that.

After a quick bite to eat during which time the cargo pod was exchanged, I lifted clear of Europa Six with a new load. Swinging about over the base, I watched the desert tilt back and forth as Delta Seven locked herself on course for Chornaya Gora. Alone for this stage of the journey, I tried to call Karin only to find she was in conference. I considered that was probably a good thing and hoped she was continuing to get a positive response from her people. It was earlier in the day at Karin's station as Europa Four was some three and a half thousand kilometres to the west of my position. I did contact Leo, though. He was flying on the night side, way up north over the great expanse of the Elysium plain. He was glad to hear from me.

'Hi, Brett, buddy!' he responded with that ever dependable grin. 'How're you doing over there on the sunny side?'

I did my best to fill him in over what had been going on - including a detailed account of our escape from the space station. I made out, though, that I couldn't figure why they had tried to stop us leaving - that perhaps it was an overreaction by those two thugs of Hammond's – something personal because of what had happened earlier in the recreation area. Of Ingvar Svendsen, I said nothing. Although my transmissions were routed via our base and meant to be secure, I was concerned over the possibility of Virgil Hammond's technicians looking to unscramble them. Had I been the General I'd be attempting to do exactly that. Maybe Leo sensed my unease because he didn't press me further over the subject, letting our conversation drift instead onto other areas.

'When all this is over, old buddy, I say we have ourselves one hell of a party - you, me, the two girls and anyone else who wants to join in.'

'Sounds a great idea,' I replied, 'but I have a feeling our party may be some way off, yet.'

'Well, perhaps we can get in a little golfing practice, meantime. And there are the teams I've been working to organise - I reckon we could get moving on it next time I touch home base.'

'I thought you might have given up on that for the time being.'

Again, the grin as he shook his head. 'Oh, no, no, no! Remember I talked about intelligent golf balls? Well I had a consignment of them arrive on *Cassiopeia*. They're the ones that emit their own signals then pop up so you can find them when they get lost in the sand. They were ordered over a year ago and I can tell you, buddy, it cost me a fortune in credits to get them out here. I spoke to some of the guys in our workshops a good while back and we have a deal going. They're already turning out sets of irons and from time to time I throw in a few bottles of vodka. Kurt Hoffman tipped me off about the booze operation so now I have a deal going with the Russians over something else. My golfing plans will be out in the open soon, you see. The only problem could be when Uncle Joe finds out what's been going on.'

'That's an easy one to get around,' I answered. 'You present him with a set of clubs and make him captain. He won't dare say anything after that.'

'Er - right, but what if he doesn't play golf?'

'Then you offer to teach him for free,' I answered. 'You know Joe as well as I do - he'll more than likely give it a try.'

'Okay, done! Then the next thing will be matting for the greens. Somewhere on this lousy planet there has to be matting - preferably green matting. I saw some once on my travels but I'm damned if I can remember where it was.'

'Yeah, I know the stuff you mean. I think they used it at some of the Asian bases. They had it laid down in their recreation areas for a time then it disappeared. If it's still lying about somewhere, maybe we could negotiate.'

Like Helen, you might think all this was crazy. It seemed that way to me as I stared out from the pod and saw little more than featureless desert with the occasional crater drifting beneath. We were living on the biggest sand bunker in the solar system but Leo wasn't letting that get in the way. We would have continued with the subject at greater length but when he was contacted by Helen I thought it best to close. Before signing off, though, I agreed to give serious consideration to his proposed golfing venues over the next few days, in spite of what was happening.

Alone once more I checked the navigation and saw that I had no more than a half hour before reaching my destination. The horizon was obscured by a pink haze but I would keep my eyes peeled for I expected that soon enough the basalt spire, the so-called Black Mountain, would appear.

***

D'mitri relaxed against the low-loader and gazed across desert emptiness. He and the tractor man had spent the previous ten minutes in idle conversation, knowing they would not be observed from the administration building. They had finished re-arranging cargo pallets and empty containers on the far side of the landing strip and the tractor man was about to climb into his vehicle. D'mitri was musing upon the less practical aspects of life when his companion's voice elbowed aside his thoughts. 'There is a flight coming in soon D'mitri. We should return now or we'll be denied access to the runway.'

'Oh, we can stay here until the wingship is down,' yawned D'mitri. 'Who is worrying?'

'I can't hang around any longer,' said the tractor man. 'I have to be over there getting on with my work before the wingship arrives. I don't want

Nikolayev on my back again. You can do as you please until the cargo needs taking off.'

D'mitri watched the blue pressure-suited figure haul himself into the steel frame of the tractor cabin then set off toward the runway, raising fine sand into a golden sky. D'mitri would stay where he was then cross the runway once the aircraft was down. In the meantime, alone with his thoughts, it would be an excuse to do nothing and to speak to no one. He didn't care in the least what the conceited Nikolayev might say. And what did Nikolayev know about working on Mars? What did Nikolayev know about anything?

Staring up at the sky, D'mitri wondered, as he so often had, what it would be like if he could remove his helmet, if he could savour the air. Would it alter with the seasons? Would it change from night to day? Would it smell of iron from the rocks or sulphur from those giant volcanoes? Would there be a tang of ancient mountains, of distant ice caps, of long vanished seas? He wished he could smoke a cigarette. They might be illegal on Earth yet everyone knew where to get them. But not on Mars. This world was devoid of cigarettes and so much else yet his contract still had over a year to run, even if it was only an Earth year. Life could be burdensome but at least there was Katya. Sometimes there was Katya.

The wind sighed through his microphones. He peered up at the sheer walls of the black mountain rising skyward beyond the main complex. At its summit, if he used his visor magnification, he could make out a crown of wind-sculpted pinnacles. D'mitri imagined himself walking amongst them to gaze out across the complex to the cratered expanse beyond. What a view that would be. What if he found himself marooned up there alone with no one to help? He tried to imagine how he would feel if he could not get down – a truly horrifying thought. But then, how could anyone get to the top in the first place unless -.

'D'mitri Mikhailovitch.'

'Who -?' D'mitri turned, shaken from his reverie. A figure in white pressure suit stood watching him by the front of the low-loader.

'Katya - what the hell are you doing here? I thought -.'

'Aren't you glad I came D'mitri?'

'Glad - of course I'm glad, but why did no one tell me - why did you not call me first? I thought you were still working at the out-station.'

'I wanted to catch you by surprise, D'mitri. I know you like surprises. I know how bored you are with this world. Our ground vehicle brought me back a short time ago. When they told me you were busy over here I kept my pressure suit. So - here I am.'

Greatly puzzled, D'mitri questioned her again about her unscheduled presence. His lovely, dark-eyed Katarina seemed reluctant to disclose the reason for her early return to Chornaya Gora until they were indoors together but there was still the cargo to deal with once the wingship had landed. Puzzlement gave way to concern when he saw her close her eyes, place one hand against the side of the low-loader and pass the other across her visor.

'Katya, are you all right?'

'D'mitri,' she replied, backing away, 'there is something wrong with my air supply, please - I need to go back. We must return at once.'

'What! How can there be anything wrong with that? Did the suit monitor not alert you?'

But as the anxious D'mitri moved toward her she stumbled to the cabin of the low-loader, grasped the handrail then lifted a foot to the first step. Intending to help, he started forward but she was already pulling herself into the vehicle. As he hurried around to the other side her voice rang inside his helmet. 'D'mitri, my breathing! It is so difficult!'

In seconds D'mitri was beside her in the cabin, his engine whining into life. On full power, the low-loader lurched forward. It was swinging around toward the strip when D'mitri hesitated and changed direction. 'Katya, crossing the runway is forbidden – there's a wingship coming in!'

'D'mitri it is getting worse. Quickly D'mitri! I cannot breath - ah - ah, I cannot -!'

How could he doubt his Katya was not in distress, that her situation was not becoming desperate? To drive around the end of the runway would take too much time and for the same reason there was no point in calling for help. In a panic, D'mitri swung the heavy vehicle about then headed up the rise to the runway. Metres from the edge, the engine died and the low-loader shuddered to a stop on its tracks. 'Katya, the security field has cut our motor! We must walk across the strip! We must hurry - Katya!'

'D'mitri - I have - no – air.' Her voice echoed loud as if she was calling from the depths of a cavern. 'No more air - no more air - no more air!'

D'mitri knew what all drivers knew but should not have known. D'mitri did what no driver should ever do. He entered the emergency over-ride code then restarted the engine. He was blind to warning lights, deaf to the alarm signal as her voice compelled him onward. In a cascade of desert rubble the low-loader surged forward over the rise then pitched onto the now forbidden zone.

In the control room they watched the aircraft catch afternoon sun as, flared out, she descended on final approach, her landing gear down. She sped low over the desert, aligned, locked in electronic precision with the runway.

'She has a heavy cargo,' said the girl at the control desk. 'Does anyone know what she is carrying?'

'More mining equipment, probably,' replied one. 'That's all that comes in here since Nikolayev took over. It's about time they sent over some decent -.'

The urgent rhythm of the alarm had their heads turning as one to the main display. Already it flashed a pair of red, pulsating circles. Circles that converged remorselessly before the eyes of those who did not wish to believe what they were seeing.

'Who is that idiot on the runway!' someone called. 'Get him off! Get him off!'

'It's D'mitri!' shouted another. 'He does not respond to the warnings! He has bypassed his safety system! He will not answer!'

The wingship's sensors had also spotted the low-loader as it drove onto the strip. It had registered the alert with her pilot as it had with the base. With her landing wheels but a metre above the ground, the ship's own systems had initiated emergency procedure before the pilot could act. Turbines powered up with demonic howl, rocket boosters roared vivid flame, her cargo container ejected clear, hitting the strip with a glancing blow as the wingship began to lift. Careering along like a sled, there was nothing to stop the container until it met its first obstacle. It slammed into the rear end of the low-loader, spinning it about, then sprang upward in the throes of disintegration to strike with violent impact against the right wing of the aircraft passing directly overhead. Her nose rising, the big aircraft heeled over with graceful ease, the tip of her left wing spewing rubble as it tore into the ground. Losing height, jetting fire at her rear, she staggered then veered aside amidst a raging vortex of sand.

No one in the control room counted those fatal seconds as the wingship careered insanely on. With dreamlike slowness she drifted from the runway. In unreal silence they watched her plough into the main storage building, rending the facade in a welter of metal tissue before being consumed within its vast space. The building erupted with volcanic rage, was obliterated in a boiling incandescence from which a kaleidoscope of glowing lights emerged to spiral skyward, to dance crazily within a turmoil of smoke.

* * *

I was circling three kilometres away, losing height, flaring out when I saw the fireball rise.

264

Smoke billowed outward in the thin air with wreckage spinning in all directions. I'd witnessed the deep-frozen horror of Europa Six but nothing could have prepared me for this vision of flaming destruction. I powered back up but kept on circling, my attention locked onto that incredible, mind-numbing sight.

Nothing burns in the Martian air so it was pretty obvious what had happened. Their liquid oxygen reserves had been in that building; tonnes of the stuff in large storage vessels. The wingship, the building, everything inside had burned explosively. It could easily have been me swallowed by that inferno. It was unusual for two aircraft to arrive anywhere so close together so I'd gone into a holding pattern to let the Asian pilot land first. His was a scheduled flight and he'd been ahead of me. What jerked me back to another reality was Delta Seven grabbing control to alter our course as she howled out a warning. I'd been heading straight for that damned spire of black rock. It was about to claim its first victim!

There were voices from the control room in the stricken base below; voices calling to each other, voices telling me to keep clear. From my vantage point it looked like the main part of the complex, the pressurised sections, had escaped the worst of it. Certainly their biodome, furthest away from the storage building, appeared to be unharmed as the pall of smoke started to thin out. It was evident, too, that Delta Seven wouldn't be able to land because of debris and the half-demolished low-loader on the strip, so I had them agree that I pancake the pallet down alongside the runway. At least the cargo would be recovered once they were feeling inclined to do that. As I drifted in low to release the container the air was clear enough for me to observe the devastation close up. The storage building was ripped apart, wide open to the sky. Of the wingship, there was nothing recognisable to be seen amongst blackened wreckage.

Understandably shocked when the Russian base issued a planet-wide emergency call, Joe's image was forming as I gained altitude. 'Get clear of there, son. Get yourself straight back here!'

After I set course for home my next priorities were to contact Karin and Leo for they both would know about this soon enough. Ahead of me was another seven and a half-hours haul so it would be well into the night before I landed back at Novamerica One. The air was alive with news about what had happened to the Russians with everybody quick off the mark to offer help where help seemed possible. There was one source, however, whose total silence no one could fail to register. The space station.

That made a number of people think real hard.

During my return journey, details of what had caused the accident were becoming known. If that ship had left the runway further along, she would have smashed into the administration building and maybe damaged the biodome. It had almost been goodbye Black Mountain and they knew it. As it was, nine people were killed, including the pilot, but the guy who drove the low-loader onto the strip survived unharmed, physically, that is. Very soon his story was out. The female friend the driver imagined he'd had on board was still at one of their out-stations. She'd been there all along. I understood well enough what had happened. So did a good many others.

Later on I tried to catch up with some sleep but with little success. What I had witnessed still burned brightly in my mind.

***

It was past twenty-three hundred hours when I arrived back over our base. To my surprise there was another wingship lifting clear. I watched her lights move against the blackness of the desert then rise up to merge with the stars and I wondered at the purpose of this unscheduled flight. It wasn't until I was down and through the airlock, however, that I discovered the turn things had taken. As I walked from the inner doors, my helmet swinging from one hand, my small case gripped in the other, there was a figure heading toward me under the concourse lights. A figure wearing a blue crew suit and a big smile. Two reactions gripped me in rapid succession. The first was a more than pleasant surprise at seeing her back again so unexpectedly but the second had me stop dead in my tracks.

'Brett, what is the matter?' she asked, hesitating wide-eyed before me.

'Karin, I -. What are you doing here right now? Why are you -.'

'Oh, Brett,' she answered, the smile returning to her face. Stepping up close, she kissed me. 'There, it really is me. Satisfied now?'

There was no mistaking her warmth, no mistaking the sensual perfume of her breath. 'Fine,' I shrugged, 'if it isn't you and you're this convincing then we humans stand no chance at all. I give up.'

'My flight came in half an hour ago,' she said as we walked over to the pressure suit storage room. 'My people have stopped all but essential operations because of what has happened. I think everyone is doing the same. As soon as Joe found out he arranged to get me on that flight over here for your sake as well as mine. He's a good man, Brett – really he is.'

'I won't disagree with that.'

'He's waiting for us now. There are things you have to know about - things he did not wish to discuss over the radio.'

**

'I couldn't say anything until you were back with us,' said Joe, 'because we, the Europeans, all remaining base commanders and acting commanders planet-wide are communicating only via light-pulse relay for maximum security. You'll be glad to hear, after this latest calamity, that we are now in complete agreement as regards deep level drilling – as well as keeping out Hammond's military.'

'I'll say I'm glad, Joe. After seeing what I did at the Black Mountain that has to be good news.'

'Your remark yesterday about another disaster, Brett - it came true, didn't it. It turns out that wingship was delivering advanced technology drilling equipment and my guess is the natives knew all about it. Anyhow, that new guy in charge at the Black Mountain – Nikolayev – did some soul searching over his relationship with Pazukhin and Hammond, especially as he couldn't get any response from either of those jokers for some time after it happened. When he did, they just told him to hang on in there until help arrives. The Asians were none too impressed with Liang's lack or response either, since they lost a pilot and a wingship. I figure we're lucky the General and none of his crew up there ever had a lesson in public relations. In the meantime, yours truly has been voted mouthpiece for the colonies and -.'

'But that's great, Joe,' I interrupted. 'For the first time we have our own voice. We can tell Hammond and his cronies to -.'

'Hold on there, son! The agreement so far is only at command level for security reasons. We can't be sure there are no committed Frontier Mining people still hanging about on the surface, though somehow I doubt they'd be in a position to do much harm without being caught out. The delay in our going public will give everyone in authority time to evaluate their personnel and their internal security.' Joe moved from his desk to procure the inevitable but welcome cups of strong coffee before continuing. 'A couple hours ago, I beamed a formal message up to the space station. The two of you may as well hear it exactly as it went out.'

I watched his image materialise, looking as grave as I ever saw him but at the same time purposeful and dignified. Only Karin and I were present but no one could have had a more attentive audience as Joe's recorded image began to speak.

'By unanimous agreement I, Joseph van Allen, have been nominated to address the representatives of the International Council, of Frontier Mining and of its Consortium associates on behalf of the

269

colonists on Mars. Whilst recognising the seriousness of what has happened and the dangers we face here on the surface, the colonies reject outright any intention to place armed men on this planet for whatever purpose. I repeat - for *whatever* purpose. Should such an attempt be made, access to all base facilities and provisions as well as to ground and air transport will be denied. As for the use of deep level plasma drills. All such operations have, of today, ceased and all relevant equipment is deactivated. We believe this course of action is necessary to avoid further loss of human life through interaction with the life forms that exist upon or within this world. We believe also that our inability to communicate with Earth is the result of a deliberate act, which means those responsible are most certainly in breach of international law. Further transmissions from the space station will be accepted and acknowledged only via myself at Novamerica One.'

Karin and I were silent for a time after the image faded. At last she remarked, 'Well, I have to say, Joe, that sounded very well-rehearsed.'

'That's because it *was* rehearsed' he smiled. 'It's the wording I and others agreed upon so - well, that's it, we've done it. We've made our first big decision as a community. We've spoken out for our own interests even if it is only amongst a relative few.'

'Has there been any response?' I asked.

Joe waved his hand with a dismissive laugh. 'Oh, sure - there's been a response - hasn't there just! Within ten minutes I had the merry trio all to myself. Virgil Hammond did his best to remain calm as he informed me that I and those with me were simply misguided and didn't know what we were talking about. Even the two thugs who attacked you and Karin up there he claimed was a misunderstanding. He offered me the chance to back down and let bygones be bygones. I told him no deal unless we could contact Earth.'

'They're stalling for time,' I said.

'I guess they are,' agreed Joe. 'Hammond said he'd have no option but to have me replaced if I didn't change my mind but we all know things have gone way beyond that. Pazukhin started banging the table and Liang appeared about to have a coronary. They actually pulled in Adelle to lay on the charm. She was cool all right but I believe she knows little of what is really going on. When I demanded to speak with Amalia Barbosa, Hammond informed me she was beginning her rest period so we'd have to wait. At that point I told them we would only continue dialogue when she was available, then I signed off.'

'We should have asserted ourselves a long time ago,' I said. 'The majority of us belong on this world. The likes of Hammond are sent out to make sure we all behave ourselves whilst Earth milks the planet dry. In his case we get the screwball missionary thrown in as well. It's pretty ironic we have to be under threat of being wiped out before the idea of having some control over our own affairs catches on.'

'And even more ironic,' put in Karin, 'that some of our own people are bringing this down on us.'

271

'Let's hope everyone keeps steadfast,' sighed Joe. 'Let's hope no one weakens and lets the military in through the back door. If that happens, I don't see any of us being around for too long afterwards - no, sir. If Hammond's gang don't have our hides then the goddamned Martians, or whatever they are, surely will.'

'Frankly, Joe,' I added, '*Aurora* will determine the fate of us all unless we have a few lucky cards in our hands but I'm not sure right now who will be dealing.'

CHAPTER 7
THE OMEN OF DAWN

During the night there arrived that for which we had so anxiously awaited: the first light-pulse transmission from Ingvar Svendsen. Joe relayed it to Karin and me the following morning whilst we were readying ourselves for another uncertain day. Viewing the image, you couldn't tell whereabouts on the space station Svendsen had been when he sent the message because it was too dark. His voice was low, his face close-up as though he was afraid someone might be hanging around nearby.

As we listened to what he had to say, there could be little doubt he was scared.

'I have been unable to speak until now because I'm sure they suspect me. You should know it is not *Aurora's* engines that have been blocking dialogue with Earth. She has positioned a mobile beacon in space between the two planets. This can only be de-activated by a code from *Aurora* or from Hammond himself.

Take note, please - Hammond's technicians are trying to disrupt Marsnet. They have not succeeded so far because I have reconfigured the limited equipment at their disposal up here to make things more difficult. They are sure equipment on *Aurora* will enable them to do it so you should take whatever measures you are able to protect yourselves. I have learned *Aurora* is also carrying deep-level penetrators with nuclear charges. They will burn down as far as the plasma drills have gone before exploding. Hammond's men will need ground facilities to operate the things because *Aurora* is not equipped to deliver them directly. You must not allow this to happen!' Glancing nervously about, his image backed away from us. 'I'll attempt to speak again later. Remember, *Aurora* is only two days away!'

***

One of the things Karin and I speculated over as we ate breakfast in the biodome cafe was why we'd had no need to fend off Roy Kendrick. The pleasure yet awaited us, myself in particular, of learning about the misfortune Roy had called down upon himself over the bugging episode.

Early that same morning Joe requested everyone's attention to reveal officially the situation as Karin and I already understood it, in good part through our own experience. Planet-wide, as the light of dawn spread across each time zone, the colonies were waking up to the same message. In no time, the air was alive with babble and many of our personnel seemed to be temporarily off duty. People gathered in the recreation areas and in the biodomes to discuss the implications. Messages were flying around the planet, official and unofficial, with rumour yapping hard at the heels of humankind.

The attempt to block planetary communications was something Joe did not mention; likewise the nuclear penetrators. That was to help protect our source of information and avoid forcing the General's hand in case he had something more drastic up his sleeve.

On a world where you don't just step outside and stroll off to visit the neighbours, the implications of losing our satellite network were not good, especially since there is nothing in the Martian atmosphere from which to bounce radio waves. Karin and I were discussing matters with Joe a little later when he confirmed a part of what Ingvar Svendsen had told us. 'Our people have locked onto *Aurora's* position in deep space – she creates a powerful electromagnetic field, like a scream in the night you might say. We pinpointed the radio beacon as well, and it's clear the two are diverging from a single point. Svendsen was right about that one and I'm damn certain he'll be right about the penetrators.'

We were headed down pathways of further speculation when his communications indicated an incoming call from the space station. We had no doubt it was Virgil Hammond so Joe filtered out Karin and myself from vision in case our presence influenced what the general was about to say. It was evident as soon as his image materialised that he was wearing his diplomacy hat, even if it was a lousy fit. But then I was biased. There, too, was that placid Buddha smile.

'Commander Van Allen,' he began. 'In view of your recent broadcast to the colonies, I respectfully suggest we consider our respective positions. To remain in disagreement amongst ourselves cannot be in the interests of our people in these perilous times. May I continue?'

'Sure - go ahead,' responded Joe, relaxing in his seat.

'Thank you, Commander. I will be frank and say first of all that we - I, must bear much of the blame for the misunderstandings that have arisen between us. Some of my earlier remarks may not have reflected my true intentions. Decisions have had to be taken in the interests of security and the common good but I realise that through pressure of circumstance, I and others may have appeared too hasty in some of our actions.' The actions of Rigby and Milligan popped into my head as he continued. 'It was never our intention to create dissent. I regret you considered it necessary to take the measures you have but I do in part understand why you felt obliged to do so. I also know you have the backing of many of the colonists. In view of that I suggest we work to achieve a reasonable accord before matters develop which might give cause for regret on both sides.'

'I'm all in favour of reasonable accords, Chief - you know that.'

'Indeed I do, Commander Van Allen,' Hammond smiled. 'Indeed I do.'

He'd now pinned on the smile he'd worn when Karin and I took leave of his conference on the space station. I didn't expect that would fool Joe.

'Then,' continued Joe, 'we can sort matters out between you, me, Amalia Barbosa and the International Council on Earth - once I can talk to them, that is. And you could hold *Aurora* back for the time being as a good-will gesture. How about that?'

'I'm afraid, Commander, that dialogue with *Aurora* is not possible for those same technical reasons that prevent our contact with Earth. As for Secretary Barbosa, I expect she will be able to join our conversation in due course.'

'Then what are you asking me to do, Chief?'

'As a gesture of co-operation, Commander, you should agree to the opening of base facilities when our team arrives. They are UAS personnel and are coming here for the benefit of the colonists.'

'Well, Chief, if you were intending to be frank, there are one or two points where you have fallen somewhat short, in my humble opinion. I don't see a basis for any kind of deal at this time.'

'But surely, Commander, now *is* the time to reach an agreement. Things cannot remain as they are. What purpose can there be in prolonging this situation in the face of the inevitable. Really, Commander Van Allen, it is my sincere wish that you accept my offer of a cordial settlement.

'What purpose do I have? Well, I'll tell you, Mr Chief Executive. It's not because of *Aurora* but through that goddamned space beacon we detected. That's why we've had no contact with Earth for three days, as well you know.' With mention of the beacon, Hammond's smile promptly quit its nest and his expression hardened.

'More lives have been lost down here,' Joe continued, 'and like it or not, we were obliged to make our own decisions. We had to stop all deep level drilling in order to protect ourselves and I figure you won't need to ask why. As for *Aurora,* we don't want those people down here and we most certainly don't need what she has on board.'

'Commander Van Allen.' replied Hammond, his voice calm but cold. 'You have taken on a great deal: unofficial representative for the UAS and others who have nothing whatsoever to do with you, as well as interfering with the operations of an enterprise in which all major governments on Earth have considerable interest. Well, Commander, that is a substantial responsibility indeed. I do hope you are fully aware of the implications, for implications there surely are. Mars is a gift to mankind, Commander Van Allen, do you not understand? It is a second chance! I cannot allow those things to get in the way of -.'

'"I," Chief?' cut in Joe. 'I wasn't aware you were responsible for colonial affairs. That prerogative surely belongs to Secretary Barbosa, with whom I have still not been allowed an interview. As for "those things," I assume you are referring to the intelligent life form we have encountered on this world. A life form that appears to have been around a great deal longer than you, me, Frontier Mining and the goddamned Consortium!'

Hammond's face darkened. 'Intelligent, Commander? Intelligent! They have destroyed an entire base. They are murderous, unthinking degenerates. They are a blasphemy, Commander Van Allen! A blasphemy you are helping to uphold!' His image moved closer. 'If we do not put a stop to them, the colonies on Mars could be wiped out! Wiped out entirely, Commander - do you not understand that?'

'We've been spreading ourselves across this planet for well over a century,' replied Joe, his voice rising as he spoke though he showed little sign of anger. 'In all that time they stayed out of our affairs. They've stayed out until *you* came along with deep level drills that probably burned through their kitchen ceiling. For all I know or for all you seem to care we might have incinerated thousands of them. Now you come up with some lunatic plan to poke nuclear penetrators into the goddamned crust! Just what do you think -.'

'Van Allen!' he snapped. 'Where did you get that information?'

'Never you mind where I got it. Think about some of the people you trust up there. Maybe one or two of your closest pals don't see things your way and decided to shoot off their mouths. Now perhaps you wouldn't mind moving over so the Administrator for Colonial Affairs can get into the act. And maybe you could have them knock off that beacon so we can talk to the folks back on Earth. Do that and maybe we have our deal!'

Hammond regarded him for tense moments before speaking. 'I will inform Secretary Barbosa of your request. You, Commander Van Allen, still have time to reconsider your position - but not much. The matter will be decided once and for all when *Aurora* arrives. Earth will thank me for it, Commander. I am the one person striving to preserve the interests of the home planet. The resources of Mars are too important for mere sentiment to alter matters. Our future on this world is pre-ordained by one far greater than us all. Commander Van Allen, mark my words. Mark them well!'

'Well, that's that,' sighed Joe as the image faded. 'It's pre-ordained, evidently.

'The guy is nuts,' I muttered.

'He will know there's someone up there working against him now.' Karin added.

'Yes,' replied Joe, 'but hopefully, the way I put it will make him suspect one of his own cronies -

not Ingvar Svendsen. And I needed at this point to let him know we're aware of what he's up to.'

Whilst we were talking, Joe had the interview relayed planet-wide. We hoped informing everyone about the beacon and the penetrators would serve to undermine any intentions Hammond harboured of trying to win back the minds of the colonists.

***

As we walked hand in hand through the biodome amidst trees and perfumed flowers, I said to Karin, 'What he must have told people back on Earth to justify the beacon I don't know. Maybe it was a case of, "leave it all to me - no outside interference and I'll sort the problems out my way." It might suit a good few people who stand to lose if Frontier and the rest of them have to wind down their deep-level operations. On the other hand I don't see the International Council backing a proposal like that.'

'Someone has to lose, Brett. Virgil Hammond thinks it will be us because when *Aurora* arrives he will cut the rest of our communications so his men can find a way in. What can we do? We know he is prepared to kill but we have no means of defending ourselves. Once every station is isolated it can only be a matter of time - then what will become of us?'

Karin was right – someone had to lose. But whatever happened, Earth would still need Martian resources. The home planet, including the IC, would still have to deal with whoever was in charge no matter what crimes had been committed.

On reaching the central fountain we sat down to continue talking. I had never seen so many people in the biodome before. That made the absence of

Roy Kendrick even more perplexing though I didn't let it play on my mind for too long. Shafts of sunlight fell through the trees, lit up the grass and danced upon water playing from the fountain. Coloured birds, calling to each other, flitted from bush to bush whilst the two small animals who recognised me chased each other about our seat much to Karin's amusement.

'Hey,' came a voice from over the pathway, 'there's the pilot who met the Martians!'

Three children came dashing over - two little boys, faces bright with enthusiasm, and an older girl who, following close behind, seemed to be in charge of them. The boys hovered a few steps away, staring at me as though I'd walked straight out of one of their epics. The older of the two moved closer and asked, 'What do the Martians look like, mister? Are they bigger than us?'

'My dad says he really didn't see them at all,' put in the girl, blandly.

'Well, yes and no,' I replied. 'The one I met was disguised as a human being so I don't know what they really look like.'

'There, what did I say,' added the girl, folding her arms smugly, 'nobody's ever seen them properly except for a dead one and that doesn't count.'

The two boys gazed at me as though I'd just handed them the biggest disappointment of their lives. Then the second one asked, 'Are you going to fly out there and blast them to bits before they hit us again?'

'That's not so easy,' I replied. 'We don't have any weapons on Mars and I figure they live out of sight most of the time.'

'It would be a mistake for anyone to do that anyway,' added Karin.

'Why?' asked the first boy. 'That's what happens to aliens when they kill humans.'

'I guess if they've always lived here,' I replied, 'they're not the aliens - we are.'

'Do they have rockets and wingships like ours?' asked the second boy.

'What a stupid question,' put in the girl, glancing upward in mock despair.

'No,' I answered, 'I don't reckon they can fly at all. We'd have seen them a long time ago if they could. Years before the first people even came here.'

'My dad flew wingships on Earth,' said the girl, pushing back her hair. 'He says they go much faster than the ones we have here.'

'Yeah, mister,' came the second boy with renewed enthusiasm, 'why don't they make our wingships go the same speed as the ones on Earth then we could catch them on the surface?'

'Well, they can go faster if needs be but it isn't a good idea. The speed of sound is over a third slower on Mars than it is on Earth and remember, there's no oxygen. A wingship would need to use her rockets to travel at high speed and that would waste a lot of expensive fuel.'

'There, I told you, didn't I,' said the girl, folding her arms once more whilst regarding the two boys with a well-practiced expression of disdain.

'Have you ever flown with your rockets?' asked the first boy.

'Sure - now and then,' I answered, 'there was one time not so long ago when I had to -.'

'Come along, you kids!' called a woman standing close by the fountain. 'Those people don't want you hanging around!'

That was the end of my small audience. All three turned without another word to scamper off quickly as they had come. As we watched them chase spider bots around the fountain I recalled there were kids just like these playing in the biodome at Europa Six when disaster struck.

'Brett, dear,' smiled Karin, 'you're becoming a celebrity. 'They'll soon be asking you to sign autographs like those old-time movie stars.'

One of them had just referred to me as, "the pilot who met the Martians." That churned up a thought that I wish had surfaced earlier. A thought that now seemed entirely obvious. I turned to Karin. 'There is something we haven't considered yet - something that could turn out to be most important of all in the end.'

'What d'you mean?' she asked, taking hold of my hand.

'The Martians themselves, that's what I mean.'

She appeared puzzled. 'We know nothing of them, Brett, except that they create illusions and they are willing to kill. And if Hammond has his way, there may be nothing left to know.'

'It seems certain they're able to enter our bases at will. Maybe they've been in and out of here since the day we opened for business. We know they can get into our minds - at least I do, and so does that

283

poor guy at the Russian base. They must long ago have figured out pretty well everything about us. Maybe they watched the first humans arrive. Maybe they even checked out the first robot probes. They must have been studying us ever since. Karin, I believe they have a presence within this base right now. I can't explain why but I know it as sure as we're sitting here. They're watching and they're waiting.'

She stared at me. I was again aware of the sounds and the colours around us, of the sunlight on her hair. 'Brett,' she asked quietly, 'are you suggesting we try to talk with them? You are, aren't you?'

'Yes, Karin, that is what I'm suggesting. I managed to do it for a time. I'm convinced now it's what they wanted me to do in the canyon. Down there, when that – that being was you, she - it, begged me to listen but I wouldn't. Right now, I'm wondering if it isn't the only chance we have of finding a way out of this mess. I sure can't think of any other.'

'How, Brett? How do we communicate with something we can't even see? How can we know where they are.'

'Oh, I think if we want them to find us they will. It's as though the idea's been here in my mind for a long time - like it was following me, like it was waiting for me to turn around and see the obvious. Tell you the truth, Karin, I'm not entirely convinced it ever was my idea.'

'You mean they could have suggested it?'

'I can't see that would present them with too many difficulties - do you?'

'No, Brett,' she sighed, 'I don't suppose it would.'

***

It was late evening when we re-entered the biodome. I had determined to go back there alone but Karin wasn't having it and would have followed me no matter what. The air smelled deliciously fresh after a recent shower. It looked as though everyone had left before the rain started though as always, lights were on in the biodome café and the main restaurant. Apart from illumination above the main routes, most of the biodome was in near darkness with the atmospheric circulatory system running so low as to give only the hint of a breeze.

We strolled away from the lighted track to find ourselves on a deserted, wooded pathway beyond the central fountain. We continued on hand in hand, talking very little but aware of an occasional furtive scurrying in the darkness. Beyond the bioplast shell, high above to the south, pallid little Phobos drifted in its lonely orbit against the stars, beating a time of its own as it had through uncounted ages.

'We should go further along,' Karin suggested. 'There are more trees over that way. It will be too wet for anyone to be about.'

'Don't be so sure,' I began, recalling that day when we stayed behind to get soaked in the rain. 'Maybe the Martians were snooping around last time when we -.'

'Now, now,' she smiled, squeezing my hand as we walked on. 'Even if they were watching us it might not have meant that much to them. At least I hope not.'

Insects began to chirp close by and Karin squeezed my hand tighter. Every sound seemed portentous with both our minds wide open to suggestion, however slight. After a while, having walked around three quarters the way across the biodome, the chirping stopped. We stood in darkness, waiting. Amongst the trees were vague sounds I took to be small nocturnal animals rummaging about in the undergrowth. But that quietened as well, though there was still an occasional patter of water dripping from the leaves. I wondered if her heart was beating any harder than mine and in the stillness I lost all sense of time. I know we shared the same feeling – one of tense expectation verging upon irrational fear.

'Brett,' whispered Karin, her hand gripping mine like a vice, 'there's something -.'

I heard it, too - a rustling as if someone pushed through the undergrowth close by. We glanced at each other then stared hard into obscurity. For a while I thought the night must be playing tricks with us. Whether my memory is leading me on now or not it's hard to say, but I sensed we were no longer alone.

Moments later I was damned sure of it.

'Brett we will speak with you.'

It sounded close though we could see nothing. 'This could be it,' I breathed.

Karin grabbed my arm with her free hand. 'Brett - it can't be - it -.'

'Where are you?' I asked. 'How many are here?'

'I am alone but others listen beyond the biodome. You cannot see me. I have not taken your form. I will stay as one with the darkness.'

The voice had no direction. It seemed to be everywhere around as well as inside my head – a kind of deep whisper. I knew Karin could hear it also. 'On that journey to the Labyrinth,' I began, 'the one I was with - she - it, looked like -.'

'That one had greater skills than most. Even so, when you flew in the sky it was difficult to continue without the presence of other minds. When you came into the canyon, the one with you was exhausted. That one could not maintain the illusion without our help. If you had stayed with us, you would have understood. We did not wish you to leave but another called you from the sky and you were afraid.'

'So - so you really were trying to communicate. But why me? Why did you lure me down there? Why did you kill Zena Michaelis? Why did you kill all those people at Europa Six?'

'When the first humans arrived, their minds were as closed to us as they are even now closed to each other. We speak amongst ourselves as if space does not exist but with humans we must be very near. We have studied you since your machines came from beyond our world but few could we speak with. Brett, you are different. You create strong images in your thoughts. Your mind is freer. It is more open to us than others of your kind. Most humans could never hear as you hear. If we made ourselves known they would not understand. They would be afraid.'

'But I hear you, as well,' said Karin.

287

'That is because your minds are harmonised. Each of you holds a part of the other in your thoughts. This we see. You ask about the one called Michaelis. That being was not as you. It was not as other humans. That one had different senses - like some of your robots. Senses we understand well because they are in some ways closer to our own. We had to reprogram Michaelis so she would walk into the desert believing it was right to do so. The purpose of that one was to see what others of your kind cannot see. She would know us if we moved amongst you and through her eyes another would watch.'

'You mean Virgil Hammond,' I said.

'Yes, the one called Hammond and others who are close to him. These humans suspected our presence when we tried to stop their intrusion into our domains. Hammond wishes to destroy us when the time comes without knowing what we are. It was through the mind of the one called Michaelis we came to know this. We entered that mind before it knew us. Through that mind we saw Hammond. Through it we came to understand how he wished to harm us.'

'The drilling!' exclaimed Karin. 'It is the deep level drilling, isn't it?'

'Your machines have passed into a part our world. They have brought destruction. This must end.'

'Is that why you destroyed Europa Six?' I asked. 'Was that meant as a warning?'

'We did not wish such great harm to humans. Our visit was meant as a warning to the one called Romano and to those who shared his guilt. We would have brought images of fear so that humans would feel our anger. We did not understand the weakness in the structure. It was not within the minds of those inside. When the power failed, we could do nothing. The one who came down from the sky to the black mountain we had to destroy. What that one brought was of great danger to our domains. They would have reached us from within the black mountain.'

'Then why didn't you appear to Hammond?' I asked. 'Why didn't you warn him off before he went into space? It's what we all would have wanted.'

'Where Hammond stays there are devices that would reveal our presence. Hammond never left his place of safety except to go from our world into the sky.'

'So,' I said, 'he set up defences to protect himself without knowing what he was up against and had Zena Michaelis sent over to do the dirty work.'

'Hammond sees us as a threat to his plans. Hammond wishes to destroy us for his own gain. We must protect ourselves. If we do not then destruction will fall in greater measure by far upon humans.'

'What the hell,' I muttered, glancing at Karin who still held onto me. 'Okay,' I continued, 'it was me you chose to contact and I blew it. What was I supposed to do? What am I supposed to do now?'

'You must understand more. You know what Hammond intends and because it is in your mind we know it also. You should know our truth. Through knowing you may find a way to save your kind.'

'And how do I do that? Show me!'

'Here is not the place for us. The one who could speak with you for a greater time died in the burning when you left the canyon. Such a one is not here.'

'I'm sorry - I thought -.'

'It is not important. Even though the body was destroyed, the consciousness remains with us.'

'But how - when?' I asked. 'We don't have much time.'

'You must return to the canyon for our kind cannot long survive on the surface. The air you need to maintain your lives is harmful to us. Outside there is radiation from space and from the sun. At the canyon we will be protected. At the canyon we will be many. There, you will understand. There you will know our true powers.'

***

Joe van Allen was alone in his quarters that morning when the chime sounded and her image materialised.

'Hi, Karin,' he smiled, putting aside his coffee. 'What are you doing up and about so soon? Is everything okay?'

'It is early, Joe, but I have to tell you.'

'Tell me what?'

'Last night in the biodome we met one of the Martians. Joe, it spoke to us. It - they, know what is happening - everything. They know what Hammond is doing.'

Joe rose to his feet. 'What! You – you mean they're in this base? Why didn't you call me sooner?'

'I couldn't until now but they do not wish us harm. Not you or me - not Brett nor anyone here. They want Brett to go where they can talk to him. They need him to go back to the canyon and he agreed to do it. I will explain everything to you, Joe - properly. When you're ready we should meet in the biodome.'

'Now hold on, Karin! Where's Brett?'

'As I said, Joe, he's going back to the canyon.'

Joe stepped toward her image, finger raised. 'Now you just tell him he can't do that! No – never mind – I'll tell him myself. It's too much of a risk and I won't allow it! I'd better talk some sense into that boy before he does something foolish!'

'I'm afraid it's too late for that, Joe. He's already on his way.'

'He's what!' Joe called up a wall-wide view of the runway. To the east, a violet glow announced the presence of a soon to rise sun. It already cast a lurid glare across the dust-hazed horizon whilst a thin sheet of white mist drifted under a purple sky. Joe watched Delta Seven rise to climb away in a wide, graceful arc. He continued watching as she gained altitude catching bright sunlight before diminishing in the morning sky on her journey south-east toward the Labyrinth.

From behind him came Karin's voice. 'Don't try to contact him, Joe. He won't answer.'

***

Gaining height, I watched the eastern sky brighten. Down to my left, the base and our precious biodome nestled in the mist of morning half-light. My destination was still in the ship's memory so there was no need to re-enter co-

291

ordinates. At five kilometres altitude I had a fine view of a deep yellow sun about to clear the horizon. I usually welcomed sunrises but for me this was a dawn of uncertainty. Was I soon to contribute something meaningful to history or disappear from it altogether?

I saw Karin's face - her dimpled smile, her blue eyes. She had wanted to come with me but I surely could never have risked that in spite of her being there on that previous evening's encounter. It was a bit late to think of it but perhaps those beings had a hidden agenda and I was the fall guy. Perhaps they wanted a healthy specimen fresh from the pen. There seemed little consolation to be had in telling myself they couldn't be any worse than Virgil Hammond.

As for secrecy – my instruments indicated I was being tracked by my own people as well as someone else Delta Seven couldn't identify. It didn't take much to work out who the other party was.

The sun was much higher when, under two hours later, I was passing over the Tharsis rise. Ascraeus was out of sight as, crossing the equator, I skirted closer than before to the sun-flamed slopes of Pavonis. Way up to my right, thin plumes of water vapour, hundreds of kilometres long, streamed northward from the crater, glowing bluish-white against a vault of smoky, gold-tinged purple. I wished I could have circled for a while to take it all in - to contemplate a magnificent desolation that was the stuff of my dreams.

I thought once more of Karin and of our adventures together. I thought of ever cheerful Leo, of his so-serious plans for the golf tournament, and of Joe to whom I owed a debt I might never be able to repay. I would gladly have spoken to any of them right then but my determination to maintain radio silence precluded that. I could not risk giving anything away to Virgil Hammond.

Pavonis was well behind and the Labyrinth only a half-hour away when I spotted something high up, little more than a speck over to the west at too great an altitude for a wingship. It wasn't a rocket coming in from Earth because there were none due and anyhow the trajectory was wrong. A shuttle didn't move that way either and, being smaller, wouldn't have been so noticeable at that height. No, this new intruder was in low orbit, no more than a hundred kilometres up and moving eastward at high speed to cross directly above my flight path. My sensors weren't picking it up so I magnified the image. When it approached the horizon to vanish into low haze, the sky was again empty.

I had witnessed the coming of *Aurora*.

CHAPTER 8
EMPIRES OF THE MIND

The desert glowed as I approached the Labyrinth and Delta Seven began her descent. Lower still and I was over the canyon with golden light fingering into the dark shadows of its upper walls. Delta Seven was flaring out, the sound of the turbines dropping a little as our speed decreased. The navigator displayed my destination clearly but on looking down I saw the deeper realms completely obscured by mist through which speared those ranks of sharks-teeth pinnacles. The sea of pallid fog rushing toward me was alarming. Unaided eyes couldn't see through it and as I plunged in I was tempted to shrink down in case it burst right in on me! Moments later I was through with the mist a mottled ceiling that sped above. The pinnacles, the rock walls, even the gaping arc of that landslip, all passed by like ghosts as I was swallowed by the abyss. The sides of the canyon vanished into darkness for in its depths the tide of night had yet to recede. Fine-tuning her descent, Delta Seven quivered like a living thing.

My faith in the ship's sensory systems at that point was total. It had to be.

I was down and rolling along the bottom but because the sunlight on the cliffs ahead was as yet no more than a thin band of orange spreading just below the rim, the chasm appeared even more sombre than I remembered. One thing that concerned me right then was the cargo pod I'd abandoned on the occasion of my previous departure. Although at that time I'd been unable to detect it from above, had it still been there I would have had a problem getting back out. Neither the ship's sensors nor my own eyes showed any such obstruction during our approach to the amphitheatre and as the chasm widened, it was obvious the container really had disappeared. As to how or to where it had been moved I could not even guess. Delta Seven slowed right down at that point because the ground was still churned where the container had dropped and where I had blasted off in such spectacular fashion. To my right was the rock fall with the cave entrance close by. Still deep in shadow, it struck me as none too inviting.

Those immense walls, their upper tiers awash with sunlight, were an oddly welcoming sight as I emerged into the open space of the amphitheatre. The mist had altogether dissipated here and everything stood out in stark clarity. To anyone looking down from the upper edge, Delta Seven would have appeared no more than a barely moving white speck. Speeding up her engines, I brought the ship around to face into the canyon in readiness for lift-off, following my earlier wheel tracks, which were barely visible.

Once stopped with the engines idling, I peered though the armaplast then rotated the view all around the ship. Nothing moved. There was no indication any form of life had ever been there other than me. Well, there was nothing to be gained in my staying on the ship but before I lowered the ramp I checked out the standard locator beacon inside my pressure suit. Should I, should it, be out of touch with the ship for a continuous period of more than ten minutes, Delta Seven would interrogate for a positive life response. In the event of there being no such response she would lift off then return to base. I didn't want her abandoned down there if anything happened to me.

Before reaching the bottom of the ramp, I switched on the recording unit in my suit. It would transmit to the ship everything I said, everything I saw, everything I heard and felt. If the ship did return on her own she'd at least have my ghost on board. I was only a few steps away when Delta Seven retracted the ventral ramp to seal herself against the world I had just entered. As I set off toward the rock fall, I imagined the pressure suit being recovered ages after I'd vanished, still bearing my nametag. I smiled at the thought of it stuffed with plastic foam, propped up in some museum display. Visitors would gape at the spotlighted relic then learn of one who had embarked upon some fruitless errand - a self-appointed saviour of humanity who was never seen again.

But who, I wondered, would be running the museum?

Once at the rock fall I glanced about and waited. Waiting was something I was never too happy about unless it was on my terms. Propped against a convenient boulder, I gazed about the amphitheatre. The sun had risen further so the walls, afire halfway down the western side, cast a warm glow over the entire vast area. My sensors, though, told me the temperature hovered at a none too friendly minus ninety-seven C and that there was a moderately blustering wind. Way up to my left I watched the sun peer over the canyon rim like an inquisitive eye, spilling light through shifting gossamer veils. A grand show just for me.

Something moved out there in the amphitheatre beyond the ship. A shapeless form, shifting, elusive, it darted across the shadows beneath an unlit section of the cliffs. I tensed, expecting this was it, yet I could make no sense at all of what I was seeing. It vanished but moments later reappeared, weaving from side to side, heading right at me! It scurried on into a shaft of sunlight to resolve itself as a translucent, spinning column of sand, swaying like some kind of exotic dancer. I breathed, 'Oh, shit,' and continued to stare, fascinated. Anywhere else and I'd have guessed straight away what the thing was. The dust devil grew in height, slowed, then collapsed lazily into a myriad drifting specks of light.

So distracted, I was quite unaware of the figure standing beyond the rock fall to my left until it spoke. 'Brett, we are with you.'

'Karin! No - not her!' I called aloud. 'I don't want that! If she was really here without a pressure suit, she'd be dead!'

'We do not wish to cause you distress,' the image replied. 'We will appear as another.'

As quickly as I could have blinked, and maybe that's what I did, the image blurred to become the woman I had once thought was Zena Michaelis. I took a big, deep breath. I needed to stay calm.

'We appeared as the one called Karin because that image is strong within your mind.'

'Who is the image I now see?' I asked.

The voice was not that which had spoken to Karin and me in the biodome but the voice of the

297

female illusion I had carried to the canyon. And although it was in my mind rather than picked up by my sensors, the figure standing before me appeared to mouth the words so that at least I had a focal point to hold my attention.

'This image was in the mind of one who died in the first days of your kind. There were three who came from the sky to the great valley you call Candor Chasm. The ground where they landed was above a void. When it opened beneath them, two were destroyed within their vessel but one who had left it to explore the canyon lived on through some of the day. That one we could not help but there were thoughts we reached into. There we found the image we now create for you. The image flowed out - such a strong, such a precious image. It filled the mind of the one for all the time life remained. We preserved the image because it was the first human mind we had entered. The image will stay with us forever.'

'Did the image have a name?'

'The image was called Elena.'

'And the man who carried it?'

'The one was called Vasili.'

'Vasili Chernushenko,' I breathed. 'That was a century and a half ago. No one ever found out what happened to those guys.'

'The one called Vasili still lies frozen by a great pillar in the chasm of Candor, sometimes hidden by sand, sometimes not. Often we look upon the human with sadness. Often we remember the thoughts. Through the mind of this one we saw your world, the cities, the green lands, the great seas. So strange did your kind seem at first, some wondered if you were not an aberration created by those among ourselves who devise such entertainments.'

'Aberration! Entertainment! But you must have known of us from the machines that came here before we did.'

'We were curious,' the image replied. 'We analysed, but we did not concern ourselves with them because they were not truly alive. We expected their creators would follow.'

'But our radio transmissions - did you not realise they were from another civilisation?'

'Your methods of communication are unnecessary to us though later we learned how to hear them. Now we sense all your machines. The one that brought you here from the sky possesses an intellect created to serve you and your kind.'

'Are there many of you here right now?' I asked, glancing aside at Delta Seven.

'Some are close but many others hear us. All can share in what another does. It is what we are. The individual is not important to us though we understand well how essential it is for humans.'

'So the one we found at Europa Six – are you saying its death didn't matter?'

'That one was a transient. It lived only in your time and space. Its kind we create for physical tasks. They removed your container from the chasm. They possess no independent means of thought and feeling. We allowed that one to remain because its existence would confuse humans. It was to be a part of our diversion until the structure failed.'

'A diversion?' I asked. 'You mean you really did see our presence here as some kind of entertainment?'

'It was more than that. Humans are unlike anything we ever encountered. You were another dimension in our dramas until your machines began to harm our world. But for the harm you are doing, we would have remained unknown to you. It was what we wished. Now that can no longer be.'

'Diversions? Dramas? I don't understand. To us this is life or death!' I was trying hard to make sense out of what it, what they were telling me but it sounded like we were little more to them than a sideshow – albeit one with regrettable habits. 'Tell me,' I asked, 'tell me what you are and how you create these illusions. Your technology must be far ahead of ours.'

'Technology, Brett? All the knowledge humans brought to this world we have added to our own yet we have no need of the material devices you rely upon.'

'Then did you never conquer the air? Did you never wonder what was beyond this world until we came? Did you never study the stars and the planets? Did you never go out into space?'

'In our earliest memories, in our first age, we have images of this world when it was as yours. It once possessed a magnetic field, there were seas with an atmosphere great enough to protect life. We flourished upon this land long before life emerged from the waters of Earth. When this planet began to die we decided to remain. Earth could not support us even had we been prepared to go there. When life spread across the land and into the air on your world, this planet had become much as you see it now. As it cooled, as it lost most of its atmosphere, as the seas were lost to space or vanished beneath the deserts, life merged then moved inward to gain energy from the core. Ours is a closed system like your biodomes but more efficient by far. By then our minds were evolving, already merging until they could share as one.'

'But how,' I asked, 'did you survive so long on this dead world? There's no food chain.'

'Humans talk of many dimensions, of parallel universes, but have yet to enter them. We have known of these from our earliest times. From them our minds gain much power though our physical forms remain transient. We pass through gateways into realms unattainable by you. This is what sustains us. One of them will become our home when this planet finally dies though we know it may alter us forever. We create within those other worlds what we choose because the choice is without limit. In our thoughts, in our epics, we journey through many planes of existence, some benign, others of great danger. We have reached out to infinity without the need to leave this world. Here we have found stability for a time.'

The being, or whatever it was, hesitated as if considering its next words. Then it spoke again.

'This you must know; what is done with little consequence in one plain of existence may bring great change, perhaps catastrophe, in another. A small stone dislodged here may cascade as an avalanche elsewhere. Even so, nothing we encountered was ever stranger than humans. Your closed minds, your method of reproduction - so strange. Each of you is a consciousness passing alone through one time and through one space. When humans die, experience and understanding die with them unless it is given to imperfect machines.'

'We're working hard on that one,' I muttered, recalling how a rough account of my entire life so far was stored in my right earlobe.

'We lose nothing we do not wish to lose,' the image continued. 'We keep all we wish to keep. You and your companion discovered a small part of it when you went to the valley within the mesa.'

'The crystals!' I exclaimed.

'As you have learned, they are an ancient repository. Others lie hidden as were those when the great volcano began to rise. The human who would destroy us wishes to know their secret but they are a part of what we are and of what we once were. The crystals were born of our ancestors though we are even now able to create them within ourselves. They, too, extend into other realities, as moving facets in the fabric space-time but never as you find them in this dimension. Without the key, which is a part of us, they will in your existence bring destruction to any that attempt to unlock their secrets by force. One has died already because Hammond demanded the knowledge they possess. Brett, the humans on Earth who use what you call dark energy to power *Aurora* have drawn it in part from one of those other dimensions. They do not know it but if they go too far it will rupture space-time in your world with results that cannot be predicted.'

'I understand how we must appear to you,' I said. 'Greedy and destructive. But humans need to search, to explore, to go beyond each horizon in body as well as in mind – always to question what is. Without the will to do that we would stagnate as some cultures on Earth have. Surely your kind must ask the all-important question - Why?'

'There are many ways of asking. Many ways of understanding. We wish to take you on a journey to another reality in space-time. If you agree, you will understand more. It is a journey you should accept.'

'A journey?' I breathed. 'Well, since you're calling the shots – yes, I'll agree.'

'We desire it for the sake of you and your kind, Brett. No harm will come to you. You will remain in contact with your vessel. We know you must do that. It will not depart without you.'

I gazed up at the sky, half wishing I was back up there then thinking what the hell, I've come this far and I'm still in one piece. I regarded the image of the girl, so real I wanted to reach out and touch. The breeze swayed wisps of hair against her cheeks and light danced in her green eyes. The guy who left her behind must have been crazy as me. I glanced across at Delta Seven then I sat down on a slab of rock. 'Okay, I'm all yours.'

Whatever version of reality I occupied wavered then dissolved.

I was minus my pressure suit, sitting in some kind of vehicle - a sort of flattened, transparent bubble. Straight away I knew I could control the thing just by willing it in whatever direction I wanted to go - the way you sometimes do in a programmed dream. But I swear I was wide-awake. I swear it because all my senses insisted this was no dream at all. But there was something else happening. Something big.

For a time I didn't understand what I was looking at or how far away it was. Before me was an ascending wall of fire - a vast curtain of glowing matter that rose in terrible majesty. Following it up I saw lightning arc in frenzied glare to illuminate a canopy of ash and smoke that billowed out high above where the sky should have been. It spread as far as I could see over a realm plunged otherwise into utter darkness. My gaze followed the rising torrent down to its base where the maw of an immense crater seethed chaotic violence. I knew right then what I was witnessing. This was Olympus - not the silent giant of today but the Olympus of a distant age, maybe a different dimension, in full eruption, vomiting the fires of some primordial hell. Nothing else could I see of this awesome world. The volcano dominated all.

I began to lose height, at the same time moving toward that monstrous spectacle from which I realised I was still some considerable distance. Descending toward the cauldron, I observed ribbons of shimmering yellow reaching from its rim to lace the flanks of the mountain in a fretwork of light. Lower now, not only could I hear but could feel through my bones the drumming of some titanic engine. Glowing fragments cartwheeled by, pirouetting on vortices of heat. Still some way above the crater, the ribbons had resolved into braided cataracts of radiance surging over the edge, leaping outward on a journey into boundless obscurity.

I must have let go all sense of danger. I should have been scared out of my wits in the face of so nightmarish a prospect but by the time I was level with the crater I didn't care anymore. I floated down until hovering directly above one of those cataracts where I could smell burning sulphur. Then closer until it sped beneath me - a cracking, heaving deluge of fire. Closer still and I swear I could feel the flames surge through me. Maybe by then I had taken death for granted for suddenly I was surfing the lava flow amidst a storm of glowing motes that spun in wild disarray about my capsule! Downwards I swept, yelling aloud like some kid on a wild rampage, forgetting that had it been as real as I was convinced it was, I'd have been blasted to cinders a thousand times over!

Some way down I took a hold on reality and lifted clear to sweep upward in a widening curve, so putting distance between myself and the inferno. I hovered further away than where I had started but for a long while I could not avert my gaze from the volcano. What I beheld might have been a vision spawned by some medieval artist, someone whose wits were steeped in traditions of hellfire and damnation; one whose mind was obsessed by images of satanic retribution.

I continued to watch, aware now of a profound silence. When I peered about expecting to find nothing but featureless darkness I was intrigued to see a dim light high above. As I peered up, it grew brighter. It seemed to be pulling me like a magnet. Brighter still it became whilst the dark skies retreated. Brighter until the image of Olympus dissolved in a tide of light that spread to fill the whole of my vision.

'Was that not fascinating, Brett?' came her voice.

I blinked at the sun then placed a hand on my visor to reassure myself I was really back in the canyon. Yes, I was still sitting on the rock with the image of the girl staring down at me. 'Quite a day this turned out to be.' was all I could manage as she spoke again.

'We shared your experience. We were with you on your adventure but what you did there was of your own will.'

'Hope I was suitably entertaining,' I muttered.

'The world you entered was before the time this planet began to die,' the image continued. 'Through us you entered realms closed to your kind. Through you, Brett, humans must learn what we are. We will preserve our domains from harm as you would wish to preserve yours. Humans do not work in harmony. Your conflicts are real. They are destructive. Some would sacrifice others for their own gain. We know of the coming of *Aurora*, Brett, because it was in your mind and you did not wish for it.'

'Most of us fear what could happen,' I answered. 'We don't want *Aurora* to come here.'

Now it seemed as if many whispered to me from a gathering of voices. 'We are of the realms beneath the deserts, beneath the mountains and the canyons. If humans from *Aurora* strike into our world, we will reach into other dimensions. We will create new realities within this one. We will awaken the furnace beneath Olympus. We will break open the gates of Ascraeus, Pavonis and Arsia. The darkness of the volcanoes will fall once more upon this world. The night will be long. The biodomes will die. For humans there will be no dawn.'

As I sat there I knew they meant it. It was why they had shown me the vision of Olympus. Through them I had witnessed our day of judgement on Mars.

'You must hate some of us,' I said, 'all of us, maybe, and yet you offer me a chance to resolve the situation.'

'What you call hate we do not experience. It is our survival we must protect, as with humans.'

I couldn't question that. I just waited.

'Soon you must return to your kind,' came the voice – once more only the girl's. 'Matters of importance have passed since you left. The one called Karin desires to see your image as the one called Vasili long ago desired the image I hold now.'

Pushing up from the rock, I faced the likeness of the young woman whose ashes must lie somewhere on distant Earth. For a time I watched her eyes shine in the sun of a world she had never witnessed. She could never have known what happened to him – to her Vasili.

'Brett,' said the image, closing her eyes as if to concentrate, 'I am alone with you. I am no longer a part of our community. I am an individual as are you but cannot long remain so. When alone we can sometimes experience pleasure, pity and anger, as do humans. Our emotions are not as yours yet from your own we have taken much. Through our entering the mind of Vasili I hold memories of the woman, Elena, and through our meeting in the biodome with you and Karin, I hold her emotions also. I understand the meaning of man and woman. I know you, Brett, and I – I wish to keep you from harm. The closeness of you and Karin is strange to my kind yet because I live it now it is precious to me and I wish it to continue.'

As she spoke it was as if I truly faced a human being, exposed even as she was to that frigid, unbreathable hostility. Maybe my imagination had gone into orbit but I swear as she gazed at me there were tears in her eyes. I wanted to reach for her hand as I might with Karin or as poor Vasili would have wished with his distant Elena in those last, lonely hours. When she opened her eyes, the illusion passed and I knew she - it had re-joined the others. But there was one thing I had to ask before I left the canyon. 'May I see you as you really are?'

For a short time nothing happened, then the image replied, 'You ask the question though you fear what might be revealed. But why should you not see, Brett – you of all humans.'

True, I'd seen what I had seen on Joe's recording as well as those contrived remains at the devastated base, but now it was to be right there before my eyes. The image of the girl wavered then dissolved into drifting lights. In its place appeared a translucent haze of glittering, moving facets. It shimmered, altering from moment to moment so I couldn't focus properly. I wondered if it was only part emerged into this world and part hidden in one or more of those unseen dimensions of which they had spoken. It did nothing as I approached and raised my hand to reach slowly out. Through my sensors it felt cold. Cold as the crystals. Yet in spite of that I was aware of a life pulse, elusive, yet burning deep within.

With the canyon depths beginning to flood with light I glanced about to see Delta Seven aglow in the sun. When I turned again I found myself quite alone.

***

Hanging motionless by the space station the sinister form of *Aurora* reflected no starlight. Within the station Virgil Hammond surveyed the recreation area. Here was not the Hammond people knew on Mars but an armed and uniformed Hammond – appearing now the true General. By him sat two stern-faced officers, each wearing the insignia of UAS special services. Before them were seated some seventy men in blue-grey military uniform, each bearing a side arm. A section of the wall glowed with the image of Mars.

Placing a hand on his belt, Hammond cast a stern eye over the audience. For long moments he said nothing. For long moments he kept them waiting. With silence absolute, he began to speak.

'You have come from Earth on a mission. A mission that is to determine the future of human enterprise on Mars. It is also an opportunity – a God-given opportunity – for greater things, and I will soon touch upon that. You are already aware we have people working on the planet against the commercial interests of Frontier Mining and the Consortium. Like a malignant cancer, there has grown within the colonies a faction that would hold everyone to ransom in the furtherance of its own interests. And what are those interests? Why, self-determination, or so it would seem. A fine state of affairs!

But let me tell you - Mars is no land of green pastures bestowed by divine hand to welcome the hardy pioneer. No, it is an arid desert - cold and devoid of breathable air. The colonies were established to change all that and whilst some on Earth have turned their backs upon the dream, I say it *can* be realised. Rule from Earth by those who have never set foot on the planet is not the answer. What the colonies need is resolute guidance, on the spot where it matters, together with a moral authority they have so far lacked.'

Hammond leaned forward, his expression hardening. 'Now, they claim to have found life down there. Intelligent life!' Another hesitation. 'Oh, they found life all right - life that wiped out a community of around three hundred men women and children. Yes, wiped it out! And to follow up, this so-called intelligent life of theirs destroyed a wingship in an attempt to kill hundreds more. Sure, it's life. But what kind of life are we talking about here? Well, it's the kind of life that jumps up and bites you when you kick aside a rock. The kind of life that crawls into your bed at night to suck your blood. Yes, I guess that does qualify as life. Yet a few misguided do-gooders want to protect this abomination from the depths – these worms festering in an empty husk. They want to convince the folks on Earth that it's great new discovery that must be protected. Protected, they say!'

Hammond gazed about with an expression of astonishment then exclaimed, 'Well right now, after all those deaths, I guess we all know who needs protecting! And a great new discovery? Why, if you came out of the water and found some fancy new species of leech fastened on your ass would you call *that* a great new discovery or would you want to get rid of the thing pretty darned quick!'

He stabbed a finger toward the image of Mars, now in three quarters daylight. 'These people hope to gain from the situation. They hope to control our means of production. Yes, sir - they want their own finger on the button and they have a ready ear with the International Council. Well wouldn't they just! Can anyone tell me what part the International Council ever played in opening up Mars? The answer is nothing. Nothing! A big fat zero! So - we had to cut off interplanetary communications for a while. We had to end the stream of misinformation coming from down there and stirring up problems back on Earth. Now they threaten to deny us access to property belonging to the Consortium. But we need only persuade one base to see sense and the problem is solved. There will be no point in them continuing to disrupt operations any further. Meanwhile, you'll not be surprised to learn that the Europeans, the Russians and the Asians are unhappy over our handling of the situation. They'd have preferred to have gotten their people out here first. Sure they would! But they did not get here first. You did! In days, not months, because we have the technology and the know-how to do it.'

At this point Hammond placed hands resolutely on his hips, closed his eyes for tense seconds then continued. 'Yet further ahead lies an even greater mission than that of taking back control of our resources. It is the opportunity of which I spoke - a mission to re-establish the faith and the values so many on Earth have forsaken. I know each of you

311

shares my faith just as *you* know how important a factor it was in your nomination. And so it was in the choosing of those on Earth who are already preparing to follow us.

On Mars faith in Almighty God is totally denied. They have not a single place of worship! But, I promise you, on this new world the slate will be wiped clean. Clean so as to accept anew the message of Christ - though that message may have to be written in fire. With justice and true belief on our side we will prevail against the wickedness that has taken hold. Increased commercial output will fund our mission. With new resources we will confound all who stand against us. I see before me a vision - a vision of a foundation from which to inspire the home planet with the truth of His word and His glorious kingdom. Through us the voice of the Redeemer will ring across space!'

CHAPTER 9
MESSENGER OF LIGHT

A manta-shadow scurried across desert sand dunes bright in the mid-afternoon sun. The wingship described a wide arc about the complex then flared out on her approach to the runway. Two eager faces watched the welcome image of Delta Seven gleam sunlight as she touched down, sped along the strip, slowed, then taxied toward the parking zone. Only now, only as the ship rolled to a standstill, did Joe van Allen make contact. 'Brett, there are a lot of people hanging about the concourse. Come in via number three cargo auxiliary. We'll meet you there and go straight up.'

The journey back had seemed quicker because images of the volcano and all that I had witnessed passed before my head time and time again. Yet in spite of that there was something nagging at the back of my mind – something I was not too clear about but needed to resolve with Joe. There were a couple of ground crew standing by when I hurried down the ramp but we exchanged no more than cursory greetings. They must have been puzzled to see me head off toward one of the subsidiary buildings rather than the main admin block. Joe and Karin were there to greet me as I pushed through the small service airlock.

'Good to see you back home, son,' smiled Joe, placing a hand on my shoulder. 'Our new sensors tell me things are just fine so we know it's really you inside that suit.'

'Yeah, and it's really me wanting to get out of it,' I answered.

As soon as I'd twisted off the helmet Karin planted a kiss on my cheek and said, 'Brett, I'm so glad you're back.'

'Karin, Joe - if only you could have experienced what I did out there! It was incredible! Just incredible!' I was all but bursting with what I wanted to tell them so as we headed into the service elevator I began by outlining what had happened. I still had my pressure suit on, intending to get out of it once we were upstairs. Joe and Karin were as keen to listen as I was to talk but as it turned out, other events were about to overtake us.

'Brett,' said Joe as we emerged from the service elevator, '*Aurora* showed up while you were out there and –.'

'Yeah, Joe, I spotted her.'

'Okay, then since you started back, Hammond, Pazukhin and company have been hollerin' after me as well as trying to muscle in on other bases. So far the other stations have all refused to hold dialogue unless I'm fronting it. Hammond will have tracked you to the Labyrinth the same as we did so you can bet they're trying to figure out what we're up to. I've avoided talking to them until we had you back here safe and sound. I need to hear lots more about what happened but there isn't time right now. Hammond's talking ultimatum.'

'What kind of ultimatum,' I asked as we continued along the corridor.

'I guess we're about to hear the finer details but we'll use the conference room - I don't want to see the guy's face in my office again.'

314

Once we sat around the table, Joe said, 'Brett, something else has come up that isn't good at all though we have been expecting it. *Aurora* is probing our communication systems. It seems as if Hammond intends to cut us off from each other. If the worst came to the worst they could louse up our satellites but that wouldn't help any since they'd need the things back again once they got their way. Our manufacturing facilities, too, even some of our maintenance bots; they're attempting to reprogram these. What the hell will happen if they succeed doesn't bear thinking about so all non-essentials are being deactivated. So far our technicians have managed to sidestep their efforts but we don't know what equipment *Aurora* is carrying and we're not set up to deal with military level technology. In the meantime, I doubt Hammond's mob know we're fully wise to them though sooner or later they will figure it out.'

Before contacting the space station, Joe put out a planet-wide alert. It was essential everyone heard what was about to be said or at least had it standing by if it came through on the night side. Joe made contact with the space station straight after but almost five minutes passed before Virgil Hammond's image materialised. When he did appear, it was to regard Joe with those nail-head eyes then for a while longer and somewhat harder, myself and Karin. This time around we'd seen no reason to filter out our presence.

It was Joe who broke a charged silence. 'Well now, Chief, I didn't expect to see you, a civilian executive, in military uniform – no sir. How may I be of assistance?'

'It is most considerate of you to find time in your busy working day to talk to me, Commander Van Allen,' he replied. 'I will reiterate the situation as now appears. You and your fellow acting commanders have responsibility for the support of our commercial installations and staff. Whether on Earth or Mars, our affairs need to be conducted in a proper manner and that has been far from the case here. We now have means at our disposal to re-establish rightful authority over operations on Mars. I assure you I have no desire to prolong what has become a standoff. I require you now to consider the position of yourself and others. Commander Van Allen, I formally require you to step aside and allow peaceful entry to the representatives of our government and of the Consortium.'

'Well, Chief,' replied Joe, 'I'm all for peaceful solutions and I'd love to discuss them right now with the folks on Earth as well as the International Council but it seems we're still prevented from doing so in spite of my earlier requests which are at very least as valid as yours. Maybe we could speak to Secretary Barbosa so everyone down here can see how happy the lady is in your company. She's also our officially designated legal representative in case anyone had forgotten. How about it, Mister Chief Executive?'

Hammond stared coldly at Joe and for a moment I thought he was going to ignore the request. Without a word he disappeared. Half a minute later, another face materialised - a face that usually offered a broad smile. On this occasion it didn't.

'Commander - Joe,' she began, quietly. 'I'm sorry I was unable to speak to you earlier. Things have been a little difficult.'

'Are you all right, Amalia?' Joe asked.

She glanced aside at whoever was standing off-vision. 'I - yes, I'm all right.'

'Look,' said Joe, 'I want Brett to talk to you for a moment. He has something you might be interested in hearing - okay?'

'Very well,' she nodded, trying to force a smile.

'Secretary Barbosa,' I began, aware that time was not on my side. 'I returned earlier today from the Labyrinth. Whilst in there I encountered the indigenous life forms. They are highly intelligent beings. They have inhabited this world since long before humans existed on Earth. I spoke with them. I understand something of what they are. We have provoked them into doing what they did through intensified mining operations. They tried to talk with me when I first went into the canyon but it didn't work out - I guess that was partly my fault. The colonies face total disaster if we allow deep level mining to go on. The colonists themselves need to control what happens on Mars and not leave it in the hands of a bunch of accountants, crooks and fanatics back on Earth who don't give a damn about what we have here.'

She stared at me then said, dryly, 'Captain Anderson, that – that is amazing I must say. Really - quite amazing. We must inform the various national authorities on Earth through the International Council. I'm sure they will all respond in a rational and constructive way once the situation is explained.'

I heard Karin whisper to Joe, 'She's not aware we have no communication with Earth. Hammond is holding her prisoner.'

Before anyone could speak again the interview was cut and Virgil Hammond reappeared.

Joe said, 'You jumped the gun there, Chief - we still had a few things to say to Secretary Barbosa. She does not appear fully informed about what is going on.'

'But you and I *are* fully informed,' responded Hammond with thinly disguised anger, 'and I do not intend to continue playing games. A conclusion has to be reached - and quickly.'

'So you tell me,' answered Joe, in a now sterner voice, 'but you, Chief, or should I say, General, are at present acting in a military role when by international agreement on Earth the military are excluded from Mars. I know the law as well as most people so I'll tell you this; *you* no longer hold legal authority over UAS or anyone else's facilities on this planet. Most of those who might have stepped in to take over are detained up there in orbit - against their will if I'm not mistaken and clearly so in the case of Secretary Barbosa! As elected representative under extraordinary circumstances, I choose to place the colonies under the direct authority of the International Council as soon as possible - and I happen to know, General, or whatever goddamned name you care to call yourself, that *is* the correct *and* legal procedure!'

Hammond's face was a mask of granite. 'So be it, Van Allen,' he scowled. 'You may think you have legality on your side but I have the reality of this situation on mine.'

With that he vanished.

'Well, that's it,' shrugged Joe. 'I guess we might as well head back to my office for coffee.'

'I could use something stiffer than coffee after today,' I muttered, thinking to get off my mind what had been nagging at me earlier. On our arrival, Joe fished out a half decent bourbon but before I could say thanks his desk communicator chimed then flashed, 'PRIORITY.'

'Commander Van Allen,' said the girl, 'I have a report on *Aurora*. She has left the space station and assumed synthetic orbit about the planet at an altitude of one hundred and twenty kilometres.'

'Okay,' replied Joe. 'Keep me informed.'

'Synthetic orbit?' queried Karin.

'She's not holding a natural orbit,' I answered. 'She has to use her power to maintain it.'

'Hammond's looking for a way in,' said Joe. 'I reckon he was on board that ship and ready to go all the time we were talking to him. *Aurora* will be tracked as she passes through each time zone for as long as we're able.' Joe attempted to raise Amalia Barbosa once more but the space station was not responding.

'He'll still have armed men up there,' I said.

Again the priority signal flashed. Thinking it must be a follow-up report from one of our operatives I wondered what could have happened in so short a time. But no - a section of the wall lit up and looming large upon it was the wide-eyed, agitated face of Ingvar Svendsen. 'I hope you got my last message. We're passing over eastern Tharsis right now so I'm transmitting direct in case your satellite links are already compromised.

Hammond is on board *Aurora* with over thirty armed men – the rest are still up here to keep control of the space station. They are trying to find out who is leaking information. I heard them -.'

Svendsen turned aside then backed away from the screen.

'What's happening?' whispered Karin.

'The guy's jumpy,' I answered. 'I sure would be.'

'It's one hell of a risk he's taking,' put in Joe. 'If he's transmitting live, it might have to be via the station control centre.'

For interminable seconds nothing happened then the face reappeared. 'Listen to me, please. I heard them mention a weak point of cntry at one of the bases. If the colonists continue to refuse him access he will exploit this to get inside. Pazukhin and the others will not sanction force against any of their bases by UAS troops because they fear repercussions on Earth so it has to be an American base that they can claim co-operated. I think I know which one it is so you should contact -. Oh, there is -!'

He was gone from the screen again but the sound was still on. There were noises like furniture being slammed about. Vague shapes darted back and forth. Voices called out in the background. Karin gave a sharp cry as the shot rang out. Then the image closed.

'Goddamned bastards,' muttered Joe. 'I guess Ingvar's time had to run out sooner or later.'

'If only he'd had a few seconds more,' I breathed.

'The poor man should not have taken such a risk,' said Karin, glancing at Joe and me reproachfully.

'I'll run a check on all our facilities,' said Joe. 'It may take a while since we aren't sure what we're looking for but I don't want to tip Hammond off by warning the others. It might push him into something drastic and that we don't need.'

Karin and I stayed put whilst Joe got on with the task of briefing our technicians. After that I pulled out what I mentioned had been nagging at me a while ago. 'Joe, something crossed my mind on the way back here from the canyon. It may be of no importance but could be worth checking out. What happens when we have a magnetic storm and there's a communications blackout with Earth?'

'Exactly that,' responded Joe. 'We can't get through. What are you saying?'

'Well there's someone who never seems to have communication problems even when the rest of us do - at least that's what I've heard. A guy who bitches about not getting interviews with people like you and me but never about -.'

'Darn it!' Joe exclaimed. 'You mean Roy Kendrick?'

'Yes - Roy Kendrick. I recall Leo commented a while back on the way he usually gets through to SolaNews even in the worst magnetic storms. How could he do that - unless it's just another rumour?'

'I once heard someone remark on that as well,' added Karin, 'but I also thought it was a rumour.'

'It could be more than a rumour now I think about it,' Joe responded. 'We can be jammed out completely but I only recall him complaining once.

321

He happened to be down here a couple of years back when conditions were real bad. We had solar flares as well as planet-wide sandstorms lousing things up. Roy'd had quite a lot to drink and bellyached about the situation because it made communications with SolaNews difficult. "Difficult," was the very word he used, I swear it. For the rest of us it wasn't just difficult, it was damned well impossible! Knowing Roy, I just took it as drink-talk.'

'I say we get hold of him, Joe. Where is he?'

'You might well ask, son. I impounded his equipment after we caught him tapping into our communications. Most of the time he's been hanging around the bar. Our Mister Kendrick is not a happy man and because the booze is his only comfort I turn a blind eye to it unless he gets to annoy somebody.'

'Happy or not,' I said, 'if we can let Earth and the IC know what's really going on out here they'll soon put a freeze on that trigger happy idiot and the rest of his crew – here as well as on Earth.'

'Yes,' agreed Karin, 'once the situation became public he would have to back down. It has to be worth a try - what else can we do?'

***

The search for Roy took longer than expected; he was not responding to his ear lobe communicator even on priority code. Joe got a location fix on it, something seldom done on base for reasons of privacy.

When we arrived at Roy's quarters, Joe had to use the emergency access code to gain entry. Knowing Roy as we did, Joe had brought along a shot of alcohol catalyser. It was no wasted gesture. The place reeked of booze and there was an empty whisky flask laying on the floor by the bed upon which Roy lay sprawled out cold.

For almost two centuries the civilised world had benefited from a genetically enhanced ability to metabolise ethyl alcohol at a greater rate than nature once permitted if, that is, it was not gulped down in excessive quantities. Roy was living proof that science couldn't keep up with everything, especially where there was a will to defeat it. I guess that might happen to the best of us now and then. Some fell foul of Pazukhin's vodka whereas others made a habit of it. Karin and Joe got him propped up and administered the shot through the skin of his left arm. Even so, it took around five minutes before Roy knew who we were or which planet he was on. Eventually his brain and mouth decided they could team up and work together. In another five, he was able to hold meaningful conversation.

'Roy,' said Joe, 'I'm going to ask you a simple question. This is mighty important and I need a straight answer.'

'You'll be lucky,' I muttered.

Karin just stared at him.

Roy spread fingers over glazed eyes, peering at us like someone just slammed up behind prison bars. Karin and Joe glanced at me in disbelief as Roy attempted to invoke that which he so readily ignored when dealing with others. 'What d'you want in here? I'm entitled to my privacy.'

'You're so right, Roy,' Joe replied, 'but like I say, this could be pretty important.'

'Roy,' I cut in, 'how d'you get through to SolaNews when all our communications are down?'

Leaning back on the bed, Roy mumbled, 'Get through? What d'you mean, get through?'

'Please, Roy,' said Karin, 'you don't know what's been happening, do you - we must find out while we still have time.'

Rubbing a stubbled chin, Roy said, 'You're damn right I don't know what's been happening. I don't know because I haven't been allowed to find out - so don't expect any favours from me!'

Feeling a more direct approach might be in order, I pushed past Joe, grabbed Roy by the collar and raised my fist. 'Okay, Roy,' I growled, 'we can do this the easy way or the hard way – I don't care which! Just tell us how you get through to SolaNews!'

Roy cringed but said nothing so I raised my fist higher. 'Roy – I'll count to ten but I'm starting at eight. Give!'

'Oh, shit!' he gurgled. 'You don't know what you're asking!'

I was about to make the point more forcibly when Joe stayed my arm and cut in, 'Roy, there could be something worthwhile in this for you - I mean a real break.'

'No kidding,' he croaked as my grip tightened on his windpipe.

'No kidding,' added Joe. 'Brett, tell him what's been going on the last twenty-four hours.'

Letting go, I explained to Roy as calmly and as succinctly as I could about *Aurora*, the beacon and my trip back into the canyon. Cramming it all into a few minutes wasn't easy but when I'd finished, Joe added, 'We need to communicate with Earth, Roy. We need to real bad if you have some way of doing it.'

'It's highly classified,' he replied. 'You've got to understand – my job depends on this. If SolaNews found out I even mentioned it, I'd be through. They wouldn't even pay my fare back to Earth.'

'We're *all* gonna be through if we don't find a way out of this pretty damn quick,' put in Joe.

'Roy,' Karin said. 'Most people know something about what Brett and I have witnessed but nothing like the whole account. As Joe said, this could be your break.'

Roy stared up at us. I could almost hear his mind ticking like that ancient clock in Joe's office. 'You mean an exclusive?' he asked, twisting upright. 'Everything?'

'I'll go along with that,' I put in, eyeballing Roy. 'You get our accounts first-hand and whatever we learn about your methods of communication we keep strictly to ourselves. We give you our word on it.'

I glanced aside at Joe and Karin. They agreed.

Roy struggled up from the bed, kicked the whisky flask aside and tapped his earlobe. 'Look, if I co-operate, there'll be no backing out on my exclusive, right - whatever happens? I want it legal. I'm recording.'

'No backing out, Roy,' I agreed. 'You get exclusive rights on everything we discussed but we have to move now.' I next offered him the small pen device Ingvar Svendsen had given me on the space station. 'Can you download from this?' I asked.

'Easy,' he replied, taking it like a kid grabbing a treat.

To clinch the deal Roy Kendrick and I shook hands - something I never imagined could happen in my wildest dreams - and I'd had a few of late. 'And,' he added as we left his bedroom, 'when do I get to talk with - with those -?'

'You have us, Roy,' I replied, 'but we can't answer for the Martians!'

Turning to Joe, he said, 'I can't do this without my equipment – and I need a clear view of the sky.'

'You just got your gear back,' said Joe. 'Follow me.'

***

Joe van Allen had moments earlier seen Roy Kendrick from his office when his earlobe pinged. 'Hi, Naomi,' he replied, 'd'you have something worthwhile?'

'There's an anomaly here, Commander,' said the girl. 'It could be what we're looking for.'

'Okay,' said Joe, 'I have the image in front of me but you'll have to explain.'

'It shows a service airlock mechanism inside Novamerica Three. The doors are a design that was tried out years ago but never adopted elsewhere. The outer and inner doors can be opened manually from each direction. This airlock connects their aircraft maintenance building to the administration block. As the maintenance building itself is not pressurised it just has a single door to the outside.'

'Goddamned manual airlocks!' exclaimed Joe. 'Now at least we have something to go on. Store that and see if anything else comes up. I mean anything!' Moments later his desk panel was flashing with another call.

***

Karin and I were on our way to the biodome with Roy, discussing what needed to be relayed when Joe pinged my ear. 'Brett, I can't join you right now. Leo just called in. I'm trying to get through to our Number Three. That's where we think the situation is but *Aurora*'s starting to foul up inter-base communications. Our people will do their best to keep things afloat but there's no saying how long we can hold out. We also have to maintain satellite alignments or we lose light-pulse.'

'What about communications with our aircraft?' I asked. 'Is Leo flying right now?'

'He's on his way over to the Asian base down south at Kepler,' replied Joe. 'Communication on wingship frequencies is still holding, leastways on the secure links. He asked about you and Karin.'

'Joe, we're at the biodome - I'll let you know what's happening soon as I can.'

Karin and I went through the airlock with Roy, who cradled that small black case of his like he'd just given birth to it. We hadn't gone far inside when he stopped and looked about. 'I don't want anybody seeing this. I think it's too busy in here.'

'Where else can we go?' asked Karin.

'Nowhere else,' I responded as we hurried on. 'We'll have to find a quiet enough spot.'

I was getting impatient, but he was right - it was busy, though no more than we might have expected that time of the day. I thought maybe Joe could signal a rain shower to get people out of the biodome but that would take up more time. Heading

327

for the perimeter track, we went on around the south side until we came upon a small clearing in a wooded area with no sign of anyone close by. Facing roughly south and just a few metres from the bioplast shell, it was on the side of the biodome where Roy said we had to be. Why in that particular area, he hadn't got around to explaining but I already had the glimmerings of a notion as he squatted on the grass to open the case.

Out in the desert, shadows were lengthening with the late afternoon sky a vivid pink toward the west. Hanging like iridescent streamers at around fifty kilometres height, slender clouds of carbon dioxide ice glowed in the sun. When flying I was often intrigued by their strange, abstract beauty. The sun also caught something lower down to the south – the spectral image of Phobos drifting eastward across the sky.

When I looked around, Roy was lifting things from amongst the electronic paraphernalia his case contained. Another flask of Scotch had its own special compartment. We watched him set up a metre-high telescopic tripod. Onto this he placed a metal object, a small silver cylinder that rotated and lined itself up on Phobos without Roy seeming to do anything at all.

'Is that some kind of micropulse transmitter?' I asked as he delved back into the case.

'Yes and it's all classified, Captain. And that little gadget doesn't exist, right?'

'If you say so, Roy,' I answered. I recalled that although there used to be a powerful relay transmitter as well as emergency supplies stored on Phobos before the space station came fully into service, it and tiny Deimos, both dead lumps of rock, were regarded now as little more than navigational hazards.

'Why is the tube thing pointing at Phobos?' Karin asked.

At first reluctant to answer, Roy must have felt a need to keep us reassured when he said, 'SolaNews has a gamma-pulse transmitter buried up there. We can beam straight to the NewsNet system on Earth without anyone knowing. One packet can carry everything you want to say and much more.'

'Roy,' Karin asked, 'why has no one detected your set-up on Phobos?'

'If you don't mind, dear, I'll keep that to myself. We're lucky Phobos is still on this side of the planet though it won't be for much longer. Normally, I'd be able to relay information via elsewhere but with communications as they are that won't be an option.'

'Roy,' I asked, 'who else d'you know on Mars who would be involved in that during a blackout?'

Roy just smiled. He glanced about to ensure no one else had appeared in the vicinity then spent the next few minutes talking close into his left hand. He obviously had something implanted there. We listened as he related, without too much embellishment, what we so badly needed them to hear on Earth.

'This message includes the information from that small device you gave me,' he assured. 'Now I'll transfer data to the unit on Phobos. It responds only to me. D'you want to add anything else before I transmit?'

'That won't be necessary, Roy; just send the damned message.' I was concerned at how the pallid little moon was getting quite low in the sky and would soon be out of sight.

'All right, Captain,' he answered, poising the index finger of his left hand close to the gadget on the tripod. The thing twitched slightly. 'We'll get verification from Phobos at once,' he added. The little cylinder pinged twice, softly. 'There!' He turned to us with a smile of satisfaction. 'Confirmation from our Earth satellite will take around twenty minutes. By then Phobos will have set, which means I won't be able to interrogate the transmitter for another five hours.'

'Is there nothing else we can do?' asked Karin.

'Nothing unless someone flies me around the planet,' replied Roy. 'We'll just have to wait. Sorry.'

'Then we have to wait,' I conceded, realising Karin's frustration must be as great as mine. I was the only one able to fly Roy anywhere but felt we had to stay where we were for the time being.

'In that case, Captain,' said Roy, 'maybe we could take up the other side of the bargain and record the first part of your account in full.'

'Yeah, all right,' I sighed. Well it had to happen sooner or later so we agreed upon a secluded corner in the biodome cafe.

After an hour and more I'd had enough of Roy's questioning and it was dark outside. He was far from finished but we agreed we would continue at the next convenient time. I'd not eaten much that day so Karin and I remained most of the evening in the cafe - minus Roy, naturally. Joe called later to say, 'We're having no luck with inter-base communications but Leo is taking an overnight break at Tien Shan station then flying back to us.'

'Any news on *Aurora*, Joe?' I asked.

'Nope, nothing. She's still circling the planet as far as anyone can say. It's my guess Hammond will stay up there until communications with our aircraft are gone in case his position is reported by a pilot. Maybe he thinks he's keeping us guessing because he doesn't realise we know about Number Three. We'll just have to hang on until Phobos sneaks back into sight.'

***

The acknowledgement from Earth via Phobos reached us before midnight together with a welcome assurance that SolaNews had relayed the information directly to the International Council. By next morning Joe had received reports from several wingship pilots in different time zones who had spotted *Aurora*. Doubtless *Aurora* had also detected them. Communication with the pilots was still holding but Joe reckoned we were fighting a losing battle with the technology they had on board *Aurora*.

He became anxious when the reports stopped coming and so determined upon a long shot that would have consequences none of us expected.

***

Morning sunlight caught the big '4' that emblazoned her wing as she lifted into a saffron sky, circled about then set course north-eastward. Below Leo's ship drifted the eroded ramparts of Kepler crater, an ancient structure some two hundred and thirty kilometres across with a smaller, younger crater tucked against the inner southern wall. Close by this smaller crater lay the Chinese base of Tien Shan from which he had just departed.

Ahead lay a journey of over six and a half thousand kilometres - nine and a half hours flying time. It would probably be his last flight until things were sorted out for, planet-wide, pilots were soon to be grounded. That didn't even happen when they celebrated Foundation Day; the day Mars had been officially declared a colony of Earth by those advanced nations having the means to place a foot on it.

Gaining height, Leo passed over a pockmarked southern landscape of sun-etched crater rims, each one a fractured chalice cupping darkness. Perhaps there would be something to report. Perhaps not. And there was a remote chance of his spotting *Aurora*. That would be important if remaining communications were lost. Still, he wouldn't mind an extended break at home base. Brett would be there and he would hear of his good friend's encounters first-hand. And there was Helen. Soon they would consider formalising their relationship - something even pilots got around to eventually. His old pal Brett was hooked. Brett of *all* people! Brett who always boasted he would reach at least fifty before he'd let that happen. Well, it might be no bad thing to admit defeat even if it meant staying longer on Mars. Then there was the golf. Everything was coming together, albeit slowly, for the first match. On considering the possibility that he might well become first champion of their world, Leo smiled. Trophies had still to be designed and that needed more planning. Something tasteful, something different from the kind of old-fashioned ones they had on Earth. Brett was involved in an arts course - maybe he could come up with -.

His thoughts were interrupted by a chime from the communications panel followed by the image of Joe van Allen in shimmering, shifting colours. 'Leo, are you reading me okay?'

'Sure, Joe, but the signal is poor, like it's being pulled apart and put together again.'

'It probably is, Leo, and it's getting worse. Inter-base communication is all but impossible. Now they're trying to foul up the rest, though I think our conversations are still secure. I want you to re-route a hundred kilometres or so but it's important you cut all transmissions and active sensors.'

'No problem, Joe, I'll go fully manual if needs be.'

'Then fly over our Number Three. Take a look and see what you can – but don't get too close. Don't be surprised if their navigation field is down and they can't talk to you.'

'I know what you're getting at, Joe.'

'I'm sure you do, Leo. If there's nothing unusual down there then try calling them. Land if you have to. Warn them about the two airlock doors between the wingship maintenance building and the administration block. Tell them to secure these from the inside! From the inside, Leo! Tell them to weld the goddamned things shut if ... be! Did you get that, Leo? ... inside! If Aurora is there then .... should try... Leo, you're breaking up! Leo, can ...'

'Okay, I got it, Joe!'

'Take it ea ... , Leo. Don't ... yourself into ...'

The image wavered, fragmented then vanished. The readout flashed: 'CONTACT TERMINATED.'

Novamerica Three was no great diversion from the route home. After leaving the cratered uplands Leo would fly over more level regions on his approach to the equator. By fifteen degrees south, he would be almost halfway home. There he would alter direction some thirty degrees to the right and proceed seven hundred kilometres north-eastwards. That would bring him to a point just south of the equator where lay Novamerica Three. By that time the sun would be well down yet even should *Aurora* be there, Leo saw no reason for undue caution. Wingships were not designed to pose a threat to anyone.

***

When Joe caught up with Karin and I at the main concourse his face expressed grave concern.

'Brett, since we last spoke all outside communications have gone – light-pulse, wingships - everything. The last report on *Aurora* had her headed south toward our number three station. Leo's on his way back from Tien Shan so I asked him to fly over and take a look. I wanted to tell him we'd got through to Earth but we were cut off.'

'And what d'you see as our next move?' I asked, fully aware of how this final break in our communications had rendered the situation very much worse.

'I'm trying to re-establish contact with Leo,' answered Joe. 'Once he knows we contacted Earth, he can go deliver the news to Hammond. If that crazy fool doesn't listen to sense and back down then they'll have his goddamned hide!' Joe rubbed his chin then added, 'I guess they're going to do that anyway.'

'Then he's got nothing to lose, has he,' remarked Karin.

'But,' I said, 'if we can't contact Leo and Hammond uses force to take that base we might end up with hundreds more dead. Joe, this idea Hammond's cooked up of running Mars as some kind of feudal overlord has fried his brains. If he controls communications and has armed men and military bots in key bases, there may be little or nothing Earth can do about it for years to come - if at all, even if there are major casualties. And try to see it from Hammond's point of view, twisted or not; as long as he delivers what they need some of the governments on Earth might consider it far easier to sit back and accept the status quo rather than embark upon military action. I doubt he's going to listen to Leo, the IC or Earth and if he starts loosing off those penetrators he'll bring the curtain down on all of us. If I know nothing else, I know that – and, Joe, I do not like the idea of Leo going in there. He doesn't know what we know.'

Whilst Karin was entirely up to date with events, I didn't want her getting further involved. I told her and Joe that I had something private to sort out, that I'd be back later then I left them in the biodome and hurried straight along to the main concourse. I'd just grabbed my pressure suit down from the recharge unit when she showed up and confronted me. 'Brett - what are you doing?'

'I have to get out there before it's too late,' I replied, wishing I had shown more discretion. 'Leo doesn't know what he could be heading into.'

'Brett, no! There's nothing you can do. You'll only put yourself in danger.'

'Karin, I'm in danger already. We all are!'

At that point Joe came striding over to ask me what the hell I was up to. Trying to squeeze into a pressure suit and argue with two people at the same time is not easy, but I was managing. Any moment I expected Roy Kendrick to show up and start grilling me. That would have been too much.

'I won't allow this, son,' Joe said. 'Now the message is through to Earth, it's only a matter of time.'

'Joe, even if Earth decided to send troops over here we are talking months when we don't even have days. We're deaf and blind without any idea what Hammond is doing or any means of forcing him to back down. We're on our own, Joe, with only one chance left to stop him. One chance!'

'Exactly what d'you imagine you're going to do against all those armed men?' Joe demanded.

'*Aurora* is Hammond's trump card. She'll contain his supplies, his military bots and those penetrators until he gets himself a base. Without *Aurora* he's done for. I'll program Delta Seven to smash into her then eject in the pilot's pod well before impact. I figured out how to do it and that's one thing he won't expect. It will give us back our communications and put an end to his plans – armed men or no.'

'Now wait, son!' Joe responded. 'Why attempt such a damn fool trick? Why not slam a cargo pod into her? That way you also get clear of Hammond since he won't be taking what you did too kindly.'

'Because I'd need to fly in real close to do that and I'd risk getting picked off by his men. Doing it my way means the ship comes in too quick and steep for anyone to act. It'll be getting dark not long after I arrive overhead so I'll steer the pod away from the base and lie low for a while. There must be a couple of ground vehicles and probably a wingship there. With a bit of luck I can hi-jack one of those.'

Joe knew I wasn't kidding. He knew I wasn't going to be stopped but I guess he needed to put up a token protest. I was about to leave for the main airlock when a new complication jumped out at me. I thought Karin had been standing close by as I remonstrated with Joe but she hadn't. She'd suited up also and with her helmet under her arm was hurrying back toward us.

'No way!' I exclaimed before she had chance to speak. 'I'll be jumping ship in mid-air. Anything could happen.'

My objections made zero impression. She eyed me coolly. 'Brett, have you ever ejected from a wingship?'

'Sure I have. In training – in the simulator.'

'Then I have as much experience as you because I have done that as well and I'm not even a pilot. Ejecting in the pod will be quite safe so you are *not* leaving me behind. Not this time!'

I turned to Joe in desperation though it was obvious from the look on her face she wasn't about to change her mind. 'Hell - this is dangerous. Talk some sense into her will you, Joe! Time is running out!'

'Brett, I don't want either of you heading out there but I'm not her boss and right now it doesn't seem like I'm yours either.'

Karin glared at me. 'You heard that, Brett. Now let's get moving!'

***

The sun was getting low when we lifted off to swing due south. Novamerica Three was less than two thousand, seven hundred kilometres to the south-west but we needed to skirt around the colossal mass of Olympus and that added another four hundred kilometres or so to the journey. Had this been a regular cargo haul, it would have meant a flight time approaching five hours - but we had no cargo and this sure qualified as an emergency by my reckoning. The tenuous atmosphere that made normal flight more difficult on Mars than on Earth could be an asset for high-speed flight. We were about to take advantage of that.

I took Delta Seven up five kilometres before reconfiguring for rocket power. Left on automatic she'd have done what she was designed to do with a good margin of safety but we didn't have time for good margins of safety and we didn't plan to sit admiring the scenery. I knew my ship, I knew what she could do and I knew we had to make it to that base pretty quick. I also knew how to disable *all* safety systems.

Neither of us spoke as the horizon levelled off. Lights shuffled around the flight status displays. Countdown passed the five second mark. Then zero!

A muffled drumming filled the pod as the rockets cut in and we were thrust back hard into our seats. The ship accelerated at one hell of a rate then began to climb rapidly with the desert landscape flowing below at an unaccustomed speed and angle. Instead of my usual modest altitude we'd be flying at well over twelve kilometres - about half the height of Olympus. I intended taking us closer in to the flanks of the great volcano than I ought, but it would cut our journey time.

We would reach our destination in under one hour.

CHAPTER 10
THE SHADOW OF AURORA

From south-east to south-west of Novamerica Three, a range of muted hills marched across the desert beneath a late afternoon sun that shimmered in pink haze. Within the control room four people sat about in idle speculation. No more flights would be coming in or going out until communications were restored. One of the staff, his mouth full of food, glanced casually across the runway to the desert beyond, turned away, stopped chewing, swallowed hard then switched his gaze back. 'Hey, what's that moving above the hill's?'

Four pairs of eyes stared out through the shell. The girl peered at her console. 'Sensors aren't picking it up. I guess we know the answer.'

'The thing's heading our way!' called another. 'You'd better raise the commander!'

'No, Alan, you do it. I need to keep an eye on our sensors. I think she's gone down to get her hair done.'

'Gone down to -!' He stared at the communications panel. 'Oh, hell!'

A flattened beetle form descended slowly in apparent defiance of gravity. They watched her hover a few metres above the runway - not directly before the base but some way back, for a low-loader positioned across the strip prevented *Aurora* moving closer. She was still for a time and then her ventral ramp began to lower.

On the control deck, Virgil Hammond hard-eyed his own communications display. Next to him stood the ship's commander, a special services military pilot responsible for the vessel's navigation and control systems. He watched in silence. Everyone in the base must now be aware of *Aurora*'s intimidating presence. Until that day only a select few on Earth had observed her up close.

Communications to the base had been enabled as they approached. Hammond had already requested dialogue but so far no one had responded. Assembled in drab military pressure suits, each with helmet clutched at his front, the senior soldiers gathered for their orders. There was limited room on *Aurora*'s control deck so the greater number remained in the corridor leading to the boarding ramp. This was their first assignment beyond Earth. Their preparation for operations on Mars had been hasty but they were, whether fully human or otherwise, among the first of Hammond's chosen few and each carried an unshakable belief in the divine purpose of his mission.

Turning to his first officer, Hammond ordered, 'Have two of your men move that low-loader then go take a look at the service airlocks inside the maintenance building. The men may need explosives.'

'Castellano, Miller,' barked the officer 'helmets on! Arm yourselves, grab a couple of limpet packs and get out there. Neutralise its security system and shift that vehicle. Check out the airlock doors inside the maintenance building but do nothing until you receive further orders. Keep your eyes open. If anyone gets obstructive, you know what to do.'

'Sure thing, sir,' drawled one, lifting his helmet, 'we won't be standing for no arguments.'

Hammond growled at the blank space above the communications desk, 'Message repeat!'

The console acknowledged transmission and receipt of his message but several more minutes passed before the woman's face materialised above it, chestnut hair falling loosely about her blue-uniformed shoulders. She eyed him coolly, seeing the regulation smile melt away ice-bound features as he spoke. 'Commander Burnham, this is Virgil Hammond, Chief Executive and acting authority for the Consortium. I wish to -.'

'Christ, Virgil - I know who you are! Why are you hanging around my base in that fancy contraption? I was about to have my hair done.'

'I'm sure you will forgive the intrusion, Commander, when you consider the importance of our mission. I appreciate you and your people have suffered no small degree of inconvenience over the last day or so but as legal authority on Mars I must re-establish control over all operations. A number of base commanders have now accepted this so let me assure you this unfortunate state of affairs will soon be concluded.'

Her head tilted quizzically, she considered his statement before moving closer. 'I'm so glad to hear that, Virgil. Do go on.'

'Thank you, Commander. Those responsible must answer for their actions but there is no reason why the rest, including yourself, should not continue with their duties. No one wishes to see a return to normality more than myself. I have two men on their way now to move that vehicle so we can bring our ship closer. My colleagues and I will walk over and discuss matters with you face to face.

If you prefer, you are welcome to come aboard *Aurora*. Either way, I'm certain we will proceed in mutual trust, just as I'm sure you will appreciate why these problems have arisen.'

'Mmm - that sounds a great idea, Virgil. It's what we've all been hoping for and - oh my, I do like the military uniform and the badges. Very nice. One small matter as we're talking trust – we still have a problem over here in the communications department. Maybe you could fix things so I get through to Joe van Allen then raise the space station so I can check out the good news with my dear friend Amalia. Only a few minutes, Virgil, for the sake of trust - while those two guys toting guns are shifting the low-loader *without* my permission.'

'Commander - Julia, we need to maintain our security situation a while longer. Forget about those other matters for a moment then we will -.'

'Forget!' she responded. 'Oh, now Virgil, one minute we're talking trust, then the next I'm still denied access to the outside world. You wouldn't be planning to double-cross little Julia would you, honey?'

'Double-cross!' exclaimed Hammond with a dry laugh. 'Julia, my dear, remember who put in a good word for you when you applied for this posting. Offer me your co-operation now and I can do yet more for you on Mars and on Earth. There are people back home who owe me more than the odd favour.'

'Yes, Virgil, I bet there are - but I still can't speak to Joe or Amalia. Is that right or is that right?'

'Julia,' he responded, 'there is more at stake here than you know.'

343

'Virgil,' she continued, though the expression in her eyes hardened, 'no speakee to outside world - no deal. I know what you're about and so does everyone else on Mars. And if things are looking that good tell me why you can't even get into your own base! Frontier Mining may have a few lackeys in its pocket back on Earth, maybe out here, too, but you don't have Joe van Allen, you don't have the International Council and you sure as shit don't have me! We stocked up with supplies in the biodome days ago. My people are already moving in there and I'll have the rest of the complex depressurised pretty quick if I have to. Now don't think I can't see those two monkeys of yours heading toward the maintenance block. If it's the service airlocks they're after, don't bother - those doors don't open any more, Virgil - I know, I watched our guys do a real neat job on them with the torches.'

Hammond gestured with a hand to the Captain. He and the men behind him fitted on their helmets, took up their weapons then began to move down the ship. The troops would need to disembark in small numbers because of *Aurora's* airlock capacity.

'Julia,' continued Hammond as the menacing form of *Aurora* settled in full view of the administration block, 'it isn't just the law we have on our side, though that alone is quite sufficient. I *will* have access to this base one way or another because it is my duty to do so. I beg you to reconsider. You and others have been misled by those who preach evil. I swear in the name of that greater power to which we are all accountable, I have no wish to see anyone hurt or any more damage done.'

'You mean you don't want another Europa Six. No, Virgil, that wouldn't go down too well with the investors, would it. You'd have a tough job explaining things if the biodome got busted and a thousand of our own people died. I bet your greater power wouldn't get you out of that one. Well, screw you, screw your greater power and screw the Consortium! Virgil, I'd rather negotiate with the Martians!'

'Julia!' he glared, 'heaven knows I have tried to be diplomatic!'

'Diplomatic! I suppose those goons I see marching down the ramp and lining up on my strip armed to the teeth are also diplomats, are they? How many more fucking diplomats d'you have in there, Virgil?'

'Be as foul-mouthed and as blasphemous as you wish, Julia, but you leave me with no choice. If we are unable to access the service airlocks, the low-loader will go straight through those main doors and into the admin building. Is that what you want?'

'Virgil, you can drive the low-loader up your ass - it should be an easy fit. And as far as being foul-mouthed is concerned – I always cater for my audience. Goodbye!'

The image vanished though her mocking smile seemed to persist a while longer.

'Blasphemous bitch,' he growled. 'You will regret defying me.'

With the troops disembarked, four armed men were left on board with Hammond. One was a senior officer, one a soldier and one *Aurora's* systems specialist. The fourth man had been an *aide* of Hammond's but not so long ago on the space station had failed to accomplish a task entrusted to himself and a now dead companion. The bruising still evident about the man's face served as a stark reminder of the one who had inflicted it. Hammond had forbidden him to remove the marks on pain of dismissal for he knew the man harboured a deep hatred that might one day be turned to good advantage.

The main display lit up to reveal the complex aglow in late afternoon sun. It revealed, too, Hammond's soldiers mustering with weapons ready.

'Do you still intend to break through the main airlock, General?' asked the officer at his side.

'Sure - if it's the only way of getting in then that's what we'll do. With the facilities at this base, the airlock can be sealed until proper repairs are undertaken. We'd be operational by morning, that's for sure.'

'And who is going to undertake repairs?' asked the officer. 'Do you expect co-operation from the people inside that base?'

Seeing his men waiting to move, Hammond snapped, 'Those damned colonists will do as I say once my authority is re-established and I'll -.' A warning sounded. He turned to the console. 'What is it?'

An image had resolved to show the sky above the desert. High up a drifting speck glinted sunlight.

'General,' announced the ship's commander, 'there's an aircraft heading our way.'

346

Above the hills to the south-west a wingship had appeared and was approaching rapidly. Gathered outside, the captain and his men had also observed it. They stared intently as it lost altitude to swoop in at less than a half-kilometre above the desert.

'Captain!' cut in Hammond, eyeing the magnified image. 'That's one of Van Allen's pilots! Watch him!'

Vivid white against a deepening sky the wingship banked, passed beyond the complex, then gaining height it sped over the desert, turned northward and in moments was gone.

'He's on a cargo run,' came Hammond's voice. 'No doubt he's recorded our presence here for all the good that will do. All right, Captain, let's get on with the job.'

The men made a final check of weapons and equipment. Soon, they were ready, soon they were beginning to move away from *Aurora*. Again, Hammond's voice over their radios. 'Captain, we have that aircraft again - she's coming around from due west. The men turned to see Delta Four aligned with the runway. 'Hey!' one called out, 'Looks like he's heading straight over us!'

'He sure ain't flaring out to land,' said another.

'Watch him!' called Hammond, 'Don't let him get too close!'

Silhouetted against a vivid horizon the wingship, lower now, approached at speed.

'He's coming right at us!' shouted one of the soldiers as the men spread apart.

'He'll drop that fuckin' cargo pod!' yelled another. 'He'll smash our ship!'

347

Hammond's voice responded loud and insistent. 'Stop him! Bring him down!'

Weapons were raised, then - 'Hold it!' shouted the Captain, for already Delta Four, the whine of her engines rising, had begun to lift and veering aside, would no longer pass directly overhead.

But there was one for whom the order came too late; one with keen eye and of an all to human mind determined to show what deadly work he might do. His weapon locked on, the soldier fired. His projectile flashed upward to punch through the aircraft wing as she banked. A bright glare flashed above the wing as the shot ripped into the right hand engine where it caused spinning blades to disintegrate. A spurt of white vapour then a hail of fragments erupted outward as the casing burst asunder, as the fin above it tore away to dance like a feather within the vortex. For only a heartbeat longer did Delta Four continue on. Metal fragments had pierced the second engine so that, too, exploded. The wingship faltered. The cargo pallet dropped away but Delta Four, fatally stricken, rolled aside and in slow, grotesque pirouette, fell from the sky to vanish behind the eroded walls of a nearby crater.

Not a voice was raised as the dull boom of impact confirmed her destruction – except from the soldier who, lowering his weapon remarked, 'Dumb bastard should have ejected.'

A pall of dust arose above the crater rim to drift lurid in the setting sun.

'Captain!' ordered Hammond. 'Proceed at once!'

348

'All right!' called the captain. 'The show's over! Let's move!'

Starting off in a group toward the main block of the complex - a distance of some one hundred and fifty metres from the landing strip, their feet raised sand in a gravity to which some were not well prepared. They had covered half the distance when from the open service door at the end of the maintenance building two pressure-suited figures emerged. Both moved out, only to stop abruptly by the low-loader they had left standing close by.

'Miller! Castellano!' radioed the captain. 'Get that vehicle to the front of the administration block! You've got work to do!'

Neither man responded.

The soldiers trudged forward. A low sun cast their shadows to spread across red sand as wavering black tendrils.

'Miller! Castellano!' repeated the captain, hearing only unintelligible babble. 'What gives with you two? Get aboard that blasted vehicle and move it!'

'Are those guys foolin' around?' cut in another.

Miller and Castellano had found themselves dazzled and confused when they stepped back into the open. The world had changed. The world was utterly wrong. From horizon to horizon, the sky seethed violet and orange flame - chaotic forms that advanced and receded at the same time to confound eye and mind. A sea of glowing embers drifted eerily by where once had been desert sand. In weird perspective, *Aurora* hung shimmering, a translucent gem against hills that boiled as angry clouds. Between the two men and *Aurora*, something writhed up from that flowing lava ground – a monstrous apparition of liquid pitch that, as it began to approach, multiplied into numerous parodies of the human form.

'Ah - shit -!' yelled Miller. 'What's happening! What is this!'

Those approaching nightmare figures swayed against an impossible sky. Eyes sprang open furnace red, mouths grinned blood-crimson wide whilst voices rattled hideous laughter.

'No - no!' screamed Castellano, an arm raised across his visor. 'Tell me it's a fuckin' dream! Wake me up for fuck's sake! Wake me up!'

'Shoot the things!' Miller yelled back in mindless dismay. 'Shoot - shoot - shoot!

In a dance of panic, both blundered to the cover of the low-loader where they raised their weapons.

'Miller! Castellano!' the captain yelled. 'What the hell are you two playing at?'

The two began to shoot with rapid bursts. The first soldiers fell, life-blood foaming into the thin air from ruptured pressure suits as, too late, their comrades realised what was happening and sought to defend themselves. The captain spun around as a projectile pierced the front of his helmet, jetting a plume of boiling gore across the visors of his companions. Several men attempted to rush the low-loader, three almost reaching the vehicle before they were hit, shaking like discarded marionettes as they tumbled in blood-hazed vapour to the ground. Some thought to flee back to *Aurora* but ended spinning in the throes of agony as the bullets struck. Others dropped to the sand, firing wildly at the hidden enemy until hit, screaming into oblivion as death laced the frigid air. The cover of the sand was not enough for the weapons they used were deadlier by far on Mars than on Earth. Men darted about in confusion, firing wildly, screaming, falling - until the shooting stopped.

For a time nothing moved. Slowly, a figure emerged from behind the low-loader. The soldier lurched forward. Gazed about. At his feet lay the contorted body of Miller, pale vapour rising to freeze above a torn and bloody chest. Castellano stood uncomprehending, oblivious of *Aurora's* ramp lifting back into the hull, oblivious of another wingship approaching from the north-east, still high enough to catch the now vanished sun. Dropping the firearm, pressing hands against his visor he began to tread a circle in the sand. Around he staggered, parading the stage as its remaining player in a bizarre theatre of carnage.

Around he staggered. Around and around and around.

***

We were down to an altitude of five kilometres, racing over moderately cratered desert when I cut back the rockets. Still losing height, only minutes from our destination, our speed was falling dramatically. Once Delta Seven reconfigured, once the turbines took over, we dropped below cruising speed to circle in a broad arc over the complex that I had magnified on vision. We were high enough, I hoped, not to be in range of the hand-held weapons I expected Hammond's men would have.

Aurora we spotted soon enough, then to our amazement the many drab-suited bodies strewn about the sand between the runway and the main buildings. We looked hard with enhanced vision but could see no sign of movement. It was pretty obvious from the grotesque sight that the men were dead. Only when we made a second pass directly over the area did we realise what lay a short distance to the east of the base.

Karin broke our silence. 'Oh, Brett, what has happened down there?'

The area within the crater was darkly shadowed because the sun was well down but as it passed below we could easily make out the big '4' on the shattered wing. I also noted the pilot's pod. It was still attached to the wreckage.

'Brett,' said Karin, 'that is Leo's ship, isn't it?'

'Yeah,' I replied, 'it's Leo's ship.' I knew Leo must be dead.

As we came about for the final run a grievous anger seized me - an anger deeper than anything I had known until that moment. I didn't understand what had happened - not then - but I knew who had to be behind it. We were still circling when my panel chimed and Julia Burnham appeared. They obviously had local communications restored. 'Brett, honey, we sure are glad to see you.'

'Julia, what's going on? What happened to Leo?'

'They shot Leo down, Brett. We couldn't do anything to stop it. I'm sorry.'

'Is it safe to land?' I asked. 'Are your people okay?'

'There's enough of the runway clear for you to land, Brett. It looks as though all Hammond's men are dead except for one. All my people are unharmed.'

'Are you're saying those men on the ground are all Hammond's?'

'Yes, they're all his. They were busy killing each other a few minutes ago. We don't know why they did it but two of their own men gunned down the rest. Some of the shots hit our biodome but the damage self-repaired. I have a team suiting up right now.'

'What about Hammond - is he down there?'

'We don't know, Brett. Maybe the dumb bastard is, maybe he isn't. We're trying to contact *Aurora* but no one is answering.'

Karin voiced concern for both of us when she said, 'It might be a trick.'

'It's no trick, sweetheart,' came Julia's reply. 'We watched everything close up from the control room. The one guy still left alive sounds like he blew a circuit.'

The sky above was darkening as Delta Seven hit the strip with her turbines howling into reverse. Hoping communications might be restored generally, I attempted to contact Joe van Allen. There was nothing so I quit trying as the ship rolled to a stop only a few metres from *Aurora*. When we descended the boarding ramp, a violet halo spread weirdly over the sky above where the sun had set behind the hills.

Lights flooded the area between the base and the runway. Julia's team, having already emerged, were busying themselves amongst the dead, turning over bodies to record the macabre scene. I figured it might take some time before anyone could be sure whether or not Virgil Hammond lay amongst them.

'We still have no response from *Aurora*,' came Julia's voice. 'Some of those morons might still be on board.'

It will come as no surprise when I tell you how upsetting Karin found the situation. Not just because of Leo's wingship laying out there but the sight of those bodies scattered about and looking none too pleasant. 'Stay here by the ship,' I suggested. 'There's no reason why you should have to see any of this close up but I need to find out what's happened to Hammond.'

She gazed at me through her visor. Tears glistened in her eyes. 'Brett I – I'm so sorry about Leo.'

'Yeah, I know,' was all I could say, then I left her to wait on her own.

I spent those first few minutes examining the hull of *Aurora*. She hung there with her boarding ramp sealed so there was no way of telling if anyone remained inside. Standing close, my skin prickled like I was stroked by a thousand electrodes. Though I could hear nothing, I sensed an overwhelming power brooding within that all but featureless hull.

We've all heard the expression, "scene of carnage," It had real meaning when I moved amongst those corpses. Pressure suits are self-sealing to a certain extent but a high-velocity slug goes through suit and man then out the other side with dramatic results in our rarefied atmosphere. Several of Hammond's men had been ripped wide open whilst two had their heads blown apart. Others were so damaged by rapid pressure loss that their innards hung out of their suits. As I walked among them, something told me I was not going to find the General – not even his nametag.

There was a guy in a military pressure suit slumped against the track of the low-loader, the survivor mentioned by Julia, so I joined the two crewmen trying to haul him to his feet. He didn't appear to be injured but his eyes were darting about like he was seeing things all around him that we couldn't. 'It's okay, buddy,' I said. 'Tell me what happened?'

For a while his mouth just opened and closed as if he was reciting to himself. Then, waving an arm out across the bodies he stared right through me. 'It wasn't our guys! No way! It wasn't our guys!'

'Where's Hammond?' I asked.

'They're gone, now,' he muttered, shaking his head from side to side. 'All gone.'

'Who are gone?' I asked but he kept on shaking his head and muttering the same words.

'This guy's totally freaked,' one of Julia's crewmen said.

I saw no point right then in trying to explain what I guessed had happened but it seemed as though the Martians had decided we were the best of a bad deal by stepping in on the side of the colonists. It was a pity they didn't show up before those bastards murdered Leo. I wondered whether to try making myself useful here or ask Julia to organise a ground vehicle so we could get out to the crater and recover Leo's body. Either way, what I had in mind first was getting Karin into the complex since we wouldn't be leaving Novamerica Three that night.

I stepped around to check the other side of the low-loader where it was quite dark in case anyone was hiding there. As I did so, my boot hit something hard in the sand. It was a medium-barrelled gun that must have been dropped by the soldier who lay sprawled close by. I stooped to pick up what turned out to be a weapon familiar from my training days. On checking, I saw the soldier had loosed off only three rounds before being killed. It was more powerful than the side-arms with which most of them had been equipped so I wondered if this could be the gun that had brought down Leo. As it happened, I hung around there a while too long.

The stars were bright as Karin rested against the landing gear of Delta Seven. From there she watched the base crew go about their grim work, a number of them carrying containers in which to place the dead. A low mist had begun to seep all about so Karin decided to call Brett and tell him she would make her way around the bodies and go to the main airlock as she, too, had realised they would not be leaving for some time. Occupied in thought, she did not notice the ramp opening beneath *Aurora*. Nor, as she began to move away from the wingship, was she aware of three figures closing upon her from behind.

'Don't use your radio,' came a voice through her suit microphone. Karin turned to find one of Hammond's men with a weapon pointed at her helmet. 'Try anything and your precious captain dies as well as you,' came the voice of another. 'That's a promise!'

'What d'you want with me?' she asked, peering at vague faces behind tinted visors. 'Look, there's no point in making things worse. We got through to Earth today. They know what has been happening.'

'Lady - don't argue!' came the reply as hands grasped each of her elbows and propelled her toward *Aurora*'s ramp. 'Move quick!'

At the ramp, Karin pulled back and would have spoken again but they forced her roughly on with further threats. Inside the airlock they released their hold to leave her facing the inner door whilst the outer closed with serpent hiss. She stood there expecting them to take her through into the ship but nothing happened. The air pressure readout showed a little below eight millibars but as she watched, it was not rising. When she turned to face her captors they were gone. She was trapped and alone.

I was about to step from behind the low-loader when a none too welcome voice came over my radio. Not just my radio but everyone else's because it was on the hailing frequency. 'Pay attention, all of you!'

It was not a voice I recognised. Not that of Virgil Hammond. Still out of sight in the shadows I froze as the voice continued. 'We are armed! Everyone, put down whatever you're holding. Move away from the airlock and line up at the side furthest from the low-loader. Do it now! We will shoot if you fail to obey!'

Moving to the end of the vehicle, I eased myself around as the voice came again. 'Commander Burnham, get suited up and come out here!'

I peered around the vehicle and saw three of them. They were standing in a line amidst the bodies of their own fallen, each man about two

357

metres from the next, their side arms levelled at the base staff who were assembling as ordered. It was fortunate that people from the base were not standing between those jokers and me. I'd not used a firearm for some time so I hoped I'd remembered the tricks they had taught me at the academy. The military suits they were wearing had image intensifiers that reacted quicker than our civilian issue, as well as fancy targeting aids. I was taking a big chance but then I had a more powerful weapon. I'd also assumed they were Hammond's close pals and so would be fully human and maybe not quite as agile in a pressure suit as otherwise. I stooped low, took aim at the nearest of them, locked onto their frequency and called, 'You three - drop your guns or I shoot!'

Scrambling apart, two of them crouched, twisting from side to side, not knowing where I was as they had only picked me up on their radios. The nearest guy spotted me first then swivelled about to aim his pistol. I felt the jolt as my own gun went off with a spurt of light. I was on a high, sure I was, and pretty confident about my aim. I'd fired, hoping for a hit before moving back but in that instant I saw the result. The bullet went straight through the poor bastard's visor and out the back of his helmet. He tottered with blood foaming out like red champagne, then fell. The sight of it must have put his two pals off their aim because one of their slugs tore into the side of the low-loader next to my left arm whilst the other zinged off into the night. I leapt behind the vehicle so quick I almost left my pressure suit standing there without me! At the same time a couple of Julia's crewmen rushed forward to take Hammond's men whilst they were distracted. They were not quick enough. One of the soldiers spun about, fired and brought the closer of the crewmen down at his feet in a spray of blood whilst his pal took another shot at me. The second crewman froze a few steps away then backed off with hands raised but Hammond's men were feeling none too generous and one of them gunned him down all the same. Worse, they were now so close to Julia's people I dared not fire again without stepping into the light.

The two split up, intending to circle the low-loader so as to catch me from either side. They might have succeeded if I hadn't hurried some way back from the vehicle where I squatted in deep shadow behind a ridge of sand and rubble from where I had a good view. For a moment they seemed to think I'd crawled under the low-loader to get away. But only for a moment - and the sensors they carried were pretty certain to locate me.

I wasn't going to give them time to do that. As they realised where I'd gone, as they dodged low in the shadow of the vehicle, I fired then rolled over in the sand, certain the shot had missed, only too aware my luck was stretching thin. Jumping aside, they started shooting again. One of their slugs spattered me with rock fragments. Gravity was still on my side though, for they over-reacted as they dodged from side to side, so spoiling their own aim. I fired again as they dashed toward me. My shot all but took off the right arm of the closest man, making him spin about as his shriek came loud over my radio. Going down, he sprawled into the path of the other guy who made a leap to avoid him. A fatal error. He jumped too hard in the lower gravity, rose up clear of the low-loader and was for a moment silhouetted against the lights of the base. I didn't see where my shot caught him but he fired into the air as he went down, choking like his head was held under water. I stayed put a while with my gun levelled in case he was fooling, aware of my life-support pack humming double time. Neither of them moved.

I stepped from behind the low-loader to find the base personnel shuffling about in nervous anticipation over who would stroll into full view after the shoot-out. An all but tangible sigh of relief came over my radio when they saw I was not military. I was intent on finding Karin when a familiar voice cut in. A voice telling me something I didn't want to hear.

'Very heroic, Captain Anderson! An entertaining spectacle though the outcome was not to my liking. What a pity Officer Blomdahl was confined to our airlock and unable to witness it. Nevertheless, she is joining us now and we're most anxious you should be here also. Very anxious indeed. Lay down that weapon then walk toward *Aurora's* ramp. Quickly now! Quickly!'

I looked about in case he was bluffing but there was no sign of Karin. 'Hammond!' I called. 'Let me speak to her!'

'But of course,' came the reply.

After some moments, a voice. 'Brett, I'm here.'

'Karin, are you hurt?'

'I'm all right, Brett, but the two of them have guns. What's happening?'

'Hammond,' I called. 'I'll come aboard if you'll let her go. We can make an exchange in the airlock.'

'A predictable request, Captain. I will give it due consideration whilst you are on your way over. Do not think me in any mood to compromise after witnessing your recent performance. Your weapon – move closer and drop the thing where I can see it!'

He had to see me throw down the gun even though the mist was thickening. I hoped he did not see what I slipped so very carefully into the life support harness at the rear of my suit before I got close enough to *Aurora*. The kind of gun I'd picked up had something fitted into the hollow stock. Something a little old-fashioned but something under the right circumstances might prove deadly as any firearm.

On reaching *Aurora*'s underbelly, I walked cautiously up the ramp, keeping my eyes peeled as the outer airlock door slid open. Once inside I found myself facing the wrong end of a gun similar to the one I had only minutes before discarded. The guy holding it leaned against the wall as the door began to slide shut. 'Nice to see you again, ass-hole,' he snarled. 'The General wants you alive but one fancy move and he's going to be so fuckin' disappointed it ain't true!'

I knew that voice even though I couldn't yet make out his face. The suit tag confirmed it was Rigby, one of the thugs sent by Hammond to prevent us leaving the space station. If I was going to do anything meaningful it had to be before we got through that airlock. Karin had said, "the two of them," when she referred to her captors. If she'd used the phrase deliberately it meant there had to be only Rigby and Hammond left on board.

From the looks of it, the airlock on *Aurora* could accommodate nine or ten if they squeezed tight together so Rigby wasn't too far away. Maybe he thought I wouldn't be stupid enough to try anything. Maybe he was stupid for thinking that. He stood back far enough to be out of reach though the barrel of his gun was only a half metre away.

'Just give me one excuse, motherfucker,' he sniggered. 'Just one.' He jabbed the gun closer to emphasise the point. That was his big mistake.

The airlock had started to repressurise when I made my move. Turning as though to face the inner door I lurched at him, knocked the firearm aside with my life support pack, twisted about, grabbed the barrel and kicked away his leg to throw him off balance. Rigby yelled out, the gun went off, the slug passed close by my helmet to crack against the ceiling then zing across the airlock. I could see his face now. By the expression in his eyes he must have realised what a risk he was taking by firing in that confined space but real as it was, the chance of being hit by a ricochet didn't concern me. I heaved him into a corner whilst reaching behind my back. All the time he was kicking out, wrenching at the gun, his other hand splayed across my visor whilst he cursed aloud with a vehemence fermented by a deep and violent hatred. With one foot levering against the wall, Rigby heaved us both across the small space so we slammed against the opposite bulkhead. But I held on, knowing if he got the chance to shoot again it could be the end of yours truly. Seeing the double-edged knife in my hand but not daring to make a grab for it in case it slashed his suit, he made frantic effort with both hands to manoeuvre the barrel of the weapon against me. Too late! I wrenched back my arm then drove the blade into his side, clean and easy the way it was meant to go, cutting like cheese through the layers of his suit, reinforcing mesh and all.

The airlock pressure hadn't reached three hundred millibars at that point but the slit in his suit would self-repair even if the guy inside it didn't and there was a chance he would hold out long enough to have another go at killing me. I could see his eyes through the visor. I saw the look of fear, of desperation, as he cursed me in a way I never heard anyone curse. This was real personal, not like the three outside. Rigby and his pal would have killed Karin as well as me up there in orbit and this man had all the more reason to do so now.

As we struggled for our lives, time spread out. In that interminable instant I might have questioned what I was about to do because I'd seen too much death. But I was thinking of what they had done to Leo and the knife went in again. This time much deeper.

The pressure was touching seven hundred millibars when Rigby died. High enough to be breathable, high enough to avoid the mess that might have resulted as the blade came out. He was already slumped against the airlock wall when the inner door opened. I weighed up the situation quick as I could. Ahead lay no more than a short passage leading directly onto the control deck. An exit either side of the passage could have concealed someone but I had to go on. I slid the door aside. By the console stood a uniformed Virgil Hammond, looking like he'd expected to go out on parade, medals glittering like an old style trinket stall. Next to him was Karin with her helmet clutched in her arms. Her eyes were wide with alarm, her lips parted as if she wanted to call out to me. Hammond had a gun but it wasn't pointed at me – the muzzle was pushed against her neck just below the jaw.

'All right I'm here,' I said, 'Now let her go.'

From the virtual window to my left I could see out across the base. People stood about in the lights, no doubt wondering what was happening within *Aurora*. Hammond glanced to the airlock then stared at me with a forced smile. 'Well now, Captain Anderson, you seem to leave a trail of death wherever you go.'

'Nothing to compare with yours, General,' I answered. 'You're way ahead of me on that score.'

'I told him,' gasped Karin, 'He knows we got through to Earth.'

'You heard that,' I said. 'What's the point in going on?'

'Oh, there is every point in going on, Captain.' he growled, glancing at Karin. 'And take notice - I will certainly shoot you both - her first if you do not keep your distance. Doing so would be entirely justified as an act of self-defence, apart from everything else. Yes, and that knife of yours – throw it back into the airlock!'

I threw the knife along the passage where it clattered down next to Rigby's body. 'Kill us,' I said, 'and you'll never leave Mars. Even if you could reach the space station you don't have enough men in orbit to back you up whether they're armed to the teeth or no. Now how about this deal?'

'As I promised,' Hammond replied, 'I have given your request due consideration whilst aware neither of you wishes to be parted from the other. I have no desire to be responsible for that now or in the hereafter. But at present this woman is my bargaining card.'

His mouth hardened, his eyes shone with malice whilst with his free hand he grasped Karin's hair from behind, wrenching back her head so that she cried out and let her helmet fall aside onto the pilot's seat. It was all I could do right then not to go for him.

'Understand this,' he snarled, 'I intend to leave here without delay. Because of you, the man able to activate this ship is lying dead out there with the rest. You, Captain Anderson, will take his place and in part make up for your meddling stupidity. As to what happened to the rest of my men, Officer Blomdahl, here, offered me the probable cause as well as informing me about your transmission to Earth via SolaNews. You have defied me, Captain Anderson - defied me and aided the work of the Devil and those obscene creatures crawling in their pit of hell below the surface of this planet! What can you say about that captain Anderson?'

He levelled the gun at me and might have been about to pull the trigger. Then he pushed the muzzle back against Karin's throat and said a little more calmly, 'It cannot end here - oh, no. But for the time being I must endeavour to make the best of our circumstances.'

'You don't have any circumstances to make the best of, Hammond,' I said. 'The UAS knows, the IC knows – all of Earth knows what's been happening. Anyway, how d'you figure I'm going to fly this ship?'

'Don't play the fool, Captain!' he barked. 'I know her navigation systems are much the same as other interplanetary ships with which you are familiar. It will take you little time to work out what to do. And without wishing to seem indelicate, both your lives depend upon it, as does mine. We will collect my men from the space station then *Aurora* can get us back to Earth. There are a number of people in our senate who would not wish to have me compromised provided we return soon. With your help, Captain, I should be able to smooth things out even at this late hour and re-establish some kind of equilibrium.'

'Re-establish!' I responded. 'After what's happened here! Don't all those lives mean anything to you - all the people wiped out at Europa Six as well as those killed at the Black Mountain? What about Ingvar Svendsen? And what about the guy laying out there in the desert with the wreckage of his ship? What did Leo have to die for? Are you going to re-establish him and the rest of them?'

Then I thought maybe I shouldn't try to convince him over the futility of carrying on. There was no way he could return to Earth with impunity. No way could Frontier and the Consortium continue digging up the planet as they had been so intent on doing. But he either wouldn't or couldn't see it. But if he did - if he finally realised there was nowhere to run, our chances of walking out of there alive were about as likely as Frontier's share values staying put.

'This is getting us nowhere!' he countered, confirming my fears. 'I have nothing more to lose unless I return to Earth and I promise both your fates will coincide with mine if we remain here. I am not afraid to face the one from whom I must ask forgiveness in my failings, Captain - oh, no! You may have done the Satan's work but his way shall never prevail. You will get *Aurora* operational now!'

'Once Karin is free, General. Once she's off this ship I'll take us out to Neptune and beyond if that's what you want.

'No, Captain Anderson!' he snapped, pushing Karin forward, still holding her hair but forcing the gun so hard under her ear she gasped in pain with her eyes screwed up tight. 'The woman stays with us. During our flight she will sit directly in front of me. The two of us will observe how well you apply your skills as a pilot. As soon as my men are on board, the problem of who keeps an eye on whom will not be so demanding. Now, *if you please* – or would you prefer to see her brains spattered over both of us before we also take our leave!'

Hammond was desperate and might at any moment lose whatever grip he still had on reason. I was desperate, too. Even if I figured out how to operate the ship, once I collected his thugs from the space station, once he had someone else to pilot *Aurora*, there was no way he could let either of us live. Each second saw him more agitated and he was hurting Karin badly with that gun in the side of her jaw.

367

'Captain,' he scowled, 'I have little patience left!'

'All right,' I answered, turning to the airlock, 'we get the ramp up and the ship secured then I'll do whatever you want.'

I made those few steps to the airlock control panel. I saw that it at least appeared to be standard layout and I hoped Hammond wouldn't insist on carrying out the operation himself from the main console. Maybe he didn't know how to do that, maybe he was scared of releasing the grip on his hostage. He may not have realised I was tuned into Karin's personal radio frequency but before I reached the panel, his voice came through my suit microphones, 'Captain Anderson - remove your helmet!'

I hoped he'd think I hadn't heard him as I neared the controls. At the same time I whispered to Karin through her ear-lobe communicator, 'Karin, have your helmet ready.'

There was a mountain of hope in those few words. More hope than ever I held onto any time in my life before then. And the safety override codes - what if *Aurora*'s were different? So much was different about the ship. My heart pounded as I reached out to touch the first of the keys. I'd pressed two of them when the red warning began to flash. He had to see it - but would he know what it meant?

Again his voice, 'Anderson! Get that damned helmet off or I *will* shoot her!'

As my finger touched the third and last key I wondered who he'd got the weapon pointed at. He would have to shoot me first. He'd have to! Then I heard scuffling and Karin yelled, 'Now, Brett! Now!'

A shot cracked out. The slug ricocheted off the wall and zinged along the side of my helmet as I stabbed at the key and spun about to see through the passage the outer airlock door begin to open. Hammond wrenched the gun barrel from Karin's grasp, hurling her violently against the console. As she grabbed for her helmet he staggered around, mouth agape, eyes darting from me to the gaping airlock. I jumped aside as the gun came up but it kept on up and didn't shoot because the invisible hand of rushing air had snatched away his breath. He dropped the gun, lurched forward to grab at me then clutched at his mouth with a high-pitched scream. A scream that became a warble as the lifeblood welled from between his fingers. He reeled about, blurting red down his medalled chest, eyes and ears blood-streaked, then stumbled in convulsion as far as the corridor before pitching to the floor where he rolled back across the deck to end up wedged against one of the seats. White vapour coiled from his jaws. His rapidly cooling blood streaked both floor and adjacent wall.

Hammond was dead; his exit from this life expressed across a polyp-eyed mask of gaping horror.

Karin was slumped in the pilot's chair, hands clutching either side of her helmet. In those frantic seconds she'd managed to fix it on so I could see that she was safe. I helped her up, wanting to pull her out of there before she had any chance to witness the appalling sight that was Virgil Hammond.

369

As we moved to the open airlock, I turned to gaze at him once more, to see the grotesque image, the gore-spattered ruin this ruthless, power-driven yet utterly deluded man had become. Hammond's death punctuated a tale of deceit and contempt for life - human and otherwise. I could summon no pity for him.

Leaving *Aurora*, we walked hand in hand down the ramp. I looked up at the stars. I looked at Karin and her tear stained smile. There were voices. From the direction of the base where bright lights shone into a frosted night, Julia and some of her people were approaching. They were calling our names.

EPILOGUE
THE NEW EDEN

Soon after Julia's crew had removed the corpses and cleaned up *Aurora's* control deck, her technicians figured out how to restore Marsnet, switch off the space beacon and re-establish contact with Earth. None too soon as it happened. It turned out the major powers back there were on the verge of breaking off diplomatic relations over the antics of Hammond and his disciples, many of whom were involved with a small group in the UAS senate. The situation might well have ended up a lot worse had it not been for Roy Kendrick. Yeah, even I had to admit that.

Before sunrise next day, I set out with a small party by ground vehicle to the crater where Delta Four had come down. Climbing the rubble slope to the crater rim then descending into the still gloomy interior, I was stuck by a sadness I find difficult even now to describe, though at the time it helped to share my thoughts with Karin and Joe over the radio. I confess I had no desire to look too close when they recovered his body. I wanted only to remember Leo as I had known him in life. The Leo who always had a smile. The Leo who so enthused over his golfing plans. A true and good-hearted friend.

It turned out a fragment of metal had killed him. It had driven through his heart. That was why he never ejected the pilot's pod before going down.

Joe readily agreed with my suggestion about what to do with his remains. We buried Leo in the centre of the crater, close to where he'd fallen. Later in the day, a team returned with tractors to clear away the wreckage. Afterwards, we took one of Delta Four's fins, still largely intact, put in a foundation then erected it by his grave as a kind of monument. It could be seen from Julia's station rising up above the crater rim with the big '4' catching the morning sun. I don't think my old pal would have minded that.

On returning to my own base Karin and I fulfilled our promise to Roy Kendrick by giving him the rest of his exclusive down to the last detail. He dug deep, though I managed to keep my cool in spite of it. SolaNews awarded itself much of the credit for having saved the situation with Roy now flavour of the month as far as they were concerned. Sending that message to Earth then getting our story made him a star.

But being a star was not enough. Roy wanted to shine out as a supernova so for several nights he hung around our biodome into the early hours of the morning, hoping to encounter the Martians. I imagined him attempting to grill their entire community through a few individuals. Now that *would* have been a scoop! But for all his efforts, as well as two thorough soakings when the rain was switched on, the Martians didn't show up. I figure good taste must have been another of their highly developed attributes.

For once, the governments on Earth saw sense and decided the International Council and only they should oversee colonial affairs. It meant deep level mining was ended for good. It also meant, in effect, autonomy. When our affairs began to settle, Joe van

Allen was nominated first president of the human community on Mars. At first he needed some persuading but the vote, predictably, was unanimous. Unanimous, too, was the election of Amalia Barbosa as our ambassador to Earth. She was over the moon about that - okay, *both* moons if you prefer! Joe wondered if I might go back to my routine of flying but things could never be the same again. Not for me they couldn't.

As for the Martians, it was suggested I should try to re-establish contact with a view to opening permanent dialogue. I turned the idea down. I was convinced they wanted no further involvement in the sideshow of human affairs when they had such a big slice of space-time to play around in. Perhaps it was they who put the notion of refusal into my head. If so I can't say I blamed them, although at the same time I was certain they couldn't remain aloof from human beings for good now each side was aware of the other.

But what of Karin and me? Well, I'll come to that. I was now a reluctant celebrity but I had my sights on other things. *Aurora*'s technology would open up the entire solar system to human exploration as it never could have been with rockets. There was also the fact that the scarce resources of Earth as well as the Martian colonies needed to be replenished from elsewhere. The asteroid belt, Jupiter and Saturn, even distant Uranus and Neptune were about to become accessible in realistic time. But it was the rich organic resources of Saturn's moon, Titan, to which the acquisitive gaze of humanity now turned for exploitation.

As far back as the early twenty-first century, probes had begun to analyse this murky world but it had seemed forever beyond human reach and much about it still remained unknown. An unmanned processing plant was already being assembled in Earth orbit for the voyage to Saturn, together with power core, life support and service modules. With International Council co-ordination the powers on Earth ordered it's completion and despatch as a matter of priority. Here on Mars would be processing facilities.

Once out there, it was intended that it should assume orbit about Titan in readiness for the arrival of a human crew, following soon after in a modified *Aurora*. The plant would serve as a factory, living quarters and as a scientific base for surveying the entire Saturnian system.

With the backing of Joe and Amalia Barbosa, I got the job of commanding *Aurora* with Karin as head of our science team. There was one task remaining for us on Mars, however: Karin and I would return to the Valley of Crystals at the same time of the day as on our first visit. There, we would replace those we had taken away. There we would stand before the crystals as sunlight descended, once more to watch them shine out in wondrous glory in this new Eden.

THE END